Praise for Debbie Burns's unforgettable Rescue Me series, where love always comes to the rescue

"Burns charms with...much more than a cute critter story. Delightfully appealing."
—*Publishers Weekly* Starred Review

"A fun, heartwarming story of love, family and trust."
—*Harlequin Junkie*

"Pet lovers will adore all the animals introduced in Burns's sweet romance."
—*Booklist*

"A ragtag cast of supporting characters, human and otherwise, shines."
—*Foreword Reviews*, 5 Stars

"A lovely and wholesome story."
—*Night Owl Reviews*

"Heartfelt and engaging... It captured my whole heart."
—*Urban Book Reviews*

"A sweet stor⋯ ⋯ ⋯ ⋯rooting for the human⋯ ⋯ ⋯ling."
⋯*k Nook*

Also by Debbie Burns

HEAD OVER PAWS

🐾 A RESCUE ME NOVEL 🐾

DEBBIE BURNS

sourcebooks
casablanca

For you, Mom,
and for all the support along the way

🐾 🐾 🐾

"The bond with a true dog is as lasting
as the ties of this earth will ever be."
—Konrad Lorenz, *Man Meets Dog*

Chapter 1

OLIVIA GRAHAM FLICKED ON HER BLINKER AND locked her hands around the steering wheel of her ten-year-old Chevy Cruze. Nervous excitement pressed against her ribs.

While waiting for a break in traffic on the Great River Road, she stared through the fat drops of rain at the choppy waves of the swollen river. Thanks to an unusually wet spring, the muddy Mississippi reminded her of a peacock puffing out its chest and fluffing its feathers. With any luck, the rains would end earlier than predicted, and the river would stay confined within its sturdy banks.

She pulled out onto the Great River Road, the Cruze's engine whirring and knocking in protest as she kicked it up to highway speed. She gave the dashboard a quick pat. "Come on, girl. You've got this." All the miles she'd spent commuting the last few months had the engine sounding like its own percussion band until it warmed up.

Behind her, within a handful of seconds, the little town of Elsah, Illinois, was swallowed by the towering bluffs on either side. The river flanked her side as she drove, the wipers keeping rhythm with the rain. Until recently, Elsah had been no more than a name on a map where a semi-estranged aunt lived. But in a twist of fate, Olivia had taken a temporary teaching job in downtown St. Louis. She'd accepted an invitation to stay in one room of her aunt's hundred-and-thirty-year-old clapboard home while she determined if she would be able to turn the temporary position into a permanent one. Elsah was an enchanting town, full of enchanting people. If it weren't for the agonizing rush-hour commute, Olivia would be happy to stay much longer.

The irony still struck her how, at twenty-five, she'd lived in three states but had never been more than a stone's throw from the muddy Mississippi. As fate would have it, today's three-and-a-half-hour drive wouldn't take her any further away from the river than she was now.

When she'd signed up to be a volunteer animal rescue transporter and had agreed to drive up to five hours in a transport chain to get some misplaced dogs into shelters, she'd hoped her first call would be a pickup in Kansas City or Chicago. Instead, her first assignment had her headed to the Missouri Bootheel where she'd grown up and where most of her family still lived.

The river was threatening here, but three and a half hours further south, heavier bands of rains had the Mississippi and its tributaries spilling over their banks, pushing people and animals out of homes, and that was where help was needed.

Olivia didn't need a map to get where she was going today. As a kid, she'd gone with her grandpa every Saturday to buy supplies from the feed store just outside the New Madrid town center, which was where the misplaced animals were being held until they could be returned to their owners or shipped to different shelters.

Using the Bluetooth system she'd gifted to herself

to help pass the time in traffic, Olivia chose one of her favorite playlists on Spotify and settled into the drive. The metal door on one of the two empty dog crates in the back seat was loose and vibrated a squeak of its own to the music. She'd bypassed St. Louis on Interstate 270 and had traveled about twenty miles down Interstate 55 when her phone rang. The distinctive chirpy tone she'd programmed just for Ava, her older sister by one year, rang out.

"Hey. What's up?"

"Are you in the car?" Ava sounded even more nasal than when they'd spoken yesterday.

"Yep."

"But it's Saturday. Where're you going?"

"You make it seem like I never go places on Saturday. And your cold sounds like it's getting worse."

Ava sniffed determinedly. "Ever since you moved up here, every time I ask you to do something on a weekend, you tell me you don't want to get in the car. When are you going to be home? I was going to come over."

Olivia made a face. "To Elsah? Is that cold making you feverish by chance?" *Quaint* and *historic* and *tucked-away, sleepy village* weren't words she'd ever associate with her sister. Ava had visited their aunt's house when Olivia first arrived in January. Looking around, her sister had done the classic folded-arms, rocking-heel, and raised-eyebrow "Quaint, isn't it?" and had never been back. Whenever they hung out, it was either at Ava's favorite coffeehouse or her luxury condo in downtown Kirkwood, one of St. Louis's popular suburbs.

"Very funny. And you didn't answer. How soon will

you be home? Should I start driving? I don't want to be alone with Aunt Becky. She's weird."

"She's not weird. You just need to get to know her better." Olivia hadn't told her sister she'd signed up as a rescue driver for a reason. Ava had taken off from their Bootheel home a month after high school graduation and hadn't looked back at life in rural southern Missouri. And she'd been in no hurry to add an animal to her life either.

While she'd never had a lit firecracker under her butt like her sister, Olivia understood. She'd dreamed of leaving too. Back home, life moved at a different pace, which could be good and could be bad. It bothered her more that everyone knew everyone else's business. Or at least they assumed they did. And sometimes they were as quick to hand out judgments as they were a helping hand.

The difference between Olivia and her sister was that since leaving three months ago, Olivia had had more than a few waves of homesickness. One of the things she missed most was having a dog or cat underfoot. On her grandpa's farm, there'd always been a few of each. Her favorite, a golden retriever named Sassy, had passed away a year ago, breaking Olivia's heart.

But even if she was finally ready to bring another dog into her world, her aunt was a vegan and borderline hermit who made a living as a potter. Her only pet was a dog-fearing cockatoo. When Olivia had heard about a fellow teacher at her school who did rescue driving on weekends, she'd thought it might be just the thing to get her through until she had a place of her own.

"I'm gonna be gone all day," Olivia added. "How 'bout tomorrow?"

"All day? But you don't even know anyone up here yet." Ava paused to blow her nose. "What's going on?"

"I know people, thank you." Olivia pulled in a breath as if she were about to blow out a hefty number of candles. There was no getting past telling her sister now. "I'm on a mission, actually. I've signed up to be a volunteer rescue transporter. I'm picking up two dogs and a cat and taking them to a shelter in O'Fallon."

"Huh." Ava was quiet a second. "I didn't even know that was a thing, but something tells me you're not kidding."

"I'm not. Honestly, I didn't know much about it, either, but it turns out homeless animals are hauled all over the place by drivers working in tandem. There's this whole world of coordination behind it. Usually it's to get them into a shelter or a foster home." Knowing full well what her sister would say, Olivia owned up to the rest. "You'll never guess where I'm headed to pick them up."

"When you say it like that, I'm not sure I want to. Death row, I'm guessing?"

"Heavens. I don't even want to think about that. These guys were caught in the floods." Her shoulders had nearly tucked up against her ears before she noticed it, and she shoved them down again. Determinedly, she shook her head, sending her long, wavy red hair bouncing back and forth. "New Madrid, believe it or not. They're holed up in Milton's Feed Store."

"Shut. Up. Did you tell Mom and Dad?"

"Heck no. I'm hoping to get in and out before anyone's the wiser."

"Fat chance in that town, Livy. Why on earth did you agree to that?"

Olivia chewed her lip. Why *did* she agree to this particular drive? As much as she missed some things about her home, she wasn't ready to go back. Not even close. It would probably take a couple of years before she could go home without feeling a blanket of shame draped across her shoulders over the way things had played out last fall.

But this had been the first opportunity since she'd been approved as a driver, and she'd been excited to start. When she'd checked her email this morning, she'd swallowed back her reservation and jumped on the mission before she'd been able to talk herself out of it. "It just sort of happened."

"What about Trevor?"

"What about him?" She'd been thinking about him all morning, had even come close to texting him. She'd gotten past it by reminding herself they were on different journeys now. "It's been almost six months. With any luck, he's dating someone by now."

"Oh, please. Not unless it's a someone who was trapped in the path of his combine or fell into his lap while he was sitting on the couch reaching for a beer."

Olivia choked back a giggle. "He was quite the catch back in high school."

"Crabs were pretty catchy back in high school, too, weren't they?"

Olivia shuddered. "You know, no, I don't think they were. I've never heard of anyone I know actually having crabs."

"It was a figure of speech." Ava let out a sigh. "If someone spots you, don't let them guilt you into meeting up with him. Swear?"

"Pinkie swear." Breaking off their engagement just over three weeks before the wedding hadn't come easily. But it had been the right thing to do, even if Trevor hadn't understood her reasoning.

"Good. That'd be a step backward you don't need to take." Ava let out an exasperated sigh. "I guess I need to find another way to drown out my sorrows with you gone today."

Olivia straightened in her bucket seat. "What do you mean? What sorrows? Ava Graham and sorrows are oil and water, aren't they?"

Her sister sniffed again but didn't say anything.

A wave of shock rolled over Olivia. "Are you crying?"

The silence extending from the speakers seemed to physically slow the Cruze down even more. Olivia searched for an exit ramp, but there was nothing in sight, just the steel-gray sky, highway, billboards, and the bright yellow-green fields of spring. She let up on the gas, and the engine knocked in protest.

"Ava, what's going on?"

"I think Wes is leaving me. Actually, I don't think; I know."

Olivia drove in stunned silence for a quarter mile before words would come. Guys didn't leave Ava. Ava left them. And even so, this was entirely different. Ava and Wes had been married just over a year. "I'm turning around at the next exit. Where are you?"

"No, don't. I'm okay. It was going to be a short visit today anyway. One of my clients wants to see property downtown at three. Maybe we can meet up tonight when you're driving home."

That was so Ava. Her marriage was falling apart, but she wouldn't let it get in the way of work. "Yeah sure, of course. If you're positive you're okay?"

"I'm okay."

"You said things haven't been great the last few months, but I had no idea you meant *this* not great."

"Turns out they were a bit less great than I thought they were." A shaky sigh resounded from Olivia's speakers. "But whatever. It's not the end of the world."

"Avey…don't." That was Ava. Whenever something got painful, she closed a lid on her feelings as if it had never mattered at all. "Don't shut down. This is your marriage you're talking about. What the heck's gotten into Wes? You guys are great together."

The bumps in the highway seemed to keep time with her sister's silence. Finally, Ava said, "Look, talking out our problems is you, not me. I just want to hang out with my sister tonight and watch a movie and maybe eat my own carton of Ben & Jerry's…after you spend six or seven hours in the car saving the world."

Olivia drummed her fingers on the steering wheel. Maybe this was Ava keeping herself together to get through the day. She didn't care if it took two tubs of Ben & Jerry's, she wasn't leaving her sister tonight until she had a better understanding of what was going on.

They hung on the phone another few minutes, but Ava made it clear through her choice of conversation she didn't want to talk about Wes any longer. Instead, she talked about some of the favorite properties she'd seen in the last week. When they hung up, Olivia was left to contemplate what might have gone wrong. Wes and Ava had been a fairy-tale couple, beautiful and successful and vibrant.

She thought of something Aunt Becky had said when Olivia was watching her work at the potter's wheel. "If you rely only on your eyes to tell you the story, you'll never know it. If you want to create something sturdy, you've got to get your hands dirty. Gotta feel the weaknesses against your fingertips and work them out."

When it came to creating pottery, Olivia was no artist, at least not yet, but she understood what her aunt was talking about. And she suspected this was her sister's problem more than anything. At one point or another, Ava had stopped wanting to get her hands dirty.

Olivia drove another hour and a half, adjusting her wipers up and down as she drove through patches of light and heavy rain without ever leaving it behind. Sometimes the world felt so soggy, it seemed as if it would never dry out. With her bladder about to get the best of her and her tank down to less than a quarter, she took the first exit with a decent-looking gas station.

Under a covered roof, she filled up her tank and stretched, listening to the dance of the rain on the metal awning ten feet above her. If the sun didn't come out soon, she was going to need a megalodon-size coffee to get her through the drive home. *Wait. What're you thinking? No, you won't.* The two dogs and cat who'd be her travel companions home would energize her more than any cup of coffee ever would.

She finished up, made a quick trip inside, and was driving out the side entrance of the gas station when her engine knocked loud enough that the steering wheel shook her hands. She hardly had time to react before the Cruze jolted forward, then died, rolling to a stop.

"Oh no. *Please* no."

Every possible light on her dashboard seemed to be lit up. A dozen thoughts raced through her mind, at least half of which were of the self-deprecating I-told-you-so sort.

She flipped the gearshift into neutral, attempting to use the last momentum to get over to the side. By the time she rolled to a stop, the smell pouring out of the vents was burning her nostrils.

Her shoulders dropped, and her heart sank into her toes. Not only was this likely to be a heavy hit to her bank account that she didn't need, but she could also keep three animals from getting where they needed to go today. Pulling her phone from her purse, Olivia frowned. She was still forty-five minutes from New Madrid, but Sikeston was only ten or fifteen minutes ahead of her and a big enough town that she'd be able to find a mechanic.

Maybe, just maybe, luck would be on her side and this would be a quick fix so she'd have nothing but a bit of a delay holding her back. Holding this hope at the front of her thoughts, she pulled up the internet to search for a repair shop in Sikeston that was open past noon on a Saturday.

Chapter 2

GABE WENTWORTH IGNORED THE PHONE BUZZING IN his back pocket as he snipped through the last of the inner padding from the cast on the back left leg of a basset hound he'd performed surgery on six weeks ago. He couldn't tell for certain, but his phone seemed to be ringing for the second or third time in a row. The calls were running together, which meant someone really wanted to talk to him. Usually his phone wasn't on him while he was working, and he was trying his best to ignore it till he was through with the plucky dog who was healing well after a run-in with a car. Tater Tot, the newly named seven- or eight-year-old hound, had been dropped off at his office by the motorist who'd accidentally hit her after she'd stepped into the road from behind a parked car.

The hound wasn't collared or chipped. When no owner could be located, the driver had paid for the bulk of her surgical expenses and was campaigning to get her adopted quickly from the High Grove Animal Shelter where Tater Tot had been transferred a few weeks ago.

"One more minute and you won't have to thump around on a peg leg anymore." He paused to readjust the scissors and scratch behind one impossibly long, silky-smooth ear. Like the most dignified of basset hounds, Tater Tot was standing with her head raised high. She'd seemed more inconvenienced than afraid of the loud

Dremel tool he'd used on the outer portion of her cast and, unlike most animals when high up on the exam table, was hardly straining to escape.

Patrick, one of the shelter staff members, was the only other person in the shelter's closet-size treatment room. He was holding Tater Tot still while Gabe used surgical scissors to cut through the remaining cast interior.

"Smells like a beast, doesn't it?" Gabe directed the comment Patrick's way.

A few deep creases appeared along Patrick's forehead. "I can't say. Beasts are fictional, and descriptions of them vary widely. If they were real, I assume they'd smell similar to their animal counterparts." He gave the air over the dog a determined sniff. "Bacterial growth?"

Gabe choked down a chuckle. Since he started taking over Dr. Washington's cases here at the shelter three or four months ago, he'd come to recognize Patrick as both the most literal and the most direct person he'd ever met. A bit peculiar or not, Patrick was also a master at keeping the animals still atop the table while causing them a minimal amount of distress—better than most vet techs at his office—and Gabe was happy to work with him.

"There's a bit inside the cast, yeah. Some of the smell is just dog odor times six weeks of no fresh air," Gabe answered. "But the scar's healing nicely. No sign of infection." Finished cutting away the foam-and-gauze interior, he peeled the last of the cast away from the dog's leg. "Give it a couple weeks, Tater Tot, and all this will be a bad dream." Now that she was free of the cast, Gabe ran his hands along Tater Tot's leg and hip. The pins had set nicely.

He nodded at Patrick to loosen his hold, then stood

back, leaving Patrick to guard over her. "It's going to feel weird for a bit, but I'm betting she'll walk without a limp."

After holding her leg awkwardly to the side long enough that it grew heavy, Tater Tot gingerly balanced it underneath her without putting any weight on it. She turned to give Gabe a look that, along with her droopy lids, seemed to say, "What now?"

After dumping the cast, Gabe headed to the treat jar, grabbed a handful, and held one out at the end of the table. After a single sniff of the air, Tater Tot shuffled over. She held the leg to the side as she gobbled it up, but then seemed to forget about her discomfort as she sniffed the air and nuzzled his palm until he produced a few more. By the time she'd munched another two more, she was standing equally on all fours.

He nodded, more to himself than to Patrick. "I'll watch you lead her for a bit, then you know the routine. Keep her kenneled today, increase her activity slowly, starting tomorrow. Call me Monday and let me know how she's doing. I bet you'll be able to clear her for adoption late next week."

Gabe's phone started buzzing again. Hands finally free, he pulled it from his back pocket. It was Yun, his study partner from vet school. They'd graduated last year and were still close. She'd called six times; a few must have blended together. "I've got to take this." He started to add that Patrick should go on ahead without him, but saw that Patrick was already lifting Tater Tot to the floor.

Gabe answered the call and stepped out into the hall. "Where's the fire, Yun?"

"You know I hate it when you ignore my calls."

"I was taking a cast off a basset hound."

"It's quarter to one. I thought your office closed almost an hour ago."

"It did. I swung by High Grove."

"Oh…*that* basset hound. How's she doing?"

"Leg's healing nicely. But you didn't call me six times for that. What's up?"

"Last week at lunch…you had that look. The one you get when it's been too long between adrenaline rushes. And those ants in your pants are only going to get worse if you ignore them."

Gabe dragged a hand through his hair. "What're you getting at, Yun? Even if you're right, life's entirely too busy of late to heed the call of an adrenaline rush."

"Didn't you say you're not on call this weekend? What're you doing this afternoon that's got you so busy on your half day off?"

"I've got Samson with me. He's been moping around all week with all the hours I've put in. I was going to take him fishing, but the rain's not letting up."

"Fishing in the rain isn't fun for human or dog. I've got something way better for both of you. Remember that closed Facebook group I asked you to join? The one that lists emergency cases needing veterinary assistance?"

"Yeah. What about it?"

"Down south near the Bootheel—New Madrid, actually—they've got a warehouse full of animals that've been caught in the floods, and they're seeking volunteer vet services for several different dogs. And you love triage work. I'd ride down with you, but I'm on call."

Gabe suppressed a groan. He could feel the *yes* rising in his throat but held it back. "Yun, I don't know. It's been a long week…twelve-hour days and a string of tough surgeries."

"Samson would want you to say yes. He loves riding in the car."

Gabe closed his eyes, thinking of all the things he could be doing this afternoon, some tasks that needed to be done, others guilty pleasures—like fishing—that he'd put off far too long.

"One of the dogs is a golden retriever like Samson," she added into his silence.

"Yun, you're killing me."

"No, I'm helping you stay connected to a giant part of you that you're trying to shove away in a box. You need this, Gabe. Trust me. Remember, it's me. I know things. This triage event has you written all over it."

He sighed. Yun was right. Ever since he'd needed to retire Samson from their search-and-rescue volunteer work over a year ago due to Samson's arthritis, weekends had been more something to get through than to enjoy. For the last six months, he'd not been honoring the part of him that missed some of what he'd left behind when he'd walked away from two years as a firefighter and EMT to enter vet school. "Tell them I'm a yes and text me the address. I take it there are supplies on-site?"

"Ahh…I think so, but I'll text you that answer."

Gabe hung up as Patrick led Tater Tot into the hall, cajoling her forward with treats a foot or two out of reach. The easygoing dog was using her leg hesitantly but without any sign of flinching or sharp limp to indicate she was in pain.

After watching long enough to feel good about her prognosis, Gabe gave her a pat on the shoulder as Patrick rewarded her with a few more treats.

"She's the last one for me today, right?"

Patrick nodded. "Affirmative."

"Affirmative," Gabe repeated under his breath after telling Patrick to have a good rest of the weekend.

He headed through the double doors that separated the dog kennels and the treatment room from the cat area, gift shop, and adoption center. Samson was sprawled on the floor in a quiet spot in front of the cat kennels. Gabe blinked in surprise to spy Trina, the shelter's resident cat, down on the floor tenaciously grooming Samson along his cheek and behind his ear. Samson was soaking it in, his eyes blinking open and closed in a partial doze.

Even in the bustling room, Samson's ears pricked to attention when Gabe clicked for him. Always at the ready, Samson rolled from his side to his feet and hoisted up with a touch of effort that was typical of a ten-year-old retriever. Looking put off at having her charge disappear midlick, Trina hopped to the adoption counter with the ease of a cat that had four legs instead of three and began to give herself a bath instead.

"Sorry, Treenz," Gabe said, stepping over to give her a scratch as he scanned the room to see if one of the senior staff was available. The place was bustling. Fidel caught his eye and nodded from the other side of the adoption counter. With no need to hang around, Gabe offered him a thumbs-up.

Fidel was with a customer but paused to give him a quick nod. "¿Has terminado?" he called, honoring Gabe's request to only speak Spanish with him.

"*Sí. Hasta la próxima semana, amigo*," Gabe said, glad at the ease with which the words came. He'd taken a few semesters of Spanish in high school and college but wanted to brush up after struggling through a few appointments at his office with Hispanic customers who spoke little English.

With Samson tagging along at his side, Gabe headed out into the rain. After Samson scent marked on a bush or two, Gabe pulled the step stool from the back seat of his seven-year-old Toyota Tacoma that enabled Samson to keep getting in and out with ease.

"I don't know about you, but I'm starving."

As Samson lumbered onto the stool, then onto the back seat of the Tacoma, he let out a well-timed grunt as if in answer. Not that Gabe could remember a time that Samson wasn't down for a burger.

Five years ago, when Samson was in his prime and Gabe was smack-dab in his midtwenties, a Saturday hadn't passed that he hadn't stopped by one burger joint or another, treating them both to a burger or two, keeping Samson's plain and his loaded. Now, four months out from hitting thirty and having learned to appreciate human health a bit more as a side effect of vet school, Gabe tended to take Samson on Saturday hikes instead.

Once Samson was loaded into the back, Gabe headed to the nearest gas station, filled up his tank, and pulled up the maps app in his phone, debating whether to swing by his house before getting on the highway. It was a two-and-a-half-hour drive south to New Madrid from Webster Groves. Depending on what sort of help was needed, it'd probably be pushing midnight before he was back. But worst-case scenario, he kept enough supplies in the back under cover of the camper shell to spend a night away without wasting the time now.

Yun texted that medical supplies were on-site and followed up with a dozen emoji prayer hands, hearts, and a few thumbs-up—he was betting just because she knew he wasn't a fan of emojis. Finished gassing up, Gabe sat in his truck and texted back that he was headed out, then followed with two periods, a l, and another two periods, the closest he'd get to sending an emoji.

Funny, Gabe. You'll thank me later.

She followed with a wink, and Gabe dropped his phone onto his passenger seat, shaking his head. After a pit stop at Five Guys, he made his way to Interstate 55. He drove through the rain, playing music loud to combat the fatigue of a long week, the soft, steady rain, and the blanket of dull-gray skies overhead. The fact that Samson was sprawled across the back seat, snoring heavily, wasn't helping.

Gabe had driven close to two hours and was fighting off a serious bout of fatigue when he grabbed his phone to dial Yun. He pressed the display to find three missed calls from her.

"Where are you?" she asked without saying hello when he dialed her back.

"Ah, no idea. Middle of nowhere, it looks like. Guess I'm about forty-five minutes out."

"Forty-five? Then you've probably not passed Sikeston? It's like a twenty-five-minute drive from there to New Madrid." From her punched breathing, he could tell she was walking.

"Ah, no, I've seen some signs for it though. Why?"

"One of the rescue drivers is stranded there. I'll text you an address. You two are going to the same place. Someone else can haul her dogs back to St. Louis, but they need her crates to move them, and everyone's got their hands full."

"Am I picking up crates or a person?"

"Both maybe. Maybe just crates. I'm in St. Louis, friend. I'm not getting all the details."

"I'll pick up crates, but I'm not hauling around a stranded motorist."

"Gabe, you're such a grouch. You can handle less than half an hour in a car with a fellow rescue worker if you have to."

"I don't know; there's a chance it could kill me."

Yun groaned. "I'm adding 'reassimilating back into humanity' to your to-do list. Text me when you get there. Let me know what cases you get. They've listed a few cool ones, but I'm not going to say and jinx it."

Gabe hung up, and a few seconds later, his phone dinged with a new address that he copied into his maps app. It was twenty-three minutes south of him.

Behind Gabe, Samson's snore crescendoed. "Sleep while you can, buddy. If we end up having a rescue worker with us to finish out this drive, I'm sticking you up front and her in back."

Chapter 3

THE ADDRESS GABE HAD BEEN TEXTED WAS TO A REPAIR shop a few minutes off the highway. The garage—this whole section of town, for that matter—looked to have been in its prime forty or fifty years ago. He knew this didn't have anything to say about the quality of the mechanics working there. Good mechanics could often be found in the most unlikely shops. There were more mechanics in Gabe's family than anything else, from his dad and his grandpa to a few uncles and several cousins. It was no wonder he spoke shop before entering preschool.

Growing up, Gabe had worked at his dad's auto body repair center and had had a free ride into managing it. In late high school, he had found himself way more interested in finding out what had happened to the people who'd been inside than he was in repairing mangled cars.

After a thousand jabs of "*You could be cut out to be a real doctor, not a car doc like your dad,*" from his family, Gabe entered college with the intent of sticking it out through med school. But by the time junior year rolled around, he was losing steam for college life and switched from biology to emergency medical services. He spent a couple years as a firefighter and EMT before switching gears again and enrolling in vet school. Despite the time commitment and cost—and despite the jabs from most of his family—now Gabe couldn't imagine wanting to be anything else.

The parking lot of the repair shop was half full, and Gabe parked in an open spot facing the building. Samson woke from his doze as soon as the engine shut off.

"Stay here, bud. I won't be long." As his dad often commented, Gabe had grown quite comfortable talking to Samson. Maybe too comfortable. Considering Gabe preferred Samson's company on weekends over any other's, maybe he was right.

Even this far south, it was still raining. Gabe jogged through the rain to the cover of the wide awning out front. Off to the opposite side at the edge of the awning, a young mechanic was smoking a cigarette a few feet from a redhead who seemed entranced with something on her phone.

"We closed at two," the mechanic called as Gabe reached for the door. "Can I help ya?"

Gabe froze with his hand paused a couple inches from the handle. A *stunning* redhead, actually. A stunning redhead, and immediately on her other side, two crates were lined against the brick building.

Oh, hell no, *she* wasn't getting in his truck. Damsels in distress weren't on his to-do list. At least, not anymore.

"Yeah, I'm here to pick up those." Gabe pointed at the crates.

The girl looked up, relief washing over her face. She was tall and had long, wavy hair that called to some instinctual part of him to lose his hands in it as he pulled her against him. He was fairly certain she had a remarkable figure to complete the package, but he did his best not to let his gaze stray south of her face.

"You're one of Deedee's rescue drivers?" she asked, her tone hopeful.

"Ah, no, but I'm guessing you are. I got a call that I needed to pick up a couple crates here."

Her shoulders sank, and her eyebrows knit together. "I thought... There must be some confusion. I was told the person they're sending is giving me a ride to New Madrid where the dogs are being held. My crates, too, I guess."

The mechanic took a drag on his cigarette. "If there's a problem, I can give you a ride, sweet thing. It ain't far." There was a hint of seediness to his tone that instantly pricked the fine hairs on the back of Gabe's neck.

The girl gave an immediate shake of her head. "I'm... No. Thanks, but no. I've, uh, got to make a call."

She stepped out from underneath the awning into the light rain, crossing the parking lot as she lifted her phone to her ear. With her free hand, she tugged the hood of her windbreaker over her head. A strong gust of wind blew the rain at an angle, and she tucked her shoulders high as if attempting to create a wind block. She probably didn't want to get in Gabe's truck any more than she wanted a ride with the sleazy guy who was clearly trying to pick her up.

Gabe looked from the crates to the mechanic, who was eyeing him like a bee who'd just interrupted his picnic. He could hear Yun the same as if she were still on the phone with him, telling him not to be an ass. Didn't it matter that he had his reasons? Aside from Yun and some of his immediate family members, women weren't in his life by design.

But leaving this one stranded wasn't going to sit right, and he knew it. He jogged into the parking lot after the girl. *So much for being resolute*. "Hey, lady, I'll give you a ride." He stopped five feet from her. "To New Madrid."

She turned around and looked from him to the mechanic, a frown turning down her lips. "Hold on a sec," she said to whoever was on the other end of her call. She sucked in one side of her cheek and shot a glance toward his truck. Relief seemed to flood into her features at the sight of Samson, who was standing in the driver's seat, watching them from the window with an easy pant curling his mouth into a smile.

She met Gabe's gaze again. "You aren't involved in the rescue?" she asked as if trying to make sense of what he was doing here.

"I'm not a driver, but I am headed down to help."

She was quiet for a few seconds before she nodded. "Okay." She lifted her phone again. "Hey, I've got a ride. We're back to the original plan. I'll see you down in New Madrid tonight." She turned away and dropped her voice, but Gabe could just make out her words. "No, not him. The other one. It's fine." A pause. "He's got a dog. It's fine. I'll text you."

Gabe returned to the spot under the awning for the crates. They were big and bulky, but he grabbed both by the handles and headed for the back of his truck. The camper shell was unlocked, and he'd slid them into the back by the time she joined him. Her arms were clamped over her chest and she had a purse with her, but that was it.

"Do you need anything out of your car?"

She gave a light shrug of one shoulder and shook her head. "I'm good. I didn't pack anything extra."

The mechanic was putting out his cigarette and watching them from under the cover of the awning. "Guess we'll be calling you about your car Monday."

"Thanks. I've got your manager's card."

As the guy headed to an old Corvette on the far side of the lot, the girl appraised the strapped-down trunk at the opposite end of Gabe's truck bed peeking out from between the crates. It was bursting open with the gear that enabled him to camp at will when he headed out on different weekend hikes with Samson.

"Thanks for the ride." There was a touch of hesitation in her tone, and Gabe sympathized with her. As much as he'd not been looking forward to a passenger, he wasn't the one about to pile into a stranger's car.

"You're welcome, but in good conscience, I can't let you get into my truck without asking you to first snap a picture of my plates and text it to someone who knows what you're doing today." He shut the gate and camper top. "Just good practice for anyone getting into a stranger's vehicle," he said, thinking how he was probably freaking her out more.

Her eyes widened a touch. They were hazel with flecks of green and gold. "Okay. Mind if I have a name to go with it?"

"Gabe Wentworth. If you want to snap a picture of my license, too, you're welcome to do so."

"Olivia." She extended her hand, and her eyes widened again at his grip. "Graham," she added, flushing pink and accenting the thin constellation of freckles bridging her nose and the tops of her cheeks. And somehow drawing his attention to a pair of full and defined lips.

"My license is up front in my wallet if you want it." Her hand was cold to the touch, probably from being stuck out in the rain. He held it just long enough to feel the warmth under the surface. "While you get settled, I'll let my dog out to take a leak." *A leak? Really? You couldn't come up with anything better than that?*

There was a thick strip of grass between the shop and the nail salon next door. Gabe pulled out the step stool and called Samson out the driver's side back door.

Samson lumbered down to the pavement and took his time with a deep stretch of his front and back legs. When finished, he fell into an easy trot after Gabe motioned toward the grass island. Oblivious to the rain, Samson sniffed around on the strip of grass before finding the perfect spot to pee. After some more sniffing, he scent marked on a scraggly bush and a broken piece of curb before trotting back through the rain.

By the time Samson was loaded into the back again, the girl—Olivia—was settled in the front passenger seat. She'd removed her wet jacket and had tucked it and her purse on the floor behind her feet. She was wearing jeans that hugged her thighs and a perfectly snug, light-green sweater that drew his attention back to that hair of hers spilling over the top of it.

Gabe paused for a second before sliding into the driver's seat. It had been awhile since someone that pretty had ridden in his truck, and a bit of tension rippled across his ribs. There was no denying he was nervous about the prospect of riding alone in a vehicle with a chick this good-looking. That was irritating more than anything else. He'd have preferred to think the last few years of being a self-proclaimed hermit had moved him past being affected by such a thing.

Clearly, they hadn't. His stomach tightened and his throat threatened to lock up.

He slid into his seat and shut the door, and dammit anyway if the smell of her—something light and fresh like flowers—didn't war with the odor of wet dog inside the cab.

Samson shoved between the seats to give her a solid sniff along her cheek and behind her ear before settling down across the back seat again.

"Cute dog. I'm a sucker for retrievers. And that gray muzzle. He's adorable."

"Thanks, and I'm pretty sure he not only knows it, but takes advantage of it."

She smiled. "What's his name?"

"Samson, but if you've got a treat on you, he'll answer to anything." He flipped on the ignition, more to keep the silence at bay than anything else, and said, "So, Olivia, huh? Nice name."

"Yep, Olivia. And thanks. When I was a kid, I always wished I had my sister's name instead, but I think Olivia's the name I'm supposed to have."

She folded her hands over her lap. Her seat belt was buckled. *His* seat belt, actually, and the way it was hugging her thighs and cradling the valley between her breasts was more action than he'd had in a while.

Get ahold of yourself, man. Has it really been that long? Actually, it had, he realized. Over a year, and that last time hadn't been anything to hang onto. Before that…it had really been awhile.

"What's her name?"

"Ava."

He nodded and allowed a direct glance at her as he slipped the truck into reverse. Her profile was as close to sculpted as he could imagine. He cleared his throat. "What's better about Ava than Olivia?" He pulled out of the parking lot and headed on autopilot back to Interstate 55.

"It's easier to spell. And it's a palindrome. What kid wouldn't want their name to be a palindrome?" When Gabe raised an eyebrow and nodded in agreement, she added, "So, is it just Gabe, or is it short for Gabriel?"

Gabe chuckled. "Honestly, if it was, I doubt I'd own up to it."

It was her turn to laugh. The sound of it rolled across the cab, warm and inviting. Infectious. She dragged a hand through the lower end of her hair, sweeping it all to one side, exposing her neck. "So, uh, thanks again for the ride. This is my first rescue drive, and it's turned into a bit of a disaster."

"What's wrong with your car?"

"They don't know yet. It crapped out a little way east, and I had it towed. By the time I got it here, the shop was a half hour from closing. They've done a few things, and they're saying it could be the transmission, which would really suck. I was hoping to trade it in a few months, not dump a few thousand dollars into it."

Gabe asked a half-dozen questions about what had happened, attempting to isolate what might've gone wrong, and none of her answers sounded promising.

"I take it you know cars," she said afterward.

"I come from a family of mechanics."

"Oh. So... You're not a driver, but you're headed

down to New Madrid to help anyway? How'd you hear about it?"

"A friend of mine. She's joined a Facebook group of some sort. I guess a few of the animals who've been brought in from the floods are more roughed up than others. The organizers are looking for the help of a few vets, so I'm headed down."

"You're a vet?" Her voice pitched a bit at the end.

"Still feels a bit weird to say it, but yeah. I've been in practice since my residency this summer."

"That's cool. I wanted to be a vet when I was growing up, but the idea of that much studying was a turnoff. It's not that I wasn't engaged in school. I was, but I'm dyslexic. Which is why my sister's name being so easy to spell was appealing."

This level of honesty with a total stranger had Gabe unsure of how to answer. He merged onto the highway after first slowing down to let a semi in the slow lane pass.

"It all worked out okay," she added into his silence. "After bouncing around in a bunch of different classes, mostly art and math, I settled on math, but then I went to work for Teach for America after graduating. Now I teach middle-school math, and I love it."

"And you're feeding the part of you who wanted to be a vet with this stuff, I take it?"

Olivia nodded thoughtfully. "I guess so. I grew up on my grandparents' farm." She shot a look back at Samson, who was dozing again, lulled to sleep by the movement of the car. "There were always dogs and cats around. One of my favorites looked a lot like him. She passed away last year. Where I live now, there's a no-pets policy."

"Sounds to me like maybe you should consider finding somewhere else to live. Where're you from?"

"Originally, a half hour south of New Madrid. I live in Illinois now, but I teach in St. Louis."

"Oh yeah? Whereabouts?"

"A magnet school in the city."

"Huh. It's a small world, and a small city. Smaller than I care for sometimes. I've lived in St. Louis my whole life aside from when I was away at school. Originally, I didn't plan on returning, but I did. Family and all. And now I'm taking over a practice in Rock Hill, so it seems I'm staying."

Gabe guessed her to be about twenty-five or twenty-six, a few years younger than him, and he couldn't help but notice there was no ring on her finger. He wondered if the call she'd made had been to a boyfriend. He couldn't imagine her not having her pick of them. Not only was she something to look at, but she seemed nice, the kind of nice you didn't easily forget.

"That's perspective for you," she said. "My hometown's smaller than Sikeston even. Growing up, I drove into New Madrid with my parents and grandparents on weekends to shop 'in town,'" she said, making air quotes at the last two words. "St. Louis was intimidating the first few months. Especially driving downtown. But I like being immersed in so much culture. Back home, it was cotton and corn and the county fair. You also won't see me complaining about such a big variety of places to eat within a few square miles of where I work."

It was on the tip of Gabe's tongue to ask if she had a favorite restaurant when he realized how easy it was to talk to her. Almost as easy as it was to talk to Yun. Ever since they'd met, for whatever reason, he'd thought of Yun like one of those friends he'd had back in elementary school before he started taking notice of things like boobs and thighs and supple neck lines.

But Olivia wasn't Yun. She was a stranger, a stunning, friendly stranger whose curves and sculpted face stood out in his peripheral vision like a bull's-eye. Only none of that was shutting him down. As easily as the conversation was flowing, he wanted to keep it going.

Before he knew it, he'd driven the twenty miles to New Madrid and was pulling off on the exit ramp, and she was telling him there was no need to navigate. She could lead him where they were headed with her eyes closed. And Gabe found himself wishing they had another hundred miles before the trip ended.

It was a curve ball he hadn't expected. There was a beautiful girl in his truck and they were talking and he didn't want it to end. Any of it.

Had someone told him this a few hours ago, he'd never have believed it.

Chapter 4

THE BIG METAL SHED BEHIND MILTON'S FEED STORE had been converted from storage to a temporary holding space for misplaced dogs, cats, and a handful of goats. With no electricity, it wasn't an ideal space, but it was March and above freezing most nights, and the animals were protected from the incessant rain that was tapping on the metal roof like a lullaby.

Years before being legally allowed to drive, Olivia could remember her grandpa asking her to drive his ancient F-150 from the main store along the winding gravel pathway to this shed so that one of the workers could fill the truck bed with shavings as he paid. Maybe time and adrenaline had embellished the memory, but the first time she'd needed to back the truck up into the open sliding doorway, she'd barely had a decent view over the rim of the back seat, and she'd been terrified of backing into one of the sides.

She'd stopped riding along with her grandpa when she was sixteen and went to work at the Dairy Freeze, a little roadside shack fifteen minutes south of here. How she'd possibly thought the nine years that had passed since then had been enough to keep her from being recognized this afternoon, she wasn't sure, but she'd been wrong. She was about to take one of the crated dogs out into the rain for a potty break when a Milton employee popped in to fill a customer's truck bed with some of the remaining bags of shavings piled high in one corner. She guessed him to be in his late fifties or early sixties. He was tall and fit for his age, so much so he rocked the overalls he was wearing. He looked familiar but not familiar enough for her to have once known his name.

He singled her out just seconds after rounding the corner. "Olivia Graham, is that you, all growed up?" he asked, tipping his faded John Deere ball cap.

Guess you'll be making those phone calls to let everyone know you're here after all. She headed over and spent the next couple minutes answering a slew of questions. With her red hair—hair that had been even brighter red when she was a kid—and freckles, Olivia had gotten used to people remembering her. The fact that her grandpa was a second-generation farmer who'd grown up in the Missouri Bootheel didn't help her slide into anonymity either.

Nor did breaking up with a Jones three weeks before the wedding. The Joneses were local legends, mostly because they'd been farming in the Bootheel since just after the Civil War and were one of the few families around here who'd held onto their land through the Great Depression.

As much as she didn't like to think about it, she wouldn't be surprised if people hung onto their belief in her poor judgment for another few decades.

"Trevor know you're in town?" the man asked, driving her suspicion home. He was tossing the forty-pound bags of shavings into the truck bed like they were filled with fluff. The driver wasn't stepping out into the rain, and Olivia hoped the woman stayed put just in case she knew her too.

"I wouldn't think so." Olivia ran the length of the leash through her fingers, refusing to say anything else. She shot a glance over at Gabe. He was squatting in front of a crate and talking to one of the two rescue workers.

It honestly didn't matter if he overheard. Her sister was most likely finishing up with her clients, and she'd be driving down to pick her up. When Gabe was finished with whatever emergency had brought him here, it was doubtful he'd stick around either. And it wasn't like she'd ever see him again. They'd met three hours from home, and there, they didn't run in the same circles. He was a vet; she was a teacher.

Her chest tightened into a knot at the thought. Even if she didn't see him again, he wouldn't be easy to forget. Neither would his endearing dog.

Samson had won her over with a single look. He was one of those dogs who'd bonded with his human so much that she'd swear he knew how to communicate like one. Even here around the kenneled dogs and cats and the playpen full of goats, he wasn't on a leash. Instead, he hung close to Gabe, veering off once in a while to sniff something that sparked his interest.

It seemed as if she'd made a friend during their short time together, because Samson left Gabe's side a couple different times to find Olivia and furtively burrow his head under her hand for a bit of scratching.

"Good kid, that boy," the man said, not dropping the Trevor thing. He tossed in a final bag of shavings and gave a determined pat on the side of the woman's truck, indicating he was finished. She waved a thanks from inside the cab and pulled away.

"Yep," Olivia agreed. Trevor was a good guy. She

wouldn't have been with him since her sophomore year of high school if he wasn't. But him being a good guy didn't mean it had been wrong to break off their engagement.

None of that was any of this man's business. She held up the dangling leash in her hand. "Well, I guess I'd better make myself useful."

He clasped her shoulder and gave a single nod. "You take care now, Ms. Graham. I'll let your grandpa know I saw you."

Of course you will. Olivia resigned herself to checking in with her parents and grandparents soon and returned to the dog she'd been about to take out. She squatted to open the crate door and hooked on the leash. The dog was midsize and cute, some sort of Lab mix, mostly black with patches of white on her chest and back feet. The poor girl was shaking, and Olivia's stomach twisted into a knot of sympathy. She didn't know this dog's story but had been told that while a few of the dogs and cats in the holding area had been dropped off by flooded-out owners, most had been found roaming loose in town or walking up to people's homes, driven to high ground this last week by the rising waters.

The rescue team, run by two middle-aged women named Rhonda and Karen, was posting pictures of each animal on social media and working with the police and animal control in an attempt to locate the owners. After seventy-two hours of being held but not claimed, the animals were listed as available for other rescues or foster groups to request.

"Come on, girl." Olivia tugged on the hood of her jacket and headed out into the light rain after cajoling the hesitant dog out from under the shelter of the metal roof. "It's not raining that hard."

From the dog's glossy coat to the way she meandered around patches of standing water, Olivia suspected she'd been an inside dog. She wanted to know if the dog had been surrendered or found roaming the streets, but there were more than twenty dogs and cats in the shed, and Rhonda and Karen were clearly inundated with coordinating the different parts of this rescue effort.

The Lab mix was one of the two who'd been cleared for transport to the shelter in O'Fallon, Illinois. Since Olivia had had car trouble, the two women were working out whether they needed to find another driver to get the dogs to the shelter this evening. Some shelters would hold kennel space in emergencies like this, but others wouldn't.

Olivia headed to an island of trees at the edge of the feed store's lot, letting the mild-tempered dog sniff around and stretch her legs. Once Olivia stepped from the gravel to the soaked ground, the water began seeping in over the top of the rubber soles of her shoes, and the backs of her calves and thighs grew damp from turning her back to ward off the wind and blowing rain.

Tugging her collar tight, she spotted Gabe headed her way with one of the dogs, a black-and-brown hound of some sort, on a leash and Samson trotting along behind them. He joined her at the island of trees but kept a respectable distance between their dogs. He was wearing a hoodie but didn't have the hood on, and raindrops were glistening on his dark, cropped-short hair and beading up on his shoulders. Samson paid neither dog any mind, instead trotting over to sniff at the base of a jumbled pile of pallets.

"Do you know what they're going to have you do?" Olivia asked, her pulse beating a bit faster now that he was joining her.

Gabe offered a crooked smile that drew her attention to a deep dimple on his right cheek. "I guess the call for help they put out turned into a game of telephone. The vet services they needed were pretty basic, and a veterinarian who left an hour ago took care of them already. One dog needed stitches for a cut on his leg, and Rhonda and Karen were trying to determine if one of the cats was pregnant."

He gave a one-shoulder shrug at her "Oh no."

"It's all working out fine. They've got their hands full, and the request was put out with a plea for help with basic care, which I can do. And it was nice that I could be there to give you a lift."

Olivia's pulse burst into a full sprint. It *was* nice. In fact, even with the disappointment of her car taking a giant crap and knowing she was going to have to face her family tonight when she'd been hoping not to, meeting Gabe and his dog had affected her in a way she hadn't felt in a long time.

"I'm really thankful you did." She debated bringing up the mechanic but decided not to. There was something intimate about standing out in the rain with him and the dogs, watching the raindrops dampen Gabe's hair and roll down his temple. He had beautiful eyes, hazel-green, and a chiseled jawline. And really nice hands. They'd drawn her attention several times on the ride here when they were wrapped around his steering wheel. Long fingers and defined muscles that she could imagine guiding a scalpel with precision as easily as catching a football.

He motioned toward the shed. "I guess I haven't been paying enough attention to the weather this spring. These guys are just from two counties. The water's higher in spots further south." He gave a light shake of his head. "If the rivers keep rising, I can only imagine how much worse it'll get. I've been in practice less than a year, and I'm still figuring out how intricately woven rescue efforts are."

"Having grown up down here, I can tell you the farmlands closest to the water flood often enough no one gives it much notice. At least not until things start getting serious. And I had no idea about the rescue efforts, either, even living here where it floods more years than it doesn't. Not coordinated ones like this. Two of my grandpa's lower fields flood whenever the tributaries around the farm back up. When it gets bad, animals come in from who knows where. They even show up on his porch. He acts all tough and says he's not about to let four-leggeds burn up his profits. But he ends up letting them stay if they don't move on when the water recedes."

Gabe dragged a hand across his damp brow. "I can relate to that. I'm renting where I live. If it weren't for the fact that my lease only allows one animal, there are a couple homeless dogs and cats I've worked with that I'd have loved to bring home."

"Oh really? I wouldn't have guessed you'd end up with homeless animals at a veterinary office."

"Yeah. It happens more than I'd have guessed too. A box of kittens by the door when we get there in the morning, or there's a client emergency—allergies or moving, that sort of thing. A few weeks ago, a guy brought in a basset hound he'd accidentally hit. No owner could be located, so he paid for the dog's surgery. When she was mostly healed, I transferred her to the main shelter I work with. I took her cast off today, so she'll be up for adoption. The vet whose business I'm taking over has developed a good relationship with the shelter that took her in. He's been out from back surgery the last two months, so it's just me now. I spay and neuter the shelter's intakes at a pretty steep discount, and they take on animals I send their way when they can."

"Sounds like a good arrangement." Olivia gave a light shake of her head. "Before I signed on to do this, I was thinking about volunteering at a shelter. I chose the rescue driving instead because I'm convinced I'd struggle with wanting to adopt every animal that comes through the door."

"I can see that. But from what I've seen, it's a pretty rewarding experience."

Once the dogs had gone to the bathroom and sniffed around another few minutes, Gabe and Olivia headed back to the cover of the shed. Before she had even pulled down her hood, it became clear the energy in the crowded metal building had changed. So far, the rescue workers had displayed a "once you've been in the business as long as we have…" attitude about things. Now, Karen was on the phone, tension lining her tone, and Rhonda was flushed bright-red and mumbling to herself.

The only other volunteer at the moment, an older woman who had only recently begun helping Rhonda and Karen with their rescue, was shaking her head. "That's not right. It's just not right," she said.

"What's not right?" Olivia asked as she coaxed the Lab mix back into her kennel with a couple of treats.

"The county fire and EMS is too busy with evacuations to respond to an emergency call about a dog trapped in rising water. There're a couple people trying to get to him, but the current's too strong. Karen's trying to find someone to help. And some bolt cutters too."

"How far away? I bet they have a pair of cutters inside the feed store."

The woman's face brightened. "Maybe five or ten minutes. You know Old Bollinger Road? It ends at the river hangout where all the kids go."

"Yeah. I know it." Olivia looked at Gabe, who was snapping the bars of a crate into place. "I'll help, but could you give me a ride?"

His mouth turned down into a hint of a frown as he stood. "I'll take you wherever you want to go, so long as you promise not to charge into floodwaters before I assess the situation."

Assess the situation? That wasn't the first thing he'd said that had her thinking he acted more like a cop or an EMT than a vet. Maybe he watched a lot of *Law & Order*. Feeling a bit like his gentle yet assertive command called for a "Yes, sir," she settled on "Thanks. I'm a strong swimmer, but I won't get into anything I'm not positive I can handle. I'll run up to the store and see if they have a pair of cutters and meet you at your truck. I know the road dead-ends at the river, but see if you can get an address."

"Yeah, okay. And if they don't have any, I've got an ax in my truck."

Olivia jogged toward the main building, her wet

shoes sloshing. It was a steeper incline than she'd have guessed. By the time she made it up there and borrowed a pair of rusty bolt cutters one of the workers had in his truck, Gabe was pulling up. She climbed into his passenger seat still breathless from the jog and in jeans that had become soaked and muddy from the knee down. Even though it would be hours from now, she promised herself she'd end this day with a soak in a warm tub.

"Thanks again." She did her best not to sound like jogging uphill an eighth of a mile hadn't just sucked the breath from her lungs and made a mental reminder to up her home cardio routine.

Samson's head was sandwiched between the seats. His long, pink tongue swept across her jaw and ear as if he was happy she was joining them again.

"No problem, but honestly, in good conscience, I couldn't have left you to head out on this alone." Pausing at the parking lot's entrance, Gabe asked, "Left or right?"

She pointed left. "It's not that far down the highway. Did you get an address?"

"No, but they said it's a ranch on the left less than a quarter mile from where the road's flooded out. They're in a Camaro out front. I guess the dog's in back in a kennel next to a shed."

Olivia's heart lurched, and she clamped a hand over her mouth. What if they didn't make it in time? "Did they say if the owners are home?"

"No, but I'm guessing not. The call was from a couple teens who were driving down to check out the flooding and spotted the dog. They're the ones who called for help."

Olivia sat on the edge of her seat, tension knotting heaviest in her shoulders and calves. It was all she could do not to urge Gabe to drive faster even though he was already pressing the upper edge of what was safe for the winding highway. The truck wipers seemed to pulse over and over to the beat of "*Hold. Still. Hold. Still.*"

When she directed him to turn on the road leading to the river access, she was thankful Gabe didn't find it necessary to slow to a crawl the way many drivers did on dirt roads. Even so, what felt like an agonizing four or five minutes later, Olivia spotted an ocean of brown water covering acres of fields and creeping past the narrow tree line a few hundred feet away on the left side of the road.

"We must be getting close," Gabe said, having spotted it too.

The as-of-yet-unflooded farmland they passed was mostly still winter-brown, but a few fields had the yellow-green of newly emerging growth. Small country houses popped up here and there. This side of town tended to be more run-down than most other areas of New Madrid, and a handful of the modest houses were in different stages of disrepair. Some needed nothing more than a few coats of paint, a power wash, or some landscaping attention. A few others were littered with long-discarded toys or broken-down cars.

They spotted the Camaro at the same time. The house that it was parked in front of was in the shabbiest condition of any house on the road, close to condemnable even from what Olivia could see through the remains of last year's overgrowth of trees and shrubs pressing up against it. Certainly, the partially collapsed front porch was a hazard. The back of the property dipped in such a way that it seemed unlikely the house wouldn't take on water before the river crested tomorrow.

"If we're too late…" She swallowed back the rest. They weren't too late. They were right on time. It couldn't be any other way.

Gabe's tires skidded to a halt on the wet gravel driveway. "Stay put, bud," he directed Samson. Proving again the almost humanlike connection between them, Samson responded with a soft whine and settled back onto the bench seat.

The teens who'd spotted the dog were nowhere in sight. "I'm guessing they're around back?" Olivia grabbed her jacket and the bolt cutters and hopped out into the rain. The soft gurgle of rushing water made the hair on the back of her neck and arms stand on end as she tugged into a jacket that was nearly as wet inside now as it was outside.

"Most likely." Leaving the keys in the ignition, Gabe jogged around to the back of the truck. He popped open the back of his camper and crawled in. In the space of a minute, he emerged with a tightly wound rope over his shoulder, a set of gloves shoved into his back pocket, an ax, and a jumbled mass of nylon that looked like a set of shoulder straps without the attached backpack in one hand.

As they headed along the side of the house together, his free hand locked around her elbow. "Look, I don't want to come off sounding like a macho prick, but there's no trusting floodwater, not the current, not what it carries. So, what I'm saying is if I don't like the look of things, I'm going to ask you to hang back. I'd appreciate it if you'd trust me. I don't want to have to choose between saving a dog and saving you."

Electricity raced up her arm at the gentle strength in his grip. His words struck a chord. She was a good swimmer, but she'd never swum in a current before. "Okay. You say it like you have experience in floodwater."

"Technically, I do. Ten hours of water rescue training and one real-time rescue."

Olivia started to ask him to clarify what he meant, but they'd rounded the corner of the house, and her heart lurched into her throat. A hundred or so feet out in the rushing, choppy water there was a dog pen attached to a small, rotted shed. From the creaks and groans emanating from it, the shed was on the verge of collapsing from the massive pressure of the water rushing into and past it.

Inside the pen, a large liver-brown and spotted-white hound balanced precariously atop a nearly submerged doghouse that must have been swept by the pressure of the water into the far corner. He was standing on all fours, his gangly legs balancing on the half-hexagon roof, his tail tucked tightly between his legs, and his head bowed low. Even as far away as she was, Olivia could spot drops of water streaming off him. He either hadn't been up there long, or he was having trouble keeping his balance and was getting knocked off.

The two teenagers were behind the house at the edge of the advancing water. One of them, a girl who looked as if she might blow away at a heavy wind, was crying. The guy with her wasn't much bigger. He had his phone out and was filming.

"You two place the call?" Gabe directed the question their way.

The girl startled, not having heard them approach over the eerie gurgle of the rushing water and creaking trees.

The teens hurried their way, the girl swiping at her cheeks and the guy putting away his phone. As they got closer, Olivia realized the guy was soaked to the bone, cropped black hair and all. The girl only seemed wet from the waist down.

"Robby tried to go in after the dog," the girl said, her voice shaky and uneven, "but the water gets really strong about ten feet in. It isn't that deep, but I thought he was going to get swept away."

"It's a good thing you turned around," Gabe said. "Water moving this fast has undercurrents, and you never know when you're going to step into a strong one."

The dog let out a giant bay that stabbed straight into Olivia's heart. She clamped her hands together and scoped out the path to the pen. The unflooded strip of yard between the house and the water seemed to fall in a steady decline, and out in the rushing water, there were areas with more ripples than others. With any luck, it was only three or so feet deep, but Gabe was right. There was no denying that it was moving fast.

"Did you guys bring a boat, or are you going to try to walk it?"

"There's no boat." Gabe's free hand locked around Olivia's arm for a second or two. "Would you want to stay back and hold the rope for me? I think we could use that tree as a pivot joint."

Olivia frowned. If she went in and the water knocked her off her feet, four years of high-school swim team might enable her to reach the pen, but there'd be no carrying out a dog that size through the water. She was willing to bet he was seventy or eighty pounds. Pushing through rushing water while holding a gangly, heavy dog would be a challenge even for Gabe, and he probably had half a foot of height and fifty pounds on her.

It was Olivia's turn to squeeze Gabe's arm, and even in the stress of the moment, some instinctive part of her responded to the solid feel of his biceps. "Just promise not to get into anything you can't handle."

"I'll do my best." He pulled out the gloves tucked into his back pocket and offered them to her along with the rope. "You'll need gloves to hold the rope if I end up fighting with that water." To the teens, he added, "Back her up, will you, guys?"

The dog let out a series of long bays. To Olivia's horror, she realized the water was close to tipping the doghouse over right underneath him. It was knocking back and forth against the metal fence of the pen from the pressure of the water. *Dogs can swim,* Olivia told herself over and over. *They're great swimmers. Even if it tips, he'll be fine till Gabe reaches him.*

Olivia tugged on the several-sizes-too-big gloves as Gabe threaded one end of the long rope through the belt loops of his jeans. His cotton shirt was lifted in the process, exposing an inch or two of remarkably defined obliques and a pronounced vee disappearing into his jeans and sending a wash of saliva over the back of Olivia's mouth.

When finished, he hooked the backpack-looking strap over his shoulders. Just before he tugged a red-handled pull poking out from its left tip, Olivia realized it was a self-inflating life jacket, just a much slimmer one than the bulky Styrofoam-filled floaty she'd worn strapped around her on float trips as a kid.

He checked his pockets, and his eyebrows furrowed together. "Guess my phone's in the truck. Keys too."

"For sure your keys are. I saw them." Before she realized she was doing it, she leaned forward and pressed a kiss onto his cheek. "Be safe." Certain her face betrayed the easygoing demeanor she hoped to portray, she flushed tomato-red. She could feel the heat of it lighting her skin. She hadn't realized till now how good he smelled—subtle but enticing, the scent warring with the earthy smell of the floodwater.

His hazel-green eyes locked on hers for a single second, then he turned and took off down the yard, leaving Olivia to unwind the rope and pivot it around a relatively young but sturdy-looking tree not far out of the water.

"Water's damn cold for late March," Gabe said when he was a few feet in. The brown water parted around his legs, rippling in a heart-shaped wave and forming soft bubbles against his jeans.

A large, floating branch struck the shed with a solid whack, bounced against it for a few seconds, then was swept away by the water. Olivia hoped the metal fence of the pen was concreted into the ground. Maybe it was because it was an open mesh fence rather than a solid wood surface, but at the moment, it seemed to be more stable than the shed it was attached to.

She wanted to keep watching, but Gabe was pushing through the water fast enough that she needed to focus on unwinding the rope and providing him with the right amount of slack. Just over her shoulder, the girl was mumbling "Oh God, what if the water sweeps him away?" more to herself than to her boyfriend or to Olivia.

The tension mounting inside Olivia quadrupled on hearing the girl's expressed fear. She blurted out the first question that came to mind in hopes of suppressing it. "Do you two know who lives here?"

"No idea," the boy spat out. "We just wanted to check out the flooding. We spotted the dog on our way back. We were down the road a way. It's a trip, man. The river access—the whole parking lot—is swallowed up by water." He pulled out his phone and started filming again.

"I kind of get the feeling nobody lives here," the girl added. She dropped her voice and shot a glance back toward the house. "The front yard already looks like a flood ripped through here."

Olivia was inclined to agree with her.

A glance at Gabe showed he was fifteen or twenty feet in, and the water was already over his knees. He still had a long way to go before he reached the dog. As a rush of fear pressed over her, all Olivia could think to do was pray harder than she'd prayed in a long time.

Chapter 5

IT WASN'T A GOOD TIME FOR GABE TO THINK ABOUT the ridiculous fear he'd had as a kid of rivers and brown, murky water. Wasn't a good time to think how, at ten or eleven years old, obnoxious little Susan Drier—who'd lived two blocks away and ridden the same bus—had insisted that everyone's biggest fear was a foreshadowing of how they were going to die.

The rushing water was sharply cold, forty-five or fifty degrees at most. Each new inch of skin experienced the shock of it as he headed in deeper. When the water hit his groin, he suspected his balls wouldn't descend again until July. Worse than the cold was the sweeping pressure of it. Gabe felt like a leaf caught in the runoff along a storm drain. If he lost his footing, he'd be swept ten feet before he could even react.

Then, too, there was the debris in the water bumping into him every few feet: sticks mostly, odd pieces of litter, and, from the way it seemed to react with a will of its own rather than just bounce off him, one sizable fish. The bolt cutters were shoved in the back of his jeans, but he had the ax at the ready. *Ready for what?* The fact was he'd seen entirely too many episodes of *River Monsters* a few years back.

He was in deep enough that the water was starting to swirl around his hips when he caught a glimpse of a hollow, plastic doll head bobbing up and down a body length ahead of him. The once-golden hair was knotted with debris, and the lifeless eyes sent a deep chill up his spine. Then the head was swallowed by the water so fast that Gabe had to wonder if he'd seen it at all.

"Come on, man, get it together."

It was the dog that kept him moving forward. The terrified thing had stopped baying and was watching from the far corner of the pen where he was still teetering on top of the doghouse. Gabe was willing to bet it was only a matter of seconds before the unstable house toppled over. The water surrounding it was high enough that the only thing keeping the doghouse upright was being held in place by the fence it was pressing against.

A glance behind him showed Gabe he'd progressed farther than he would have thought. Olivia was feeding the rope one wrap at a time, her wavy red hair, long, lean body, and bright-blue jacket reminding him of a brilliantly colored bird in a field of dull brown and faded green. She and the two kids were fifty or sixty feet away now, but with the rush of the water filling his ears, they could've been a quarter mile away instead. Soaked as he was from the river and the soft, incessant rain, the small circle of skin where she'd pressed those remarkable lips of hers against his cheek still tingled.

He should've said something, a thanks at the very least, but he hadn't. He'd clammed up and headed into the water like the crotchety old man Yun threatened he was on the path to becoming.

It had been a good-luck kiss, that was all. There was something in her eyes though. Something more than just wishing a near-stranger to be safe. A connection—a knowing—he'd not felt since Claire. "This is right, pursue this," his body seemed to be saying, something it hadn't communicated in years.

Considering the way things had ended with Claire, he'd been pretty determined not to listen the next time his body attempted to do the talking for him. It had taken long enough to get over her when she'd walked away. They'd met at a gala fund-raiser for his firehouse that he'd been talked into attending at the last minute by his captain. She'd looked like Cinderella on the night of her ball, and she'd wanted him. Unequivocally.

She'd come at the urging of her parents after a tumultuous breakup. Rather than having her head turned by one of the eligible bachelors in attendance as they'd hoped, she'd homed in on him. He'd not been introduced to her parents that night, but from getting to know them later, Gabe had no doubt of the looks they'd exchanged when Claire told them she was getting her own ride home.

She'd only been out of college a few months and had still been living with them. He'd parked in the circular drive in front of the remarkable home in a part of the county where he'd never been and figured ten or more of his parents' house would fit inside.

"It's just a house," she'd said, seeing the direction of his gaze and picking up on the quiet that swept over him. "Just a facade. The only real thing is the little bubble of space right around you. It's the only thing that matters."

He'd been thinking about kissing her but had decided when he pulled up that he was better off just letting her get out and forgetting her. A voice inside him—probably his father's—made it clear that a girl like her would have a vision for her life that didn't include him. Then she'd said that bit about the bubble and thrown him off. He asked her what she meant, and instead of answering, she leaned over the seat of his truck and brushed her lips against his. "You have a nice face, Gabe Wentworth. And really good lips." She gave him her number and waggled her pinkie in front of him till he locked his finger with hers and promised he'd give her a call.

The next two years were work and Claire and dating and an engagement. Then he headed into a beast of a fire and nearly lost his life and found Samson in one fell swoop. And when he couldn't pick himself up—when he couldn't be the man who walked into fires again— Claire walked away.

Even stepping cautiously through the water as he was, Gabe kicked a rock protruding from the ground, and just that slightest bit of variation in stride had the torrent of water threatening to topple him. He got his balance, stepped carefully around the rock, and pressed on along the uneven ground.

Claire's walking away hadn't only been because of him. By then the phase that had led her onto a path of mindfulness and minimalist living was over, and she wanted a bigger life than he'd be able to give her.

He'd loved her and her eccentricities, and he would have tried to work through anything, but the life he was living now was more authentically him than the life he'd shared with her. He'd been the square peg that had never been to Florence or Montenegro or Santiago, and he didn't grow up golfing or attending polo matches. All those things she'd loved about him at first, she'd been growing to resent.

The truth was that for the last several years, he'd been happier without her than he'd ever been trying to fit in with her family.

Gabe was midstep when the dog tumbled into the murky water. After creating a splash that reached all the way over to him, the hound disappeared underneath the water. Gabe was moving through water deep enough that it reached the top of his jeans, and every step was an effort to stay on track to the pen. He pressed forward, holding his breath for the dog to reappear. He was navigating around a dip in the ground when he was pulled to a halt from behind. He turned to see that Olivia was out of rope. She was holding onto the end, shaking her head helplessly. The rope was wrapped around the tree and stretched out as far as it could go. He still had another eight or ten feet till he reached the pen.

And without the tree as a brace, if he lost his balance, he'd sweep Olivia off her feet and into the water in a fraction of a second. And that was without the added weight of the dog in his arms.

Gabe searched the flooded pen again, hoping to find that the dog had resurfaced. Relief swept over him when the dog's face popped above water and he began to tread frantically. The rushing water was stronger than the dog's paddling strength, and in the space of a second or two, the terrified animal was swept against the fence. As much effort as the animal was extending to stay above water, it was obviously something he wouldn't be able to maintain long.

Barely conscious he'd made the decision to do it, Gabe yanked at the knot on the rope till it released and tugged it free of his belt loops. He heard Olivia yell in protest, but the rush of the water was too loud to make out her words.

Adrenaline propelled him through the water the last of the way to the pen. Grabbing onto metal fencing, he traveled along the side to the door and felt for the submerged latch. Perhaps the water had been lower when the kids first came by, but they'd been right about the pen being locked. A medium-weight chain was wrapped around the latch and secured with a dead bolt.

Lifting the chain as high as it would go, Gabe twisted it so the rusted dead bolt was just above water. He wasted precious seconds whacking it with his ax but couldn't get the momentum to break it free while holding it. Realizing it was a fruitless effort, he tucked the ax into his jeans and yanked free the bolt cutters. He needed both hands to work the cutters and therefore had to cut through the chain while it was underwater. The cutters were crap, and Gabe struggled to get a strong enough hold on the chain. Finally, it broke and he was able to yank it free and pull open the door.

The dog was struggling to stay afloat, dipping below water and popping his head into the air for a few seconds before disappearing again. A stainless-steel bowl clanked and bounced in the water against the fence, sounding a bit like a wind chime. Gabe allowed the rush of the water to sweep him inside. The current seemed to double in strength as the water pressed around the side of the shed. No wonder the dog hadn't been able to break away from the current to try for the doghouse roof again. It was all Gabe could do to lock his arms and legs against the fence as he was swept into it so as not to smash against the dog.

Even over the rush of the water, an eerie groan resounded through the air, reminding Gabe of the humanlike hisses he'd heard emanating from planks and boards as they succumbed to fire. It wouldn't be long before the shed collapsed under the weight of the rushing water, and there was a good chance of it taking the whole pen with it.

Determined not to be inside when it did, Gabe hoisted one arm underneath the long-eared dog who'd not only noticed him but was attempting to climb onto his shoulders. Once Gabe had hold of him, he flipped around, collapsing against the fence as the floodwater swept past them.

The dog was a big, gangly, long-legged pointer and awkward to hold under perfect conditions. Soaked and slippery and shaking as the animal was, Gabe struggled to find a position in which he could carry him across the water without losing his grip. Even in the chaos, it struck him how underweight the dog was. The ridges of his ribs stuck out like the keys on an accordion.

As soon as Gabe had a decent enough hold, he pushed off. To get out, he needed to head straight into the current. Doing so reminded him of a winter trip to Chicago a couple years back, being at the intersection of Michigan and Oak and walking into the wind and moving absolutely nowhere. The dog whined in his ear but held still. Thankfully. Considering the effort he was spending just to move through the water, Gabe would have a hard time keeping the hound in his arms if he didn't.

"Easy, boy. Gonna get you out of here in no time."

He kept his voice low and soft and kept talking, certain the dog was listening. "Get you to solid ground and then maybe swing by a drive-through and pick you up a nice, juicy burger. Something tells me you may not have had the luxury of a decent burger that many times."

The solid weight of the dog combined with the head-on rush of the floodwater had Gabe's muscles burning by the time he cleared the pen door. Relief swept over him once he turned toward the house and was able to walk perpendicular to the current again. The ax and cutters were no longer digging into his back, and Gabe suspected he'd lost them in the water.

Ahead, on the bank of the yard, Olivia had waded in as deep as her knees and was watching him with hands clamped over her mouth. He was too focused on moving through the water to take much notice of the teens hovering behind her at the water's edge.

"I've got it. Just stay put." He yelled but wasn't sure if she could hear him. Out here, he certainly couldn't hear her.

Aside from shivering in fear, the dog was quiet in his arms. The frightened animal was frozen in place and curled toward his chest, one paw over his shoulder and his long snout wrapped around his neck in a pseudo embrace.

When Gabe was halfway between the pen and the edge of the water, Olivia bolted forward, screaming and pointing ahead in the current. Gabe craned his head over top of the dog to spy a massive branch tumbling his way. Without a doubt, it was sizable enough to take him out. And in water this deep, he didn't have time to outrun it.

Just before it hit, he turned to block the dog from

the blow, afraid the animal's dangling back legs might otherwise be crushed. Gabe's lower back took the brunt as the floating mass slammed against him. A shock wave of pain raced up and down his spine as he was knocked into the water. The thick branch tumbled over him, a dozen twigs and offshoots tugging at his clothes and gripping hold of him like a thousand barbed tines. The branch dragged him along underneath the surface of the water. The slim life vest that ran down his chest and torso pressed up against him, but it wasn't enough to overcome the weight of the branch keeping him submerged.

To overcome his body's natural inclination to suck in air, he locked down his fear and focused on releasing the air in his lungs in a slow, controlled stream. The terrified dog fought to free himself, and Gabe released him, knowing the animal had a better chance if he did. Seconds ticked by as Gabe struggled to be free of the deathly embrace of the branches. He was being dragged along and running out of air. He fought to reach underneath the giant limb and tear away at the branches entangled in the back of his shirt.

The craving in his lungs for his next intake of breath was more intense than anything he'd experienced in the densest of smoke-filled buildings in a stifling fire mask. The pressure in his head became so intense that he could hear a roaring buzz in his ears and knew he was close to passing out or involuntarily sucking in a breath of water.

He was losing focus when something knocked into one side of the branch, dragging the bulky thing down his back and yanking it free from him.

Jutting up, he gulped in air and floated downstream

for another few seconds as his head cleared. The massive branch had struck a tree and was now floating sideways beside him, seeming far more benign that it had a moment ago.

Once his head cleared, Gabe swam toward the bank. He'd been swept downstream enough that the house was blocked from view by a strip of trees at the water's edge. When he got close enough in, he stood and finished exiting at a walk. As the adrenaline began to wane, pain tore across his back and exhaustion slipped into his spent muscles.

Movement in the far edge of the tree line drew his attention as he sloshed out of the water. It was Olivia, weaving between the trees.

"Gabe! Oh my God, I thought… I thought you were swept away." She was running toward him, and now that he was out of the roar of the water, he could hear the sloshing noises from her shoes and drenched jacket. She was soaked, completely. Water streamed from her hair and off her clothes. She didn't stop running until she reached him and all but jumped into his arms. "Oh my God, I thought you were gone."

She was shaking wildly. Gabe allowed his arms to lock around her waist. He held her against him as he caught his breath. The life vest acted as a blockade above the navel, making her hips and thighs and arms stand out more acutely as they pressed against him, enticing and yielding, the only seemingly real thing in the world for too short a time.

She pulled away half a minute later, swiping at the tears running down her cheeks as if they were the only wet parts of her. "Are you hurt?"

As the adrenaline wore off, the scratches on his back were burning, and his spine felt somewhere between hot and numb from the direct smack by the branch. He'd probably feel it even more tomorrow than he did now. "I'm fine," he said aloud. "Thanks to that tree. What about the dog? Did he make it out?"

She nodded. "He's okay. Thanks to you. But he came out too far away for us to catch him. When we saw you coming out of the water over here, the kids left to try to chase him down. He ran in the direction of the river access, and unless he runs back into the water, he won't be able to go far."

Gabe followed her as she wove through the strip of trees and over sloshy ground. Water was falling off him in sheets. When they reached open grass, he closed his palm over the small of her back. "Let's get to my truck. I've got some dry clothes in back. They may not be the best fit, but they'll feel better than what you're wearing. And Samson can help us find that dog."

Chapter 6

MAYBE SHE'D NEVER REALIZED IT BEFORE, BUT THERE were few things in life more rewarding than a good heater when you needed it. Especially the ones that blew from dashboard vents onto your face and hands with the strength of a blow-dryer set to medium.

Twenty minutes after hauling herself out of the chilly water, Olivia's shivering was still emanating from deep in her bones. She leaned closer to the nearest vent, certain she could give a massage chair a run for its money if someone sat on her lap. When the branch had knocked Gabe under, she'd run in after him, tripping in a dip in the ground and coming close to being swept away herself. Thankfully, she'd been able to grab onto a tree limb that had been protruding into her path.

Gabe seemed to be warming up faster than her, which made no sense considering she'd had enough of a glimpse as he'd tugged off his ripped shirt to confirm how low his body fat actually was. And maybe she'd ogled a bit too. When he'd come out of the water, his lips had been light blue, but they'd transitioned to light pink. Color was coming back to his face too.

Olivia had changed into one of his spare hoodies. It was big and comfy, but her soaked bra was creating softball-size circles of dampness right through the cotton. After debating between ignoring it and hoping he didn't notice or clamping her hands over her boobs until they dried, she chose the former. Hopefully the high heat would help dry the material out.

She was also wearing a pair of too-big flannel lounge pants that Gabe had tied around her waist with a strip of twine after realizing the tie string was missing. They were long and oversize, and there'd be no keeping them up without the twine's help.

"I don't think this smell is going to wash out of my hair in one wash," Olivia said, sweeping a damp lock over one shoulder. She was also pretty sure even the deftest of scent hounds couldn't distinguish her smell from that of the bottom of a pond.

She found a bit of reassurance in the fact that Gabe had to smell the exact same way. And aside from a dozen thorough sniffs of both of them, Samson didn't seem to mind.

"Try rinsing your hair first with baking soda when you take a shower. It works well with dog odors." As soon as Olivia glanced his way, he shook his head. "Sorry. I'm out of practice when it comes to talking about anything that isn't vet-related."

"Why?" Olivia studied his profile as he drove down the dirt road toward the river access in search of the dog.

"Why what? Why baking soda?"

"No; I'm already a believer in home remedies. Why are you out of practice?"

He pursed his lips. "Is the rigor of vet school enough of an answer?"

"If you need it to be."

He looked her way, his bright hazel-green eyes standing out starkly from the gray skies behind him. "If you'd said anything but that, that's the only answer you'd have gotten."

"My sister tells me I'm good at cutting through the bull and getting to the point."

"I've got no reason to disagree." He drummed his thumb on the steering wheel. "Aside from a close friend who went to vet school with me, you're the only girl who's been in that seat for a while. By design."

Olivia nodded and waited to see if he'd offer more. She had so many questions. They'd reached the end of the road, but the parking lot to the river access was a hundred feet away and underwater. The floodwater was flowing over the road, swallowing it up and reaching halfway up a signpost. If the dog had come this way, most certainly he'd angled off in another direction away from the river.

"I had a fiancée," Gabe added after a bit of silence. "A serious one. Before I entered vet school. I was a firefighter-EMT with the city. We got engaged a little over a year after getting together." He shrugged one shoulder. "Half a year into that, I had a bad experience in a fire. Things were going downhill between us before then, I guess. I just didn't see it." He scanned the horizon at the water's edge. There wasn't a living thing in sight. "Want to get out and walk around, or would you prefer I drive along the road in the other direction first?"

She'd do it if she had to, but Olivia was less than excited at the idea of getting wet again. If only it would stop raining. "I'm good to drive up and down the road once or twice, then we can reconsider our options."

Gabe slipped the truck into reverse and turned around in the direction of the highway. Samson sat up on his haunches and looked out the window. Without seeming to give it any thought, Gabe cracked the window next to Samson several inches, and the retriever sniffed the air deeply before letting out a little sigh.

A wave of envy washed over Olivia about how perfectly used to each other they were. She'd never had that level of closeness with a dog, even though she'd loved several over the years. Her grandpa's dogs had been farm dogs, lazing around outside all day and sleeping in the garage at night. She didn't have anyone—person or animal—in her life like that. She and Trevor had had some semblance of it. Maybe. He'd known which pair of cozy pants she slipped into after a long day during the winter and how she liked fresh mint leaves in her iced tea in summer. And there were a hundred things she'd known about him without giving it any real attention any longer.

But when it came to people, knowing someone wasn't enough reason to commit to a life together. After months of looking within as the wedding loomed closer, Olivia had realized that over the years they'd been together, she'd become someone who wanted something out of life that Trevor didn't.

"Will you tell me what happened in the fire?" So many things had clicked into place at learning he'd been an EMT and firefighter.

He released a sigh like steam releasing from a teapot. "I stepped away from the line and got lost in the smoke. It was an old brick two-story house down near Lafayette Square. I'd have been a goner had it not been for Samson. I opened a door and found him in a room, locked in a kennel. I wrapped some kids' pajama pants around his neck, and he led me out. Even with his help, I barely made it. It was the smoke and the heat. Me and two guys who'd been trying to find me were hospitalized a couple days. And while we were in there, one of our buddies died in a warehouse fire."

Gabe swallowed and gave a light shake of his head. "After that, I was done. I couldn't do it anymore. And *not* being able to do it knocked the wind out of me more than anything I'd ever experienced. It took a month for her to do it, but my fiancée walked away." He shook his head. "By then I had Samson. The family he'd been with couldn't bring him to where they'd relocated. He was taken to a shelter and treated for second-degree burns on his paws.

"When I got out of the hospital, I made for that shelter and tried to adopt him, but he was in treatment and wasn't cleared for another few weeks. I went by every day to check on him. Then one day I showed up and he'd been cleared and they'd waived all the fees. That was five years ago. His paws still needed care, but they trusted me to do it. Being witness to his recovery was one of the things that started me thinking about vet school. I don't think anyone there remembers it any longer, but that shelter is the main one I work with now."

Olivia shook her head, closing her hands over her mouth for a second or two. "Wow. Absolutely wow. I don't know what to say except no wonder you two are so bonded."

"We've been a good team. When I gave up firefighting, I wasn't one hundred percent ready to walk away from the emergency-rescue world. Once Samson was fully healed and had his strength back, I went through search-and-rescue training with him. It took about six months, but I was able to get him certified to find cadavers both on and off leash."

Olivia turned to give Samson a look of appreciation. He was still looking out the window, but she had a good view of his faded-gray muzzle. She'd never have guessed he'd once had such an impressive career. That either of them had.

"And believe it or not, he was pretty good at it," Gabe continued. "He once found an old guy who'd walked out of an extended-care senior-living home in Festus. The guy had Alzheimer's. He was dehydrated and had done a number to his bare feet, but he was okay. Most of the time, when it comes to search and rescue, that isn't the norm. Samson had a few other successes, too, but they weren't as rewarding, if you know what I mean."

"I think I do. That had to be hard. And by 'was,' I take it Samson's not doing it now?"

"No, he's been retired a little over a year. He gave it his all every time we went out, but after a couple months of him being super stiff in the hips most of the week afterward, I figured I needed to be the adult and find something else to do on weekends. School was pretty rough then, so I started taking him on hikes and camping trips just to get away from it all. He's a trouper, and he's got his own sleeping pad in back of the truck for when we camp." He cocked an eyebrow. "His is twice as padded as mine. I've considered fighting him for it, but when he gets a good night's sleep, that snore of his is a few decibels quieter."

"That's sweet. Really sweet." Olivia was quiet a moment, picturing Gabe and Samson camping in the back of the truck under a star-studded sky. "So, this explains you asking me to take a picture of your license plate. And you having an ax and rope and a self-inflating life vest in the back of your truck. I thought maybe you'd been an Eagle Scout or something."

Gabe chuckled. "I was in the Scouts but didn't make it that far. But you know what they say…once a fire-fighter, always a firefighter."

Olivia wasn't convinced it was her place to bring it up again now that the conversation had taken a turn, but she couldn't stop herself. "Your, uh, fiancée leaving… I'm sure that was hard."

He brought the truck to a stop by a narrow strip of woods off to his left between two newly planted fields and scanned the trees. "It's a deer. See it? Behind the cedar, a hundred feet in."

Olivia leaned over the center console and followed the direction he was pointing. On the second sweep, she spotted a fleck of white that turned out to be the under-side of a swishing tail. "Oh. There she is. She's pretty. Want to stick around here a few minutes and see if the pointer shows up? Maybe he'll catch her scent and come to investigate."

Gabe made a face that seemed to say it was worth a shot. He pulled to the side of the empty road but left the ignition running, for which Olivia was thankful. Without the heat blowing on her, her shivering would certainly return full force.

She was beginning to think he wasn't going to respond to her comment about his ex-fiancée when he spoke. "Her leaving was hard. At the time at least. I have to admit I'm pretty sure we'd have been among the fifty percent of marriages that wind up in divorce a number of years down the road. Probably not even very many years. So, I guess it all worked out in the end."

His answer only made her want to know more. "Do you say that because you two were too different…or too much the same?" It was on the tip of her tongue to tell him she'd walked away from a guy and an engagement, but she couldn't bring herself to do it until she knew his answer.

Gabe fell quiet and studied her for several seconds. Olivia let her gaze travel from those remarkable eyes to a pair of equally remarkable lips, and her heart pounded like a bass drum in her chest. When he wasn't smiling, she could just barely make out the dip in his cheek from his dimple.

She was pretty certain she'd never wanted to be kissed more than she did right now. Only she'd been submerged in floodwater a half hour ago and probably still very much looked the part.

Even so, she suspected her hormones weren't the only ones racing because he cleared his throat abruptly and looked back into the woods.

"There's another one," he said a moment later, nodding toward the deer who was chewing on a long, thin twig. "Curled up on the ground a few feet to her right. Based on the size, I'm betting it's last year's fawn."

Olivia craned to see but couldn't. She unbuckled and leaned over the center console for a better look. "Oh, there. What a cutie. I bet they're tired of all this rain."

She was still leaning over the console when he looked her way again. She swallowed, realizing that mere inches separated them. Inches that would be so easy to claim as her own. The skin of her face tingled as if there were an electric field between them.

She could hear her grandpa's voice asserting that no one liked a woman who was too forward, but she took a leap that surprised her, brushing her lips over Gabe's. Maybe he met her partway. Maybe it was all her. It was hard to tell because she closed her eyes just before they connected. It was a gentle kiss, subtle and with enough hesitation to fit the circumstances. Gabe's thumb traced her jawline, creating a thin trail of pleasure along it.

She pulled away enough to meet his gaze. She'd just kissed someone in his truck mere hours after meeting him.

Gabe's lips stayed parted slightly, and his eyes searched her face. This time, there was no doubt about it. He moved toward her, deepening the kiss and awakening a heat that swept through her veins on a superhighway she hadn't realized was a part of her. His hand slipped from her jaw to the back of her head. His tongue brushed against hers with a subtle, unimposing force that Olivia let herself savor.

This. So much this. She'd dreamed of kisses like this back when she was a kid who believed in princes and happily-ever-afters. Dreamed of wanting and receiving and giving all blended into one.

With an ease that seemed impossible considering the bulky center console and the protruding steering wheel, Olivia made her way onto his lap. Maybe it was so easy because his hands quickly locked around her hips to guide her.

This is crazy. This is so crazy. You don't even know this guy. But Olivia wasn't listening to caution. She brushed her lips along the side of his neck, letting them trail over the smooth skin underneath a shadow of stubble, pausing over his Adam's apple.

This wasn't her. She didn't do this.

Even so, it didn't stop her from dropping her mouth lower and savoring the skin in the dip above his sternum. His hands slid underneath the hoodie, circling her bare back and then locking around her hips again, pulling her even closer.

She wasn't entirely sure where she wanted this to go, but she didn't want it to stop. It didn't matter that her knee was digging painfully into the door and Gabe was wearing a seat belt and Samson was suddenly very interested in what they were doing. The curious dog gave Olivia's ear a sniff and followed it with a solid lick across it. A few loose strands of her hair got caught in his mouth in the process. Olivia pulled back from Gabe, laughing and dragging her wrist across her ear. "Talk about a wet willy."

"Samson, bud, lie down." When Samson obeyed and sank back onto the seat with a grunt that seemed a touch exaggerated, Gabe unclicked his seat belt. After releasing it with obvious care so as not to catch her up in it, he sat up straight and kissed her with an intensity that made her feel as if she were melting into a puddle. "You're so damn beautiful it hurts."

So damn beautiful it hurts. No one had ever said anything like that to her. Ever.

She and Trevor had been in tenth grade when he'd asked her to homecoming, and they'd been friends as kids. She suspected she could've dyed her hair gray and sported a pair of baggy overalls at their wedding and Trevor wouldn't have noticed.

Gabe's hands slipped underneath her hoodie again, confident and searching and respectful at the same time. Olivia was savoring the sensation of running her lips along the edge of his jaw and over to his earlobe when Samson woofed and Gabe jerked back abruptly.

"What the… Looks like we have company."

Olivia sucked in a breath as she glanced out Gabe's driver's-side window. They *did* have company. And not just anyone. Her stomach flipped full circle. An instant queasiness settled in and her face burned hot. "Of all the luck."

The man from the feed store was idling directly across from them in a truck, a look of clear disapproval on his face. *I'll be telling your grandpa I saw you.*

Now he wouldn't just be telling her grandpa. He'd be telling the whole town.

Olivia scrambled off Gabe's lap and dove awkwardly to her seat, a considerably more difficult feat on return.

Gabe cleared his throat. "You okay if I see what he wants?"

Olivia pressed her eyes closed for a split second. "Yeah, go ahead. It can't make things any worse."

He rolled down his window. "Can I help you?"

"Looks like you two are helping yourselves, you ask me. I got off work and thought I'd drive down and see if you were able to save the dog."

"We got him out of the pen," Gabe said, ignoring the loaded comment, "but he took off. We've been driving around looking for him."

"Have you, now."

It was a declaration, not a question, and it was sharp

and stinging. Gabe tensed enough that Olivia could count the muscles in his jaw.

She could hardly summon the courage to look the man in the eye but recognized that hiding wouldn't help this not become the talk of the town. "There are a couple deer in the woods," she offered over Gabe's shoulder. "We think the dog might be drawn to their scent."

"Hound, was he?"

Olivia had presumed so, but Gabe spoke up. "A pointer. German shorthaired, if I were to guess. Reddish-brown face and ears and a flea-bitten look to his coat. Pretty sure his tail was docked."

The man nodded and ran his tongue along his front teeth. "I'll be on the lookout for him."

Gabe popped open his door and hopped out. "Got a pen and paper? I'll give you my number in case you spot him."

With Gabe blocking her view, Olivia sat back in her seat and released a tired breath. Conversations with her parents and grandparents were already playing out in her head. The same way she could hear Ava telling her she had a knack for creating chaos. Her muscles tensed in reaction to words that hadn't yet been spoken. It wasn't true. She really wasn't one to cause chaos. Except for calling off her engagement less than a month before a wedding this entire town had been anticipating, perhaps.

Besides, she could make out with Gabe—or anyone else, for that matter—any day of the week and not be in the wrong. She'd broken things off with Trevor six months ago. With the exception of one major fail of a blind date that Ava had talked her into, she'd not so much as thought about dating. Or climbing onto some really hot, amazing guy's lap hours after meeting him for the sexiest make-out session she'd ever had.

As Gabe stepped back into the cab, Olivia waved a humiliated goodbye.

"You okay?" he asked after shutting the door.

"Yeah… He, uh, keeps in touch with my grandpa pretty regularly, I guess."

"Sorry about that. If you think it would help to put a face with the gossip, I'm happy to stick around and introduce myself."

Olivia folded her hands on her lap. "It don't think it would. Thank you though."

Her hands were shaking, and she wasn't sure if it was still from the cold water or from being caught in such a compromising position when it had seemed to be just her and Gabe and the rain, or maybe both.

The sky was growing dark in the east, and it occurred to her she hadn't eaten since breakfast. The shakiness in her hands could also have something to do with the ravenous hunger sweeping over her.

She released a tired breath. "This sucks."

"I'm sorry, Olivia. The road seemed all but deserted. I didn't think we'd have company. If there's anything I can do…"

This whole thing was her fault, not Gabe's. And she didn't want him beating himself up over it. "There's one thing maybe." She forced a lightness into her tone she didn't yet feel. "I don't know about you, but I haven't eaten since breakfast, and I'm the queen of stress eating. If you're hungry, it just so happens the world's best shake-and-burger joint is down the road a little way.

Maybe we could circle another time or two, then if we don't see him, grab something to eat and check back in a little bit?"

"Olivia Graham, you know how to speak my language." He cocked an eyebrow, his gaze dropping to her lips before he turned his attention to the road. "In more ways than one."

Chapter 7

A HALF HOUR HAD PASSED SINCE OLIVIA HAD abruptly shimmied off his lap, and Gabe's blood was still running hot. It could very well be seventy-two and sunny instead of fifty-one and drizzling. Considering he'd come closer to drowning in chilly floodwaters than he wanted to think about, he debated offering Olivia the kudos she deserved. Considering how their short make-out session had ended, he wasn't convinced he should. It wasn't just those remarkable lips or the body that sent his thoughts in a thousand wild directions. There'd been something exceptionally real and raw in those few quiet, unexpected minutes.

And a part of Gabe that had been slumbering the last several years had stirred to life to salute with a *hell yes*.

The tree-house-size shake-and-burger joint she'd suggested was the takeout-only sort that seemed to thrive in small towns. Even before Gabe got a whiff of grilled beef spilling out into the parking lot, he knew he wouldn't leave disappointed.

As they'd waited for their order, Olivia had admitted to working here at the Dairy Freeze for two years when she was a teen. Gabe could envision a younger version of her working behind the window, her striking red hair drawn up in a ponytail sporting one of the blue ball caps embossed with cheeseburgers, handing out white paper bags stuffed with greasy burgers, and that smile of hers sending a town full of guys into a tailspin.

On an afternoon as dreary as today, he was surprised to find business as steady as it was. It was sunset and the clouds were thinning to the west, a sharp contrast to the blanket of gray, endlessly dripping clouds overhead. With any luck, this wet spell was finally about to break.

After being caught midembrace, and sensing that Olivia was worried about the ramifications she'd face in a rural area like this, Gabe wasn't eager to suggest they eat in his truck. Instead, they sat side by side on the dry half of a picnic table under a narrow awning near the walk-up window. Aside from him and Olivia—and Samson, who planted himself attentively between them in the event that even the tiniest morsel fell to the ground—everyone else was taking their food to go.

As he bit into the burger, Gabe stifled a groan of pleasure. They'd prepared it just as he'd asked: cheese, lettuce, pickle, ketchup, and mustard. "Damn." He swallowed and took another bite before shaking his head. "Worth a much longer drive if you ask me."

Olivia mumbled in agreement and wiped the corner of her mouth with a napkin even though nothing had been there. Had there been, he'd have been tempted to swipe it off with his thumb. Any excuse to connect with that mouth again.

"I know," she agreed. "I make it a point of stopping by every time I come home."

"I can see why." He swallowed a few more bites and washed them down with a mouthful of root beer. "How far away is your family?" She'd been visibly tense on the drive here, but she seemed to be calming down. He wanted to keep the conversation away from what had happened in the truck, but he also wanted to know more about her. A lot more.

Olivia nodded in the direction of the road toward the west. "My grandparents' farm is another ten miles away. It's where I grew up. My parents didn't get a place of their own until after my sister and I moved out. It was a different upbringing than most of my friends had, but it worked for us. My parents lived in town a year or two, but last summer they moved into a prefab house on one corner of my grandparents' property. They aren't the best at adulting, I guess you could say."

"There are all sorts of normal anymore, if you ask me. So, your grandpa's the real thing? A full-time farmer? Growing up in the city, I can't say I've known anyone who's managed to make a living that way."

Olivia nodded as she finished chewing a bite of her burger. "Yeah. Cotton mostly, but corn too. He inherited the land—about a hundred acres—from his dad. My uncle's in the process of taking over so my grandpa can retire, though everyone says he won't stop farming completely till the day he dies.

"My uncle lives in town with his family and still works the night shift at a bakery three days a week. At some point, he'll move his family onto the property, but not for a few years. He wants his kids to finish high school where they are. My dad and my aunt are the only other Graham siblings, and neither of them are interested in farming. I guess you could say my dad's a dreamer. He's always working on the next big thing, which drives my mom nuts."

Her fingers, long and delicate, were wrapped around her burger. Gabe had a feeling it would be awhile before he forgot the feel of them brushing over the ridge of his jaw.

"Yeah, well, neither of my parents are dreamers, and they still drive each other nuts."

Her tense shoulders fell as they talked. Gabe took it as a good sign that she was relaxing again, the same way she had on the drive down when they'd fallen into easy conversation. Between bites of burger and fries, Olivia filled in the silence with what she'd loved best about growing up in a such a rural area—the night sky; crisp, clean air; and the county fair—and what she'd loved least—the isolation and everyone knowing pretty much everything about everyone else, or assuming they did. Gabe listened intently, distracted only when their fingers brushed as they reached for fries at the same time and by how her long lashes framed her hazel eyes.

Her sense of humor, a touch dry blended with a heavy dose of realism, was refreshing. Unlike a couple of single women his age who worked at his clinic, she didn't seem to be tailoring her answers to what he might hope to hear. It was this as much as the fact she was so damn beautiful that had him reaching out to brush the tips of his fingers down her temple. She could probably read it on his face, but he wanted to do much more than that.

He was impossibly close to leaning over and kissing her again—and he was confident she'd open her mouth to it the same way she did earlier—when a truck pulled into the parking lot and slipped into an open space ten or so feet away. The look that passed over her as she glanced that direction sent an alarm through Gabe.

"I, uh…" Bowing her head, she pressed her middle

and index finger against her forehead. "Wow." She sucked in a breath and looked up.

He followed her gaze and was only half-surprised when it landed on a guy about his age behind the wheel. He had dirty-blond hair and was wearing a faded hoodie, and his mouth had fallen open in surprise at the sight of Olivia.

"Everything okay, Olivia?"

"Yeah." She swallowed hard enough that he heard it, then broke into a flurry of activity, lifting their empty fry container off the table and folding it flat into her wrapper along with a bit of her discarded bun. He didn't think it was his imagination that she'd gone a few shades lighter.

"I was trying to find a way to bring it up. I guess this is another thing about life out in the middle of nowhere that I'm not crazy about. You end up running into the one person you'd enter a half marathon to avoid even though you hate running." She gave Gabe a pleading look. "It's getting pretty dark. We should look for the dog again while we can still see. I'll, uh, be just a second though."

When she reached for the trash, Gabe waved her off. "I'll get it."

Old boyfriend, he guessed as she headed over to the driver's-side door of the guy's truck. The guy didn't seem that eager to get out. It wasn't until Olivia came to a standstill by his window and a few awkward seconds had passed that he opened the door and stepped down from the cab.

Gabe gave the last bite of his burger to Samson, gathered the trash, dumped it, and returned to his truck with the dog trotting along at his heels. After getting Samson loaded with help of the stool, he checked his work email on his phone. He skimmed the subject lines to see most were sales pitches by drug companies and a few were responses from clients to the automatic follow-ups they received after bringing in an animal for a visit. He'd look at the messages later.

He kept tabs on Olivia in his peripheral vision. Gabe didn't need to be an expert at body language to know she was stressed. Her whole body seemed stiff and tense. Her arms were tucked over her chest, and she shook her head abruptly a couple of times, sending that remarkable hair of hers tumbling over her shoulders. The guy didn't seem to be antagonizing her or Gabe would've stepped out. His head was tucked, and he was staring at the ground more than he was at her. Finally, the guy tipped his hat and took off for the ordering window.

Gabe gave her time to get settled in the truck before reversing and pulling out of the lot. Once she was buckled, he asked, "Back to where we came from?"

She nodded, tucking her hands under her thighs.

When she didn't seem ready to broach what had just happened, Gabe decided to focus on the dog. "I was thinking he might try going home after he calms down and runs off some energy. Not to his pen, per se, but to the house."

"That makes sense. A lot of sense, actually."

They rode in silence, and when she didn't seem ready to talk, Gabe turned up the radio, scanning stations until he landed on one with good reception. It was bluegrass, and whatever was playing had a catchy fiddle and banjo melody.

By the time they were headed down the dirt road again, it was close to fully dark, but mercifully the rain was ceasing. "What do you know. Maybe we won't be building arks after all."

As she smiled, Olivia's white teeth were illuminated by the soft light of the dashboard. "That'd be nice. It's been so long, I can't remember the way it feels not to have the ground squish under your feet with every step you take." Gabe was pulling into the tattered driveway of the house when she added, "And around here, I bet everyone's ready to not have rivers filling people's backyards."

He slipped the truck into park and shut off the ignition, scanning the heavily littered front yard for any sign of the dog. The windows were dark, without even a hint of digital light shining out of any of them, causing Gabe to suspect the power was out. The level of trash strewn about the front yard and the general disrepair of the home made it difficult for him to give the benefit of the doubt in terms of a caring pet owner residing here. Maybe there was a genuine excuse for why the dog had been left behind. Maybe there wasn't.

Perhaps the owners were out of town and not keeping track of what was going on in their hometown. Perhaps it was the fault of someone else entirely. But whoever was responsible for that pointer should've pulled him out yesterday at the latest.

"Dogs are smart, but do you ever wonder how much they understand about how much of their condition is the responsibility of their owner?"

"I was wondering the same thing," Olivia said as she unbuckled her seat belt. "If he knows that human error left him nearly drowning in a locked pen. The other thing I thought of was I don't think those kids were telling the whole story."

"How so?" Gabe asked as they stepped out.

"The dead bolt. From what I could see, it looked like it was submerged a foot at least."

"It was. Maybe a little deeper. I wondered that too. How those kids knew to ask for someone to bring bolt cutters when they didn't get more than halfway to him."

"Yeah, the river's rising fast, but not that fast."

"The truth of the matter is that dog was probably dealing with floodwater in his pen for more hours or days than I care to think about." Gabe headed around to the truck bed, opened it and the camper, and crawled in again. He rooted around in the camping tub until he found the metal tin where he kept a couple days' worth of Samson's kibble and a stainless-steel bowl.

When he shimmied out with the one arm full, Olivia let out an appreciative "Oh." She stepped to the side as he swung off the gate. "Drawing him in with food is a great idea." She raised her hands, crossing fingers on both of them. "Let's hope he's in hearing distance."

Leaving the gate open, Gabe shot Samson a look through the back-seat window as they passed by. He could just make out his loyal dog in the darkness. Samson was watching them intently, ears perked forward. "I know, bud. You'll get your dinner in a bit. Promise."

Olivia laughed softly. "He's the cutest dog I've seen in a long time."

"Watch out; he knows it." He offered the tin in Olivia's direction. "Want to shake it as we walk? I'm hoping he knows the sound. Most dogs recognize it, regardless of what their food's kept in."

"Sure." She took the tin, an old two-gallon popcorn one with a snowman family on the front, and shook it as they fell into step across the yard.

"Gabe?" Her voice was punctuated by the effort she was putting into shaking the tin. "That thing I was trying to tell you before…before we kissed…"

She stopped shaking the tin and paused midstep. Her words tumbled out, the weight of them visible on her shoulders. "I did that same thing. The same thing your ex-fiancée did. Only it was worse. Three weeks. That was all we had left before the wedding. And everyone here knows it. What's worse, he didn't do anything wrong. It was me. All me. I just couldn't do it." She stopped to collect herself, shifting the tub to rest on her hip. She clamped a hand over her mouth and gave an abrupt shake of her head.

Gabe was determining whether to kiss her or let her finish first when he heard a long, drawn-out yawn that finished off in a whine, just audible over the gurgle of the floodwater. They both froze instantly. The sound had come from the front of the house.

Gabe scanned the littered, darkened porch. In the corner, nearly lost behind the haphazard lawn furniture and a knocked-over table, the pointer was cautiously rising onto stiff or wobbly legs.

From the confines of the truck, as if sensing he was in danger of losing his dinner, Samson let out a baritone woof.

The pointer looked from Gabe and Olivia to the truck, whined, and turned his attention to them again.

Gabe was debating what to do next when, in the darkness, he was just able to discern that the gangly pointer was cautiously wagging his docked tail.

Moving slowly and deliberately, Gabe set the bowl down on the ground and glanced at Olivia. "Let's finish this conversation when we've got nothing but time to do it justice. For now, how about you fill that bowl with kibble, because I think we're just a step or two from making a new friend."

Chapter 8

THE DOG RECOGNIZED THE MAN BY HIS SCENT. IN THE still night air, it blended with the woman's and the sharp metallic odor of the object she carried. His stomach cramped and his mouth watered at the sound of the kibble clanking inside it.

Weakened from the swim as the dog was, his legs would hardly heed his command. Instead, they shook underneath him, threatening to collapse without warning. So much time had passed since the dog had munched kibble between his tongue and the roof of his mouth. Now that he was safe from the rush of the river that had swept into his pen, threatening to swallow him up, the thick fog that had been clouding the dog's thoughts returned.

He watched the man dump a mound of mouthwatering kibble into a bowl at his feet and listened as the man beckoned him with clicks of the tongue and motioned with his hand. This same man had lifted him up out of the water, kept him from sinking until the river had tried to swallow them both at the same time.

He was pleased to know the man had been spit out the same way he had. Terror had kept the dog moving when he'd reached the water's edge. He'd run and run until he was certain the river was too far away to catch him.

As the fear abated, the dog had felt the pull of his master's whistle, even though he'd not heard it on the wind—he'd not heard his master's whistle for some time now—and he'd returned home on legs so weak they were hardly under his command.

Upon return, the dog had discovered that the only home he'd known—the quiet pen behind his master's home—had been swallowed up and swept away. The dog had been dozing up here where his master had stayed, hoping for his return and dreaming in fear of the river swallowing up the house just as it had his pen. The people returned and woke him, and the smell of food drifted across his nose.

Hunger beckoned the dog forward. When the man and the woman retreated several steps from the mound of food awaiting him, the dog became emboldened. He wobbled forward off the porch. From inside the big, rolling thing that carried humans from place to place, a caged dog barked.

The dog had no fear of the caged dog; there'd been no real aggression in his warning bark, just an attempt to claim a dinner that couldn't be reached.

"Good boy," the man called out over and over, beckoning the dog forward with words his master had used when he was young. As he'd grown older, he'd learned "Here, boy" and "Come, boy" and "Sit, boy."

This man's tone was softer than his master's. The gentleness in it guided him forward in spite of his hesitation and weakened body.

Hunger and solitude had been his companions since the long quiet at winter's end when his master had stopped coming, had stopped bringing him food and fresh water. That had been before the rains began.

The dog had lived here in the pen behind the house

since he was small and weak enough that munching a single piece of kibble in his sharp milk teeth had been nearly impossible. That was too many seasons ago for the dog to have kept track of.

For so long, life had been easy and predictable. The dog had counted on a short visit from his master each morning that ended with a bite or two of the man's food—something grainy and greasy and delicious and nothing like his dry, plain kibble—and a second visit toward the end of each day as the sun dipped low in the sky. It was during this late-in-the-day visit that his master would open the dog's pen and let him run about the yard and in the woods all the way to the river. These were the dog's happiest times, as he stretched his legs and left his scent in his favorite spots: bushes and tree trunks and rocks and human things that had been abandoned in the tall grass. In too short a time, his master would whistle and call the dog home. Waiting inside his pen would be a bowl spilling over with fresh kibble and another with water.

Rather than rush inside, the dog would sit at his master's feet, his tail wagging in anticipation. Most nights, his master would reward him by stroking one ear for a short time. Then he'd point to the kibble and dismiss him with an "Eat, boy."

The dog learned to heed his master's whistle and to return with haste, no matter how far he'd run or what scents beckoned him to explore. The faster he returned, the more likely he was to be rewarded with this bit of gentle stroking. The few nights that scents had held the dog's attention too long and he'd not heeded the man's whistle, he'd been greeted on return with a swift kick in the haunches instead.

His master's visits had become less and less predict-able, stretching back to when the days were the longest in the year and the scorching heat was nearly intoler-able. Some nights, he wouldn't come at all. Others, he wouldn't open the pen to let the dog run free while he filled his bowls with food and water.

Then, as winter ended and before the rains came, his master stopped coming altogether. The dog's hunger had become so immense, surely he would've succumbed to it had he not had been lucky at catching a squirrel and then later a large bird who'd come in to scavenge on remains of kibble that was no longer there.

When the rains came, he preyed on a few small frogs and bitter-tasting moths. When the river had first swept into his pen, the dog drank and drank until his belly hurt. He waited and waited, but his master didn't come.

And now his pen had been swallowed by the earth and this docile stranger was offering him a heaping mound of kibble.

The dog crept forward, lulled by the kibble and the gentleness in the man's tone. The man had tossed a piece or two of it in his direction. He swept them up with his tongue. His mouth watered as the meaty, salty kibble disintegrated over his tongue and ignited a fresh fire across his taste buds. His empty stomach knotted in anticipation. More, more, the dog wanted more.

He crept forward and sank onto his haunches as he reached the bowl. He dipped his head and tried to gulp the food in the same way he gulped in air after an exhausting run, only the individual pieces lodged in the back of his throat, and he coughed and choked and needed to try again.

He was eating just slow enough not to choke again when he realized the man was kneeling beside him, stroking the length of his body the same gentle way his master had stroked his ear. The dog wagged his tail but didn't lose a beat in consuming this unexpected meal. Before his hunger was satiated, the man clipped something onto his collar and the woman slipped the bowl of food from his reach.

The dog whined for it, but the man patted him reassuringly. "Easy, boy, easy. Thin as you are, we don't want to end up shocking your system."

The man's tone was soft and nonthreatening, and the dog knew he meant him no harm, nor did the woman with the salty-smelling water rolling down her cheeks.

He wagged his tail and waited, hoping the bowl would be placed within reach again. Instead, the man swept him up in his arms again. This time, the dog trusted that the river wouldn't separate them.

Chapter 9

BY THE TIME THEY CRATED THE DOG, TIED THE CRATE down in back, and Olivia had a minute to check her phone as they headed to the feed store, she found four missed calls and a slew of texts from Ava. Her heart sank into her belly. She was grateful her sister had driven all this way to pick her up, but she wished for a bit more time with Gabe. She desperately wanted to explain herself. To say something beyond "Oh, someone broke your heart and called off a wedding? Well, same here, only I was the caller, and we were much closer to heading down the aisle." But as it was, her sister had pulled up to the makeshift rehab behind the feed store a few minutes ahead of them and was getting out of her Jeep when they pulled up.

As Gabe slipped the truck into park, Olivia resigned herself to chalking up any sort of follow-up conversation as a missed opportunity. She probably wouldn't have been able to find the right words anyway. For any of it. How did she tell him the few minutes they'd spent making out had seemed more real and more relevant than anything had in longer than she cared to remember? The truth was, it was naive to hope an impromptu make-out session in Gabe's truck hours after they met might actually lead to something.

Leaving her purse and jacket inside the cab, Olivia jogged over to her sister and pulled her into a tight hug.

Bad timing or not, it *was* good to see her. "Thanks for coming. I know driving down here wasn't what you envisioned doing today, but at least we'll have time to talk on the way home. I want to hear everything, starting from the beginning."

Ava groaned into her ear before they pulled apart. "If I start there, we'll need more than three hours."

Olivia gave her sister a closer look. She was dressed for a day of showing property in pressed pants that flared at the ankle, four-inch heels, and a fitted suit jacket, and she clearly knew some sort of miracle cure because her perfectly made-up eyes didn't look puffy at all.

"You look great, Sis."

That was Ava; her marriage was falling apart, but looking at her, no one would have a clue. If Olivia had cried like that earlier today, she'd still have a stuffy nose, and her eyelids would resemble a pair of used tea bags. While she sometimes had to work at not feeling insignificant around her year-older sister, she also knew that Ava deserved all the amazing success that had come her way, especially in terms of how far she'd gone in her career as a real estate agent.

Aside from their height—they'd both topped out at five feet, eight inches—and similarities in face shape, most notably in the eyes and nose, people rarely guessed they were related, much less sisters. Ava had blue eyes and raven-black hair and spotless skin. Olivia's hair was bright red, her eyes a muddy hazel, and she had an abundance of freckles.

It was no surprise that back in high school, guys had looked her over like a pheasant hidden in the grass whenever her sister was around. Ava had known how to make their secondhand clothes look fashionable, how to project a you-could-complete-me vibe, and somehow perfected the best angle to turn up her chin to look ridiculously but genuinely demure.

But as put together as her sister seemed—even now—one of the dozen texts she'd sent had been to declare that they'd be swinging by the nearest Wendy's on the way home for a giant Frosty, her number-one comfort food. For Ava, Frosties even topped their grandma's chicken pot pie, which was famous countywide. Not Olivia. When trouble mounted, Olivia couldn't think of anything better to drown her sorrows in than that pot pie.

Thinking of the pot pie reminded her of how much flack they were going to get when their family figured out they had been this close to home and hadn't stopped by. Earlier, Ava had made it clear she wasn't in the space to see anyone tonight. Not with what was going on with her marriage.

Even though Olivia knew avoiding her family wasn't going to help douse the rumors that were most likely already beginning to circulate, she wasn't about to object. Starting out, she'd had no intention of showing up at the farm today. Knowing her intense make-out session would soon be the talk of the town didn't make her want to show up there any more than before. Besides, it had been a long day, and she had a lot to process.

Behind them came the solid *thwack* of a truck door being shut. Olivia was pretty sure even a toddler would've caught something significant in the look Ava directed her way after setting eyes on Gabe. "Uh, yeah, you know I'm going to want the full."

It was a whisper but not the quietest, and Olivia

hoped it didn't travel far. Head angled away from Gabe, she gave her sister her most ferocious glare, which only produced the slightest of eye rolls. "He didn't hear," she added an octave lower.

Gabe headed over, stretching out his hand in Ava's direction. "Gabe Wentworth. Nice to meet you."

"Pleasure's all mine." Olivia couldn't remember ever shaking her sister's hand, but she was willing to bet Ava's handshake was a confident one. "Ava Graham."

It was Olivia's turn to roll her eyes. *Pleasure's all mine.* Did anyone honestly say that anymore? At least one person did, it seemed. Thankfully small talk was kept short since there was a dog needing their attention.

Olivia helped Gabe haul the bulky crate inside, and Ava trailed along after them. "Oh, he's a pointer, isn't he?" As much as her sister worked hard not to acknowledge her rural upbringing, Ava still knew a thing or two about hunting dogs.

They headed through the open sliding doors of the big shed, and Olivia spotted Rhonda and Karen in back feeding the crated dogs.

"Well, I'll be… You two did it!" Rhonda dropped the scoop back into a giant bag of off-brand kibble, and they walked over together for a look inside the crate. "When you didn't come back right away, I wasn't sure what to think."

"You wouldn't believe what a close call it was," Olivia said, giving them a shortened version of Gabe's heroics and sharing how the dog had run off after making it out of the water. "There were two kids with us, watching as well," she added. "The ones who reported it. I'm hoping they resurface because the guy was filming the rescue, and Gabe and I both kind of feel like they may have more information on the dog than they shared."

Rhonda looked at Gabe appreciatively. "I'd never recommend anyone walk into a flood, but it sounds like you saved a life, for sure."

"He absolutely did." A new rush of admiration swept over Olivia as she made eye contact with Gabe. He was confident, heart-stoppingly cute, and kind. How crazy was it that she'd kissed him with no reservation like that?

With a blush heating her cheeks, she found it safer to focus on the dog who was standing with his back pressed against the top of the crate, balancing on all four legs as if he were on a ship sailing through stormy seas. His head hung low, and he looked from her to Gabe with warm-brown eyes that seemed both cautious and gentle. "I'm pretty sure this poor guy's strength was closer to giving out than I care to think about."

Gabe nodded to an empty place at the end of the third row. "Over there okay?" He looked at Rhonda for an answer, all but ignoring the comments about his heroics.

Rhonda nodded. "Sure." She looked at her coworker. "Have we got any blankets left? The poor fellow looks like he could use a bit of comfort right now."

"There's one or two left," Karen said, heading for one of their supply tubs. She sorted through it and returned with a faded-blue plaid blanket and offered it their direction. "I'll let one of you two do the honors."

Gabe cocked an eyebrow in Olivia's direction after they'd set the crate a foot or two from the crated dog at the end of the row. From Olivia's best guess, it was a border collie/Dalmatian mix. "Be my guest. And here," he said, fishing through his pocket. "Might as well give him the last of these."

Olivia ignored the rush from their fingers brushing together and sank to a squat in front of the pointer's crate, letting him sniff the blanket through the bars. When he didn't seem frightened by it, she opened the door slowly and placed it at his feet. Then she rewarded him with the last two treats, which he inhaled in the space of a second or two. He looked at her hungrily, clearly hoping for more, but Olivia scratched him behind the ear instead.

It had taken most of the ride here for her tears to stop flowing. She was a sucker for hunting dogs anyway, and this one seemed so docile and sweet. And he was clearly underweight. By quite a bit. If the owner had pulled up while they were there, it would've been all she could do not to give him or her a swift kick in the shin. What sort of person kept a dog locked in a pen and didn't provide adequate access to food?

The same sort who left him to drown.

Olivia shuddered. Thank goodness he was safe. She couldn't imagine a greater horror than watching helplessly and Gabe not being able to get him out in time. "He's *so* thin." She swallowed hard. "There's no excuse for a dog to be this thin."

"Agreed," Gabe said. "Underweight as he is, added to the fact that he was left in a locked pen during a flood, is enough to warrant a neglect confiscation, I suspect. And if you'd seen the house... I should've taken pictures. I didn't think about that until now. It looked abandoned. Worse than abandoned. More like a junkyard. And I suspect it wasn't any cleaner inside the pen before it flooded than it was in front of the house."

Karen gave a disheartened shake of her head. "I can count his ribs from here, though I've been in this business long enough to have seen worse. But I know when you risk life and limb to save one of these fellows like you two have, it gets personal. I'm sure you'd like to hear otherwise, but we'd risk our license being called into question if we didn't follow procedure." She turned up her hands and looked at the dog who was still standing on all fours and looking between them. "Like it or not, his owner has seventy-two hours to claim him. What I *can* do is list your grievances with the county. When there's a neglect complaint, sometimes it can move things faster. Don't hold your breath on it though." She gave an apologetic shrug of her shoulders. "In the meantime, I'll post this guy's picture online. Maybe someone will come forward with more information."

"I know the perfect shelter to take him if no one comes forward," Ava piped up. "I went to a fund-raiser there recently. It's no-kill, and they vet adopters heavily, so he'd be sure to be in good hands."

"Near you?" Olivia asked.

"Yeah, like ten minutes away, maybe less."

"You know, I'm going to have to come back for my car," Olivia added. "If that works out, my sister and I could come get him when we do." She hooked a finger around one of the bars, and the pointer leaned close to give her finger a sniff. His nose was warm and dry. Hopefully he wouldn't get sick from having expended so much energy in his already-weakened condition. "He's such a sweetheart. I'd adopt him myself, but without a place of my own, that's out of the question."

Rhonda patted Olivia's arm as she stood up. "If the

shelter will take him, call me. I could use one more animal off my plate. Most days I feel like I'm playing solitaire when it comes to finding places to take these guys."

"So that you know, underweight as he is, we stopped him short of a full meal tonight," Gabe said, hooking his thumbs in the back pockets of his jeans and drawing Olivia's attention to his wide, rounded shoulders. "I'd recommend smaller meals more frequently over the next few days. Plenty of water and a real checkup as soon as he gets where he's going."

Rhonda agreed before pulling Gabe to the first row of dogs to look at one that had come in this morning, an energetic Lab-collie mix who was running a fever. Olivia took the opportunity to walk her sister around the other cages and share some of the rescue stories she'd heard this afternoon.

"These dogs are adorbs, Livy, especially that pointer." Ava dropped her voice and nudged her in the ribs. "But I want deets on the hottie. I take it he was the one who picked you up? Which begs the question, *why* didn't you find a way to mention how phenomenal looking he is? And what am I doing here? You should've asked to ride back with him."

Olivia gave her sister another he'll-hear-you glare and pulled her over to the cat kennels on the opposite side of the shed. "Hush, will you? I'll fill you in in the car. And I didn't know how things were going to turn out."

Ava was stubborn and determined, but she was also a cat person, and luck was on Olivia's side in terms of adequate distraction from her sister's train of thought.

A few particularly adorable cats had been brought in. Two had been wandering the town, and one was rescued off a tractor in a flooded field. Ava seemed especially drawn to a silver-and-cream long-haired tabby with bright-green eyes. "They don't know how she came to be there, but she turned up at the filling station. She slipped inside with one of the customers, and she seemed terrified of the outdoors."

"Can I hold her?"

Olivia nodded. "Rhonda told us we could so long as they don't fight it."

When her crate was opened, the dainty cat practically hopped into Ava's arms, and Ava let out a heartfelt coo. "I forgot how much I love cats." Her sister smoothed the cat's long, silky coat, sending tufts of fur flying into the air. "Her coat's soft and tangle-free like an indoor cat."

Olivia ran her hand along the cat's smooth coat. "She seems to be in great health, that's for sure. And she's not underweight either."

"Oh, Sis, I want a cat. And not just a cat. I want *this* cat. Don't you think my failing marriage entitles me to a cat?"

Olivia choked back a laugh. "Yes, definitely, but I think you should sleep on it first." Hearing a deep, thrumming purr erupting from the cat, she shook her head. "Though something tells me you two are a great match."

Ava wasn't one to make impulsive decisions often, but when she did, she could forget to take things into account, and right now, that included who was going to be getting the house, and if it wasn't her, where she was going to live, among other things. Fortunately, this kitty would still be in limbo another day or two. It would give her sister time to take stock of some of the big decisions awaiting her if she and Wes were in fact calling it quits.

The next several minutes passed in a blur. After seeing that the pointer was curled atop his wadded-up blanket at the back of his crate and falling into a doze, Olivia figured it was best not to disturb him with a goodbye that would serve her more than it would him.

"Sweet puppy, you're safe now."

She refused to let herself think she wouldn't see him again. The shed was full of deserving dogs with their own touching stories, but this one now mattered to her more than any dog had in a long time.

"I'll check in with you tomorrow," she promised Rhonda and Karen as she and Ava joined the group before heading out. "I understand everything has to be done within the confines of the law, but I have huge reservations against him going back to that house."

"Me too," Gabe agreed.

Rhonda gave them a reassuring look, complete with a gentle smile and a little nod, reminding Olivia of how she herself must appear at parent-teacher conferences when meeting with parents of kids with bigger-than-average struggles. "With that pen of his collapsing like you said, and the fact that yard won't be habitable for some time after the water recedes, there's a chance he could be surrendered even if his owner does come forward."

With nothing else to do, Olivia determined to hold onto this.

Her sister jangled her keys, switching them from hand to hand. Suddenly Olivia realized she wasn't just leaving the dog, she was leaving Gabe too. She cursed herself for bringing up her past and not finding time to finish the story. Now she was leaving him with two very distinct images: the girl who'd initiated a make-out session in the middle of the day on a public road that culminated in her crawling onto his lap, and the girl who'd walked out on a guy three weeks before a wedding.

Why did you blurt out that you had, you idiot? The truth was, even if she'd had another ten or twenty minutes to explain herself, there was a good chance she wouldn't see him again. Not only did they live on opposite sides of metro St. Louis, but he was a new vet taking over a practice and working exhausting hours, and she was still establishing herself as a teacher and crossing her fingers her contract would be extended and she wouldn't need to come crawling back here where she'd forever be the girl who all but left Trevor Jones at the altar.

She swallowed hard. The thought of never seeing Gabe again had her throat tight and dry and tears stinging the backs of her eyes for the second time in a half hour. But crying over a guy she'd only known for a handful of hours seemed a touch more pathetic than crying over a mistreated dog.

She hugged Rhonda and Karen, promising again to call tomorrow to check on the pointer, then turned to Gabe awkwardly. She sucked in the side of her cheek and stuck out her hand. "It was really nice meeting you."

He gave an almost imperceptible shake of his head, causing Olivia to wonder whether or not to pull her hand back. Before she determined what to do, he closed his hand over hers but didn't shake it. His gaze shifted from her to Ava, then to her again. "Do you have a minute?"

Ava's eyebrows nearly disappeared into her hairline. "She can have several. I'll be in my Jeep checking my email…assuming I'm lucky enough to get reception."

Olivia's palms broke out in a sweat. "I need to grab my things from your truck anyway." Doing her best to appear more confident than she felt, she trailed outside after her sister with Gabe following just behind her. Her pulse began to sprint.

Gabe followed her around to the passenger-side door. As she grabbed her things, he opened the back door and placed the stool for Samson to hop down. "You probably need to stretch your legs a minute, bud."

When's the last time you met someone sweet enough to always make sure his dog had his needs met like that? Never, that's when.

Olivia tucked her jacket over her arm but left her purse clutched in front of her like an added layer of protection against the wave of uncertainty rocking her.

"Look," Gabe said, dragging one hand through his hair. "I want to apologize."

"You don't have to," she burst out before he could finish. "It was clearly me who started it."

A crooked smile lit his face, tugging Olivia's heartstrings. "Olivia, I'm not apologizing for kissing you. I'm apologizing for being the guy that gave serious consideration to leaving you stranded at that gas station because of a bunch of stupid baggage that's been weighing me down."

Olivia smashed her lips together. There was no denying it now; she was *very* close to crying. "It's okay. You didn't know me from anything."

"That's what I keep thinking. I could've missed this

opportunity. I could've missed out on today. And it was the best day I've had in a long time." He swept his thumb over the corner of her eye, brushing away a stray tear she'd not realized had slipped out. It was so dark out here, just a single floodlight shining onto the pavement, and he'd still spotted it. Maybe it was because he was looking at her as if he couldn't see anything else.

"You saved that dog's life today."

He blinked abruptly, and the set of his shoulders visibly stiffened. Had she said the wrong thing? She'd have sworn he'd been about to kiss her, but he stepped back half a foot.

"Tell me the truth, will you? The truth you wouldn't normally tell someone at this stage in the game."

She didn't understand it, but there was something very raw and real happening right at this moment, and as scary as it seemed, she committed to complete honesty. "Yeah, okay."

"When did you first want to kiss me?"

She forced herself to breathe through her thoughts rather than spout out an answer. When *had* she first wanted to kiss him? There'd been so many little things, from him asking her to take a picture of his license plate to his soft, easy laughter and that irresistible dimple to the way he treated Samson, and of course there'd been the heroics in the water.

Finally, she gave a resigned shrug. "It was a dozen little things more than any one big one. If I had to put it to one thing, I guess it would be the way you treat Samson. The stool to help him get up and down. The incredible bond you two have. The way it's so clear that he sets his world by you."

To her surprise, a look of sheer relief swept over Gabe's face. He pulled her to him abruptly, smashing her purse between them, and pressed his lips against her temple. He let out an easy chuckle, then pulled away just enough to find her lips. His hands locked at the back of her head and he kissed her, soft at first, then harder as a rush of hunger swept into it.

Olivia decided that she didn't care Ava was certainly spying through the windows and opened her mouth more fully to his. If she'd said the wrong thing, then surely she'd followed it up with the right one. This reminded her that she barely knew him. It was crazy to feel such a strong connection with someone she'd only known for a handful of hours.

And from the way he was kissing her and the way that rock-hard frame of his was shaking ever so slightly, she was certain he felt it too.

A high-pitched yawn carried up from knee level, and Samson could be heard settling down onto the ground beside them. Apparently, he'd had enough adventure for the day.

Gabe pulled away and kissed her forehead. "If your sister wasn't ten feet away, I'd have a hard time stopping this here." He brushed fresh tears from the corners of her eyes. "What you were trying to tell me back at the house before we spotted the dog... I want to hear it. All of it. I'll call you."

She nodded and fought back a flood of fresh tears. It was the weirdest feeling. She was wildly happy and impossibly sad at the same time. Why did this feel like hello and goodbye at the same time? And why the hell had she called Ava to take her home? She could've ridden back with him and had a few more hours before they went back to their separate lives.

"I—I haven't given you my number." She stepped back and opened her purse, sifting through with a shaky hand for a pen and a piece of scrap paper.

"I'll just put it in my phone."

"That makes sense." She waited as he pulled up his contacts and typed in her name.

"*G-r-a-h-a-m?*"

She nodded. "I forgot I told you my last name."

"I didn't."

She shook her head, laughing and fighting away the tears that were still pressing in. She recited her number, waiting as he typed it in and showed her for confirmation, then nodded.

She bent down and wrapped Samson in a whole-arm hug. "Bye, buddy." He licked her ear, and that was all it took for Olivia's tears to rush forth unchecked. "Dammit. I hate goodbyes," she said, standing back up.

Gabe pulled her in to his chest again. "If I have anything to say about it, it's not goodbye, just good night."

Somehow Olivia made it through another kiss without falling into full, blubbery oblivion—*What the heck was wrong with her anyway?*—and over to her sister's car. She plopped into the passenger seat and shut the door, wiping the stream of tears from her cheeks.

"Don't ask, just drive, okay?"

Ava squeezed her knee before flipping on the ignition. "Yeah, okay, Sis. But I'm pretty sure I don't have to ask a thing. I know the real thing when I see it."

Chapter 10

GABE WAS STILL A HALF HOUR FROM HOME WHEN HE determined he couldn't drive another mile without a pick-me-up of some sort. Spotting a gas station, he pulled off the highway and filled his less-than-half-empty tank simply to stand in the chilly night air for a few minutes. As it filled, he let Samson stretch his legs and take a leak on the grass at the far end of the parking lot. Afterward, Gabe headed inside for a king-size Snickers and a 16-ounce coffee that he suspected couldn't have been accurately described as fresh for half a day at least. Normally, he liked his coffee black, but after a cautious sip, he decided he wouldn't be able to choke it down without a spoonful or two of sugar.

Welcome company that Samson was, the tuckered-out dog proved to be no help in the final stretch of the drive. The methodic, heavy snore that lulled Gabe to sleep most nights filled the cab and counteracted the soft buzz he got from chugging the coffee.

By the time Gabe finally made it home, he couldn't recall the last time he'd been so bone-tired. He found an open parking spot on the crowded street half a block from the old redbrick home—now divided into apartments—in Tower Grove South where he'd been renting the last several years. He'd been running short of sleep for weeks, no question. Added to that, he was sore, bruised, and exhausted from the struggle in the cold, flooded river.

He trudged up the steps inside the main entry. When he didn't hear Samson's toenails hitting the wooden steps behind him, he turned around to find his dog stretched over the bottom three steps. Meeting his gaze, Samson let out a well-timed whine and pumped his tail.

"Too stiff, bud?" Gabe jogged back down and carefully lifted his dog into his arms, craning his head to avoid a mouthful of dog hair. Considering Samson's size and weight—close to eighty pounds—carrying him up the steps wasn't a thoughtless feat. A support sling tucked away in the hall closet enabled Samson to climb the stairs on his own with Gabe lifting the sling, but his dog moved at a snail's pace when they used it, and Gabe wasn't in the mood to delay collapsing on his bed another minute.

Samson thanked him with a wag of the tail when Gabe set him down on the stoop. Gabe entered the often glitchy code to his apartment, willing it to open without the usual struggle. "You know, bud, we're gonna have to find a different place if your hips get any worse." Samson was on Rimadyl and chondroitin supplements, and Gabe could perform a hip replacement on him if necessary, but there was something uncomfortable and daunting about the prospect of doing surgery on his own dog. If it came to it, he'd probably place Samson in Yun's capable hands instead. But he'd have to move before then. Samson wouldn't be able to take the steps during recuperation.

Gabe kicked off his shoes and debated how badly he needed a shower tonight instead of in the morning. *You went swimming in floodwater. Is there any question?*

He stripped out of his clothes in the middle of the

living room, headed into the bathroom, and flipped the shower knob to hot. Thoughts of Olivia floated through his head the same as they had most of the drive home. Would it be too early to text her tonight?

Yun had been telling him for months he needed to get back out there again, and Gabe had all but dismissed her as not knowing what he really needed. He liked being able to eat whatever called to him in the moment and shoot away for the weekends with Samson. He still got satisfaction in not picking up his messes until doing so suited him. And he already had to fight Samson for adequate space on the mattress. But maybe Yun had been more right than he could even begin to comprehend. It was as if a long-slumbering part of him was stepping out of a nearly impenetrable fog.

Hot water washed over him as he stepped in, stinging the scrapes on his back and sending a cascade of floodwater residue down the drain. How come he'd never realized his shower was so heavenly? Tonight, it didn't even matter that the showerhead was partly calcified from hard water and beat down on him in an irregular stream.

Olivia's face was burned into his mind as clearly as if he were looking at a high-resolution photo of her. Those remarkable hazel eyes with flecks of gold and green, the delicate speckling of freckles across the bridge of her nose and tops of her cheeks, the long red hair that beckoned him to bury his hands in it, the long curve of her neck, the gentle point of her chin. And her lips... Just thinking about them sent a rush of blood to his groin. He could still recall the subtle hint of citrus that floated off her when she was against him. Then there was her body, long and lean and supple and yielding.

There was also the way she'd opened up around him, the way she'd let him in, telling him little bits about her life with rare and refreshing humility.

And possibly more important than any of this was what she'd said about him and Samson. Fear had rocketed through him when he'd spotted the unchecked admiration on her face about his heroics in the river. He'd not realized it at the time, but that's what had initially drawn Claire to him, the allure of connecting with someone stronger than life, stronger than death. Then he'd walked into that fire, and she'd realized no one was stronger than either of those. Instead of accepting that the human experience was inextricably woven into both, she'd walked away in hopes of claiming a life more under her control.

What would he have done if Olivia had answered differently? Or if the answer she'd given had only been one she'd wanted him to hear? But he'd seen the truth of it in her eyes; she'd spoken from the heart.

Maybe Olivia hadn't been in his immediate plans, and maybe the idea of letting her in was about as daunting as walking into a four-alarm fire, but the way he'd felt around her today made it worth exploring this new, unexpected path.

He lingered in the shower until the tank emptied of hot water, then dried off and headed into his room. Samson was sprawled across the center of his bed, snoring the snore that Gabe had committed to memory, even and peaceful and unreserved. Gabe tugged on a fresh pair of boxers and collapsed beside his dog after shoving him over a foot with his hip. Samson slept through it undeterred, and his warmth soaked into Gabe's side, a wash of familiar comfort.

Gabe's bed was nothing more than a mattress on the floor now. He'd moved the box spring and frame into storage after Samson had twice tumbled off on his way down in the middle of the night for a drink.

He'd be asleep in seconds if he didn't fight it, but Gabe debated getting back up for his phone. He was pretty certain he'd left it in his jeans pocket, not in the truck. It had been a long time since he'd entered into a new relationship with someone, and he was a few months away from turning thirty. He wasn't interested in playing games. Wasn't afraid to let her know his thoughts.

Struggling out of the enticing pull of dreams, he cleared his throat, got up, and headed into the living room. After fishing his phone from the back pocket of his jeans, he pulled up her number and typed out a text.

> Hope you two made it home safely. Odd as it may sound, I'm thankful for the car trouble you had. Good night, Olivia. I'll call you tomorrow.

He left his phone on the nightstand that he'd cut down to the height of his mattress and, finding that Samson had stretched out again, fought for the slim pickings at the edge of the bed. He fell into a doze as soon as he'd tugged enough of the blanket from under his dog to at least not wake up frozen.

"Full disclosure, I'm not used to being spooned." Olivia wiggled underneath the straitjacket-like embrace of her sister. "Trevor slept on his back. He wasn't much of a cuddler."

"That's sad. Not even as you fell asleep? Or after sex?"

"He fell asleep in two-point-two seconds. Even after sex."

"I'm so glad you didn't marry him." Ava released her death-grip-like hold on Olivia and rolled onto her back. "But I can't fall asleep without connection. Your hair's wet though. It's getting in my face. Can you do something with it?"

Olivia flipped around on the double bed where she'd been sleeping in her aunt's loft bedroom the last few months and faced her sister, sweeping her still-damp hair behind her and flipping her pillow over for a dry spot. "I could've not showered, and you could put up with the smell of river water all night."

Ava let out an exaggerated sigh and settled deeper under the covers. "I don't know how I'm going to do this."

Olivia gave Ava's forearm a squeeze. "You're going to rock it the same way you do everything."

After Olivia had gotten out a good cry and explained the crazy, unexpected turns of the day, they'd talked about what was going on in Ava's marriage. At least, as much of it as Ava understood. She'd kept silent about it, but she'd sensed Wes had been growing distant for the last few months. He'd claimed it was because Ava was too controlling, and maybe her sister did have an above-average share of control issues that could use some working through, but from all the things Ava had mentioned, it seemed clear Wes was working through something deeper of his own.

"How do you fall out of love in your first year of marriage?" Ava swiped angrily at a few stray tears. "We were doing all the right things. Sex on the counters and in the shower and in the bathtub. Dinners out at least once a weeknight and on weekends. We cooked together most of the other times. At least when I wasn't showing property. I snuggled in the crook of his arm while he read before falling asleep. We have a laundry service, so he can't blame me for screwing that up."

Olivia was considering her answer when Ava shot up into a sitting position and slammed her fists onto the bed. "And I have grievances too. No matter what he eats, he leaves skid marks in the toilet, and he *never* notices them. He's always forgetting to use a coaster or an insulated mug. And it's politics, politics, politics. Can we *not* listen to the news for one day?"

Fighting off a wave of exhaustion, Olivia sat up and cradled her sister in her arms. She suspected that right now, Ava wanted an ear more than she wanted answers. Not that Olivia had them. Instead of answering, she smoothed her hand over Ava's back after draping her long, dark hair over her other shoulder. It was obvious, too, that her sister was holding back. Ava had never been one to talk out her problems. Mostly she bottled them up like they didn't exist. Until things like this popped up.

Gradually, the tension in Ava's muscles began to relax, and she let out a soft sigh. "Thanks. That helps. Can you rub my shoulders, please?"

Olivia felt a bit guilty for letting her thoughts travel there during her sister's hour of need, but her sister's declarations had gotten her thinking about Gabe. Again. What would she find out about him if she was lucky enough to get to know him better? She could deal with water rings and skid marks if she had to. But what differences between them would arise if she did really get to know him?

There was no doubt that Gabe loved his dog. He was caring and conscientious and protective, and he was extraordinarily brave. But what if, after a month or so, he turned into a Trevor? If he turned into someone who wouldn't notice when she walked out of a room for ten minutes or ten hours. Or worse, what if he'd somehow hidden darkness inside him that she'd not glimpsed today?

The way she'd reacted internally this afternoon... She'd never felt like that about anyone. Ever. She'd known Trevor since they were kids, and they'd started dating so early. She couldn't remember ever feeling the tingly newness of a crush with him. She'd had one or two mild crushes over the years on other people, crushes she'd somehow worked through before they became anything serious enough to threaten her and Trevor's relationship or even to bring to Trevor's attention.

But the feelings that had popped up for Gabe had been colossal. Hours later, it was as if her body was still humming with energy. She'd not been prepared to experience anything like this. *Which is probably why you climbed onto his lap. In the cab of his truck. In the middle of the day. On a public road.*

Stewing in embarrassment wasn't going to change anything or stop the rumors from circulating back home. Or help her figure out how to deal with Gabe. He'd said he was going to call tomorrow. Would he want to see her? If so, would it be something like asking her out on a date next weekend?

"You can stop rubbing now. Thanks." Ava twisted

around and wrapped her in a tight hug. "You were totally zoning, weren't you?"

"A little maybe."

"He's zone-worthy. I'll give you that."

Olivia laughed softly. "I was just thinking how weird it would be to go on a first date with someone I've already extensively made out with."

"That just gets the awkward stuff out of the way."

"Yeah, maybe, but you know me. I'll find a way to make it awkward."

Ava smiled as she curled up underneath the covers again. "You're the kind of awkward that draws people in, Livy, not sends them away."

Not entirely sure what to think of that, Olivia slipped out from under the covers and stepped around the creaky floorboards to the dresser where she'd put her purse.

"What are you doing?" Ava yawned lazily.

"My phone's probably about to die. I want to charge it in case he calls tomorrow morning." She sifted through her purse, promising herself she'd take time to clean and organize its contents this week, no more procrastination. When she didn't see her phone, she lifted out her wallet. Nothing. "Crap. I must've left my phone in your Jeep."

It wasn't raining any longer, but it was cold outside and up here it was warm and cozy. And they'd managed to come in without waking up Aunt Becky. Over a long breakfast seemed like a much better time to tell her about Ava's rocky marriage than close to midnight.

"I guess I'll get it in the morning."

Olivia crawled back into bed, giggling as she fought Ava for the perfect amount of covers just like they did when they were kids sharing a bed. "Love you, Sis."

"Love you too."

After a big, contented sigh, Olivia drifted off to sleep with the image of a gorgeous pair of hazel-green eyes, a slow, sexy smile, broad shoulders, and wonderfully toned abs burning in her mind.

Chapter 11

THE SUN WAS HIGH ENOUGH IN THE SKY THAT ALARM washed over Olivia as she opened her eyes, squinting in the bright light. How many days had it been since she'd woken up to full-on sunshine? Too many.

She was groping across her nightstand, feeling for her phone, when she remembered two things. First, when she'd gone to bed, Ava had been cuddled beside her, and now the other half of the bed was empty. And second, she'd also left her phone in her sister's Jeep.

Olivia sat up and stretched, smelling something that was neither bacon nor sausage, but was likely a half-decent replacement for one of them. Aunt Becky was a vegan, had been for nearly ten years, and while Olivia ate whatever she wanted outside the home, she'd grown accustomed to eating vegan here. While she liked a well-dressed bowl of oatmeal and had a big soft spot for avocado toast, Sunday breakfasts were a change from the ones she'd grown up with on the farm.

Shoving her feet into a pair of fuzzy slippers that Ava must have overlooked or would've confiscated, she shuffled down the narrow stairs and into the open kitchen and living room below. The whole place had a rustic country feel—packed with a hodgepodge of unique furniture and decorated with a variety of antiques—and was somehow a perfect complement to the pottery her aunt sold for a living.

Ava was seated on a stool at the counter with her knees tucked in to her chest, sipping on a mug of coffee. The mug was one of her aunt's trademark creations, solid yet delicate with a watercolor-blue glaze and a rounded rim. She sold similar ones in her store and on Etsy for thirty dollars apiece.

"Morning," Olivia said, heading over to her sister. On the way, she passed by Coco, her aunt's full-of-herself cockatoo, who was on a perch between the kitchen and living room, feeding on a long spring of asparagus that she held in one foot. Olivia paused to run one finger along the two smooth, gray front toes on the bird's perched foot. "Morning, Coco Puff."

"I thought it was just Coco," Ava asked.

"It is," Aunt Becky answered. "But she seems to like Olivia's nickname. I even heard her repeat it the other day."

Aunt Becky was dressed in the sleeveless tee and cutoff sweats she wore under her button-down potter's cape, and her dark-gray hair was pulled back in a bun. Knowing her aunt liked best to work in the early hours of the morning, Olivia's best guess was that she'd already been at the wheel for a few hours.

Coco responded to Olivia's attention by bobbing her head and raising her crest to a half salute. A previously one-owner bird who wouldn't tolerate anyone's touches aside from Aunt Becky's, Coco had grown to like Olivia enough that she tended to squawk at her when she walked in the room until Olivia paid her a bit of attention.

After offering Coco a fresh spring of asparagus, Olivia plopped onto the stool next to Ava. She ran her tongue over her lips, mulling over why they were so chapped until she remembered all the kissing she'd done yesterday. Her heartstrings tugged at the memory of the perfect lips she'd gotten a taste of. *Please let him call today. Please, please let him call.*

"I thought we were going to have to wake you." Aunt Becky flipped the row of meatless sausages in the frying pan.

The oven was on, and Olivia could smell something else in the air, a hint of rosemary possibly. She hoped it was her aunt's perfectly roasted potato wedges. They nearly made up for the lack of eggs in this place.

"What time is it?" Olivia stretched wide, yawning.

"Almost ten." Ava set her mug on the butcher-block counter and slumped forward.

"I haven't slept in this late in years." Olivia looked at her aunt for confirmation as to whether or not she knew why Ava was here.

"I got the rundown," Aunt Becky replied with understanding. "I pretty much told her what I told you back in October. You're both young and resilient, and you have a lot of life ahead of you. And figuring out how to go it on your own for a while never hurt anyone."

Ava sat up straight and stuck out her lip in a pout. "Do you think we've been married too long to apply for annulment?" Her voice was shaky. "It just hit me that if we don't get back together, I'm going to have to check 'Divorced' when I fill out forms from now on." She slumped forward again, covering her face with her hands and shaking her head wildly. "Wes said... He said he knew before we exchanged our vows. He said he decided whether or not to go through with the marriage based on a coin flip."

Tears stung Olivia's eyes instantly, and fresh, hot anger raced through her veins. Who the hell said that to someone? She'd have more than words with Wes when she saw him next. "Oh, Ava, then thank God you're not wasting another few years with him. Or worse, you could've had kids with him. This side of him you're seeing, it proves he's not the person you thought he was."

Ava shook her head and swiped at fresh tears. Olivia sensed that she was ready to say some of the things she'd hinted at last night but had not been able to voice. "He...he said I'm too superficial to start a family with."

What a low blow. Olivia wrapped her sister in a ferocious hug. "What an ass."

"Ass!" Coco parroted across the room.

With a stern look from Aunt Becky, both Olivia and her sister suppressed a few giggles. Courtesy of her first owner of seven years, Coco knew every curse word ever spoken in English and a handful in Spanish and German. It had taken Aunt Becky months of training and positive attention to change Coco's go-to vocabulary. Though she'd heard stories, Olivia had only heard the attention-loving parrot curse a few times, though for some reason, *sixty-nine* had remained one of her go-to phrases, along with *jet plane* and *ring, ring*.

Seeming relieved by the distraction, Ava plopped her hands flat on the counter. "I don't... I can't talk about this now anyway. I'm showing property at one out in the county. I just want to drown my sorrows in those potatoes this morning, and tonight, I'll go for a long run to make up for all the calories last night and today. I don't think I've ever had a Frosty and Ben & Jerry's in one night."

Olivia frowned but decided to let her sister take the lead in terms of what she was ready to talk about and when. She set the table while Aunt Becky finished cooking, and the breakfast conversation switched to filling her aunt in on the daring rescue and answering a handful of questions about Gabe.

After a giant helping of fresh bread, hummus, avocado, the sausages, and roasted potatoes, Olivia cleared the dishes while Ava showered. Afterward, she jogged outside in her slippers and the fleece pants and thermal T-shirt she'd slept in to grab her phone.

It promised to be a beautiful day, sunny and springlike and not a cloud in the sky. The flooding she'd seen yesterday suddenly felt very far away even though Olivia knew most of the rivers—including the Mississippi—still had another day or two before they crested.

As she groped underneath the front-passenger seat of Ava's Jeep, her thoughts went to the sweet pointer. Thank God he was safe. She felt like she suddenly had so much to pray for, including that his owner didn't come forward to claim him if he was as neglectful as she suspected.

She wanted to see that sweet dog again almost as much as she wanted to see Gabe. But what was suddenly alarming her above all else was that her phone seemed nowhere to be found. She bent forward, sweeping her hair out of the way, and scanned the metal supports under the seat to see if it had gotten lodged underneath.

She racked her brain, trying to remember the last time

she'd used the phone. Surely, she'd checked her texts or emails in the car on the way here, but she had no memory of doing so. The last she could remember was dropping it in her purse on the way back to the feed store with the pointer when she was still with Gabe.

Her heart thumped in her chest. Could it have fallen out when she was saying goodbye to him? Wouldn't they have heard it hit the ground?

Attempting her best to keep panic from setting in, she jogged back inside and up the narrow steps to the tiny bedroom at the back of the house. She dumped her purse onto the dresser. A dozen or so receipts. Three ChapSticks. Enough pens to write a thesis. A mangled in-the-wrapper tampon. A wallet. The remaining keys on her key chain that she hadn't left with the mechanic.

But no phone.

If she'd lost it, she'd lost the only means she had of Gabe contacting her. And worse, what if he was calling her and she didn't answer? *Please Gabe, don't doubt how much you mean to me*.

Olivia sank shakily onto the bed. If there'd ever been a time in her life when she'd wanted to lose her phone the least, surely this was it.

———

There was a list of things that Gabe savored about being in surgery, and at the top of it was when he knew it might save or dramatically improve the quality of an animal's life. On this Tuesday early afternoon, after finishing a two-hour-long cesarean section on a Boston terrier who proved too high a risk to handle a vaginal birth—and successfully delivering her five pups, Gabe thought of another benefit.

Being in surgery kept him from checking his phone.

He couldn't remember experiencing such a sharp swell of both hope and disappointment each time he reached for it as he had the last few days.

He left the operating room while his assisting staff was still cooing over the cuteness of the five square-nosed black-and-white pups.

In the prep room, Gabe stripped out of his mask and surgical gear and headed to the sink to scrub down. Standing there, he spotted his phone on the shelf above it, facedown. In surgery, he'd been too focused to think about how it was closing in on seventy-two hours since he and Olivia had shared that remarkable goodbye kiss in the parking lot behind Milton's Feed Store.

Maybe she'd called while he was in surgery. Maybe she hadn't.

What if she never did?

Swallowing back a rush of nerves, Gabe dried his hands and flipped the phone over to find a handful of new texts from his brother, his dad, and one of his fire-fighting buddies. And no new missed calls.

Doubt flooded him, but he pushed it down. She'd felt something too. He'd never been more sure of anything in his life. Maybe what she needed was time. And challenging as it was proving to be, it was the least he could give her.

Holding onto this hope, he tucked his phone in his jeans' pocket. He'd give it a few more days. She'd call. She was definitely going to call.

Thankfully, there was the distraction of an over-loaded work schedule this week to keep him occupied. Holding onto that idea, he headed up front to tell the

Boston terrier's anxious owners the news. Their much-loved dog had come safely through surgery, as had her five newborn pups, which was another one of those everyday blessings he'd promised himself he wouldn't take for granted.

Chapter 12

THE CLOCK ON THE WALL SIMPLY HAD TO BE BROKEN. The same went for the digital one on the bottom-right corner of Olivia's computer screen. The fact that they were perfectly in sync with each other was a fluke. The seconds ticked away like minutes, and minutes like hours. Olivia drummed her fingers on her desk and scanned the classroom full of kids who were just as ready as her for Tuesday afternoon's final bell and caught a glimpse of a spitball lodging into the back of the new girl's hair. The girl shook it out of her long locks and cast a somewhat flirty glare into the back corner of the room.

Earlier in the period, Olivia had given out a practice test after a short review on polynomials. The eighth graders had spent most of the fifty-minute class on it, but now, four minutes before the final bell, they were finished and whispering among themselves.

Spying a fresh spitball shooting across the room, Olivia headed over to the group of boys in the back corner. She held out her hand, palm up, and wagged her fingers. "Straw."

The three boys exchanged innocent looks. "They don't have straws in the cafeteria anymore."

"Yet somehow you managed to find one, didn't you?"

Brody, who was thirteen but could pass for seventeen with his broad shoulders and patchy facial hair, reluctantly passed it her way after pulling it out from underneath the desk. "Sorry."

Olivia pinched the straw at the center and looked at all three boys one by one as she spoke. "While I applaud any attempt at communication that doesn't involve a smartphone, there are other ways to get a girl's attention."

There'd been a rush of detentions in seventh and eighth grade during the last month or so of boys who'd been caught mooning other students. Though it had taken Olivia by surprise, it seemed that mooning had blossomed into popularity again. Or perhaps it had never gone out of it.

She was thankful not to have caught that happening in her classroom this afternoon, or she'd be staying after to write up a detention of her own. Not only was she ready to get on the road, but Ava had emailed five minutes ago to say that she was waiting in the school parking lot.

As the three boys mumbled fresh apologies, Olivia nodded. "It's just a couple of minutes till the bell rings. How about we agree not to cause any more trouble, and we'll start fresh tomorrow?"

Under normal circumstances, Olivia was one of the last teachers in the building after the final bell rang at 3:05 p.m. She loved to linger in her quiet classroom as the late-afternoon sun streamed through the windows, planning out her lessons for the next day and responding to an inbox full of staff and parent emails.

Some teachers ducked out quickly and did lesson planning from home. Olivia found she had the most confidence in her lessons when she walked out of school fully prepared for the next day. This was partly because procrastination had never worked for her, but also because of how she savored the peace and quiet of her classroom after dismissal.

She'd decorated the walls with a few dozen inspirational posters when she took over the class this January. From Einstein, Voltaire, and Carl Jung to Helen Keller, Jane Austen, and a handful of others, she'd acquired an eclectic variety of poster quotes that spoke to her in one way or another, and she loved the way her students connected with individual ones as well. Nerdy as it might be, surrounded by a sea of motivational quotes, Olivia was, well, more motivated to be the best version of herself that she could be.

This afternoon, there'd be no time for after-school lesson planning. And it was unlikely she'd have time tonight either. That meant tomorrow morning she'd be winging her lessons until she had time to catch up in fourth hour, her open planning time.

Regardless of the little bit of stress she'd face tomorrow, this afternoon's escapade with Ava was worth it. Olivia had been counting the minutes till the bell rang for more than one reason. First, at five thirty tonight, that beautiful pointer would've been held for seventy-two hours, and he'd be cleared for relocating to a shelter.

Ava's favorite animal rescue and adoption center, the High Grove Animal Shelter, had heard his story and had agreed to take him in. And since Ava had reassured Olivia that High Grove would find him the perfect home where he'd be loved and cared for and not dead-bolted in a pen, Olivia was crossing her fingers no owner came forward at this late hour.

Second, as of last night, her car was ready for pickup.

Hopefully, $843 later, her little Cruze would be repair-free for a while, and she could go another several months without having to trade it in for something newer. Third, even though Rhonda had looked and hadn't found it, Olivia wanted a chance to scour Milton's Feed Store parking lot for her missing phone. Not knowing if Gabe had been trying to call her was driving her batty.

If she didn't find it tonight, she'd head to the phone store after work tomorrow and sign a contract on a new one. She'd been overdue to do so anyway. And while it would be another unexpected knock in her budget this month, at least she'd know if Gabe was calling.

If he didn't call, she wasn't quite sure what to do. What if he'd tried once or twice and was giving up? This worry threatened to tip Olivia into a wave of panic. He'd promised to call on Sunday, and tomorrow would be Wednesday. How much time would he give her to return his call?

Thanks to last night's internet search, she was pretty sure she'd found a way to contact him. When she wasn't riding a wave of wild panic, she was determined to wait it out until Friday before doing so. She'd linked Gabe to a veterinarian's office in the Rock Hill area. He'd mentioned he was taking over the practice of a retiring vet, and she'd found an article at his alma mater, Mizzou, linking him to the practice almost ten months ago. If he'd moved from there to a different veterinarian's office, perhaps someone at the office could tell her where. The veterinary office she'd linked him to was owned and operated by a Dr. Albert Washington. Based on his picture, he was certainly at or near retirement age.

With any luck, she'd find her phone tonight and

wouldn't need to go that route, but it was reassuring to have a backup plan. She'd hardly been able to get Gabe out of her mind unless she was fully focused on something like teaching.

The final bell mercifully rang, and Olivia waited for her seventh-hour students to file out before logging off her computer and grabbing her already packed canvas tote and lunch bag.

As directed, Ava was parked at the back of the school, and Olivia spotted her bright-blue Jeep right away. Thankfully, her sister had promised not to show any property after two o'clock today. Sometimes Ava's real-estate dealings could run three times longer than expected. And as far as Olivia was concerned, waiting any longer than she already had for both the dog and a sweep search for her phone was close to torture.

"You aren't going to like this," Ava said as Olivia tossed her bags into the back seat.

"Like what?"

"We're having a late dinner with the fam."

Olivia pulled open the front-passenger door. "Who called who?"

"Mom called this morning."

Olivia had gotten a dozen Facebook messages from her hometown friends since Saturday attempting to confirm if the rumors were true. She'd known it was only a matter of time until her parents found out, but without her phone and having had to use Aunt Becky's phone half-a-dozen times to coordinate her car repairs, she'd not had the energy to initiate a call to them yet.

"I knew I was going to regret not calling her first." Olivia drummed her feet into the floor rapid-fire in frustration after buckling her seat belt. "So, did you tell her about Wes?"

"No. I will tonight. She was too consumed by who you were snogging in New Madrid Saturday and why."

Olivia plopped heavily enough against the back of her seat for her head to thwack against the headrest. "Nobody in America uses the word 'snogging.'"

"Maybe not, but it's a touch more satisfyingly graphic than just saying 'kissing' or 'making out.'"

"It irks me that she went to you to ask about me."

"Uh, you don't have a phone right now. Besides, I'm sure she knew you wouldn't tell her anything."

Olivia sucked in a giant breath and did her best to release it in one slow, controlled stream, only to find that did nothing to calm her nerves. "What'd you say?"

"That she'd have to ask you... Thus dinner tonight at Gramps and Grams's."

"Great. I can tell everyone about my snogging escapades at once. Did you tell her about the dog at least?"

"Yep. She wanted to know why we were driving down. Better for a dog than a boy."

"Why is it that I'm twenty-five but feel sixteen? I mean, seriously, Mom was pregnant with you by my age."

Ava rode the brake through the congested parking lot. Both the front and back lots were pandemonium at dismissal due to the slew of parents picking up their kids and aides and other nonteaching staff making a prompt exit. "If it helps, I'm sure the attention won't linger on you long."

Ava was right. Regardless of what was circulating through the rumor mill, what was happening to Ava right now was top priority. Feeling more than a touch inconsiderate, Olivia placed a hand over the top of her sister's. "Any news?"

Ava's lips squinched together for a second or two. "Does him texting to ask if I'd consider using a mediator to save money count as news?"

"Oh, Avey. Why is he being such a dick?"

Ava pressed a little too hard on the gas before pulling out, and Olivia was jerked backward against her seat again. "Sorry." Her sister tapped Olivia's knee point-edly. "Software engineer with a master's degree or not, I outearned him all three years we were together. I put so much money into that wedding. And into that condo— the one he's suggesting we sell so we can both have a fresh start."

Olivia mulled this over a few seconds before respond-ing. "Have you thought any more about what *you* want?"

"Yes. I want to adopt that cat. I want to sell the house and start fresh. And I definitely want that cat."

Her sister hadn't stopped talking about the cat in three days. Olivia racked her brain, trying to remember when the cat had come in. She'd learned so many animal stories at once that they were blending together. She was fairly certain the cat had come in Saturday morning after spending Friday night at the gas-station attendant's house. If so, there was a chance the cat had just been cleared today and hadn't been picked up or transferred anywhere.

"You've had enough time to think it over. If you really want the cat, then you should have the cat. Just keep in mind, as much as I've been enjoying our sleepovers this week, staying at Aunt Becky's long-term won't work with a cat. Or dog for that matter. Has she shared any of how Coco was almost featherless when she took her from that family? They had both dogs and a cat, and from what Aunt Becky says, the poor thing was traumatized."

"Believe me, I'll lose it if I stay there much more than another week. But I can't see why you couldn't give a dog or cat a try. I'm sure the bird would learn to cope with it."

"I'd love to adopt a dog—the pointer, actually—but I know not to push my luck. If Coco so much as sees a dog or cat through the living room window, she goes berserk. And Aunt Becky loves that bird. Coco's in her will, you know. She's good with the dog staying over-night tonight, as long as he's only in my room."

Ava rolled her eyes. "I don't know how you've made it there for the last three-something months. Aunt Becky can be such a head case. Just like Dad."

Anger flared, fresh and ripe. "Dad is *not* a head case. And neither is Aunt Becky. She's just happy with her solitary life…with her cursing cockatoo."

Ava snorted. "Yeah, well, how do you explain Dad?"

It always came down to this between her and Ava. Irreconcilable differences about their family.

"Why do you have to be so hard on him, Ava? Just because he's not as driven as you doesn't make him a bad person."

"I didn't say he was a bad person. I said he was a head case. A dreamer, if it makes you feel better. You know what Mom told me? He hasn't managed to bring in more than a four-digit income since the midnineties when he was working at the feed store. No wonder why

Mom resorted to scams like that honey fraud to make ends meet."

Olivia's happy optimism was teetering. Even if she didn't want to talk about it, her sister had valid points. They weren't the only kids in hand-me-downs and Goodwill scavenges growing up, but it was widely accepted that without their grandparents' help, their family of four would probably have been living out of a car. Thanks to Gramps and Grams, neither she nor Ava had ever gone without an abundance of love and attention or even a healthy meal.

Ava had always been quick to dismiss her dad's efforts over the years. And even if she didn't want to admit it, Olivia knew she couldn't entirely blame Ava for it. Like their aunt, their dad was a creative and talented artist. He'd just never been able to earn a living at it, and he'd never attempted a different career. His medium was stained glass. He created original pieces that sold at a small studio in New Madrid and had also done restoration in most of the churches in the Bootheel. Not only had his inability to make a somewhat decent living created a point of contention between him and their mom—a countless number of their late-night arguments were burned into Olivia's memory—but the strain on their family had been evident.

It was no secret that this was a big part of the reason Ava had taken off as young as she did, and why she was so driven to be successful.

Ava had left home in the throes of the scandal that had nearly cost her mom her twenty-year job at Carla's diner. She'd been selling customers honey for over a year after the hive she invested in failed to thrive.

Someone caught her buying honey in bulk at the local Walmart, and within a couple of days, everyone in a hundred-mile radius had figured out that the cute jars of local honey she'd been selling were fraudulent.

Because she was the best server in the place, she'd managed to keep her serving job, but it was a long time before anyone forgot what she'd been doing.

Probably remembering just the same as Olivia that this subject was tough for them to navigate, Ava turned up the volume to her speakers and passed her phone. "Pick something to play, will you? Something fun."

Olivia flipped through the "fun and upbeat" playlist in her sister's Spotify account. In the spirit of what her sister was going through with Wes, Olivia chose Sara Bareilles's "King of Anything."

After figuring out what it was and letting out a happy snort, Ava joined her in belting out the song into the sunny afternoon. By the time Ava merged onto the highway, they were both laughing and the tension that had spiked so abruptly was ebbing.

After a pit stop for a late-afternoon snack of fries and chocolate shakes, they made good time. Before Olivia knew it, they'd reached the service station where she'd towed her car.

Avoiding the lusty-eyed mechanic who had his head just as turned by Ava as it had been by her, Olivia paid for her car and was happy to find that it was driving smoothly.

Rather than drive around in a second car, she left it parked in a nearby commuter lot and would pick it up on the way home tonight.

It was just after six thirty when Ava pulled into the

entrance of the feed store. Olivia's pulse burst into a sprint. It made no sense to hope for sight of Gabe's truck around the corner in front of the shed where the rescue efforts were taking place. Certainly, he was somewhere in St. Louis wrapping up a day of work. Even knowing this, her heart sank in disappointment at not spotting his truck. What would she give to see him here with Samson trotting along at his side? An awful lot, that was certain.

Being here, her lips tingled fresh from the memory of his mouth against hers. It seemed like only seconds rather than days since she'd experienced the striking and unexpected pleasure of his strong torso pressing against her. He was sexy, yes. It radiated from his persona and was so clearly visible in his heroics. But he was so damn sweet too.

Please, phone, be here.

After a quick scan of the area, she headed inside. She'd give the area a closer look once she checked in.

Rhonda was alone in the big shed, resting on a folding chair over at the side. "Boy, am I glad to see you two!" She stood up, pressing both hands into the small of her back. "A couple of the pups we've got in here are about as wound up as they can get, and that pointer of yours is one of them. He was a bit punky Sunday, but as of yesterday afternoon, he's been acting more like a racehorse at the starting gate than an underweight dog."

"Is he? That's a good sign, right? I've been counting the minutes till he was cleared." Olivia scanned the crates. "And you never heard anything from his owner?"

"Didn't Karen tell you when you called?"

"Tell us what?" Olivia and Ava chimed in at once.

"You were right about them kids knowing more than

they were letting on. They tagged us in a post that they'd taped of that rescue of your friend's. Karen sent a friend request, and not ten minutes later the girl's mom called. Turns out she was a cousin of the homeowner. Says she had next to no contact with him. No one in her family did. He passed away a little over three weeks ago."

"Did they say who's been caring for the dog?"

One side of Rhonda's mouth turned down in something between a frown and a grimace. "From what she said, her cousin lived alone. And he didn't leave a will. His property's in limbo." She sighed and tossed a rag over her shoulder. "The really sad part is apparently none of his relatives knew he had a dog till her daughter and boyfriend came to check out the flooding and poke around in his yard. That was the day before they called us. They were concerned that the dog wasn't being cared for, and the woman spent the afternoon making calls to see who'd been left in charge of the dog, but no one was. When the kids went back to check on him the next day, the water had come up and they couldn't get him out."

Olivia locked a hand over her chest. Her knees were on the verge of buckling. "You mean the beautiful dog was locked in that pen with no one caring for him for over three weeks?"

Rhonda squeezed her shoulder. "I'd like to say time in the business makes these things easier to hear, but it didn't for me. Heartbreaking as it is, it was twenty-five days if you take into account the man's hospitalization before he passed."

Ava clamped a hand over her mouth. "*How* did he survive without food and water?"

"In cases like this, all I can say is put it to God or good fortune, whichever drives you."

"Where is he?" Olivia took off for the center row of crates where she'd last seen him, but he wasn't there.

"He's on the end by the door. Thought it might help him to see out."

Olivia noticed his spotted-liver paw pressing against the metal door of the crate and headed over with Ava following close behind. "There you are, sweet boy." Olivia sank onto her heels and tucked a lock of hair behind her ear. "Remember me, buddy? Probably not, I'm guessing."

As if asserting that he did, the pointer stood up and let out a single baritone "Woof."

His docked tail was wagging with the consistency of a set of wiper blades set to high, making Olivia laugh.

"I think he does," Ava said. "Look at the way he's looking at you."

"Can I walk him?" Olivia directed to Rhonda.

"Be my guest. But have your sister stand guard behind you while you clip on his leash. If he gets away, I don't think he'll stick around. And be aware. He pulls hard enough to lead a sled team when he has the mind to."

Olivia let him sniff her hand through the bars first, then she jogged over for one of several leashes hung on an eyebolt sticking out of the wooden frame at the edge of the sliding doors.

"Give it your best linebacker look behind me, will you?"

"Why do I feel like you and I are both about to get bowled over?"

"He's a sweetie. I bet he just can't stand to be stuck in a crate." Olivia pinched open the release and opened the door just enough to slip her hand through. After a gentle pat on his smooth, lean shoulder, she clipped the leash to his so-new-it-was-stiff blue nylon collar. Locking her other hand inside the hand grip of the leash, she opened the door and popped up to her feet.

Much like the thoroughbred Rhonda had compared him to, he leaped out of the crate with a force that nearly swept Olivia off her feet. She winced at the jolt to her shoulder. Under no delusions about who was leading whom, she hung on as he dragged her outside and over to a short, stubby tree. He peed a long stream at hip level, then trotted off immediately toward a couple shrubs on the opposite side of the driveway.

He glanced her way as if he was a bit unsure why he was being followed but then dismissed her as he became absorbed in sniffing and scent marking the shrubs. Olivia scanned the gravel, grass, and bushes as he did, but her phone was nowhere in sight.

Halfway to one of the nearby big trees, he stopped short and stared off into the grass with such intensity that Olivia stiffened. His tail stuck out straight behind him, one front paw curled in against his chest, and he became as still as a statue.

Olivia followed his gaze till she spotted a robin hopping about on the hunt for worms or insects. She giggled and turned to Ava. "He seems full pointer, doesn't he?"

Ava nodded. "Yep. Brace yourself in case he bolts for it. He shouldn't, but you never know."

Seconds ticked away, and the dog did nothing but stare at the robin. Olivia kept her legs braced and her hands wrapped tight around the leash, but after half a minute passed, all he did was take another step and curl his other paw into his chest.

After watching a bit longer, Ava whispered. "Looks to me like you've got this. You good if I go see a woman about a cat?"

"Sure. We're good. But he's a doll, isn't he?"

"He is. For a hunting dog. Though I'm pretty sure they're bred to be useful more than they are cute. Cute's a hammy-legged corgi or pug or even a boxer."

Olivia rolled her eyes. "Beautiful, then, if you're going to be a stickler. I think he's as beautiful as a dog gets. Especially when he puts another ten or so pounds back on."

Ava shook her head as she took off. "And which of us needs a reminder about Aunt Becky's place being ruled by a parrot?"

"Cockatoo," Olivia replied before adding a nearly silent "Me." She smoothed her hand along the top of the dog's head and down his neck to his long back. If he even noticed, he didn't let on. A second robin had joined the first, and he was oblivious to everything else in the world, including her.

Olivia didn't care. She couldn't remember feeling this way about a dog in a long time. And Ava's words were a reminder she needed about Aunt Becky's small, cramped place; it just wasn't the right home for this remarkable animal who'd been through so much already. As much as she might like it to be.

Chapter 13

WHETHER HE LIKED IT OR NOT, GABE WAS PRETTY sure not being able to sleep in past a quarter to six was a sign of maturity, not insomnia. As much as he'd enjoy lazing in bed this morning and hopefully dozing until his alarm went off at seven, he figured he was better off getting his ass moving instead. Wednesdays were his one free weekday morning. And this was only because his office was open late on the hump day for clients needing that option.

He didn't need to be in until eleven since he'd be there until seven or eight tonight. He'd gotten into the habit of going out to breakfast on Wednesdays with his brother, who was a second-shift security guard at Wash U, but today his brother and sister-in-law were headed to an assembly at their daughter's school.

After disregarding a pile of dirty laundry for another day, Gabe tugged on a pair of somewhat-clean athletic pants and a T-shirt and chugged a glass of water. Samson was still in a heavy doze and would be fine waiting to go to the bathroom till he got back, so Gabe headed out for a run.

In high school and undergrad, he'd played baseball. Had he been forced into track at gunpoint back then, he would have chosen sprints over distance runs any day of the week. For the last year, committed to adding something to his exercise routine besides weights, he'd

taken up jogging. At first it had been small-scale torture.
But he'd worked his way up to seven-mile runs a few
times a week. Doing so made him feel better about the
two or three cheeseburgers and the fourteen-ounce steak
that typically ended up being a less healthy part of his
routine each week. Eventually, he was going to have to
expand his cooking skills beyond baking frozen foods,
grilling, boiling water for pasta, and managing to not
massacre a pan of scrambled eggs.

Yun was quick to point out that all the things he
resisted would keep presenting themselves over again
until he figured them out, and he couldn't say he dis-
agreed with her.

At a couple of minutes until six, it was still dark
except for a sliver of royal-blue horizon in the east. And
as much as he'd resisted running, he'd grown to enjoy
the light smack of his feet on pavement and the consistent, controlled tightness in his lungs and windpipe
when he fell into the rhythm of it.

He also liked the way his thoughts came and went like
clouds while running. Claire had been into meditation
and had always been on him to make a habit of working
it into his days. He'd attempted it with her enough times,
but he'd never been able to keep his mind from racing.
Outside on the pavement, he was pretty sure this was
as close as he'd ever be able to get to true meditation.
Sometimes a half mile would pass, and Gabe would realize he'd been in a state of presence he couldn't explain.

When he got back, the sun was shining brightly over
the horizon and Samson was in the galley kitchen, lapping up water.

"Morning, bud." Gabe leaned over, still a bit breathless,

and gave him a doubled-handed scratch of his ears and throat, which Samson leaned into, directing Gabe where to scratch. Samson panted, his mouth agape in an easy smile. "That morning breath of yours isn't getting any better."

Gabe took him downstairs for a short walk, appreciating the way his dog stopped along the way for a series of deep stretches, then meandered from bush to bush without hurry. When he'd had his fill of sniffs and had done his business, Samson headed for the back door of the building with no cajoling. Gabe dropped the poop bag into the dumpster and trailed up the interior building steps to his apartment after him. Unlike the other night when he'd needed to be carried, Samson took the steps slowly but without hesitation today. This was good to see.

For the last couple days, when Gabe jangled his keys, indicating it was time to head out for the day, Samson had retreated to Gabe's bed and circled up for a nap. And while Gabe trusted that Samson knew what he needed, seeing his dog choose a quiet day of napping over a day at the office stabbed at his heart.

Aside from when Gabe had gone to class, Samson had gone pretty much everywhere with him for the last five years. Like it or not, he needed to face the fact that Samson was a senior dog now.

And accepting this was causing him to take a hard look at his life. In the chaos and stress of school and in the wake of Claire leaving, it had been easy to choose the companionship of the most loyal dog he'd ever met and ignore the fact that he was keeping everyone else at a distance.

In taking this hard look, Gabe was realizing that, unexpectedly, he'd met someone he very much wanted to let in. Even as he accepted the truth of it, fear threatened to incapacitate him, binding his intestines into a knot whenever he let the awareness in.

Olivia had rocked his world with her genuineness, her refreshing honesty, and that kiss. So much so, she'd come close to shaking it off its axis.

And now, she wasn't returning his calls. Or texts.

He'd done his best to give her whatever space she needed. She'd call, he was certain. Pretty certain anyway. He couldn't accept that he'd read her wrong. She'd felt a connection too. He'd experienced it in her kiss and seen it in her eyes.

But she wasn't calling. Or texting. Not even a *Thanks but I need some time to think things through*. Nothing.

He couldn't fathom that she was being coy or playing hard to get. Just as he couldn't fathom he'd read her wrong.

Which put him at a stalemate. In a moment of weakness, Gabe had done an online search and found her name in a school newsletter recognizing her for being teacher of the month for her dedication to helping students with dyslexia. She was working in a magnet prep school downtown in Soulard, less than five miles away. She'd told him she taught eighth-grade math, just not where. But now he knew. And she was closer than he'd imagined.

After he showered, ate a semirespectable skillet of scrambled eggs topped with cheese and salsa, and was ready to leave, Samson gave him a pointed look and a yawn and headed off to his room and the bed again.

"Sweet dreams, bud. I'll do what I can to swing by here this afternoon when I run out to the shelter. Otherwise, it'll be a long day of not much for you."

Carrying a thermos mug of fresh coffee, Gabe gave Samson a final pat and headed out. It wasn't until he was seated inside the Tacoma and flipping over the ignition that he realized he didn't have anywhere he needed to be right now.

And while there was no place he *had* to be, there was one place he very much *wanted* to be. And he was coming up with very few reasons not to at least give it a try.

If ever she'd been so mesmerized by a pair of sable-brown eyes that had shown this much disinterest in her, Olivia couldn't remember. But this dog had had her even before their first real hello. And now that she had an inkling of what he'd been through in the last month, her compassion for him had increased tenfold.

Last night, Ava had assured her she was making progress breaking through that indifferent exterior of his. Olivia wasn't convinced. In fact, she was afraid her attempts at showing him genuine compassion hadn't even made a dent.

Fighting off a sleep-deprived hangover from their late night, Olivia sat out on the grass in Aunt Becky's backyard and fed the pointer spoonfuls of kibble out of her hand. The damp grass soaked into the old jogging shorts she'd slept in, helping her resist the temptation to lie back and close her eyes. The only way she'd make it through this day was with copious amounts of coffee.

It had been after midnight by the time she'd gotten home to her aunt's, and another hour or so after that before she'd gotten the dog settled and crawled into bed. Since Olivia was mobile again and could get to work on her own, Ava had gone home—newly adopted cat in tow—to her house in Kirkwood. If Wes was there, which she'd figured he would be, Ava intended to kick him to the couch for the night. Fair was fair. He was the one initiating the divorce. He could wake up with a crick in his neck for a few nights while they figured out the next steps.

And while Olivia had only been sharing a bed again with her sister for four nights, the tiny guest room she'd been sleeping in since January had seemed just a bit lonely for the first time. Her sister had left their grandparents' home so many years ago, Olivia had forgotten how all-encompassing her larger-than-life presence was.

Dinner at her grandparents' had taken just as long and been just as draining as Olivia would've guessed. The best parts had been the breaks to get the dog out of his crate and let him explore the farm. He'd been fine with the other dogs, though his real interest had been in the birds he'd spotted hopping along the ground before it got dark.

"It just seems like you're rubbing it in Trevor's face," her mom had said when they were alone in the kitchen spooning ice cream into sundae bowls. "Coming home unannounced—engaging in romantic escapades that turn into the talk of the town."

The hair on the back of Olivia's neck had prickled. Her parents had said they understood Olivia's reasons for calling off the wedding, but Olivia suspected that if they'd had their wish, she'd have gone through with it. "I didn't *plan* a romantic escapade. Just like I didn't *plan* for my car to break down or to need a ride from a really amazing guy. It just sort of happened."

"You could've called us."

"If I'd called you, I wouldn't have met Gabe. And there's a good chance that dog on your porch would've drowned in his pen."

It had been enough to stop her mom from any further protests. After they finished scooping the ice cream in silence, she asked, "Does this mean you're dating him?"

"It doesn't mean I won't, given the opportunity." Olivia set the scoop on the counter a little too hard. "Losing my phone hasn't helped things be any less complicated."

Her mom had wiped up a few drops of ice cream melting on the counter. "Just move slowly, will you? Those city boys have got a whole slew of problems nowadays. From painkiller addictions to that dark web they're always talking about. The world's a good deal more complicated than it used to be."

Although she knew it wouldn't make a bit of difference to her mom's beliefs, Olivia had replied that addictions were popping their ugly heads up in rural areas too.

She sat on the grass in the soft morning light and rolled her shoulders, trying to dispel the tension setting up there. The truth was as obvious as the bright-yellow petals of the dandelions popping up all over the place. The longer she was away, the more obvious it was that a part of her had left the Bootheel for good.

Once the pointer had vacuumed up nearly half a cup of kibble from the palm of her hand, Olivia led him over to the back porch where she scooped out the rest of his breakfast. Coco spotted him through the window and let out a series of raucous squawks. Before dipping his head into the bowl to devour the rest of his breakfast, the nervous dog barked a single booming woof that sent Coco into a fresh tizzy.

After inhaling the rest of his kibble, the pointer licked his empty bowl. Olivia patted his back. "Good boy. Good...whatever your name is. I guess we'll never know, considering no one even knew you existed."

It wasn't so much that she wanted the dog to bond with her; it was that she wanted him to bond with someone. She couldn't imagine a dog more deserving of a bit of pampering than he was.

It didn't even make a difference if his owner had been kind and caring or tough and stern or something in between. He'd been locked in a pen for nearly a month and had been slowly starving. What mattered now was that he end up in a loving, caring home and have a chance to bond with someone the way Samson had with Gabe.

Gabe. *Ugh.* Just thinking of him got her insides in a twist. It would've been so much easier if she'd found her phone. But she hadn't. So tonight she'd be headed for the phone store after work. Ava had helped her feel better by reassuring her that if he'd left her any voice-mails, she'd be able to access them on a new phone. If he hadn't, she could even see about having her phone company download her recent texts for her.

Or you could just stop by his office. Let him know you lost your phone and give him an update on the pointer.

As the sun climbed up in a pink-and-orange sky,

promising a beautiful spring day ahead, Olivia was feeling optimistic enough to want to try it. To put aside any worry over being the one who'd initiated the kissing or who'd confessed to sharing something pretty scarring in common with his ex-fiancée.

She could even stop by this morning instead of putting it off until Friday. She had a sub coming in for the first part of the day so that she could take the dog to the shelter when it opened at eight. Shaving another half hour off her school day wouldn't inconvenience anyone.

Seeing that the pointer wasn't losing interest in licking his empty bowl, Olivia scooped it up and set it on the table. She sank onto her heels and switched the leash to her other hand. She held her flattened palm up to show it was empty, and to her surprise, he began to lick it as well.

"Look at that. I'd almost swear you've noticed I'm here."

To Olivia's delight, the pointer wagged his short tail hard enough to sway his hips along with it. His solemn brown eyes even connected with hers for a second or two.

"You know, you're so gorgeous it just about stops my heart. What do you say I get dressed and take you for a walk before we go check out your new digs? Temporary digs, anyway. I'm holding fast to the hope that you're adopted before you even have time to settle in."

As if in answer, his tongue swiped across her chin and nose before he turned his attention to the yard and the birds in the trees.

"On an affection scale of 'largely indifferent' to 'joined at the hip,' that might not be much, but it's good enough to make my morning."

———

Gabe had no memory of being at the Soulard Farmers Market first thing on a Wednesday morning before. In fact, he couldn't remember the last time he'd been here, though he'd come often enough as a kid with his parents on Saturdays when the market had seemed like a chaotic, bustling metropolis. Today, the old open-air building was quiet enough that his footsteps carried a light echo, just like the stillness carried the coughs of one of the vendors who was setting up a selection of handmade soaps on a nicked-up table.

The ten or so vendors who'd be selling on this early-spring weekday were mostly still unloading out of vans and truck beds. He spotted a woman unpacking an oversize tub of bouquets and headed over to her table. She'd already put out a couple different varieties of rose bouquets—whites, pinks, and reds—and a few bouquets of bright-yellow sunflowers. But he was drawn to three bouquets boasting a selection of subtler colors: muted whites and a variety of pale greens.

"See anything to suit you?" She was close to his mom's age, he was guessing, and had deep-set wrinkles around her eyes that she'd gotten from a good deal of either smiling or squinting, and he wasn't about to guess which.

He nodded toward the muted-looking bouquet. "What would you say that type's appropriate for?"

The woman was placing the bouquets into open round holders and appraised him over the rim of her glasses. "How old's the person you're buying them for?"

"Ah, midtwenties, I'm guessing, maybe mid-to-late twenties."

She nodded. "Then the answer's easy. Just buy what you think she'll like. There are no rules with millennials when it comes to buying flowers. The succulents and eucalyptus in those arrangements pair well with the cream roses. You can't go wrong with subtle elegance like that."

"Subtle elegance, huh? I'll take one. Know any vendors who sell cards?"

"If you'll hold on a minute, I've got a tub of 'em in my van that I still need to unload."

Gabe chose his favorite of the three bouquets and debated what he'd write in the card as the flower vendor traipsed back across the long hallway with a smaller tub. He was happy when the wire rack of cards she pulled out were blank inside with St. Louis photographs on the front. He'd not been in the mood for anything sappier than the flowers he was buying. He was close to choosing one with a view of Forest Park when he spotted a card with a golden retriever sprawled out on the steps below the Arch.

"This and the bouquet. Do you take credit cards?"

"I do. Give me a minute to get everything pulled up."

According to his phone, Olivia's school was just a few blocks away, so Gabe decided to leave the truck parked on the street here and walk. Based on a few recent visits to his niece's elementary school, he knew schools weren't as receptive to visitors as they used to be. If he tried to see Olivia in person without an appointment, it was unlikely he'd be able to get past the front desk.

But that was fine by him. All he wanted to do this morning was deliver the flowers to her and let her know he was thinking of her. Maybe it would tempt her to call, maybe it wouldn't. But at the very least, it was a try. And right now, that was the best he could do.

Chapter 14

OLIVIA HAD PLANNED TO ARRIVE AT THE HIGH GROVE Animal Shelter just as the building opened at eight, but traffic had been light, and she was a few minutes early. Aside from a single truck that reminded her a bit of Gabe's and gave her heart a pang, the parking lot was empty. If ever a building could radiate happy energy, this one did.

The single-story redbrick building had already been freshened up for spring with new mulch. Bright-yellow daffodils lined the mulch bed. Popping out between the groupings of flowers were brightly colored metal cat and dog sculptures. The two parking spots in front were reserved for in-progress adoptions and had metal signage with pictures of storks carrying blankets with kittens and puppies spilling out that brought a smile to Olivia's face.

As welcoming as the shelter was at first look, tears still stung her eyes as she opened her back-passenger door, pinched open the door of the crate wedged in between the front and back seats, and clipped a leash to the pointer's collar. Goodbyes had never come easy. And even in the span of one short night, she was more drawn to this reticent dog than ever.

If she knew for sure Principal Garcia was going to renew her contract for next year, and she wasn't going to be back to the drawing board in terms of a job, she'd jump through hoops to move out of Aunt Becky's right now and find a dog-friendly place to rent.

She swallowed hard and cleared her throat, which caught the dog's attention. He brushed his nose across her hand before stepping to the edge of the seat and taking in his new surroundings. He licked his jowls a bit nervously and flattened his tail between his legs. Olivia's heart might as well be being shoved through a wringer. Even nestled in between the residential and business sections of Webster Groves in a seemingly quiet part of the city, the sights and sounds here would be a far stretch from what the dog was used to. Olivia knew Old Bollinger Road well enough to know that aside from weekend traffic at the river, the dog had had a quiet life, especially alone in a giant backyard with nothing but woods and the river behind it.

She stood straight and cleared her throat determinedly as he jumped out. If she went in teary-eyed, odds were good she'd break down into sobs upon leaving.

"You're going to get a new home before you know it. And until you do, you're going to be pampered while you're here." Luckily, Olivia's tone carried the confidence she was hoping to relay to the dog, and the threat of tears abated. For the moment, at least. "I checked out the website; this place is like a Hyatt for dogs. You'll get walks every day. You'll even get a fresh blanket to snuggle up with at night. And I've seen how you like blankets."

Proving his level of discomfort by completely ignoring a bird on a branch not that far away, he stepped closer to Olivia.

"It's going to be okay, bud. There's even a dog park

here somewhere, though something tells me once you settle in, if there are any birds in sight, you won't care much about playing with the other dogs." She gave him the most confident pat on the shoulder she could muster. "Here goes nothing."

He trotted along at her side till they got close to the building, then started to pull backward. He was jerking hard enough that Olivia was panicking he'd slip his collar when the front door jangled open. A guy about her age was in the doorway; his head was cocked to the side as he studied the dog with a serious look on his face.

Olivia attempted to introduce herself as the pointer jerked her away from the entrance. "I'm…Ol—livia Grah—am. I'm here to…"

Without giving her a second of his focus, the guy slipped a small handful of treats from a pocket in his cargo pants and sank into a squat as the door fell closed behind him. He called the dog by making a series of soft clicking sounds with his tongue.

To Olivia's surprise, it worked. The pointer stopped jerking backward, and his ears pricked forward. The guy moved one of the treats around on top of his fingertips until the pointer's mouth opened in an excited pant, then tossed it a few feet in front of him.

After the treat was inhaled with a quick flick of the dog's tongue, the guy opened the door again. He stuck a doorstop into the bottom of the frame with his foot, then headed inside, dropping treats every few feet as he went.

After looking her way as if to make sure she was coming, too, the dog walked in cautiously, eyeing the counters and bright gift shop and the mural on the far wall as if any of them might come to life at any second.

Perhaps because he was still adjusting to having regular meals again, the treats proved enticing enough to draw him inside.

"Kick out the doorstop once he's all the way in."

Stretching her leg behind her as far as it would go, Olivia managed to kick out the stop while the attentive pointer munched a fresh treat. As the door swung closed, the dog's tail tucked tighter against his rear, and he let out a plaintive whine. Olivia felt a pang in her heart as his solemn brown eyes bore into hers before darting around his new surroundings.

"He was close to slipping his collar," the guy said, focusing on her for the first time. "We bring adult dogs in through the back. It's less stressful on them. And we can get them directly into quarantine."

Quarantine? While that sounded less than pleasant, Olivia determined to remain as nonreactive as possible. Ava had given her word that the staff here would take great care of him. "Thanks for your help. I guess his collar needs to be tightened. I'm not sure how used to situations like this he is."

"You mean being surrendered?"

She felt about two inches tall and fully responsible for his impending abandonment even though she wasn't. "Ah, yeah, and honestly, just being indoors. He lived in a pen outdoors in a very remote area."

He nodded. "That's a considerable change of environment."

"I, uh, believe you knew we were coming?"

"Yes. This is the German shorthair from Rhonda and Karen's rescue. And you're Olivia Graham."

Olivia blinked. Maybe it was just her, but he seemed

a touch socially awkward, just not in a gawky, insecure way. More like in an I-prefer-not-to-talk-to-people-unless-I-have-to way. "It's nice to meet you, er…"

"Patrick Wobrice, facilities manager and intake coordinator." He nodded in her direction but returned his attention to the pointer. "Do you want to see quarantine? He'll be in there a minimum of three days. Once he gets a clean bill of health, he'll be brought up to the main kennels."

"Ah, sure. I'd love to see it. The whole place, actually." With no escape route now that the door was closed, the pointer clung to Olivia's side but followed her without further struggle. He sniffed the air incessantly as they passed the cat kennels, bringing a smile to Olivia's lips.

"What a sweet-looking group of cats." A few were awake and watching the new arrival, but most were curled up in napping slings. To the side of the kennels and empty at the moment was a floor-to-ceiling kitty play area that looked like it would entice even the most stalwart of cats into a bit of playful roughhousing.

She was still gawking at the cute cats when she realized Patrick had doubled back and was tightening the dog's collar. "The dog kennels are next. You'll want to walk him through the center of the aisle. Once he's out of quarantine, he'll be able to be introduced to the other dogs."

"Yeah, sure." Olivia wrapped a bit of the extra leash around her hand as Patrick pushed through a set of thick, glass double doors.

"Is he compatible with other dogs?"

"He lived alone as far as I know, but he did fine at Rhonda's."

Olivia wished she had more time to take in the various dogs that rose to their feet to greet the newcomer. There was a motley crew of big, short, fluffy, smooth, young, and old. Most barked eagerly and wagged their tails, a few growled warnings at the newcomer, and one or two of the more timid-acting ones tucked their tails and moved to the backs of their kennels.

As if hopeful their destination was a less chaotic one, the pointer stuck even closer to Olivia's side and slunk past the long row of kennels. She thought maybe he was whining but couldn't be sure over all the barking.

After they'd passed through the kennels, they entered the back of the building. It was an open area with a few soft chairs, lots of fun pictures of cats and dogs and even a rabbit or two, leashes and coats hung by the back door, and it opened to several doors marked with purple nameplates.

Dread threatened to lock Olivia's feet to the floor as Patrick headed for the door labeled QUARANTINE.

Run, run, run. Don't let them lock him up. Tears stung her eyes instantly. She was certain she wasn't getting through this without shedding a few but did her best to swallow them back. *You know this is for the best. It's his ticket into a loving home.*

Olivia wouldn't attempt to deny that she wanted his loving, forever home to be *her* home. If she had one of her own to offer him. It wasn't that she minded living at Aunt Becky's. Waking up to the smell of chickpea pancakes, tofu omelets, or cinnamon French toast and Coco's continuous chatter had its merits, and she was grateful. Escaping the bustle of the city at the end of the day and tucking herself away in a town that time seemed to have forgotten also had merit. For the most part, she could go on living there indefinitely.

It just so happened, this remarkable and deserving dog was the first thing causing her to question how long this "indefinite" should be.

"Do you have any idea how long dogs his size and age typically stay here before they're adopted?"

Patrick held open the door, motioning her inside. "Yes, I've done some compilations of body size and age to average length of stay."

"Oh. Cool." Olivia checked out the room, waiting for him to offer more. Only he didn't.

As welcoming as the rest of the facility was, she still managed to be taken off guard at not finding the quarantine room cold and indifferent like she imagined a quarantine room could be. The walls were a muted purple-gray, soft music played through a set of speakers, and an essential-oil diffuser filled the room with the inviting but subtle scent of lavender. The kennels in the small room varied in size and were divided with cats sectioned off from the dogs.

"I've got our largest kennel in here ready for him. Once he's moved up front, he'll have more room. The big kennels in the main area are just under thirty square feet. With any luck, he won't be here long enough to be moved over to the kennels with outdoor runs. But those are sixty square feet including the run."

"How long is it that you think he could be here?" she asked, rephrasing her earlier question.

Patrick eyed the pointer with discernment. "How old?"

"Ah, four or five was the best guess."

"Then he's thin but still in his prime. Since our main kennels aren't maxed out at the moment, he'll be available for adoption as soon as he's neutered and clears quarantine. He's a hunting breed, so a home visit will be required unless it's a repeat adopter who wants him, and there's always a chance of a home visit falling through. Assuming that doesn't happen, my best estimate is thirty-two days."

"Thirty-two days." Just over a month ago, Olivia had filled out the application to be a transport driver. All the days and hours since then seemed like such a long stretch of time.

"Yes, based on the season, his breed, and his age," Patrick added as if he thought she were questioning him.

She shifted the pointer's leash from one hand to the other. "Would it be possible for me to come by and walk him while he's here?"

Patrick looked up from the dog for a brief moment before reaching out for the leash. "To walk a dog, you either need to be a staff member or a volunteer. We aren't hiring now, but we are accepting new volunteers."

In one swift movement, Patrick guided the pointer into his temporary kennel. It was three times the size of what he'd been in overnight, and while he didn't fight going in the same way he'd tried to back out of his travel crate, he looked up at her and whined a loud, plaintive whine.

Olivia's heart twisted into a knot. "What can I do to become a volunteer?"

"There's an application online. We hold volunteer interviews every other month."

She swallowed hard. *Olivia Graham, you are not*

going to bawl in front of this guy. "I don't suppose there's any way to fast-track an application?"

His forehead knotted into a near-scowl as if she'd just spoken another language. "Who is it that you know here?"

"Um, I don't think I know anyone here. My sister knows a few people. Ben Thomas and Mia Chambers. And she went to one of your fund-raisers a few months ago."

He nodded slowly. "I've seen a few volunteers fast-tracked over the years because they were brought in by staff or other volunteers and don't need to wait for the interview process."

Olivia pressed her lips together. Was he hinting that she could be fast-tracked or just telling her the facts? She wasn't sure.

His near-scowl deepened. "You volunteer with Deedee?"

"Sort of. My first drive for her was last weekend, only it didn't quite go as planned. I ended up not transporting the animals that I was supposed to transport because of car trouble, but it worked out for the best. I and, ah…a friend of mine ended up being involved in this guy's rescue. He nearly died in rising floodwaters."

"You were involved with Dr. Wentworth's rescue of him?" Patrick's face brightened abruptly. "I couldn't place how I recognized you. Your hair looks different. For a few seconds, you're in the video we were tagged in yesterday when we agreed to take him." Patrick pointed to the dog.

Olivia tried to shake off her confusion. "Dr. Wentworth?" Suddenly her pulse burst into a sprint.

"Oh! You mean Gabe. Yes, I was there with him. I didn't realize you knew him. Or that I was in a video. I've not actually seen it. I'm winding up a month-long social media hiatus with some of my students."

Patrick gave her that look again as if she were speaking a foreign language but didn't pursue it. "He's taking over Dr. Washington's practice."

Olivia nodded, not sure of the significance of that to any of this. Suddenly it clicked. "Is he your vet?"

Gabe had said he worked with two different shelters. From her rural, hometown population mind-set, St. Louis was a big city full of countless people she'd never meet, and she knew for a fact there were dozens of shelters in the city and county limits. She'd never considered she might be bringing the pointer to one Gabe was associated with.

"He's the shelter's primary vet. He's taking over for Dr. Washington, who's retiring. We work with two other vets too. If he were to introduce you to our volunteer coordinator, you could be fast-tracked into the program."

Olivia could feel the blood rushing to her cheeks, and suddenly it felt as if she were standing on stilts.

"Then you could start walking him," Patrick added, nodding toward the dog as if she hadn't understood.

She cleared her throat to keep it from locking. "That would be…incredible. Do you know when Ga…Dr. Wentworth will be here next?"

"He typically comes in the late afternoon on Wednesdays. Last week he got here at two fourteen. The week before it was at five to three."

Olivia did her best not to blink over the bit about

the time of arrival. "Would it... Could I leave a note for him?"

Patrick nodded and looked around the small room. "I can take you back up front. There are paper, pens, and counter space to write."

Olivia froze as he opened the door. The pointer was staring right at her and whining. She knelt in front of his kennel and pressed the palm of her hand against it. "This isn't goodbye. I'm going to be back before you know it. Promise."

His answer was a whine and a wag of his short tail. Sucking in a breath, Olivia stood up and followed Patrick out of the room, surprisingly able to keep her tears at bay. Suddenly, this didn't feel like a goodbye at all.

It was more like a thrilling and unexpected hello.

Chapter 15

BY THE TIME HE MADE IT BACK TO THE TRUCK AFTER dropping off Olivia's flowers, Gabe had well over an hour until he needed to be at the vet office and decided to swing by the shelter first. If he had a light caseload there today, perhaps he could block out some time later for the much-overdue conversation with the business consultant he'd hired to review the draft documents for the purchase of the practice.

Things had pretty much gone as expected at Olivia's school, aside from the fact the front-office secretary had let it slip that a substitute was filling in for her this morning due to a personal matter, and the flowers would be waiting in her classroom upon her return. She'd followed it up with a "But I'm not supposed to tell you that." Although he hadn't wanted to press, he'd overheard a woman at another desk comment that Olivia was expected to be back around third hour.

At least that confirmed Olivia had made it safely back from New Madrid, a worry that had crossed his mind once or twice when she'd not returned his three calls.

Those few minutes in the truck were starting to feel like a dream, like the best dream he'd ever had. It wasn't just her kiss or the brush of her body moving against his. Sure, he'd not experienced that in a long time, and he was overdue. Way overdue. His body was stirring to life like a long-slumbering volcano. But something bigger, more meaningful had awoken in him as a result of their conversation, her honesty, and their laughter.

If she'd had a change of heart, he'd accept it. But in those few hours together, he'd felt a connection stronger than anything he'd imagined could've happened in that short time span. And he was almost certain she'd been just as moved as him.

He pulled into the High Grove Animal Shelter parking lot and pressed down a wave of doubt that maybe he'd been wrong. Assumed things she'd not felt. Deep in thought as he was, he didn't spot the Cruze backing out from behind a minivan until it was nearly too late.

Gabe slammed the brake pedal and tapped the horn as the Cruze continued moving toward the front rim of his bumper. The Tacoma jerked to a stop hard enough that everything on his passenger seat—his phone, a few receipts, and his sunglasses—went sailing to the floor. Thankfully, the driver heard the horn and hit the brakes fast enough to avoid a collision, coming to an abrupt stop with just a fraction of an inch of space between them.

He released a big breath—he could imagine few things he wanted to do less this morning than exchange paperwork and wait for the police to fill out an accident report. Through the tinted back windows, he saw the driver, a woman, wave a hand in an apologetic plea. Offering an easy wave in return, he drove in an arc around the stopped car and parked in an open spot a couple spaces down.

He unbuckled and stretched across the bucket seats to fish for his phone and glasses and realized something else had been shot forward with that hard stop. He blinked in surprise. It was an older-model iPhone in a purple two-toned case, and Gabe had seen it before. Cradled in a pair of delicate hands that he'd wanted to draw against him and fingers he'd wanted to entwine in his own.

A laugh bubbled up from deep in his gut, and a rush of relief swept over him. Olivia wasn't returning his call *because she'd lost her phone in his truck*. It must have fallen underneath the seat. And she'd not even had his number to tell him so.

At least he knew how to get the phone to her.

He snatched his own phone off the floorboard as well and sat straight again. While reaching for the door handle, he did a double take. Maybe too much blood had been draining to his head while he was bent over. The woman who'd almost collided with him was standing beside her car door, her long, fiery hair glowing in the sunlight. She was biting her lip, and an awkward grin was spreading across her face. He gave a light shake of his head as if any second the mirage might vanish. There was no explanation for it, but the very person who'd been occupying his thoughts the last three-and-a-half days no longer seemed so impossibly out of reach.

He practically tumbled out of the truck, fisting her phone in one hand and slipping his into his pocket. He headed over, leaving his keys dangling from the ignition and his truck door open. His pulse was racing a thousand miles a minute. The only thing stopping him from greeting her with a kiss as passionate as the ones they'd exchanged on Saturday was the day-care-class-sized group of preschool kids hopping out of a van directly behind her, all squirmy and wriggling in anticipation of their visit.

"A part of me wants to ask what you're doing here, but anything that brought you here is good enough for me."

She still had that irresistibly shy grin on her face. "I just finished writing you a note. And I can't believe I almost smashed into your truck! I'm so sorry. I was steering clear of the kids and not paying attention to what was behind me."

"It happens. And trust me, this truck has its share of dings and dents." He shook his head lightly, still trying to step out of his disbelief. Was it possible that he'd nearly memorized the pattern of faded freckles over the bridge of her nose? He held up her phone. "I'm guessing your note may have been about this?"

Her eyes went wide. "Are you serious? I could've sworn I'd dropped it into my purse as I was grabbing my stuff. I thought I'd lost it in the parking lot at Rhonda and Karen's or later when Ava and I stopped for food."

"The funny thing is, until I slammed the brakes just now, I had no idea I had it." He gave her a wink. "Kind of makes you not calling me back a lot easier to swallow."

The kids had all jumped out of the van and were being herded inside like goats by two women. The van door was making a grinding sound as it automatically slid shut. Olivia looked from him to the van and back. She dug her top teeth into her lower lip again, drawing his attention straight to her mouth. "If it helps, it makes my day to know you called."

"Then I'm hoping you'll think it was romantic and not at all stalkerish that I left you some flowers at your school this morning."

She laughed, closing her hand over her chest. "You did that?" She let out a breath and shook her head. "I, uh... Romantic. Definitely romantic. No one's ever done anything like that for me before."

He wanted to kiss her. But the next time he kissed her, it was going to be hard to stop, and with a split-second glance through the shelter windows, he could see they had a bit of an audience. Megan, the director, was by the door, addressing the kids. Patrick and Tess, one of the newer employees, were behind the main counter. It wouldn't be the most professional thing he could do as the new vet who was still proving himself here.

"You, uh, you made an impression, Olivia." He stopped and shook his head. "More like carved out a canyon. I'd like to get to know you."

As if wondering about the audience they were drawing as well, she looked over her shoulder and into the building. "I'd like that." She held up her phone. "Now that I've got this, I'll be answering your calls. Once I charge it, that is. The battery sucks," she added with that brilliant grin of hers.

"So, what are you doing here, anyway?"

"Stalking you," she said with a laugh. "Kidding. It's the dog, the pointer. Ava took me to get my car yesterday afternoon, and we picked him up. Turns out it's a small world up here too. This is the shelter she was talking about bringing him to. Can you believe it?"

"I'm pretty sure that's what you call serendipity. So, the pointer's here? How's he doing? I've been thinking about him."

"He's good. I can already tell he's picking up weight. But I feel about two inches tall leaving him here. I had him overnight, and I have to say I haven't felt this way about a dog in a long time."

"He's a good-natured dog, that's for sure."

"And this seems like a great place, but considering what he's been through, I hope he doesn't have to wait too long before he's adopted. I asked if I could take him for walks, and Patrick, the employee who showed me around, told me about their volunteer program. I ended up filling out an application. I hope you don't mind, but when Patrick found out I knew you, he said you could kind of sponsor me. Then I wouldn't have to wait until the next round of training."

"Oh man," Gabe said, feeling the grin spread across his face even though he was going for mock serious. "Sorry, but the only way I could vouch for you would be if you let me go for a couple of those walks with you. You know— that way I could get a clearer idea of your character."

A laugh bubbled out of her, and she crossed her arms over her chest. "Is that how it is?" She gave him a glower that mutated into another laugh. "I think I'd be okay with that. But in the fine print of the volunteer application, I'm pretty sure there was a line about needing to take your sponsor to dinner as a thank-you."

Gabe reached out for a handshake but ended up holding her hand in his and not letting go. "It's a deal, Olivia Graham. So long as you let me take you to dinner later as a thank-you for taking me to dinner."

She laughed again, her remarkable hazel eyes shining with flecks of gold. "Deal." She made no move to pull her hand away, which was fine with Gabe because he was pretty certain he was never going to want to let go.

Chapter 16

LOCKED IN THE KENNEL, THE DOG SNIFFED THE AIR, testing it for the fresh scent of the woman who'd brought him here, but he couldn't detect it. Countless new smells assaulted him with each sniff, some enticing, others fear-inducing. This new place was bustling with the unfamiliar. As far back as the dog could remember, he'd lived out his days in solitude, watching the birds and squirrels in the trees, the hawks in the sky, the deer that crossed the back field at dusk, and the rabbits, mice, and snakes that moved through the grass.

In this new place, everything was different. Fresh scents didn't blow in on the wind but were circulated through the holes in the walls. The smells of so many dogs blended together, overwhelming him. There were other creatures here too—rabbits, though they seemed quite different from the ones who'd hopped in front of his pen from time to time, and cats.

Before coming here, the dog had only encountered a few cats on his evening runs near the river. He'd loved to give them chase, even if it was a different sort of chase than when he turned up a rabbit or squirrel. Cats were hunters and had sharp claws, and after a short run, the dog had left them alone. Here, the cats were caged like him, but they weren't taken outside to relieve themselves like the dogs or the few cats the dog had previously known.

The dog curled into the side of his kennel, thinking again of the woman who'd slept near him for one night. Sleepless as he'd been, he'd listened to the sounds she made in sleep and watched the rise and fall of her breath through the bars of his kennel. Separated by such a short space, he'd longed to experience the sweep of her hand over his back and down his ears again.

In the morning, when she'd woken and taken him from his kennel, a rush of pleasure had swept over him at the chance to go outdoors walking with her again. When something he did pleased her, his heart had beat faster at the change in pitch in her voice, making him want to please her again.

She was different from the master he'd known all his life. Her eyes lingered on him, and her tone was gentle enough for the dog to never worry she'd treat him with the same rough hand as his master's if his actions were to displease her.

The dog longed for her to return. Hoped she'd take him away again. There were other humans here, many others. Perhaps because he'd done nothing to displease them, they'd only shown him kindness. Still, he tucked his tail tight against his haunches when he was being directed into his kennel, bracing for a kick he might not feel coming.

For the most part, the men and women here hurried about, always busy with something, delivering food and water, taking dogs out to relieve themselves, and scouring the kennels, refreshing the sharp scent that clung to them and burned his nose.

And while he longed to be elsewhere again, here he was no longer hungry or thirsty. There was water to drink whenever he wished, and a bowlful of food was delivered each morning and evening. The bustle of activity occupied his day, and in the quiet that fell over the place as evening came on, the dog's attention was held by the carryings-on in neighboring kennels for longer than it took the sun to sink in the sky.

Finally, he curled deeper into his blanket and gave in to sleep. The dog's thoughts drifted back to the woman, and when he began to dream, he dreamed of her coming to take him away with her again.

Chapter 17

TWO DAYS LATER, OLIVIA FOUND HERSELF JUST AS excited to leave school as she had been earlier in the week when she'd headed to New Madrid. Only today, instead of embarking on a long drive, she would soon be headed to the High Grove Animal Shelter and her first shift as a newbie volunteer. And she couldn't wait.

To make things even better, after a couple hours there, she'd be meeting Gabe for dinner. *Dinner with Gabe!* The thought had kept a smile on her face and a happy warmth radiating inside her all day. She couldn't remember experiencing a bubbling-over-with-excitement feeling this intense since a few days before Christmas when she was little.

All day, her students had been picking up on her unusually good mood and had done their best to wheedle out the reason behind it. After finishing a lecture on solving simultaneous linear equations in her last-hour class, the one in which the kids were notoriously more rambunctious than any other class of the day, she finally gave up trying to keep their attention on algebra and pulled up the shelter's website on the oversize digital screen on the front wall of the classroom. Under the available-for-adoption-soon page were a few pictures of the remarkable pointer.

Olivia had forced herself not to randomly pull up the shelter's web page over the last two days. Not only did the pictures of the pointer warm her heart, but there was also a link to the video of Gabe's daring rescue. The adorable photos of the pointer reassured her he was doing just fine. Someone had taken a couple pictures when he was outside in a play yard. One was a close-up of his handsome face and his incredibly warm-brown eyes. In the other, he'd clearly spotted a bird because his short tail stuck straight out, one front paw was tucked up, and he was doing that stalky thing he did.

She'd had to fight off the temptation not to watch his touching and tense rescue video on replay too. As she pulled it up for the class, and the video filled the five-foot digital screen, Olivia was tempted to allow her gaze to linger on the definition visible in Gabe's broad shoulders and the toned muscles underneath his soaked shirt. Instead, she savored the determined intensity in his face—which moved her but didn't get her blood to boiling—and appreciated his surefooted steps as he headed through the rushing water.

"He's hot," several girls exclaimed as the video played.

Olivia clamped her teeth over her bottom lip to keep from agreeing. She didn't need to give these rowdy and hormonal teens any fuel with which to tease her. Even though she kept quiet, the girls knew what they were talking about.

Gabe *was* hot. And caring and kind. And it seemed that he wanted *her*.

And we're having dinner in a little over three hours.

Heat rushed to her cheeks at the thought of sitting at a booth or table across from him and having the freedom to stare straight into those hazel-green eyes or savor the slow curl of his smile when she said something to please him. And maybe afterward...

Attempting to curtail her thoughts, she smacked a hand down onto her desk a little too hard. Things had gotten heated in his truck. In that crazy, wild way she'd never felt before. But everything that day had seemed to be a bit of a fairy tale. Now they were back in the real world. If something was actually blossoming between them, they needed to get to know each other. Sleeping with him wasn't the answer. Not tonight, at least. Maybe she wouldn't wait the better part of a year like she had with Trevor. She was an adult now, and if she kept her head on straight, she'd know when it was right.

Being committed to abstinence hadn't kept her from making sure she was freshly shaved and wearing her sexiest matching bra and panties under her jeans and Westbury Middle School long-sleeved T-shirt. After all, there was the off chance they'd fool around. Okay, *hopefully* there was the off chance they'd fool around.

She rolled her neck to keep her thoughts from trailing down the road of desire.

As the video ended, the entire class began begging for a field trip to the shelter to see the dog in person, and a few kids were tossing around the idea of a service project.

"We could do a towel drive," Addison said. "Shelters always need towels. And blankets."

"And cat litter."

"What about dog food? My mom works at the pet boutique. They donate the food that's about to expire to places all the time."

"Guys," Olivia called when she caught a glimpse

of the principal craning her neck to look inside as she walked past the room. There was no denying that the overzealous eighth graders' excited murmurs had swelled into an overly loud buzz. "These are awesome ideas," she said once most of them were listening to her again. "Truly. But just a heads-up. I'm not entirely sure I've got the clout here to propose a field trip. Especially one that's not tied into algebra."

When her declaration was met with a chorus of groans, she added, "I'll tell you what. If you stay serious about it, we'll come up with a proposal, and I'll give it a shot. And maybe we can figure out a way to tie it to algebra."

A few kids groaned. "Or we could just go there and *not* do math," one of the boys suggested with a grin.

"It's all a matter of perspective. Working math into a service project is better than, I don't know, a pop quiz on Monday, isn't it?"

Amid a new chorus of groans, Olivia began to pack up for the day. Her heart skittered as she closed the shelter's website and turned off the computer. Hardly any teachers stayed late to plan lessons on Friday, and Olivia felt justified in putting her lesson planning off until Sunday. For the first time in months, she had something to do on a Friday night. The thought brought a happy smile to her face.

Last fall, she'd felt trapped in rapidly thickening cement, and it had seemed as if there'd been no way out. But now, six months later, her life was starting to flow again. With any luck, things were only going to get better.

Her teaching contract at Westbury Middle had only

been for one semester—she was filling in for a teacher who'd taken a spill and broken a kneecap and needed corrective surgery. With any luck, another position would open up. Fully contracted teachers had one week left to notify the school if they weren't returning next year, and there were rumors milling around the staff lunchroom that one of the other math teachers was in a second round of interviews at a private school. If he left, as a current teacher, Olivia could have a first-round shot at an interview. Even though she'd sent off applications to half-a-dozen open positions elsewhere, some even closer to her hometown, her real hope was to return here next year.

Westbury Middle had a great vibe, and she'd felt included from the get-go. The kids were passionate and determined—for the most part—and so much more worldly than she'd been in her small, rural middle school. One of her favorite things about Westbury Middle was that it had a book club tailored to kids who were dyslexic, and Olivia had gone to all the meetings since she was hired. She loved bonding with the kids and being able to be sympathetic to struggles she knew so well.

If she was lucky enough to get a year-long contract from the school, she'd be comfortable getting an apartment lease of her own, maybe even something around here in the historic Soulard area just south of downtown. She loved the character in the quaint and historic red-brick homes and buildings around the school.

She could almost taste the relief of what it would be like to know for certain that the life she was building here in St. Louis could turn into something permanent.

Not just be a Band-Aid to get her through until something opened up in southern Missouri, which she'd called home for so long. To live here where not only Ava and Aunt Becky were, but also Gabe.

It was premature, she knew, to assume he'd be in her life long enough to worry about her permanency in St. Louis affecting their relationship. But it would also be a lie to deny that what had passed between them last weekend had been something not quite ordinary.

When the bell rang, she headed for the door and gave high fives to any of the kids who wanted them, which ended up being most. A few, like Brody, were too cool and just gave a curt nod.

"Remember to see what service projects they need," Addison reminded her as she left.

Olivia promised she would. Once the class emptied, she packed up and headed out for the weekend. To stave off the afternoon munchies and get her through till dinner, she choked down the last of the Triscuits in her lunch bag and rationed out the last of the water in her Contigo water bottle.

Without traffic, it was just over a twenty-minute drive to the shelter, and the closer she got, the more excited she became. She wasn't usually so quick to make decisions, but just the same as with Gabe, something about volunteering at the shelter had felt right during the impromptu tour Megan, the director, had given her after she and Patrick had gotten the pointer settled Wednesday morning.

As soon as she walked through the entrance of the shelter for the second time that week, Olivia was swept away with the feeling that she was right where she was supposed to be. A senior-aged, stout-looking dog—a cairn terrier, she thought—sauntered over from where he'd been lapping up water from a stainless-steel bowl. Olivia knelt, letting him sniff her hands and jeans, and his tail wagged back and forth like a metronome.

He had tan, wiry hair and cloudy gray eyes, cloudy enough that she wondered if he had a hard time seeing.

Tess, one of the staff members that Olivia had met last time, wandered over. She seemed to be about Olivia's age, had long, dark-brown hair, and from what Olivia had seen last time, somehow radiated the perfect amount of peppiness without being over-the-top. "Hey, Olivia, welcome back! Did you get to meet Chance last time?"

"No, I didn't. He's a cutie though."

"He's one of our permanent residents. It's just him and Trina, a cat, who are intentional lifers here." She craned to look over by the kenneled cats at the back of the room. "I bet she's napping in back on top of the fridge in the break room. She's either there or sprawled out in front of the cats, flaunting her freedom."

Olivia laughed. "I was wondering why this guy was walking around freely like this."

"Chance gets full roam of the place during the day, but he's typically kenneled at night. He almost always hangs out in the front room, and he tells us when he wants to go outside. He's ten now and sleeps in later than he used to."

"That explains why I didn't meet him last time."

Chance clambered up, bracing his front paws on her knee, and stretched to sniff her face. Olivia tipped forward to give him easier access. "What a sweetie."

"You've definitely passed the Chance test. We think

maybe it has something to do with him being blind, but he's great at reading people's energy. Maybe it just comes down to him being able to tell a dog lover, or he interprets the smells people carry, or both, but we take his responses to potential adopters seriously. When someone really sets him off, which is rarely, we almost always set up a home visit."

"Huh. That's cool. Like a doggie lie-detector, I guess."

Apparently finished with his greeting, Chance plopped his front paws heavily back to the floor and sauntered around one of the adoption desks and over to a cushy bed near the gift shop.

"He's totally blind?" Olivia asked as she stood up.

"He may be able to see some shadows, but he's memorized where everything is."

"That's impressive."

"Yeah, it definitely is. *So*," Tess said, "Kelsey, our volunteer coordinator, is out of town this weekend. But we've got a name tag ready, and you get to pick out a shirt. There're a few forms to sign as well. And I know you want some time with the pointer, but Megan said you'd be open to doing other things too."

"Absolutely."

"Dogs or cats?"

Olivia shrugged as she followed Tess over to the main counter. "I'm a bit more partial to dogs, but cats are great. Just put me where help is needed most."

Tess fished through a stack of folders until she found the one she was looking for. Inside were Olivia's application and a handful of additional forms. "Sorry, but we can't escape getting your signature enough times to give you a hand cramp. Legalese and all."

"Not a problem."

Tess gave her a rundown on where to sign and summarized the volunteer work that was most needed as Olivia signed the papers.

"The shelter's one of those places where the work is never completely done, but you get used to it. We have a list of big, special projects, monthly projects, weekly projects, and daily ones. Most of our focus goes to what needs to be accomplished every day. And we're building a good list of volunteers who like to help with special projects like construction and stuff, but the truth is, the dogs can never get enough attention or training. The more they have, the better they act, and the easier it is to get them adopted. Sometimes they come in with a mess of bad manners and a lack of training. You said you grew up on a farm? I'm guessing you're pretty good with dogs then?"

Suddenly it occurred to Olivia how *not* well versed with dogs she actually was. "You know, I've been around dogs my whole life and have never really thought about it before, but it was my grandparents' land. The dogs had free roam of the farm, so they didn't need leashes, and my grandpa has always been the one to do all their training, so honestly, a bit less than you might think. I'm a quick learner, though, and I'm comfortable around dogs of all sizes and breeds."

Tess nodded encouragingly. "If you're comfortable around dogs, then the rest will fall into place. We have a basic-training-and-care video series on our website. It may be helpful to check that out if you have time. Until then, one of the staff will show you what we ask of the dogs while working with them."

"That sounds great."

Olivia finished signing the last few papers, and when she was done, Tess did a two-handed, double-gun point in her direction. "Now for the fun part. You get to pick a shirt from the gift shop, then we'll head to the dogs. Because so many volunteers are coming and going every day, we ask everyone to wear name tags, but most end up wearing shelter T-shirts too."

Olivia followed Tess over to the gift shop and took in the bright array of colorful shirts. A few had the shelter logo, and others had moving sayings. Two of her favorites read "Adopt" with a dog paw print in place of the O and "Until there are none, rescue one."

After a bit of debate, she chose a cornflower-blue short-sleeved logo T-shirt and a long-sleeved purple "Adopt" one after sorting through to find her size. "I'm assuming it's okay if I buy one too?"

"No complaints here. Most of us end up with a closetful of High Grove apparel. And both those will go great with your hair—which is beautiful, by the way. When I was a kid, I was under the impression that with the right combination of lemon juice and sunlight, I'd end up a redhead. It was a bit of a disaster, actually."

"If it helps," Olivia said, laughing, "I was once under the delusion that if I suntanned long enough, I'd freckle evenly enough to look really tan."

Tess shook her head. "That's usually how it goes, isn't it?"

For the next half hour, Tess led Olivia around, detailing some of the ins and outs of being a volunteer, like how and where to sign up for special events, where to put her things when she was working, and where the small break room was. Olivia loved the fridge inside the break room that was covered in magnets from places all over the world where the staff and volunteers had traveled, including a few places she'd always dreamed of going, like Rome and the Australian outback.

Trina, the resident cat, was in the room as Tess had guessed, napping in a cozy bed atop the fridge. With a bit of cajoling, the senior-aged cat woke up and joined them for a bit of petting. Olivia was surprised to see how dexterous she was for being a three-legged cat.

"Do you know what happened to her back leg?" Olivia asked, giving the striking cream and silver-gray cat a thorough scratch along the side of her chin and atop her spine when she arched her back.

"No, but it was an accident of some sort when she was a kitten. She was found with her mom and several other kittens floating on debris in the aftermath of Hurricane Katrina. She was young enough when it happened that she doesn't know the difference."

"Wow, what a story."

"Kind of like with the dog you brought in, there are lots of incredible stories of animals who've come here after being saved from natural disasters. Which reminds me, you're probably eager to see him."

Olivia flipped her hands palms up. "Guilty as charged. I guess I've always been a sucker for those gangly-legged hunting dogs, but he really stole my heart. I've been thinking about him all week."

"I can see why. He's a sweetheart. He's pretty timid, but he doesn't act as if he was abused. On the other hand, he doesn't seem all that used to affection either."

"That fits what we saw and then heard about him. It

seemed as if he had a pretty isolated life, most of which was spent alone in a pen."

"Poor guy. On the bright side, we're guessing he's fairly young," Tess said. "Maybe three or four. At least he's got a lot of years ahead of him once he's adopted to have that turned around for him."

"That's about how old Gabe thought he was. He said he'd feel better about narrowing it down if the dog wasn't so underweight."

"Hopefully he won't remain that way long. He's gained nearly a pound since he came in." Tess paused and clamped her hands over her thighs. "So, Patrick's out back working in the dog play area. He's going to take over from here and show you the ropes of taking the dogs in and out of their kennels for walks. The pointer will be out of quarantine tomorrow if his test results come in clean, but until then, quarantined dogs are limited in where they can go when they're taken outside. But like I said, Patrick'll show you the ropes. You met him when you brought the dog in, right?"

Olivia nodded. "Yeah, he's the one who told me about the volunteer program."

"Good," Tess said, nodding. After a short struggle in which she seemed to be deciding whether or not to say something, she added, "You may have picked up on it, but he's a bit more direct than the average person. Sometimes new volunteers take it personally, but hopefully you won't. He's a great guy, just a little different."

"Thanks for the heads-up. I, uh, kind of noticed. He remembers every German shorthaired pointer who's come through the doors since he started here."

"That doesn't surprise me. He can't remember every

animal who has passed through our doors anymore, but he's still pretty spot-on with his favorite breeds. And he's been here five or six years."

"That's impressive. This is my third year teaching if you count my training, and at first I thought I'd never forget a student, but I can see how that's going to be a challenge the longer I do it."

Olivia followed Tess outside. There was a small parking lot, then a fifty-foot section of ground that backed to a row of trees and scraggily shrubs. The area had been divided into a few fenced pens and a large gravel island.

"That's what we call the Island of Many Smells," Tess said, pointing to the gravel area as they passed it. "Once the pointer is out of quarantine, it'll probably be his favorite place to scent mark."

Patrick was outside one of the fenced areas that contained a small agility course and was packing up tools into a toolbox. "This area is our newest addition out here. It's used for basic training and agility. There's a one-dog-at-a-time policy for this pen. The other two are the play areas. The big one up front is for adoptable dogs, and the smaller one in back is for quarantined dogs and has a similar one-dog policy."

Olivia looked over the pens, nodding appreciatively. From all the enrichments in the cat and dog kennels inside, the fun kitty play area, and these pens for the dogs, this place wasn't like any shelter she'd ever been to. And she couldn't escape the feeling that she'd found just the place where she needed to be.

"You ready for us, Patrick?" Tess asked.

"Yes. I'm seventeen minutes behind schedule, but the loose section of fence is repaired."

"Great. I'll tell Fidel and Megan that it's back in business. I know there's a handful of dogs who could still really use some work today, time permitting."

Feeling a bit like a kid who was being shuffled between babysitters, Olivia followed Patrick around for the next ten minutes, doing her best to commit to memory his concise and literal instructions. While she'd been around dogs her entire life, there were so many things she'd never thought of before. Not only did the shelter have established protocols on how to approach the dogs, but each animal had an individual care plan. Some dogs were fine with collars, while others needed a variety of different harnesses. Some dogs could be walked with others, some needed to be walked alone, and a few needed to be walked in the presence of two volunteers or staff members at a time due to health issues or questionable temperament.

It was a lot to take in, but there were directions at each kennel for each dog, and Olivia was happy to know she wouldn't need to rely on memory while getting used to everything. In addition to handling instructions, there was a short bio on each dog. Olivia loved scanning them as Patrick led her around the kennels, pointing out things she needed to know before they took the dogs out.

When they got to quarantine and Patrick finished giving her the rundown of its specific procedures, she washed up and knelt in front of the pointer's kennel.

"Remember me, buddy?" He'd been dozing but lifted his big, liver-roan head off his giant paws and opened his eyes. Olivia flattened her hand against his kennel. "Because I sure missed you."

The pointer rose to all fours, tail pumping and ears

forward, and licked the bit of her hand that he could reach through the mesh fence.

"He does," Patrick said, watching. "He's more hesitant with the staff and other volunteers who approach him."

"I kept him overnight," Olivia said, talking in an effort to press back an unexpected rush of emotion. "I wouldn't have guessed that he'd paid me much notice, as nervous as he was, but maybe I was wrong."

"He's timid, but he hasn't been labeled a behavior risk. If you want to hook him up, you can. These kennels aren't big enough to step into with him in it, so you'll have to hook him up at the door."

Pretending to have a bit more confidence than she felt that the dog wouldn't slip past her, Olivia opened the door, using her body as a block, and offered him a treat from her open hand. After he'd swiped it up with a flick of his warm tongue, she slipped his collar around until she found the ring, then hooked him up.

"Correct." Patrick's tone was as matter-of-fact as they came.

I wonder what he'll say if I do it wrong? Releasing a breath of relief, she stepped back and opened the door. The pointer wasted no time rushing out. Instead of bolting for the door, he pressed into her side and let out a whine that melted her heart.

"Do you approve of the name we've given him while he's here? It means 'sea chief.' One of the volunteers suggested it after seeing the video of his struggle in the water."

Olivia looked back at the kennel. *Morgan* was written on top of his bio.

"Morgan, huh?" She stroked the silky-smooth fur atop his head. He glanced upward, meeting her gaze for a split second. His tail thumped steadily. "Morgan, the sea chief. I like it."

"Even when the names are new to them, we use them repeatedly in training sessions. It doesn't take the dogs long to connect with them."

Olivia nodded. "That's fine by me."

"Can you attempt to get him to sit using the signal I showed you before exiting the room?"

"With a closed fist, right?"

"Yes, but say the command as you make the fist. If he's not listening, you may need to show him a treat first."

Moving the leash to her left hand, Olivia made a fist with her right one and gave a "sit" command that came out with more confidence than she felt.

Morgan glanced at her again for a split second but then looked toward the closed door expectantly. "Morgan, sit. Sit."

Olivia waited, hoping he'd respond, but the pointer simply stared at the door, wagging his short tail expectantly. She had a sinking feeling that dog training was harder than she'd anticipated.

"Step in front of him. You need to distract him from the door."

Olivia did as instructed, repeating her command and attempting to draw the pointer's attention to her closed fist. At first, he attempted to step to the side to look around her, but when the taut leash prevented it, he glanced from her fist to her face and back to her fist. "Sit, Morgan. Sit."

With a lick of his lips and a grunty little groan, Morgan sank back onto his haunches. Once he'd held the pose for a couple of seconds, Olivia rewarded him with a treat and an encouraging pat on the shoulder. "Good boy!"

Happiness radiated through her. Sure, it had been a small success in the scheme of things, but it was still her first win in this new, structured world of professional animal care. "Now what?" she asked Patrick.

His brow furrowed just the slightest bit. "Now you open the door."

Suppressing a giggle, Olivia said, "Of course. I open the door."

When Morgan hopped back to all fours and wagged his tail hard enough for his whole body to wag along with it, Olivia opened the door. "Come on, Morgan. Let's go for a walk."

Chapter 18

FOUR MONTHS AGO, WHEN ALBERT WASHINGTON HAD proposed the sale of his practice to Gabe, the "real and honest" food for thought he'd given was that if Gabe wanted his own practice, he'd best sign on for long days and late evenings. Gabe didn't mind the demanding schedule or even the fifteen-minute appointments late in the day on a Friday that morphed into emergency surgeries—especially when they saved lives.

But this afternoon, two things were in the back of his mind when he took radiographs of a middle-aged Yorkie in distress and found several small stones, one of which was lodged in his urethra blocking urine flow. Neither of them had anything to do with his confidence in saving the dog. Even new in practice as he was, Gabe had begun to lose track of the cystotomies he'd performed. As far as surgeries went, an emergency bladder-stone removal tended to be relatively simple, and he went into most of them with confidence when he gave owners reassuring odds of success and recovery.

He'd gotten the all clear to do the surgery from the older woman who owned the Yorkie, and his concerns this afternoon were regarding Olivia and Samson. Tonight was his and Olivia's first real date, and he didn't want to keep her waiting. Especially considering she didn't exactly have a place to go once she finished her first shift at the shelter. Perhaps she could go to her sister's, but considering what she'd shared about her sister's life right now, he didn't want to assume that was an option.

His other concern was regarding Samson. Yesterday, his dog had been raring to come to work, and he'd had an active day—at least for him—lounging behind the front counter, soaking up the unbridled affection given to him by the vet techs and assistants on staff, and occasionally hopping up to greet some of the dogs or cats as they came through the door. For a reason Gabe had yet to understand, some animals caught Samson's attention from the get-go, even waking him from his periodic deep dozes. Yet, there were countless animals he didn't have even the slightest interest in. Considering how Samson was wearing down easier now, perhaps it shouldn't have been a surprise this morning when he'd chosen to go back to bed rather than head out with Gabe for the day after breakfast and his morning walk.

And since Gabe actually had plans after work that with any luck would stretch well into the night, he was going to need to head home before meeting up with Olivia. Samson had a strong bladder and bowels, but not that strong.

As Janice, his lead surgical assistant, readied the Yorkie for surgery, Gabe shot off two texts. The first was to Yun, telling her he was heading into a late-in-the-day surgery and asking if she could swing by and let Samson out on her way home. She knew the door code and had done this favor for him often enough, just as he did cat duty for her whenever she headed out of town for the weekend. The second text was to Olivia, explaining what had come up and letting her know there was a good chance he'd run a little late but that he'd text as soon as he was out. He also sent her the address of his office and told her she could feel free to wait in the waiting room if she finished up before him.

Knowing the Yorkie's owner was in a clear state of distress, he headed into the front room where she intended to wait out the surgery. "You're welcome to stay, Ms. Bonner, of course. But once he's out of surgery and in recovery, he won't want to do anything but sleep. We'll keep him in recovery through tomorrow morning, and so long as there are no complications, you should be fine to pick him up before noon tomorrow. The best thing for him will be to sleep it off for several hours and through the night as much as possible. You remember Janice? She'll be assisting me, and she's here till eight. She'll make sure he's on the mend before she takes off for the night."

After a bit more reassurance, Ms. Bonner agreed the best thing for her would be to head over to her daughter's house where her grandkids could keep her busy until her beloved dog was out of surgery. Gabe promised to call with an update once the Yorkie was in recovery, and she headed out after enveloping him in a hug he'd not expected.

"God bless your caring soul," she said, patting his cheek with motherly pride as she pulled away. "I know why Dr. Washington looked to you to take over his practice."

Letting the compliment roll over him, Gabe headed to the back to scrub up, then slipped on a sterile surgical gown, gloves, cap, and mask and headed into the operating room.

The whole building was in dire need of updates, some things more than others, but the operating room had been remodeled a little over ten years ago, and the equipment and supplies were high-quality. This was one of the main reasons Gabe was excited to take over the practice at the price Dr. Washington was asking. That and he liked the clientele the older vet had built up over a forty-three-year career. When it came to the building itself, a long-ago converted home that had been built in the late 1800s, Gabe still wondered what he was getting himself into. In a dream world, he'd purchase the business only and move into a newer building, but in every discussion they'd had to date, Albert hadn't been willing to consider splitting the sale. Before Gabe ended up signing on any dotted lines, he still needed to have the building inspected and to carve out time for a lengthy discussion with the business consultant he had on retainer to guide him through this.

As was typical, as soon as he was scrubbed and gloved and in the surgical room, Gabe's thoughts quieted, and he lost himself in the routines that had been instilled in him both in lectures and labs and during his internship. He liked the working relationship he was developing with some of the assistants and techs who assisted him in surgery, and today, Janice, a middle-aged vet tech who'd worked for Dr. Washington since she graduated from high school, was assisting him. She knew where to stand and what to pass and what to clip usually without Gabe having to ask. Unlike some of the less-experienced techs, she also knew not to ramble on. She was quiet and focused.

Once he'd cut through the lining of the abdomen and

into the bladder, Gabe easily found and scooped out the stone that was causing the blockage and a few others that were bouncing around in the Yorkie's bladder. If the Yorkie's owner had waited until Monday to bring him in like she'd considered doing, there was a good chance the dog's bladder would've burst. Thankfully, once the stone was removed and the dog was on a round of antibiotics, he'd be able to make a full recovery in a short time.

When Ms. Bonner picked him up tomorrow to take him home, Gabe would have a talk with her about some changes she could make in the dog's diet to help prevent more stones from forming. Middle-aged and older Yorkies could be prone to kidney and bladder stones, and now that her dog was proven to develop them, the little guy was going to need to be monitored every six months from here on out.

By the time he had finished and the dog was in recovery, it was nearly half past six. Gabe stripped out of his surgical gown, mask, and gloves and headed to the adjoining scrub closet where he'd left his phone on a shelf. Olivia had texted back, but Yun hadn't, and Gabe decided not to follow up with her. Hopefully, Olivia would be fine swinging by his place before they headed out to dinner.

Gabe opened up Olivia's text to find that she'd replied with nothing more than a simple okay. Determined not to think anything of it, he dialed her number as he stepped out into the back hallway. He was more than a little surprised to hear her hello echo through the empty hall just before it rang out in the receiver.

"Hey, you're here?" Suddenly the night seemed to be shining a lot brighter.

"I hope that's okay."

Gabe headed down the hall and pressed open the swinging door that separated the staff-only section of the office from the two patient rooms, the front desk, and the waiting room. While it had been bustling all day, the front room was now empty aside from one gorgeous redhead who was seated on the wooden bench at the side, a dog magazine on her lap and a smile lighting her face that made his heart swell.

She was in jeans, a pair of heels that were low but just sexy enough to send a rush of heat to his groin, and a silky purple blouse that dipped in a vee and called his attention to her cleavage like a beacon.

"Ah... Wow, you look great." He dragged his fingers over his chin. "It's good to see you. Really good. And I feel like a schmuck making you wait. But there was this Yorkie who had a bladder stone that was too big to pass. It was obstructing his urine, so there was no putting the surgery off."

"Believe me, that's definitely more important than being on time for dinner." Olivia bit her lip as her smile dropped to that just-a-little-bit-shy demeanor of hers. "So this is you just coming out of surgery."

Gabe glanced down at the dark-blue scrubs he was wearing today. He'd taken off the surgical gown, but the paper breathing mask was still hanging around his neck. And there was a cap still on his head. "Uh, yeah, I may have checked my phone right away."

Olivia laughed, shaking her head. "You look great. I don't know why, but it didn't fully hit me till just now that you're a vet. I'm glad you were in jeans and a T-shirt when we met, or I'm sure I wouldn't have had the nerve to talk to you, much less…" Her voice trailed off and color rushed to her cheeks. "Are we the only ones here now?"

Gabe tugged the cap off and dragged his fingers through his hair, probably making a bigger mess of it than it already was. "Ahhh, no. Janice assisted me. She's in back with the Yorkie, getting him set up in a post-op kennel for the night. I bet you're starving, but would you like a quick tour before we head out?"

He smiled over how she returned the magazine to the pile stacked on the table, rather than just dropping it anywhere. "I'm a little hungry, but I'd love to see where you do your magic."

It was Gabe's turn to feel a dose of modesty wash over him. He dropped his voice so that Janice couldn't hear. "If you want the truth, there are a lot of days when I feel more like I'm playing doctor rather than actually being one. Though I'm getting more used to it all the time." He waved her toward the main exam room. "Still. Dr. Washington was right when he said I'll come across things just about every day that no one can train you for."

"I can only imagine." She trailed after him, her hands flattened against the back of her hips as she looked around.

"The hardest parts have had to do with putting a terminally ill or a geriatric dog or cat to sleep. Even when I'm convinced it's the best thing to do, I don't think expressing that to a grieving family is something I'll ever be comfortable with."

"I'm sure that's tough. Really tough."

"Yeah, well, the good outweighs the bad. By a long

shot. And some other less heart-wrenching things throw me off too. Like when my clients want my opinion on things that don't have anything to do with their pet."

"Like what do you mean?" Olivia asked, rolling her right foot in a circle by the tip of her heel as she listened.

It was her easy smile, Gabe decided, that drew him to her most. Maybe next it was the attentiveness in her gaze. Like she couldn't see anything but him. Whatever the case, he was glad to hear Janice shuffling around in back. Knowing they weren't alone kept him from pressing Olivia into the exam table with a kiss to match the one that had steamed up his Tacoma windows last Saturday.

"Ah, like today a client asked what kind of shoes I like to wear since I stand on my feet all day. A couple days ago, I felt like I was getting cross-examined as to which publicly traded pet care companies were the best to invest in in this market." He searched for another example. There were so many every day. "Here's a tough one. I've lost track of how many times I've been asked if I believe animals have souls, and if they do, if they share our heaven."

Olivia's delicate eyebrows arched high. "How do you answer that?"

"Carefully."

As Olivia laughed, he motioned across the room. "So, this room and the one next to it are where we see most clients. Dr. Washington ran the place as a small, intimate practice from the time the doors opened in 1979. To tell you the truth, this building is a bit inadequate in some ways, but he never outgrew it. One of the biggest things I'd love to have, aside from a third exam room, is a separate waiting room for cats. We do our best to keep them out of the waiting room when there are dogs in it, but sometimes it's just not possible."

Next, Gabe gave her a tour of the back rooms. There was an X-ray and ultrasound room and the operating room. In what might once have been a closet or mudroom in the old house, there was a small recovery and observation room. In it were ten kennels of various sizes, with the cats sequestered in the four smallest ones at the far end. The dog kennels ranged in size from Chihuahua- to Great Dane–sized.

This evening, only three animals were being kept overnight—a dog and a cat, both of whom Gabe had spayed this morning, and now the Yorkie.

After he'd introduced her to Janice, who was freshening the water of the two who'd come out of surgery this morning, Olivia lowered her voice so as not to disturb the animals and asked, "Are they sick?"

Even as undefined as their relationship was, Gabe would happily introduce Olivia to any of his staff, but he was thankful the only one working tonight was Janice. All but one of his six-person staff were female, and Janice was the least likely to join in on the gossip that sometimes permeated the front room. Like him, she didn't seem that interested in fanfare.

"This is the Yorkie who had the stone taken out of his bladder just now. He'll probably doze another few hours. The other two were spayed this morning. They should go home tomorrow, so long as they're still doing well. As long as their owners are able to keep their activity levels under control, I'm a firm believer that animals recuperate faster in the comfort of their own homes."

Olivia nodded. "Makes sense. Though I'm sure keeping an animal still is harder to do with some than others."

"Especially with the hyper ones," Janice added with a wink as she locked the cat's kennel. "For the most part, animals are better than us at knowing when to lie low."

They stepped out of the room and talked for a few more minutes; then Gabe used the very real excuse of being famished and asked Janice to text him an update before leaving.

"Sure. Are you calling Ms. Bonner, or should I?" Janice asked. "Her number's on the front counter."

"I promised I would. Thanks. I'll give her a call from the truck."

Janice nodded. "Then I've got it covered here. I'm not here again till Tuesday. If the Yorkie hasn't woken by eight, I'll stick around for a while and make sure he has his wits about him before I leave." To Olivia, she added, "Some of the smaller dogs tend to stay groggy after anesthesia longer than the bigger ones."

"That makes sense." Olivia offered her a half wave. "It was great to meet you."

Gabe locked hands with her as Janice waved them out. As they headed toward the front of the building, Olivia let out a big breath. "This place is great. But I should probably admit I'm more than a touch intimidated."

Gabe chuckled. "Whatever for?"

She leaned into him, her shoulder pressing against his triceps. "You just saved a dog's life…while I was flipping through the pages of *Dogster*."

"You teach math to eighth graders. Don't downplay your own talent."

"Thanks, although sometimes I feel like all I do is

speak a foreign language to them." She gave a small shrug. "But I love it. I love the breakthroughs, especially with the kids who've put up barriers as dense as cement."

"I can imagine." Gabe dropped her hand to swipe the Post-it with Ms. Bonner's number off the counter. "So, for tonight, you can stay parked here, or you can follow me to my place. It won't take long, but I've got to let Samson out."

"I can follow you." Suddenly Olivia turned bright red. "Or I can leave my car here. I guess it doesn't matter."

Gabe brushed a lock of hair back from her face. "Hey, just a heads-up. There'll be no pressure tonight. But I should warn you that once you see my place, you'll probably be a touch less intimidated by my togetherness than you are right now."

"Why?" Olivia's playful smile returned, and she shook her head lightly. "Does Samson do the decorating?"

Gabe's thoughts went to his mattress on the floor and his sawed-short nightstand and the saggy middle cushion on the couch where Samson napped. "You have no idea how right you are. And what wasn't done in his best interest just hasn't been done."

She shrugged. "You know what they say. 'There's a time for everything.'"

"They do say that, don't they?" And with Olivia in his life, Gabe realized it might just be time to focus a bit on making the place where he spent over a third of his days a little more like a home.

Chapter 19

IT SEEMED TO OLIVIA THAT EVERY FEW WEEKS SHE was discovering a new area of the city that she'd had no idea existed. She'd driven by the tall, rectangular redbrick homes surrounding Tower Grove Park once in February when she'd met a sixth-grade history teacher for a Saturday walk through the park but had had no idea how expansive the area was. The actual park was massive, stretching well over a mile long. Having grown up in the midst of the flat, fertile farmlands of southern Missouri, she couldn't recall ever before visiting a park that had been designed for the purpose of being an arboretum, and she'd never walked among such exotic-looking trees as she had that afternoon.

Now that signs of spring were showing—flowers blossoming and many of the trees beginning to bud—Olivia was determined to walk here again. *And with any luck, it'll be with Gabe*. Her heart did a thump and a skitter. She could perfectly envision walks with Gabe under the fresh blossoms, holding hands and laughing and tossing a ball around for Samson. Suddenly, Morgan popped into her daydream. She wondered if the shelter might give her permission to take him for walks here too. The thought of how challenging that would be brought a smile to her face. There were probably so many birds around here that it would be more of a stop and stalk than a walk.

Most of the homes they were passing as they drove to Gabe's apartment seemed to be single-family, but she followed him to a side street near the park that had an equal number of multifamily units. When his brake lights lit up, her pulse began to race. She knew that having followed him here could open the door later to something a part of her was really craving.

He'd said that bit about there being no pressure tonight, and she'd seen that he meant it. Asking her to park here wasn't an attempt to get her into bed at the end of the night. But what if she was the one applying the pressure later? Where she came from, girls weren't the ones who initiated sex. And they didn't say yes on a first date. But she wasn't a girl anymore, and she wasn't in the Bootheel any longer. And the fact was that the rural mind-set of girls needing to be chaste mixed with a "boys will be boys" attitude needed some major revamping. Maybe it was the extra decade and maybe it was the city versus country mind-set, but she saw a refreshing bit of progress in the students she was teaching.

The sight of Gabe tapping his brakes brought Olivia back to the present. She could just make out through the camper shell that he was pointing for her to take the open spot at her right between an SUV and a Prius. Olivia's stomach filled with unease as she sized up the opening. It seemed just big enough to park in—at least for those who knew how to parallel park and hadn't learned to drive in a place where parallel parking was almost nonexistent.

Olivia was pretty sure she'd make the list of worst parallel parkers in the brief history of automobile driving, and typically she went to extreme lengths to avoid it. As she glanced up and down the crowded street, her palms began to sweat. There didn't seem to be anything bigger than the spot he was waving her into.

Tension set up in her shoulders, but she did her best to shake it off and pulled forward next to the front car, the SUV, until her mirror was adjacent to the back tire. Then she slipped into reverse and did the hard turn she knew she was supposed to do. Perhaps her inadequacy had something to do with poor depth perception because she immediately began to feel as if she were angled all wrong.

Seeing that Gabe was busy parking fifty feet up the road, she slipped her car into drive and started over, determined to get it right. After toggling between forward and reverse several times, her confidence swelled. She had managed to park parallel to the curb and equidistant between both cars.

It wasn't until she stepped out that she realized she'd done everything else right, but she was a good two and a half feet from the curb, and Gabe, who had parked and was headed for her, seemed to have noticed but had the expression of someone who was trying not to.

"Ah, yeah, full disclosure. If my survival ever depends on my ability to parallel park on the spot, I'm pretty sure my odds are dismal."

Gabe laughed, a deep, rolling laugh that reverberated through his chest and sent pleasure all the way down to her toes. "It's not so tough once you get used to it. And what you did here isn't bad, but drivers cut through this street, and I'd hate for you to get clipped. Why don't you get back in, and I'll give you a few pointers so it's easier next time?"

Before she knew what was happening, Gabe was jogging around to the passenger side and hopping in. Too late, Olivia spotted the lip balm, mascara, and vanilla-scented vegan perfume—a bottle gifted to her by Aunt Becky—on her center console from when she'd freshened up after leaving the shelter. Oh well, she determined, not everyone was able to step out of surgery looking like they were auditioning for a role on *Grey's Anatomy*. It was those hazel-green eyes, that dimple, and that smile. They melted her into a puddle every time she had a moment to really take him in.

"It works best when you start the ignition," Gabe said, chuckling.

Get a grip, Olivia!

She cleared her throat and started the car, then reversed so she could pull back onto the street. "I know to start with my front tire next to the SUV's back one."

"I've heard that, but want to try something else?"

"Uh, you just saw how I parked. I'm open to suggestions."

"Pull up even with the Highlander, then start backing up straight, no turning your steering wheel. Glance behind you, and when you can see the Corolla's bumper in the small side window of your back-passenger door, start turning."

Olivia did as he suggested, then took his advice again when he said to look out her driver's-side mirror for the next step, then began to straighten the wheel as she backed up.

"You've got this," Gabe said. "All you have to do now is watch for the moment when your passenger-side mirror blocks the Highlander's bumper, then steer to the left, and you're in."

Somehow everything he said made sense, and Olivia parked as smoothly as a knife slicing through warm butter. "Wow," she said after pulling forward to get centered between the cars again. "Can you be in my car every time I need to parallel park?"

"Something tells me you won't need me next time, but yeah, I'd be good with that."

Olivia turned off her ignition as his words sank in. Not just the words, his tone. There was heat in it, and it lit a flame inside her, racing down her belly and pooling between her legs. He was *so* damn sexy.

"You know, there's a benefit to getting in your car that I didn't think about."

Was he was reading her thoughts? She suspected she knew what he was going to say but asked anyway. "What's that?"

"Getting a chance to kiss you before Samson butts in."

She nodded slowly. "He's a doll, but I'd be okay with that."

Burying the fingers of one hand in her hair, Gabe leaned in. Olivia met him, pressing her lips against his, delight budding across her chest. It hadn't even been a full week, but it felt as if it had been months since she'd savored his kiss, experienced the firmness in his lips, and inhaled his scent. Everything about it was as foreign as it was familiar. She reached for him, letting her fingers cradle both sides of his neck and her thumbs trail along the ridge of his jaw.

Just as his tongue was brushing against hers, there was a smack against the passenger-side window that was hard enough to shake the car.

Gabe jerked away, and Olivia let out a half-stifled scream before realizing a dog had pounced with his front paws against the pane. And not just any dog. A senior-aged golden retriever. Samson. A few feet away, a woman was holding his leash with a look of complete shock on her face.

"What the—" Gabe's surprise quickly morphed into recognition. "Samson, you nut! Down, buddy." He squeezed Olivia's hand before pulling open the door handle. "I may not have mentioned this, but Samson's got a bit of a jealous streak. Come on out. There's someone I want you to meet."

Shaking off the heat of the kiss and a swell of confusion, Olivia stepped out to the woman's apology.

"Sorry, man. I had no idea you were in there until he jumped at the window like that. So, I'm guessing this is her?" The woman looked from Gabe to Olivia and back to him as Samson whined and did a whole-body rub against the jeans he'd changed into before leaving the office.

Her? The way she'd said it, that single word carried a lot of power.

"Yeah, it is. Thanks for swinging by. When you didn't text back, I wasn't sure if you could."

"Didn't I reply? Sorry, it's been one of those afternoons."

Gabe waved Olivia over. "Olivia, this is Yun, one of my best friends. Yun, this is Olivia."

Free of the leash, Yun met her halfway around the car. She was shorter than Olivia by a few inches but average height, and she was as cute as she was striking with shoulder-length silky, straight black hair, warm, brown eyes, and a great smile. She was in a lighter-colored pair of scrubs similar to what Gabe had been wearing earlier.

"Yun and I went to vet school together," Gabe said as Samson dragged him closer to them. "I'm pretty sure without her, I'd never have made it through."

"It's nice to meet you." Olivia noted the easy confidence in Yun's handshake. "Gabe mentioned you when we met last week." As soon as he was in leash reach, Samson pressed against Olivia, pushing in between her and Yun and dragging the full length of his body against her leg. His hips and tail wagged happily as he did.

"Someone's happy to see you," Yun said. Then she shot Gabe a pointed look. "If he's talked about me, he probably told you I spend way too much time attempting to manage his life. It's a control thing; there's no denying it. I get it from my mom, but I'm in recovery mode."

Gabe chuckled. "I didn't tell her anything close to that, but Yun's not kidding. We almost had a parting of ways a couple years ago when she gave me a thesis-length study schedule for final exams."

Yun gave him a dismissive wave. "He can be a little too fly-by-the-seat-of-his-pants, in case you haven't noticed yet."

Olivia laughed, and the unease slipped away that had formed at the realization Gabe had such a close friend who was clearly both beautiful and brilliant. The more they talked, the more it was obvious that while Gabe and Yun were close, it was a familial sort of closeness. "Is he? Based on all the equipment and supplies he keeps in the back of his truck, I wouldn't have guessed that."

"You've got a point. He's a well-prepared free spirit. So, I don't want to be a third wheel, but I ran by my parents' on the way here. My mom had the day off work, and she turned it into one of her big cooking days. I dropped off a couple containers of gimbap and kimchi. They're on your counter."

Gabe had been reaching down to unclip Samson's leash, and when he stood back up, he flattened a hand over that washboard stomach visible through his shirt. "Ahh, gimbap. Man, I love your mom." To Olivia, he said, "It's my favorite thing she makes. If you're up for it, we could hang out in the park and have some appetizers before we head out. You ever had it?"

"That sounds great, and I don't think so. The name isn't familiar. I like kimchi though." Her sister had been on a kick recently of having a small serving of the spicy pickled vegetables before each meal. Each week, she bought a few jars from a global grocery store down the street from her house. Whenever Olivia was over for a meal, Ava almost always served a plate of kimchi as an appetizer.

Yun cocked her head to the side as if debating how to answer. "Gimbap looks like the rolls you find at sushi places, and it's wrapped in seaweed, but the stuff mixed with the rice is different, and instead of fish, the meat is usually Korean ground beef, and everything is fully cooked."

Olivia shrugged. She'd once been squeamish about sushi rolls because of the seaweed factor, but she'd gotten over it. "Sounds great."

Yun glanced at Gabe. "Why don't you two head for the park with Sambo, and I'll run in and throw a plate together."

They headed off in separate directions, and after looking back and forth between them, Samson trotted along next to Olivia, sniffing the occasional tree or miscellaneous spot on the grass as they headed down the sidewalk. Gabe slung his leash over his shoulder and locked his hand around Olivia's.

"You good with this? I promise not to let it derail our night, but this way we can pick a place to eat without being in a rush." He squeezed her hand affectionately. "It's not often a beautiful woman wants to take me to dinner, and I want to make the most of it…first by making her wait, then by forcing her to hang out with a friend. Yeah, guess I'm not making the best impression, am I?"

Olivia laughed and leaned into him. "You're making a great impression, and I'm good with this. Absolutely. Yun seems really sweet. And it's a good way to see a different side of you."

He pressed her hand against his lips. "Next time I'll head out your way and check out that town you've been talking about. And meet that aunt of yours."

Olivia's heart warmed at the easy declaration of days to come. She'd been so young when she started dating Trevor. Everything had been wrapped up in the world of high school and homecomings and football games and student council events. This…this was adulting and very, very real. And also not what she'd expected. She'd had so many friends talk about dating nowadays and how guys acted indifferent for so long. But Gabe seemed so confident in this new togetherness they were experiencing that she wasn't entirely sure how to handle it. Not knowing what else to say, she went for the truth. "I'd like that. A lot."

When they neared the end of the sidewalk and the busy street separating them from the massive park, Gabe told Samson to heel, and with surprising ease, the dog trotted around to Gabe's side without the slightest hesitation.

"Wow. I see why you're so forgiving of a leash with him."

"We did a lot of search-and-rescue work together. To pass the exam, he needed to be obedient off leash. He knows when he's free to do his business and when he needs to listen."

"A lot of my grandpa's dogs have been like that, though they've never been through any formal training, and he never really takes them places. I don't think any of them were half as obedient as Samson."

"I suspect he's the greatest dog I'll ever have. I've been putting it off, but I realized yesterday I need to make a call in the next month as to whether I'm going to extend this lease. I'd like to stay here another year while I get more established, but the stairs are getting hard on him. Some days he's fine; other days, I'm carrying him up."

After crossing the street, they trailed along a winding sidewalk deeper into the park. Olivia recognized the magnolias and redbuds with their bursts of purple and pink lighting the pathway, but not many of the other more exotic trees were beginning to bloom. The park was expansive enough that even with dozens of people walking, biking, and even playing soccer, their walk still felt intimate.

"Will Yun know where to find us?"

Gabe pointed to a group of picnic tables ahead of

them. "We always eat in this general vicinity." As they neared, he added, "Take your pick."

Some were out in the open, and others were under a covered pavilion. Olivia chose one out in the open at the end, three tables away from a family with three young kids. The evening sun was beginning to turn the western sky into a wash of warm, bright colors, and the breeze was soft and gentle.

Olivia took a seat facing in, but Gabe straddled the bench, facing her, and leaned against the table. He cocked an eyebrow. "So, you've heard about my day. Tell me about yours."

At first it felt as if there'd be nothing to say except "I taught algebra to temperamental eighth graders who think they know everything already," but no sooner had she started than the bits and pieces she loved most about her job came to mind. Like the little breakthroughs and aha moments as her kids figured out patterns they could solve confidently over and over again if they took the care they needed and trusted themselves, and the more personal parts, like when they dropped their guard and showed the real, intrinsic parts of themselves and gave Olivia hope for the world of tomorrow.

She was finishing up telling Gabe about her last-hour kids' big plans for a supply drive for the shelter when she spotted Yun heading up the path, carrying a loaded-down canvas bag.

"That'd be a really cool thing to do for the shelter— and for the kids," Gabe said when she was done and as Yun arched around them to the open other side of the table. "That looks heavier than just appetizers."

"You know my mom. You'll have appetizers all

weekend long." Yun shot a glance Olivia's direction as she unpacked the bag, setting a few containers and three mismatched plates on the table. "So how do you feel about ginger?"

"Um, do you mean as opposed to being called a red-head?" As soon as she saw the look of confusion washing over Yun's face, she realized her mistake. "You mean the spice, don't you?"

"I do." Yun laughed. "And I'm direct, but not that direct. Korean ground beef is spiced with ginger and hot pepper paste, as are most other traditional dishes. When it comes to ginger, it's my experience that some people love it, while others, not so much."

Olivia tilted her head in consideration. "You know, it's growing on me, as are a lot of other things I didn't grow up with. I come from a meat-and-potatoes-and-whatever-grows-in-the-garden family. The most exotic thing in my grandma's spice rack is a jar of bay leaves, and my mom's not much of a cook at all. There's just not the same variety of food in southern Missouri as there is up here."

Yun paused in pulling the lids off the containers to point a finger her way. Standing beside her as if he were ready for a show, Samson wagged his tail, his mouth agape in an eager smile. "I hear you on being deprived of different types of foods growing up, and it's not like I grew up in the middle of nowhere. My family lives in the suburbs in the county. The food and restaurant selection out there isn't exactly as diverse as it is around here, but there was a lot more variety than I was exposed to. We ate out once a year on everyone's birthdays. The rest of the time, we ate my mom's cooking. Her family is all Korean, while my dad's a mix of pretty much every European country there is, but my mom only cooks what she knows, which is Korean. Except she loves fettuccine Alfredo and figured out how to make it, but it never tastes quite right."

Olivia noticed the magnificent colors inside the gimbap rolls—from the bright white of the rice to the brown of the ground meat to the yellows and oranges of the thinly sliced vegetables. The rolls were remarkably different from anything she'd grown up with, but her mouth watered in anticipation. The second container was filled with a variety of kimchi, the spicy pickled veggies Ava was always telling her were good for gut health. The third container was filled with pale, puffy dinner rolls that looked to be the homemade sort.

Gabe voiced Olivia's thoughts. "Yeah, Yun, somehow this spread isn't making it seem like you led a deprived childhood."

"Says the guy who got to hang out at a family-run pizza parlor every Friday and Saturday night of his life," Yun said with a playful roll of her eyes. "I can count the number of times on one hand that I had pizza before turning eighteen and getting my first job."

Gabe swung his leg around to face the table and pulled plates in front of him and Olivia. "My dad is best friends with the owner of a pizza joint," he said in explanation with a wink in Olivia's direction. "I told you he runs a collision center. They were right across the street from each other, and they were always throwing freebies each other's way. When I wasn't fixing cars, I was eating pizza."

"Yet somehow he's still got that body." Yun hiked a

thumb toward Gabe's abs. "With all the burgers he eats, I kept waiting for him to get a potbelly when we were in school. I've since given up. I'm convinced he's just one of those genetic anomalies who functions perfectly on being lethargic five days a week and busting his ass the other two."

Gabe's look was pure exasperation. "Shouldn't you be trying to talk me up? Because I'm pretty sure I'm coming across like a slug with intermittent ADHD and a cholesterol problem."

Olivia laughed and held out her plate as Gabe dropped a couple of rolls onto it.

Finished unpacking everything, Yun plopped onto the bench opposite them. When Samson seemed to have given up on freebies from her, he trotted around to Olivia's side. "Fine. I'll behave myself." Yun smiled at Olivia, showing mismatched, deep dimples on both cheeks. "Gabe's pretty much the big brother I never had. But enough about me. I was so psyched when he told me about you."

"I can't remember if I told you or not, Olivia," Gabe said, "but Yun's pretty much the reason I ended up meeting you, more proof that a few good things have come out of her attempts at micromanagement."

"Yeah, you said she was the one who encouraged you to drive down to volunteer. And you won't hear me complaining," Olivia said, burying the fingers of one hand in the silky fur just below Samson's ear as he planted his head on her lap.

"For a while there, I thought it might take an intervention to get him to do something outside of work that didn't involve camping trips with Samson."

"You're forgetting how many times a week I hang out with my brother and my nieces."

Still soaking in their easy conversation, Olivia popped one of the rolls in her mouth. An explosion of flavor burst across her tongue, and her stomach cramped in anticipation. No wonder these were Gabe's favorite.

"Family not included," Yun added at his declaration. "Oh, guess what I got to scrub in on today."

"Torn ACL?"

"I wish. A total hip replacement on a six-year-old Rott." She looked at Olivia and added, "The dog had severe hip dysplasia in his left hip. And it's super-tricky surgery."

"Impressive, Yun." Gabe cocked an eyebrow and popped a roll into his mouth before stabbing his fork at a hunk of pepper on his plate. "Damn, these are good. So, how'd you do?"

"Good enough to know I'm officially ready for a change." With a floret of cauliflower paused an inch from her mouth, she added in Olivia's direction, "I let my parents talk me into accepting a position at an emergency vet hospital and surgical center that's big enough to take up one wing of a mall. 'For the insurance and the benefits and the stability,'" she said, making air quotes with the last part. "While Gabe took a risk and got hired on with a single owner. And he's gotten ten times the experience I have since we finished our internships."

"I can see how doing something stable like that would be tempting, especially considering the loans that I bet came with vet school," Olivia said.

Yun let out a little groan as she munched her kimchi.

"You're not kidding. It's going to be like paying on a brand-new Jaguar for the next fifteen years while I try to breathe life into my ten-year-old Corolla."

"I hear you there," Gabe said. "So, you're serious? You're going to look for something else?"

"My wheels are officially spinning. Any chance Dr. Washington will let you out of buying that crappy old building? That place of yours is too small to bring in another vet. If you weren't working alone, I bet you could more than double your business."

"What're you saying?" Gabe asked before popping another roll into his mouth.

"I don't know for sure. Just keep your eye out for vacant buildings before you sign your life away on any dotted lines."

Gabe sat up straight, tapping the fingers of one hand on the tabletop. "You know, the longer Dr. Washington is away, the more I find myself wishing I had another vet working with me to take some of the calls we end up not being able to fit into the schedule. I hate having to refer people out."

"My sister's a real estate agent," Olivia piped up. "She's mostly residential, but she does a bit of commercial too. If you'd like, you can let me know what sort of thing you're looking for, and I can ask her to keep an eye open."

Yun's warm, brown eyes widened as she looked between Olivia and Gabe. When Gabe shrugged and said it couldn't hurt, Yun flattened her hands on the table. "That'd be great, Olivia, as long as she understands it's just exploratory right now."

Olivia shrugged. "Sure. She won't care. And it never hurts to look. You never know what might come of it."

———◆◆◆———

From where Gabe sat, he was fairly certain he'd never had a more stunning view in all his life. And some of the most incredible ambiance in St. Louis was only partly to do with it. The rest was all Olivia, and it wasn't just her looks, even though he couldn't remember ever being as drawn to someone physically as he was to her.

After they'd eaten a hefty share of appetizers and Yun had taken off, Gabe had thrown out half-a-dozen dining options only to confirm that neither of them were that hungry any longer. With the weather about as perfect as a spring day in the Midwest could get—having dropped to the low sixties now that the sun had set and with no humidity—Olivia had liked the idea of going for a walk through Tower Grove Park first as they talked.

Later, after a bit of debate—there were so many places she had yet to discover as a new resident to the city—they'd opted for the Boathouse at Forest Park, and Gabe couldn't think of a more perfect place to get to know her better tonight. Now they were seated at a table on the outdoor patio, facing Post-Dispatch Lake. The big, sprawling lake was quiet and serene tonight, and reflections from the lanterns in the beer garden set Olivia's hair aglow in the dark and reflected off the pair of lips Gabe found more enticing than any he'd ever known. The sun had set more than an hour ago, and only a hint of lighter blue remained in the far western sky.

They were slowly finishing off a bottle of Australian Shiraz and savoring a few of the lighter appetizers from the Boathouse's selection. Olivia was halfway through her second glass of wine, and Gabe smiled at the way she settled back in her chair and let her eyes fall closed for a moment, a happy smile lingering on her face. He wondered what it would be like to fall asleep to that smile. Or even better, to wake up in the morning and have it be the first thing he saw.

"I'm so glad spring is here," she said. "Ava's always telling me I need to do things like this, but I came up here in January, and honestly I pretty much gave everything I could to making the best start in Westbury Middle."

"I can see why you would. I've done that with work for nearly a year now. But you're just getting started. Now that the weather's better and you've got the routine down there, you'll probably have more time than before."

Eyes still closed, Olivia raised a hand and crossed her fingers. "Let's hope."

"What do you mean?"

She opened her eyes and sat up again, giving a little shake as if it was an attempt to step out of her buzz. "If it weren't for the fact that I just finished my second glass of wine, I might not have the nerve to tell you what I mean."

Gabe didn't want her telling him anything she'd regret later. "There's nothing you have to tell me before you're a hundred percent ready."

Olivia sucked in a long breath, her shoulders rising and falling with it. "I want to tell you. I need to tell you, because there's a chance it could affect things."

Tension knotted his stomach in anticipation. "Okay."

"The thing is…I hate endings. Always have. When I see them coming, I go into survival mode. I'm not talking about you. I'm talking about my job," she said, probably picking up on his anticipation.

He nodded, relaxing a bit, and took a swig of wine.

"Finding a well-rated school around here willing to hire a Teach for America–trained teacher with only a couple years' experience in a rural school district wasn't the easiest thing to do. And don't get me wrong; I loved teaching those kids down there. I just wanted something totally different, and when it came to moving across the state and into a city, I wanted something I was confident I could handle."

"I can understand that."

"I lucked out with the position I'm in, but it's temporary. There's no guarantee it'll turn into anything permanent. If I knew for sure it would, I'd go adopt that amazing dog like this," she said, snapping her fingers, "and rent a place of my own closer to the city. I love the town of Elsah, but it's a commute, and most of the residents are over sixty-five." She paused and took a sip of wine. "And then there's you."

Gabe considered his reply before speaking. "There is me, isn't there? I'm glad you said that, because as far as I'm concerned, there's no denying there's you now either." He tapped his fingers on his thigh. "As to the rest, I don't know what to say except I have faith everything's going to fall into place. From everything I've seen, you're the sort of teacher that principals would want teaching in their schools."

"Thanks. But—what if they don't?" She motioned back and forth between them. "With everything in my world so undefined, this is just...scary."

He leaned forward and closed one hand over hers. "It's been my experience that the important things are always scary. If it helps, I like you, Olivia. A lot. I did from day one, and I like you even more as I get to know you better."

"I like you too." Suddenly, she shook her head, suppressing a laugh. "Let's be real. I think me crawling onto your lap gave that away already."

"Yeah, full disclosure, you've got my permission to do that anytime you want. Day or night."

She pressed her lips together and shook her head. "Good to know."

"So, when will you know? About your job?"

"Soon. One of the tenured teachers keeps insisting it's a good sign that they haven't announced who's coming back next year. She heard a rumor they're trying to add a class, and if they do, the math department is maxed out in its student-teacher ratio already."

He nodded slowly. "Then let's trust that."

After he let go of her hand, she dipped a wedge of pita bread into the hummus. "Okay. And thanks. I feel better having told you."

"It's my experience that things tend to have a way of working out." He shifted in his chair. "I, uh, also want to thank you for how good you were with Yun earlier."

"She's great," Olivia said after swallowing a bite of food.

Out on the lake, just visible in the glow from the lanterns, a couple of long-necked swans were slowly making their way across the still water. "Do you ever feel like your life's a couple of completely different stories roughly sewn together in the same binding?"

Olivia's lips pressed together a second before she shook her head. "I think of some people's lives like that. Like my sister's. Mine has always seemed like this slowly crescendoing song where nothing much is happening and maybe once or twice it's been playing the entirely wrong melody, but there's always been a promise it's building into something worth hearing. But from what you've shared about your life already, I can see why you would describe yours that way."

"Small things bridge it together, I guess. Like the search-and-rescue work I did with Samson while I was in vet school. And the buddies I've kept in touch with after walking away from the life. But without heading into that fire, I can't imagine a way in which I'd have become friends with Yun. I had close to a dozen guys, most of whom I still keep in touch with, that I considered my best friends. A couple are from childhood, but most were buddies at the firehouse. The thing is, in rescue work like that, you tend to move through an unbelievable amount of tragedy every day nearly unscathed. There's just no end to it, and not just the fires. It's the car wrecks and heart attacks and freak accidents. The list goes on. Before you know it, you feel like you're wearing this coat of impermeable armor. At least you think you are. Then the world shifts, and you realize you never really had it at all."

Olivia's eyebrows knit together as she listened. "I can see that."

"After the fire, after Claire broke off the engagement, I pretty much lost interest in connecting with people. As far as I was concerned, the world could go to hell. All I needed was Samson. I even pulled away from my family for a while. I didn't drop them entirely, but it wasn't the same. Not for a while."

Olivia placed a hand over his and gave it a light

squeeze. "It was the same way with my sister when she left home so young. For a while it was like she cut all ties, except with me maybe, but even with us, when we talked, she just wouldn't open up anymore." She shrugged. "I guess she opened up again so gradually I didn't realize she was doing it."

"Yeah, it was like that for me, too, with my brother. The thing is, if I hadn't been through all that, I never would have become friends with Yun. She's organized to the point of being maddening sometimes, but—I don't know—somehow I recognized she's that way to stave off vulnerability. Me, I shut people out. She gets meticulously organized. And I'm telling you this because earlier tonight you didn't seem to care that my closest friend at this stage of my life is a woman, and I appreciate that." He flipped his hand over, locking her fingers in his. "But I also want to lay all the cards on the table and make sure you don't have any questions or concerns about it."

Olivia's top teeth dug into the side of her lower lip, and she sat up a little straighter. "No questions really. I mean, I hope that if there was anything unresolved between you, you'd tell me. You don't seem like the type to play games that way."

"Thank you, and I'm not. There's nothing unresolved because there's never been anything like that between us. When I met her, she was dating this guy her mom was crazy about. I guess Yun's mom is a lot like her, because she'd all but planned out their life for them. The way Yun tells it, her mom's pretty much been planning out her life since she was a kid. It just took Yun awhile to realize it. Which is why tonight when she said she was ready to try something new, it meant something."

He traced his thumb along the soft skin of Olivia's hand and underneath her wrist. "But regardless, I can't remember ever seeing her as anything but a friend. By the time she broke it off with that guy, she was more like a kid sister who was a hundred times smarter than me than anything else. And that wasn't an exaggeration earlier; I really do credit her with helping me get through vet school. I did pretty good in undergrad just winging it, but somehow I never acquired study skills."

Olivia smiled and let out a little huff. "I suspect you're being hard on yourself, but it's awesome you have a friend like that. And thank you for telling me about her so openly. There are no worries here."

"That's what I was hoping to hear."

"What you shared—it brought some stuff up." She sipped her wine and gave a little shrug of her shoulders as she set the glass down. "I've known for a while now I paid a price in getting so tightly locked into a relationship as young as I did. I had friends, of course. But there was always somebody else in the picture who took precedence over them. Not that I blame him. I blame me. But whatever the case, the last six months I've enjoyed just answering to myself and—this might sound a bit lame—figuring out what it really means to be Olivia Graham."

"That's not lame. Trust me. I went through that while deciding to enter vet school. In my family, college was pretty much for other people. Everyone calls my dad 'Doc' because of everything he knows about cars, but he's entirely self-taught. I took a lot of jabs from all of them when I decided to go for it and applied. I think I'm the only one on either side of the family to have gone further in school than a bachelor's, and honestly there are only a couple of us who've earned those. It took trusting myself and shutting down a lot of voices inside shouting that I was a Wentworth and wasn't going to cut it."

"How are they now?" Olivia twisted in her chair and slid her hand up the length of his forearm. Her touch was tender and affectionate but still warmed Gabe's blood.

"The voices or my family?" he winked.

"Your family," Olivia said, laughing. "I'm hoping those voices got quiet when you did it."

He smiled. "Quieter anyway. And my family's good. I'm 'Doc Junior' now to all my cousins, but since most of them are bringing their pets to me now, I'm okay with that."

"Good for you."

Gabe swallowed the last of his wine as the server approached, offering a polite reminder that the kitchen would soon be shutting down for the evening.

"You in the mood for anything else?" he asked as the server pulled out her order pad.

Olivia gave an emphatic shake of her head. "I couldn't eat another bite. I honestly could've gone without this, even as good as it was."

When Gabe asked for the bill, Olivia fished through her purse and pulled out a card. "This one's on me, remember?"

He fought back the urge to debate her. "So long as you let me get it next time."

"Deal."

Looking relieved when ownership of the bill didn't escalate any further, the server took off with Olivia's card.

"I'm just glad we're both in agreement about there being a next time," Olivia added once they were alone, a smile tugging at her lips.

Gabe gave in to the desire and let his fingers trail down the length of her hair. Her eyes blinked closed a second and she suppressed a shiver, but from the way she leaned in just a touch closer, he was confident what it meant. "If you want the truth, I'm hoping there are enough 'next times' that we lose count."

"I'd like that." Her gaze dropped to his mouth, and he could just make out her clearing her throat.

Suddenly, the server couldn't return quickly enough for Gabe. The light but steady evening breeze that had caused Olivia to slip into a cardigan hadn't relented, but he would swear the temperature had swelled twenty degrees.

"I, uh, know it's dark, but I thought it might be fun to walk by the lake." He pointed toward the trees lining the western edge. "There's a trail running along it over there."

She craned in her seat to see where he was pointing. "Sure. I'd love to." She excused herself to the restroom and wove around the now-half-empty tables, headed to the main door of the restaurant. By the time she came back out, the server had returned with her credit card slip.

"How about I get the tip?"

Olivia looked up from signing to give him a wink of her own, causing an internal reaction that snaked all the way down into his groin. "Next time."

He wasn't about to argue with that. She flipped the receipt book shut and added, "Ready if you are."

You've no idea how ready I am. Gabe locked his hand against the small of her back as they headed out, the soft, flowery scent of her perfume blending with the smells wafting from the kitchen and off the lake. He'd been in hermit mode for so long, he wondered if there was a chance the time of year had anything to do with why he was suddenly so very *ready*. He knew from experience that even spayed and neutered domestic animals tended to be friskier in spring. *That's it; tell her you can hardly hold back because your internal clock's ticking, even though you promised there'd be no pressure tonight.*

She fell into stride beside him as they took off around the building, the top of her shoulder finding that spot against his lower deltoids again. There was hardly a cloud in the sky, and stars and a few planets shone brightly enough in this darker section of the park. The moon was three-quarters full and bright enough to light the ground when it wasn't blocked by the towering oaks. Off to their left, moonlight danced across the water, and the soft lap of the waves was just visible. Ahead in the grass, a small group of people sat in the dark at a picnic table, filling the night with their laughter.

"Considering your first-aid training and how prepared you were to walk into that flood, am I right to assume there's no need to wonder about the safety factor of heading away from the crowds in a public park at night?"

Gabe chuckled. "I wouldn't say that goes for any park or even all sections of this park, but this area's pretty well traversed. And it's not that late yet."

After a second, Olivia gave a little nod. "I'm good

with that answer." She slipped her arm underneath his and locked her hand around his waist just above his jeans, her thumb tracing his side just over his shirt.

They walked in silence along the trail for a few minutes before she spoke again. "Is it too forward to tell you that I love the way you feel against me?"

"Ahh, no, definitely not."

She laughed softly and tucked her head against his shoulder. "Good, because I do. And it's not just that you're tall and fit and—you know, that sort of stuff. I just feel like I'm exactly where I'm supposed to be when I'm close to you."

If she could've said anything else to hit home like that, Gabe wasn't sure what it could be.

As far as he could see ahead and behind, they were alone on the trail. Gabe stopped walking and turned to face her, brushing the tips of her knuckles across his lips. "It's that way for me, too, Olivia. I don't know how or why, but the first time I saw you, something about you felt so right. I guess that's why everything rose up in me to declare it was otherwise—so much so, I almost panicked and left you stranded at that garage with that asshole."

"You're forgiven for that. Almost." She traced her thumb along his lower lip, then with her other hand, she pressed the flat of her palm against his abdomen smack-dab between the button of his jeans and his belly button.

An inferno of heat raced up and down his abs, and his cock struggled to salute against the fabric of his jeans. *Stay cool, man.* "Almost?"

"Yeah, almost. But if you spend a few minutes kissing me, I bet it would morph into full forgiveness."

"I'd be good with that, but fair warning, there's something else on the verge of morphing here too." He pressed her back against the base of a thick tree a few feet off the trail. Her purse thumped against his side as she locked her arms around his neck. Rather than holding back, this time he let himself be free, drawing her tightly in toward him and opening his mouth fully to hers. She met him with the same eagerness, their tongues and hands as ready to join in the dance as their bodies.

Her sweater was open, and he tugged down the shoulder of the silky shirt she had on underneath until it was halfway down her arm and one half of her satiny bra shone in the night, perky and taut from the beautiful swell of the breast underneath it.

He swallowed hard. It was going to be all he could do not to explode right here on this path.

Confident he was blocking her from the view of any chance passersby, he slipped the cup of her bra down, freeing her breast. "Dear God, you're beautiful." He wanted to take his time, to savor the way she looked in the moonlight, but his hands and mouth proved more eager than his eyes.

Her fingers dug into his hair at the back of his head, and he felt the heat of her breath against his ear. He was still savoring the sweet taste of her when he heard the roll of soft laughter up ahead on the path. Covering her with one side of her sweater, he pulled her around to the other side of the tree facing out to the lake.

As soon as he had her pressed against it again, she moved her sweater to the side and arched her back. He had just enough time to appreciate the glow of the moon against the bare skin of her breast before she locked her hands on the sides of his head and drew him toward it.

"Full disclosure," she whispered in his ear, "I think I'm still a little tipsy because a part of me doesn't even care who might see."

It had been so long that a part of him was impossibly close to exploding, but her words sent a wave of warning over him. He rose back up and closed his hands at the sides of her head. After brushing his lips against her forehead, he said, "I don't want this to be something you might regret later."

She tugged up his shirt and locked her hands over his bare waist. She looked him in the eye without fear or embarrassment. "I said tipsy, not drunk. I'm in full control—sort of. When you kiss me like that, I kind of lose my senses. At least all of them but the feeling ones."

He dropped his hands to her hips and brushed his lips over hers. "If you're sure, absolutely sure, we could go back to my place."

"Ah, it wasn't going to be, but that's a yes. A hard yes. Only can we stay here a few more minutes? Because this—out here, with you—just happens to be the most beautiful thing that's ever happened to me, and I want to savor it a little longer."

Her words struck a chord, reverberating through him. He nodded and looked up and down the path, confirming that the couple had passed by and were on their way back to the Boathouse. "We can savor it as long as you want."

Until now, it hadn't occurred to him that one of the advantages of all those hours and hours of practice with his hands the last several years, learning to use them with delicate precision performing countless incisions and sutures, could be making them useful in an entirely different way.

With a few deft movements, he unbuttoned her jeans and slid down her zipper, his eyes still locked on hers. He opened his hand and spread his fingers wide, placing the flat of his palm against her low abdomen as she'd done with him, only he was against her flesh.

Her jaw fell open, and she let out a half-stifled gasp.

"Still okay?"

She nodded and closed her eyes as he stepped closer and moved his hand lower, cupping her, savoring her mound and her heat. He'd never wanted to lose himself in anyone more than he did her. Right now. Only this wasn't the time or place for what he really wanted to do. He raised his free hand and dug his fingers into the bark of the tree to keep from losing himself. Her breath against his ear was almost enough to drive him over the top.

He moved his fingers back and forth inside her, let them dance in a slow circle, searching for the rhythm that most moved her. He could tell when he found it by the way her body arched and her hands locked over the back of his neck.

"Oh God." The words came out against his ear as a soft, stifled whisper, too quiet for anyone walking on the path to overhear.

He gripped the tree over her head hard enough that a hunk of bark disintegrated in his fingers, but they were both too lost in the rhythm to care about the tiny pieces that rained down.

"That a girl," he whispered when her climax rocked

through her hard enough that she buried her face against him, stifling a cry into his chest. He kept on, making sure she could fully ride it out, till she pulled away, a few tears streaming down her face.

Finally, she clamped a hand over her mouth, stifling a laugh. "I can't believe that just happened."

Releasing his grip on the tree, he brushed his thumb over her cheek, drying those tears. "Yeah, well, for the record, being here with you is the most remarkable thing that's ever happened to me too. And if I know nothing else, it's that I'll never forget it."

Chapter 20

THE WINE BUZZ HAD WANED BY THE TIME THEY WERE back at Gabe's apartment, leaving Olivia a bit in shock over what had just happened. They hadn't exactly reached the level of closeness where she could explain how out of character it was to lose herself like that. With Trevor, climaxing hadn't been an impossible task, but it had never happened even close to so easily.

Just the thought of Gabe's easy, understated confidence warmed her blood as she ascended the wooden steps leading to his top-floor apartment. It wasn't just what he'd proven he could do with his hands; it was what he'd said afterward about how affected he'd been too.

Her mind kept trying to downplay it, but her heart told her this was the real thing. Realer than anything she'd experienced before. How was it that exactly this time last week, she'd had no idea Gabe Wentworth even existed? And now, thoughts of him filled her chest like a giant hot-air balloon, threatening to sweep her away on winds she had no idea how to navigate.

He was sexy and kind and caring, and if there was any doubt about his character, it had been washed away by how he was with Samson and with Yun. And she wanted him. Olivia's thoughts flashed back to the park. Along with a fresh wash of desire, insecurity swept in. He'd grown up in the city and had a blossoming career and a life that was chock-full of friends and family. She grew up in the sticks and didn't even have confidence in her ability to keep employment here in the city. What if she gave her heart to him and nothing worked out?

Oblivious to her thoughts, Gabe unlocked the door to his apartment and swung it open. Samson was waiting there, wagging his tail so hard his whole body rode along with it in a dance.

"You still good with coming in? Because if you've changed your mind, we can take him for a little walk, then I'll see you to your car."

Somehow Olivia's hands had found their way to her back pockets; they were shoved deep inside and facing palms out. "I'm good."

He opened the door wider and flipped on a light in the main room. "Make yourself at home. I'll run Samson outside. I'm not sure how much you saw earlier when we dropped him off, but have a look around. Let me warn you now. My housekeeping skills leave a lot to be desired, and I know it."

In a flash, Gabe and Samson were gone and Olivia was alone. Her body was humming with unspent energy. She did a slow circle of the living room, doing her best to calm down.

As nervous as she suddenly was, she was still able to both appreciate the old architecture and get a sense of Gabe's understated decorating skills. Unlike Aunt Becky's place, which was decorated to the hilt, Gabe's walls were largely bare, but the hardwood floors, tall ceilings, molding, and exposed brick on the outer wall made up for it.

Judging by the way a single throw blanket was

wadded up and flattened in the center of the couch, Samson had most likely been snuggled there. On the adjacent coffee table was a nearly empty glass of water, a well-worn book of Missouri state parks and less-explored hiking trails, and several issues of the *Journal of Veterinary Medicine*.

The rear portion of the living room had a long dining table, four chairs, and a bench on one side. Based on a water ring and the fact that one end of the table was clutter-free, she could tell where Gabe ate. On the oppo-site end of the table, there was a laundry basket filled with clothes, a laptop, and a stack of paperwork and mail, all of which brought a smile to Olivia's face.

She was getting a real look into the place where Gabe lived out the monotonous parts of life—the bill paying, the laundry folding, the resting and reading, and the snuggling with Samson. And her heart warmed even more.

Guessing the bathroom had to be toward the back, she headed through the short, wide hallway that opened to a narrow galley kitchen and then two doors, the first of which turned out to be the bathroom, the second, his bedroom.

Suspecting a surge of panic would fill her if she gave the bedroom any real attention, she headed into the bath-room and shut the door. It was a small space and, prob-ably out of necessity, tidy and organized. His toiletries were on a shelf to the right of a pedestal sink, and the only item on the sink base was a jar of hand soap.

She peed and washed up and smoothed out her hair in the mirror. Spotting a bottle of mouthwash on his toiletry shelf, she was half-tempted to use it. After a bit of debate, she opted not to and just rinsed her mouth with water. Right before she stepped from the room, she heard the patter of Samson's paws trotting across the floor.

"Hey, buddy," she said, pulling the bathroom door open.

Gabe had flipped on the kitchen light and was at the sink filling an ice tray with water. He put it in the freezer and gave her a wink. "So, in addition to not being the most domestic of nearly thirty-year-old guys who live alone, I'm also not the best host. I wish I had thought about it earlier, but after a quick look in the fridge, it seems I can offer you a glass of water with the two ice cubes that clung to the tray this morning, milk from a gallon that expired yesterday, a bottle of ginger ale, or a Guinness, but I remember you said you don't like dark beer."

Olivia's laugh reverberated down into her fingers and toes. "No to the glass of milk for sure. I like ginger ale, but I'm happy with a glass of water right now."

He nodded and pulled two glasses from a cabinet near the fridge. "Next time you come over, I'm going to be ready for you."

"For the record, I like that you didn't plan on entertaining me here. And this place is sweet."

He finished filling the waters and cocked an eyebrow. "I don't know that I'd go with sweet, but it's cheap and enabled me to get through vet school without racking up a lot of additional debt. It's on my to-do list to find a new place, but it's clearly not as much a priority as a bunch of other stuff. However, like I said, with Samson having a hard time with the stairs lately, I need to make it one."

It was too early in their relationship for her to have the thought that they both needed to find new places to live, but the thought was there regardless. Hoping it couldn't be read on her face, she headed for the living room and the couch. Its seat was low enough to the ground that Samson hopped up next to her with no effort. When she was seated beside him, he was every bit as tall as she was. Actually, he was a bit taller. He panted in her face, his mouth agape.

"You're such a good boy." She did a double-handed rubdown of his ears. "But that breath."

Gabe laughed and took a seat on the opposite side of Samson. He set the glasses on coasters and settled back against the couch, draping his arm across the top and closing his hand on her shoulder.

"There's something else I should probably tell you."

"I'm all ears." Olivia twisted in her seat to face him, dipping to the side to look around Samson before he dropped down to curl up beside her. In one big, floppy movement, he rolled onto his back, his feet up in the air.

With Samson's furry belly exposed, there was nothing else to do but scratch it as she listened.

"This feels a little abrupt just to get out in the open, but considering our earlier talk, I feel like I need to say it. It occurred to me on the way here that I've never, uh, *entertained* here. By the time Samson was healed and ready for adoption, Claire and I were separating. I'm not saying I didn't have a couple, uh—you know what I mean—but I've never brought anyone here."

Gabe's hand was still on her shoulder, and hearing his declaration, it was so easy to lift it in hers and press it against her lips. He had amazing hands, sculpted and muscular, and she wanted to memorize every swell and bend and curve. Turning it over, she brushed her thumbs along the length of his palm, appreciating his slow groan of pleasure.

Samson shifted and leaned his head on her knee, fully aware that he was being ignored. When she was too slow to find his belly again, he let out a long sigh-whine combo in what couldn't more clearly be a "No, no, not him. Pet me."

"Case in point," Gabe said, laughing. "I'm telling you this because he's a bit like having a toddler in the bed, and I don't think he has any concept he could be shoved out for, ah, something other than sleeping to take place. Which I guess most likely means this mission—should you choose to accept it—is probably going to involve a very spoiled senior-aged golden retriever whining at the door."

Olivia pressed her lips together. So it seemed they were having a conversation about what in a moment of desire she'd nearly begged to come here to do. Only now she was fully sober and a bit nervous, and her blood flow was no longer pooling south of the border.

"Not that there's any pressure to end up there," he said as if reading her thoughts. "I just figured I should give you the heads-up in hopes that if we do, it'll be a bit less distracting." He shook his head, a slight smile passing over his face. "He used to howl at the door when I was leaving for class."

"You survived a fire together. It's no wonder you're bonded." Olivia ran her hand along Samson's belly again, and his tail thumped between Gabe and the back of the couch in thanks. "I can't imagine how terrifying that was. But look at the good things that happened because of it. You found him and he saved you, and now you're paying it forward with all the animals you help every day."

"There's no regret on my part, that's for sure." Gabe locked his hand around Samson's big paw. "Which reminds me... Earlier, when you were talking about the pointer, I know you said your world isn't set up to take him right now, but what you said about him struck a chord. I felt that way about Samson—this need to do more than make sure he was okay or that he'd be cared for and treated well the rest of his life. I sat with it awhile, but after some time, I grew clear about it. I knew he fit into my life and I needed to do whatever it took to make sure I got him. Thankfully, some of the shelter staff saw that even before I spoke it aloud."

A few tears unexpectedly stung the backs of her eyelids. She cleared her throat, trying to shake them off. "I'd be lying to pretend I didn't feel that way about Morgan. There are so many other dogs out there in need of loving homes, and a lot of breeds—smaller ones—that would be better suited for the life I'm going to be able to offer, whenever I can actually offer it. I keep telling myself he'll be better off if he's adopted by a family with land or, at the very least, a big fenced-in backyard.

"And I love volunteering at the shelter—so much more than I could've imagined—but the truth is, I don't know if by volunteering there I'm doing myself any favors in terms of getting over that dog. I had him out for a half hour this afternoon. By the end, he was sitting at attention and walking by my side, thanks to a handful of pointers from Patrick. But when I went to put him away, he whined and scratched at the door to his kennel, and my heart felt like it was breaking in two."

For a moment, silence hung in the air, and Samson lazily looked between them, his head relaxed and resting against the couch and his gums sagging open in a deranged-looking smile.

"I wish I could keep him for you until you get settled, but the owner of this building has a hard stop at one animal per apartment. I know because I tried to foster a few animals after I started working with Dr. Washington."

"That's a sweet offer, but I wouldn't ask you to do that. I've been thinking about asking my grandpa. He always has a couple dogs around, but it's a farm life. He gives them dinner every day and freedom to roam, but his dogs aren't pets. I just keep thinking I'd rather see Morgan land in a home where someone could really dote on him. Kind of like you said, I'm just sitting with it until I get clear, or at least clearer than I am now. In the meantime, I'm going to keep enjoying the shelter and doling out as much love and affection to him as I can. And no matter what happens, I intend to keep volunteering once he's no longer there."

As long as I have a job and don't have to tuck tail and go home, that is. But that fear was one she refused to voice. The night was too perfect for that level of indecision to creep in.

"Yeah? That's great. It'll be cool to see you there. I'm there twice a week at least for rechecks and physicals. When it comes to the more complicated stuff, like surgery, the animals are brought to my office. Dr. Washington's office, technically. For a little while longer, at least. So, I take it you've met most of the shelter staff?"

"Most, I think. Tess and Megan and Patrick. Fidel, too, but he hasn't done more than nod in my general direction."

"Yeah, Fidel's a little shy till you get to know him."

Olivia chewed her lip a second. "Mostly I've been working with Patrick. How well do you know him?"

Gabe cocked an eyebrow. "How well do I know Patrick? That's a bit of a loaded question. I guess pretty well, considering I've picked up on the foods he packs in his lunch, and I never fail to be amazed at his knowledge of the animals who've passed through the shelter doors."

She debated a second or two before saying the rest. "If I'm being honest, I feel a touch incompetent around him. I realize I'm new and all; he just seems to know *everything*."

"His knowledge of the shelter and the dogs and cats that've moved through there—and baseball, too, I guess—is unbeatable. I'm not sure if anyone mentioned it, but he has high-functioning autism."

Olivia pointed a finger his direction. "I didn't know that, and it makes everything so much clearer. I'm surprised I didn't make the connection. I've worked with quite a few kids with that diagnosis over the last couple years."

"It's easier to miss on him than some. But regardless, I know him well enough to assure you that if you treat animals well and have compassion for what you do there, he'll not only respect you, he'd move mountains to help you if you ever need it."

"This helps. Thanks. I'm not going to feel so bad

about all that I don't know next time. Or how much less efficient I am."

"Yeah, well, just remember, Megan says even with being such a stickler for routine, he averages about a hundred and fifty percent productivity compared to everyone else."

"I don't doubt it." Olivia shook her head in disbelief. "It's still so weird to me, how I was worried about reconnecting with you, yet we found each other again through the shelter."

"I think that's what they call synchronicity. But, if you think about it, it makes sense. A love of dogs brought us together. Why not a shelter too?"

"You have a point."

Gabe's hand was resting on Samson's rib cage, and she brushed her fingers over it. Earlier, after they had meandered back along the trail and ended up at Gabe's truck, things had heated up again before they were interrupted by a carload of people who'd parked next to them. Now that they were here, she was getting the sense that Gabe was holding back out of respect and concern for her comfort, not because he'd lost interest in starting something up again.

Knowing the longer it went between steamy kisses, the more likely she was to lose her nerve, Olivia took a leap. "So, full disclosure. I could live to be a hundred and not forget how incredible you looked carrying Morgan out of the water." After a second of debate, she added, "At the time, I think I had too much adrenaline flowing through my veins to appreciate that fact, but thanks to YouTube and Facebook, I've had a few more chances for it to hit home."

Gabe chuckled softly. "Thanks, but I saw the video. Morgan very deservingly stole the show."

"His struggle in the water was heart-wrenching, that's for sure. But I think that's what makes your efforts so much more compelling. And it isn't just me. Have you seen some of the comments under the video link?" She rolled her eyes in exasperation. "I'm pretty sure you were proposed to at least once."

Even in the dim overhead light, Olivia thought she noticed his cheeks darken a touch. "I chose not to read them. Let's hope it's short-lived and I remain anonymous." He traced his thumb slowly across her wrist. "Because I'm only interested in getting attention like that from one person, and she's right here in front of me."

After letting the compliment roll over her, Olivia shifted in her seat and rose up on her knees. Bracing a hand on the back of the couch, she leaned over Samson and brushed her lips over Gabe's. She kept the kiss light, lingering long enough to warm her blood all over again. Next, she trailed the kiss along the ridge of his jaw, savoring the hint of late-evening stubble against her lips before moving down his neck to his sternum. She let her lips linger in the hollow before returning to his chin. Below her, Samson shifted and pressed a back paw into her belly.

Gabe locked his hands in her hair and let out a soft murmur. "I wasn't sure… I thought maybe you'd changed your mind."

She pulled back enough to look him in the eye. Suddenly it hit her. Even though it didn't seem like it, technically, this was a first date. *Sleeping with someone on a first date's a rebound thing, isn't it?*

Maybe it was sometimes. But she'd been broken up with Trevor for six months now, and there'd been no rebound dating except for the pathetic setups by Ava. Besides, she wasn't looking for rebound sex. She wanted to sleep with Gabe. And not just tonight. Still, a thousand I-told-you-so's rose up, words she'd heard from her family and Sunday school teachers and who knew who else, pressing down her excitement with the weight of a sandbag.

"It's just now occurring to me that the fact that I hadn't changed my mind might make you think less of me."

She was just starting to sit back when he cupped his hands under her elbows. "Not a chance, Olivia. You've rocked my world. If you're ready to take the next step tonight, I'm in. If you want to wait six months, I'm a big boy. I'll wait."

"Is it crazy to trust myself that I know what I want?" She gave an exasperated shake of her head. "The truth is, I've never felt this clear before. And now that I realize it, it's a little bit terrifying."

He cocked an eyebrow. "No pressure, but you know what they say—there's a fine line between terror and excitement."

Olivia sank back on her heels in consideration, a smile rising to her lips to match his playful one. He wasn't going to pressure her, that much was clear. If she decided to head home right now, he'd let her go without giving her an ounce of guilt. "I think that's pretty much it in a nutshell. I'm terrified by how excited I am at the idea of being with you."

His laugh was soft and easy. "Would you believe me

if I said I get it? I'm battling my own round of nerve demons."

"I believe you, but I can't possibly imagine what you'd be afraid of."

"It's like I hinted earlier, it's, uh, been awhile. I'm a little panicked I'll disappoint you."

Gabe Wentworth, one of the sexiest, most steadfast and genuine men she'd ever met, was worried about disappointing her.

Unexpected happiness blossomed in Olivia's chest. So, this was what it felt like to have an honest-to-goodness partner, to have someone who wasn't just on the same side, but who confided in you, and in whom you could confide in in return.

She leaned close and brushed her lips over his ear and let her words fall out in a whisper. "I'll tell you right now, you aren't going to disappoint me. Though maybe we can give ourselves permission to set the bar higher after we get the awkward stuff out of the way."

Their kiss was just beginning to get heated again when Samson decided he'd been slighted long enough. He let out a grunt and rolled over with such a considerable amount of struggle that he passed a long stream of gas. Once he had his legs underneath him, he stood up and planted himself smack-dab between them.

"Whoa," Olivia added, fanning her face and leaning back. "I'd almost guess he timed that."

"I'm not kidding about him being put out. But the gas thing—that's just him and old age, and it's always worse at night." Gabe reached for her hand and pulled her a safe distance from the couch and straight into an embrace. Olivia loved the feel of his arms wrapping tightly around her.

"Next time I come over, I'll bring Samson a giant Kong filled with enough peanut butter to keep him busy for hour or two, and maybe he won't even realize he's missing out on something."

"That's a good idea," Gabe said between kisses, one hand at her back, the other cupping the curve between her ass and the back of her thigh, making her want to melt even closer into him.

She felt the swell of him pressing into her low belly again, and her body heated all over in response. She ground against him, ready to melt the last of that fear away.

Gabe pulled back as things got heated and released a breath. "You know, that reminds me. I've got a dental chew that'll buy us twenty minutes tonight."

Olivia slipped her hands underneath Gabe's shirt, running them along the ridges of muscle along his abdomen and sides, her knees going weak as they locked around his deltoids. "Twenty minutes? Considering you already rocked my world in about five, I feel like we could get a lot accomplished in that time."

Gabe's easy laugh reverberated through his chest and against her hands. "I'm ready if you are."

She reached up and brushed her lips over his. "I say we do this."

As if anticipating he was about to be ousted, Samson let out a single baritone woof.

"Yeah, we're going to need that chew." Gabe cleared his throat and shot a glance toward the kitchen. "I'll get it and lock him out here. You, uh, want anything? Like your water?"

Olivia pressed her lips together but couldn't stifle her

laugh. "I'm sorry, it's just… How much cardio is this going to involve?"

After a grimace, Gabe was laughing along with her. "Yeah, guess that didn't come out right."

Sensing her nerves had her close to slipping into the out-of-control laughter zone, Olivia took off for the back of the apartment. At the last second, she grabbed her purse in case she needed to dig out the condom that had come in the emergency survival bridesmaid pack she'd gotten from the December wedding she'd been in.

After finding the light switch, she flipped on the light and did a double take. Gabe's room was tidier than she might have guessed. The bed was made, and no clothes were strewn about. But the mattress on the floor, and the sawed-off legs of the nightstand next to it threw her.

Samson's hips, she guessed after spotting a flattened circle in the middle of the bed where the dog likely slept. A smile lit her face. All these things only endeared Gabe to her more.

She slipped off her sandals and, after dropping her purse on the dresser, fished out the condom from the bottom of the side pocket. Clasping it in her palm, she headed to the bed and sank onto the edge of the mattress, her bent knees nearly as high as her shoulders.

She'd hardly given the condom a thought over the last several months, except for the few times she was fishing for change or a package of ibuprofen. Now that there was occasion to make use of it, the words "Nirvana Collection" stood out in stark detail, and her heart thumped with the vigor of a brass band.

Suddenly, Gabe was walking into the room and closing the door behind him, looking exceptionally tall from her spot on the floor. She might as well have been caught with the hot potato by the way her palms began to sweat. *It's too late to hide it now*.

"I, uh, figured we should get the protection talk out of the way right off the bat." She held it up between her thumb and forefinger.

Gabe kicked his shoes off next to hers. Rather than taking a seat beside her, he sank into a squat at the end of the bed, facing her. He locked his hands around the backs of her calves, and she could feel the heat of them even through her stretchy denim jeans.

"Yeah, sure. Nirvana, huh? Looks a little nicer than what I was going to be able to offer on the fly."

"Yeah, well, it was in a bridesmaid gift awhile back."

He nodded. "I'm good with that. Wearing it, I mean. And about the bed. In case it comes across a little teenage boy, there was a frame and box spring till last fall when it got too hard for Samson to get up and down."

She brushed one fingertip over the ridge of his chin, savoring the hint of roughness. "I figured as much."

Suddenly it seemed everything had been said, and it grew quiet enough to hear Samson on the other side of the door chomping on the chew he'd been given.

She swallowed back a laugh that would probably sound a touch hysterical if it slipped out. "Just a heads-up—if you don't start kissing me soon, I think I'm going to lose it."

Gabe didn't need any further encouragement. He leaned forward, and her legs opened reflexively as his body pressed against hers. His mouth met hers in a kiss with pressure as light as when he'd swept his fingers through her hair. Soon their tongues and hunger for more deepened it, and Olivia found herself sinking back onto the mattress.

She was glad when her blood started to boil again and those capable hands caressed her in all the right places, turning the soft heat into an inferno and helping her fight back the three little words that had been doing their best to push to the surface. Three little words that should never be said to someone she'd only known a single week. Three little words that were suddenly the biggest truth she knew, even when they remained unspoken.

He slipped her shirt over her head, and their eyes met. He gifted her with a little wink before his mouth found her neck. Olivia lost her fingers in his hair and wrapped her legs around his hips, pulling him closer. The light was on, and if he looked, he'd see all her imperfections.

But enmeshed in that same feeling that had her wanting to shout out those three words that couldn't be taken back was the confidence that even if he noticed them, he wouldn't care, solidifying their truth even more.

She loved the way he was with his dog and with her. Loved that he'd found his calling in the throes of tragedy. Loved the small cleft in his chin, the sheepish grin that popped up when she didn't expect it, and the brilliance of his bright, playful eyes. Loved listening to the couple of voicemails he'd left when she didn't have her phone and looking at the flowers on her desk that he'd dropped off at school.

And just like she knew she would, when their bodies joined together as one, she loved him even more completely. And for that instant, the only other thought that pressed to the surface was that everything in her life had been leading her to this moment, right now.

Chapter 21

THE CONSTANT DIN OF WEAK MEOWS FILLING THE shelter's small exam room could pass for a badly remixed sound track but was coming from the eight tiger-striped kittens Gabe was examining. In turn, each kitten was making it known how unhappy he or she was about being poked and prodded. They were supposed to be settling down in the blanket in the laundry basket that had been used to bring them in from their kennel in quarantine, but each protesting kitten continued to set off the rest.

It was a lucky thing the kittens were as vocal as they were. Their feral mom had moved them under a broken grate into a shallow storm drain behind a QuikTrip, and an employee had heard their plaintive meows while emptying the trash. Had they not been found and brought to safety, it was likely the drain would have flooded and drowned them when this afternoon's storms rolled in.

Fortunately, a feral cat rescue group had come to their aid. Luckily, with a bit of cunning, the group's members had even been able to catch the anxious mom by luring her into a trap with a heaping bowl of tuna fish. Gabe had already examined her, pulled some blood, and done a fecal exam. The young tortoise-shell cat was a feisty thing, and Gabe wouldn't be surprised if she was feral born. For a nursing wild cat, she had good muscle tone and weight, and as a result, her exceptionally large litter was healthy too. There were two runts who were nearly identical with their darker color patterns and shorter fur. Although names were being tossed about for the rest of the litter, it seemed Abbott and Costello had been decided on for these two.

Costello, whose meow sounded a bit like his head was stuck inside a tin can, fought Gabe's gentle prodding with a fierce determination. "Sorry, little guy." Gabe did his best to get the kitten's temperature on the first try after he finished checking inside his mouth and ears.

"This one's a bit on the anemic side, based on how light his gums are. Just like the other one his size." Gabe glanced at Patrick, who'd become his go-to helper in the exam room when it didn't interfere with Patrick's nearly set-in-stone routine. "He has his share of fleas. They all do, but it seems like I spotted more on him. Since they can't be treated for another week, you'll have to remove them manually. Have you got enough staff for that today?"

After a second of contemplation, Patrick nodded. "There's a woman coming on at two who makes a point of helping to bathe the cats whenever she can."

Gabe pursed his lips. "Interesting woman, I bet, but good timing. Considering the color of his gums, I'd like to see these fleas off him sooner than later. And no soap, as I'm sure you know. Just warm water and a flea comb."

After a nod, Patrick said, "Your girlfriend can help. If she wants to."

"I bet she'd like that, but I'll let her answer that."

"I wasn't asking you to."

Gabe glanced up from Costello, who was just as unhappy at having his belly gently stroked to determine abdominal and intestinal health as he'd been at having his temperature taken. Gabe wasn't sure if he was expecting to spot a touch of indignation on Patrick's face, but it was completely free from it. It seemed, as usual, Patrick was just stating what seemed obvious to him.

He'd never intended on dating someone in his work-place environment, but Gabe didn't mind that everyone here was figuring out he and Olivia were a couple. He was a young, single vet, so it shouldn't have surprised him when a handful of animal-loving women about his age had seemed to have more than an amiable interest in him, both here and at his office. He was hopeful that as word got out he was in a committed relationship, that sort of thing would quiet down.

Gabe and Olivia had just entered their second offi-cial week of dating last night, a Friday night, and they'd celebrated with a trip out to the Missouri wine country where they'd had a relaxing dinner on the patio of the Hawthorne Inn. He couldn't remember being so eager to be around someone he was dating before, with the pos-sible exception of his first girlfriend at seventeen. He'd seen Olivia eight of the last nine days, though two of them had been for mere minutes. One of them had been when he'd dropped her off a surprise lunch at Westbury Middle, and the other time she'd swung by his office before going home with a loaf of vegan zucchini bread she and her aunt had made the night before.

The rest of the times had been actual dates, two of which were supposed to have been quick dinner dates but had turned into three-hour meals. The rest had drawn on longer, culminating at his place and resulting in a lot more treats for Samson. In addition to the Kong, Gabe's freezer was now stocked with a couple packages of doggie "ice cream" cups—a blend of Greek yogurt, bananas, and peanut butter—that bought them almost the same amount of time as the Kong.

And his sawed-off nightstand was now stocked with a much bigger variety of condoms and a eucalyptus massage oil that about sent him over the edge each time he applied it to Olivia's supple body.

As crazy as he was about her, it shouldn't have come as much of a surprise that his sex drive had kicked into hyperdrive. Clamping a tight lid on his libido the last five years to get through vet school and enmesh himself in a new practice certainly hadn't caused any harm now that he was active again. Thankfully, Olivia was matching him stride for stride when it came to the desire to find new ways to keep Samson busy on the other side of his bedroom door.

Finished with Costello's exam, Gabe returned him to the basket of roly-poly, uncoordinated kittens. After a few wobbly strides, the kitten collapsed next to his creamy-colored, much bigger sister and began to lick his paw with what came across as a clear look of indignation.

"These last two could use another few cc's of formula three times a day, assuming Mom keeps allowing them to nurse. Now that she's hydrated and eating her share, her milk production should pick up. Still, with eight mouths to feed, it'll be good to keep a watch on all of them. You know the signs of anemia?"

Patrick nodded. "Pale gums, lethargy, loose stools, high pulse."

"Sounds like you've got it covered. Considering the litter size, you're fine to supplement the rest with formula if you feel the need... You guys know how to raise kittens."

"Yes, there've been three litters so far this year. Last year, there were nine, two of which were bottle-fed."

Gabe peeled off his gloves. "Any others today?"

Patrick shook his head. "This is the last for today."

"Then I guess I'll see you Tuesday."

"If you want to stick around, there's a film crew expected in fifteen minutes. Do you remember Pepper, the Rottweiler who was one of the rescued fighting dogs from the Sabrina Raven estate?"

"Yeah. She was adopted awhile back, right? She was one of the first dogs I examined here. Sweet-natured dog."

"Yes," Patrick replied with a single nod of his head. "She's being honored for her bravery."

Gabe was about to ask for clarification when Patrick lifted the basket of kittens off the table and headed out of the room.

With a shrug, Gabe headed out as well. He didn't mind hanging around to see for himself, especially with Olivia here.

Although she hadn't planned on it, she'd ended up sleeping over last night. It hadn't made sense to head back to her aunt's at midnight, then turn around and drive back to the shelter this morning. Gabe had done nothing but welcome this next step, especially when she made it a point to let Samson in the room after they'd exhausted themselves with a few rounds of intercourse that topped out as their best yet. "I don't mind cuddling with you so Samson can have his usual spot," she'd said, sliding under the sheets next to him after coming out of the bathroom.

After enjoying bachelor life so long, he was surprised by how easy it was to welcome in this new phase. It was too early to say it aloud, but as far as Gabe was concerned, she could sleep over indefinitely. In addition to getting to lose himself inside her as the first rays of sunlight filtered through the blinds in the east window, there'd been the intimacy of showering together, then scrounging through his picked-over pantry contents to assemble a breakfast of the last of the oatmeal, some stale Honey Nut Cheerios, and a smoothie made from a very ripe banana and a bag of blueberries she'd found in the bottom of the freezer. Tomorrow, he had every intention of doing some serious restocking.

When he'd left for his office at a quarter to eight, she'd headed out to the park with Samson. Her shift at the shelter hadn't started till ten o'clock, and she'd be here through three today.

He'd gotten a glimpse of her taking out one of the dogs awhile ago but had stuck to the business at hand. In addition to the new cat and her kittens, he'd done physicals on the six new dogs that had come in this week. Now that he'd finished up for the day, he figured he wouldn't be skirting any duties by hanging out with her for a while. With no animals in critical condition staying overnight, he didn't need to head back to the office today.

After a quick scope of the kennel area without finding her, Gabe headed through the back door and outside under the mostly sunny midday skies. He spotted her long, red hair right away. Her back was to him, and she was a few hundred feet away in the new training pen behind the play area. Tess was out back as well, supervising two Labs in the nearby play area.

Even from where he stood, he could tell the Labs had some energy to dispense. They were chasing each other with enough exuberance that he heard the impact when they crashed.

Not to his surprise, Olivia was in the pen with Morgan, reminding of him of what Megan, the director, had said earlier about Morgan only having eyes for her. "Do you think he's the jealous type?" Gabe asked, stopping outside the gate.

Olivia looked over, and a happy smile lit her face. "Hey there! And no, I wouldn't go so far as to say he's the jealous type, but if dogs can have OCD, he's definitely a candidate. His focus is out of this world."

"Too many birds nearby?"

"Not today. He's decided he likes these salmon-flavored treats. A lot. Watch."

Gabe hung by the gate as Olivia walked through a series of basic commands, successfully getting the long-legged, floppy-eared pointer to sit, stay, shake, and come. And the whole time, Morgan's attention was unwavering, just like when he was a stalking a bird.

"Don't you just love him?"

"He's something. And Megan was right. He's done a one-eighty. Though I suspect it's more him wanting to please you than anything else. The way he was acting two weeks ago, I wouldn't have thought he'd bond with anyone without a struggle. And certainly not this quickly."

Finished with the commands, Olivia walked over to open the gate and waved him inside. "Missed you."

"Missed you too." He planted a light kiss against her lips as he stepped in. "And nice training skills. I would never guess you're just learning this stuff too."

"Thanks. It's got to help to have such a smart dog to practice on."

"He is smart, isn't he? Smart enough to make a good search-and-rescue dog. Young enough too."

Morgan stepped over and gave Gabe's jeans, shoes, and hands a thorough sniff. Gabe wondered if the dog knew he'd been the one to pull him from the pen during the flood. His guess was that he would, but who knew, especially considering the dog's state at the time. After a thorough sniff, Morgan refocused on Olivia, looking from her to the treat pouch clipped to her waist.

Olivia gave Gabe a curious look. "Are you thinking about doing that again with another dog?"

"I haven't given it much thought, but maybe some-day. After Samson... You know. I don't think I could bring myself to leave him at home while I went out to do that with another dog. Too many memories. I can't remember if I told you, but we logged over three hun-dred miles of real-time searches and another few hun-dred in training."

"I can understand why you'd want to wait." She sank onto her heels, and Morgan stepped forward to sniff her hair and the side of her neck.

"Olivia, if he's the dog for you, you just need to make it happen."

"How?" There was a pitch in her voice, and she cleared her throat.

"Talk to your aunt."

She gave a light shake of her head. "I can't. She's been so generous letting me stay. And me not bringing in a pet was her only rule."

"You don't think she'd make an exception?"

Still on her heels at Morgan's side, Olivia glanced up at Gabe, then back at the dog as she stroked one long, silky ear. "She loves that bird of hers. And Coco was a giant mess when she was rescued from the house where she lived before—mostly from being antagonized by the other animals living with her."

"That's no surprise, though with the right training, most birds can live comfortably with dogs or cats in the house. Think it would help if you kept them apart?"

Olivia's expression was as hopeful as it was somber. Leaning closer to the dog, she draped her hands around his thick neck and pulled him close. The doting dog stepped closer and wagged his short tail.

"If there was a way to work it out...I'd like that. A lot." With her face pressed into Morgan's neck, her words were muffled.

With a wave of nerves snaking across his gut, Gabe took a leap. "If it helps, with the problems Samson's been having on the stairs, you can let her know I'm overdue to start looking for a new place. I decided for certain not to renew my lease. And whatever I get, I'd, uh, like to make sure it accommodates more than me and Samson comfortably."

Even in the shade, he noticed a hint of color darken Olivia's cheeks. When she didn't say anything, he continued.

"It may not be anything to write home about, with

my loans and the debt I'm taking on by taking over Dr. Washington's practice, but I'm tired of leasing. I've been thinking I could have your sister show me some houses. When she's not out with Yun showing her every possible commercial space on the market, that is. I think they're seeing twenty buildings today alone. Yun keeps texting me pictures of all the places that would never work."

Olivia let out a huff of laughter and stood up, sweeping her hair back from her face. "My sister texted me a picture of their list. It's impressive. I know she'd be all over showing you some houses, and I bet Samson would love that."

"What about you?"

She pressed her lips together and seemed to study his face for all the things he wasn't saying. "I'd, uh, really like that too."

He reached for her hand and squeezed it in his. "You know, *I* like that you'd like that."

That remarkable smile of hers returned as the mood lightened. "Goof."

He shrugged. "Goof, huh? I guess that shoe fits. But a gluttonous amount of sex and cuddling can do that to you. Trust me; I learned it in vet school."

Her eyes went wide, and she shot a look across the pen toward the play area where Tess was corralling the spazzy Labs. She dropped her voice, but the smile didn't leave her eyes. "I really don't want everyone here knowing I'm having a gluttonous amount of sex with their new vet, if we can help it. And you didn't *really* learn that in vet school, did you?"

"No," he said, chuckling. "The opposite actually. You've heard of Maslow's hierarchy of needs, right?"

"Yeah, back in college."

"I guess it's the curse of self-actualization, but human beings tend to rule the roost when it comes to gluttony. Animals hardly ever obsess when it comes to reproduction, though I did have a woman come in with a Yorkshire terrier this week who wouldn't stop humping one of her stuffed toys."

Olivia shook her head, laughing. "Now that's a visual I'll have a hard time getting out of my head. What did you tell her to do?"

"I told her to get rid of the toy, first off. Secondly, she's upping the dog's exercise regimen to tire her out. We're looking at some diet changes too."

Olivia pointed a finger his way. "Is this your way of telling me that you're suggesting *we* up our exercise routines?"

"Ah, that's a hard no. I can't say I've ever been as happy with the status quo as I am right now."

A second light blush colored Olivia's cheeks as she stepped in for a hug. "Me too, Gabe Wentworth."

Gabe locked his hands around her hips and pulled her against him, smashing her small treat pouch between them. "God, you smell good. Have I told you that?"

Her lips brushed against his neck. "Five or six times a day maybe. But thank you."

Suddenly, two big paws plopped on Gabe's arm and shoulder, and Morgan was staring him down, his look more curious than threatening.

"In case you were wondering if we attract dogs with jealous streaks… Down, boy." To encourage him, Gabe stepped to the side. When all four paws were on the ground again, Gabe pulled a treat from his pocket and gave it to Morgan along with a hearty pat on the shoulder. "Good boy."

From down in the play area, Tess could be heard yelling their way over the barks of the now-leashed Labs she was cajoling out of the play yard. "Hey, guys, I just spotted the news crew about to pull in."

"Cool! We're coming," Olivia yelled back. She reached for the leash hanging by the side of the gate. "Come on, Morgan. Back to your kennel. Hopefully we can go on a quick walk before I leave for the day."

"So, what's going on with the Rottweiler and the news crew? Patrick mentioned something but didn't elaborate. No surprise there."

"I'm surprised you didn't hear about it. It's been all over social media the last couple days. It turns out Pepper's a hero, and since she was adopted out of here a couple months ago, Channel 3 wanted to film the interview here." She clipped on Morgan's leash, and Gabe opened the gate to let them file out first.

"What'd she do, save a baby? Rotts are always saving kids."

"I've heard they have a good reputation as babysitters. Not this time. Her new owner took her for a walk and didn't lock the house. When she got back, Pepper started acting all weird and followed a scent trail straight to a hall closet where some creep was hiding. Thankfully, she was barking adamantly enough that the owner stepped outside to call the police with the closet door still closed."

Gabe shook his head in wonder. "What a story. Though I shouldn't be surprised. I remember that dog pretty well. Seemed like she had a great temperament."

"That's what I've heard. According to Patrick, her story's outperforming the video link of your rescue of Morgan, and that one was the best-performing post in three months."

"Between me and you, I won't be sad to slip back into anonymity."

Olivia leaned in against his shoulder as they neared Tess and the Labs. Considering the two playful dogs together likely outweighed her, Tess was doing an impressive job of keeping them in line.

"Want a hand?" Gabe asked.

"If you could just get the door. Thanks."

Gabe jogged ahead and pulled open the back door.

Tess filed in with her dogs first. "I'm so excited to see Pepper again." She gave a little shrug of her shoulders. "She's one of my all-time favorites. Dogs are a lot like tea leaves that soak into the heart, I guess. Some of them leave behind a stronger wash of color than others."

"If that's not a quote on a tea tag somewhere, it should be," Gabe said.

When Olivia added that she couldn't agree more, he knew the direction she'd be looking even before glancing her way.

As if to prove canine hearts could be colored just as easily, Morgan paused before stepping into the building to glance back at Olivia as if in reassurance she was only a step or two behind.

And considering the way he felt about Samson, Gabe would never be one to argue with a statement like that.

Chapter 22

CONSIDERING IT WAS ONLY HER THIRD OFFICIAL DAY volunteering, Olivia figured the moments of awe that kept washing over her were to be expected. Even so, the High Grove Animal Shelter was so much more than simply a place to adopt a pet. She'd heard enough remarkable second- and even third- or fourth-chance rescue stories to have been more deeply moved than she'd have imagined possible. But beyond rescue and adoption, the shelter was a place of connection.

She was already losing track of how many families had popped in with previously adopted pets to grab something from the gift shop or simply to say hi and share their post-adoption training successes. The shelter was a popular spot for other reasons, too, like the birthday parties and training classes that seemed to go on several times a week.

And even knowing this, Olivia was still in awe witnessing the group of people who'd congregated in the front room as the two-person news crew set up for filming. Pepper, the stout Rottweiler, clearly had a special place in many hearts. She'd been one of nearly forty confiscated dogs from a large-scale fighting ring last fall.

Tess, who was standing next to Olivia, said, "Obviously we're all about spaying and neutering, considering how many animals are still put to sleep each year, but she was pregnant when she came in. I was lucky enough to be there when she delivered her pups."

"That must've been something."

"It really was. And she was a great mom."

Pepper looked completely relaxed being in the shelter again, and she didn't seem affected by the small group of people gathering around her. Mostly, the sweet-looking dog just appeared to have eyes for her owner, a middle-aged woman with striking silvery-gray hair.

The Channel 3 reporter, a twentysomething brunette, was giving the owner a rundown of how the interview would likely go once they started filming. "I'm thinking of 'from disposable to indispensable' as a tagline. Of course, *we* know she was never disposable, but clearly the people who wanted to fight her thought so, and I like the way it brings the story full circle."

Pepper's owner, who was tugging nervously on her zipper, nodded. "Makes sense to me."

"Great. And I know what a hard time this must be for you. The man who broke in was carrying a knife, and without your dog..." She broke off and shuddered. "I can only imagine. I know my producer spoke to you about keeping the focus on the dog, and we'll do that, but I just want you to know that wherever your emotions take you during filming is fine. If you don't like how something comes out, we'll film it again. And when we're done, we'll go outside and do some mock footage of you arriving and Pepper getting out of your car. Maybe let her sniff around the parking lot. This was her home for what...?" She glanced at Megan, but Patrick answered.

"She was here for twenty-three days. If you count

her time at what used to be our off-site property, it was a hundred and thirteen days total."

Patrick's directness clearly caused the reporter to do a double take. "A hundred and thirteen days. How about we round up to four months?"

As the reporter continued to run through the basics, attempting to ease the nerves of Pepper's owner, Olivia's attention was caught by two women standing nearby waiting for the interview to begin—but they weren't paying any attention to the reporter, Pepper, or her owner. They were whispering to each other and had sly looks on their faces as they checked out something or someone in the rear of the room.

Curious what had their attention, Olivia followed their gaze and felt a shot of alarm when she realized it was Gabe they were staring at. At least, she was almost certain it was Gabe. They'd gotten separated a few minutes ago when Fidel had pulled him to the side to ask something about one of the older cats.

He and Fidel had finished up with whatever they were discussing and were watching the interview preparations like everyone else. And there was enough distance between Gabe and Fidel that Olivia felt convinced that it was one hundred percent Gabe who had the women's attention.

Her heart thumped a touch faster. One of them was facing in Olivia's direction, and even though she did her best not to stare, she couldn't help but watch the woman's lips to see if she could catch what she was saying. "I could make a meal of that, no question."

The words were just loud enough to make out a few of them, but watching her lips, Olivia felt confident she'd understood most of it. Palms sweating and blood rushing to her face, she looked away. Maybe that wasn't what the woman had said at all. Who was she kidding? *It was, and you know it.*

Olivia took a calculated breath, trying her best to refocus. Who cared if some woman wanted to make a meal of Gabe?

The truth of it was, *she* cared. Her thoughts flashed to early this morning when he'd found release inside her, and she'd savored the way the muscles along his torso tensed as he rode it out. She'd not known she could want someone the way she wanted him.

Those women probably didn't know he had a girl-friend, and they certainly didn't know his girlfriend was eavesdropping on their conversation, she told herself. Olivia could feel the heat rising up her neck and the sweat blossoming on her palms.

Before she knew what was happening, the two women headed to the back of the room, planting themselves in front of Gabe and Fidel.

Even from fifteen feet away and in a crowd of other people, Olivia heard enough to make her stomach flip. "We just wanted to tell you how moved we were by that amazing rescue of yours." They sounded like chatter-ing birds in mating season, introducing themselves and gawking over how terrible it would've been if he hadn't broken through the bolt in time.

Olivia cleared her throat and did her best to focus as the reporter ushered Pepper and her owner into position.

"It gets easier after awhile," Tess said, offering her a sympathetic smile. "Believe me."

"I don't..." But she stopped herself. She knew, and

clearly Tess knew too. The thing was, Tess's tone was lined with both compassion and understanding. Olivia had heard that Tess, the newest shelter employee, was dating the Red Birds' third basemen. For the most part, Gabe was just getting proposals in the comments section of a YouTube video. Tess was dating an *actual* celebrity. "Thanks, Tess. Everything's just happening so fast, you know?"

"It's been my experience that some of the things that matter most hit you before you even realize they're happening."

Olivia forced her shoulders to relax. "I won't disagree with you there."

"And if it helps," Tess said, dropping her voice, "there've been girls here doing their best to flirt with him ever since Dr. Washington first introduced him. But until you, I never spotted an ounce of flirt coming off him in return."

Olivia brushed Tess's arm. "Thanks. That sounds like him, but it's nice to hear it from someone else. And honestly, I get it. You can't blame a girl for trying."

She was about to ask about Mason, Tess's boyfriend, but all of a sudden everyone was getting quiet and Pepper was being asked to sit for a treat as the cameraman panned in on a close-up of her. The laid-back dog munched a treat and wagged her nubbin of a tail in hopes of another as the reporter dove into her story, making quick work of bringing her tagline into her spiel early.

Suddenly, Olivia felt a hand close over her low back, and Gabe was stepping in at her other side. She glanced up to a quick wink before he focused on the interview in progress.

The last of the doubt and insecurity that had been
threatening to rock her off her axis ebbed away. Other
women wanting to make a meal of her boyfriend didn't
have to become a flaw in their relationship. Not if Olivia
refused to let it. And being the recipient of such easy
devotion made that a whole lot easier.

Chapter 23

GABE HAD JUST FINISHED A MOLAR EXTRACTION ON A Greyhound and was drying his hands after scrubbing down when he heard his phone vibrating on the shelf above the sink. By the time his hands were dry, he'd missed the call.

Picking up the phone, he saw two missed calls from Yun and three texts.

10:58 Hey. Call ASAP.

11:43 What? Are you in surgery or something?

12:51 Gabe.This.Is.Torture.

What's gotten in your head now? He stepped out of the scrub room and out the back door of the building onto the sorry excuse for a patio at the back of the building. Even if the broken concrete and privacy trellis were repaired, the commotion, smells, and noises of the shopping mall his office backed onto weren't going to change, leaving compelling enough reasons for the patio's continued neglect.

"Where's the fire, Yun?" he said when she picked up.

"I take it you were in surgery? When's your lunch break?"

"Ah, now, I guess. And yes, I was."

"Anything good?"

"A molar extraction—the four-o-nine. And some of the surrounding bone."

"My heart weeps with envy at all the things you get to do by yourself. I spent the last three hours of my day shaving and prepping animals for surgeries I haven't even been brought in on."

"Is that what you called to tell me?"

"No, but you took too long. My break's over. Now I'm getting ready to shave the balls of a hairy cairn terrier so he can get the old snip-snip."

Gabe chuckled. "I'll think about that as I shove down the sandwich one of my techs just picked up for me. Wait, what am I saying? No, I won't."

"Yeah, well, I wouldn't be thinking of me if I could help it either. Listen, I only have a minute. What time do you get off?"

"I should be finished around five. Why?"

"Do you have date with Olivia tonight?"

"Yeah. Again, why?"

"Because I want to show you something. It won't take long. Forty-five minutes max. Bring her along. Chances are she'll know about it before you do."

"Know about what?"

There was a rustling sound, followed by silence. A few seconds later, Yun was back. "I gotta run," she whispered. "I'm supposed to be in the prep room, and I just got the stare-down from Godzilla Lady. Meet me at High Grove when you get off, okay?"

Gabe agreed—to no idea what—and hung up. Before calling Olivia to confirm she was fine switching things up for a bit to start out their night, he spent a minute

searching for ball emojis and sent off a quick parade of
tennis balls, basketballs, and a round, furry purple grem-
lin emoji to Yun. When she didn't respond, he figured
she already had her hands full.

Whatever it was his friend had in mind for tonight,
he had a strange feeling that it was going to turn out to
be something good.

———⁓———

"I'm starting to think about switching careers." Olivia
transferred her phone to the other hand to adjust
Samson's leash.

"Seriously?" Ava asked on the other end of the line,
clearly too immersed in packing her stuff to pick up
on the sarcasm in Olivia's tone. "You've only been a
teacher for a year." Her words were nearly drowned out
by the high-pitched, sticky sound of packing tape being
unrolled across a box.

"I'm thinking I might make it as a lady-in-waiting,
since that's all I seem to be doing anymore."

"Oh, that was sarcasm, I see. Have you really got
grounds to complain? You've just hooked up with the
perfect guy."

"This isn't about a guy."

After she finished prepping for tomorrow's classes
at the end of the school day and still had time to kill
before meeting Gabe, Olivia had texted him that she'd
be happy to take Samson for a walk. He'd given her the
door code on their second date, but it was still something she wouldn't have done without his permission.
Luckily, he hadn't been in surgery and had texted back
that doing so would be great.

Since she still had a half hour before she needed to leave to meet Gabe and Yun at the shelter for who knew what, she headed with Samson toward Tower Grove Park.

"It'd be weird if it was, considering it's obvious you're crazy about him. I mean, you're even walking his dog before a date."

"That's because I happen to be crazy about his dog too."

"So, what's this lady-in-waiting thing about then?"

"I can't stand not knowing if I have a chance at a position next year. Principal Garcia told the few of us who aren't guaranteed to return that she'd let us know by last Friday. Now it's Tuesday and still no word. Then on top of that, there's Aunt Becky. I asked her about keeping Morgan there till I figure things out, and apparently she's thinking about it."

"Do you have any reason to talk to her?"

"Aunt Becky?"

"No. Your principal." Loud clattering on Ava's end made Olivia wonder if her sister was using an adequate amount of packing paper. "Crap," she mumbled into the receiver.

"Not really. Maybe. My last-hour kids are putting together a proposal to do an end-of-year supply drive for the shelter. Once it's finished, I will."

Samson lumbered along as they headed deeper into the park along a pedestrian trail. He hoisted a back leg to pee on a light post, then hoisted it again in another two feet to mark a LEASHED DOGS ONLY sign.

With the late-afternoon sun warming her back and a picture-perfect view at every turn, Olivia was in no hurry to urge him along. She'd known the park would be incredible in full spring, and it was. Brilliantly colored flower beds lined fountains and mulch islands, and the redbuds were in full bloom.

"Well, I suggest you help those kids finish it up and get in there," Ava said. "Once you're face-to-face, just ask if there's anything she can tell you about next year's openings."

"That's actually a good idea."

"I'll pretend I didn't hear the 'actually.' And I know you like it there, but any other callbacks?"

"Not a one. I think it would be different if I could get a year or two of experience at one school. Switching midyear like that in my first year out of Teach for America didn't do any favors for my résumé."

"You shouldn't be dinged for taking temporary positions."

"My thoughts exactly."

Ava was starting up about all the junk Wes had accumulated in their basement storage when another call came in on Olivia's line.

"Oh crap, Ava. Someone's calling from Westbury Middle. I'll call you back."

Olivia switched over without waiting for Ava to respond and offered up her perkiest hello.

"Olivia Graham?"

"Yes, this is her." *Or is it* she? *Damn, I can never remember.*

"Olivia, this is Principal Garcia. Am I interrupting anything?"

As Samson pulled in his haunches to take an impressively sized poop, Olivia replied that she wasn't.

"I wanted to apologize for the delay in getting

back to you about next year's returning teachers. I suspect a couple of you have been waiting on pins and needles."

"I'm sure it's a complicated process." Her ribs seemed to be locking tight around her heart. It was Principal Garcia's tone—stiff and formal. Olivia knew before she said it. This wasn't good news.

"The thing is, we're such a small school that we have to make the most accurate call we can when it comes to anticipated class sizes for the next school year."

The ground at Olivia's feet began to spin. All those desperate hopes toppled like a row of dominoes even before she spoke again, confirming her fears.

"We were close to being able to add another group of core classes for our eighth graders, but we can't do it. I'm sorry I'm not calling with better news."

Olivia stumbled through a few minutes of awkward conversation. She'd come close but not close enough.

Samson had finished taking his poop and turned to look at her as if to ascertain why she'd not yet begun to bag it like every other poop he'd ever made. But Olivia's feet were frozen in place, worse than in those dreams in which she really wanted to run but couldn't make herself do it for the life of her.

"Everything will be announced officially tomorrow." Principal Garcia's words had gotten high and soft. Far away. "I wanted to tell you personally. You've done a remarkable job with our students and acclimating to our school. If a position opens up next spring, I hope you'll apply. In the meantime, I'm happy to give you my highest recommendation."

Somehow, Olivia managed to thank her and keep the

tears of frustration and disappointment at bay. She hung up and fished the pet waste bag from her back pocket on autopilot. Instead of stepping forward to bag it, she folded over, bracing her hands against her knees, the less-than-pleasant smell wafting across her nose, making her even closer to being sick than she already was.

"Oh shit. Total shit." She looked at Samson and he gave a single wag of his tail, his head cocked as he watched her. "Total, total shit."

Chapter 24

BY THE TIME GABE PULLED INTO THE SHELTER parking lot at a quarter after five, he spotted Ava's Jeep, Yun's Corolla, and Olivia's Cruze parked in the lot along with the cars of a few staff members. He was heading for the entrance when he heard someone calling him from the narrow strip of woods off to the side of the property.

Suspecting there might be a loose dog, Gabe jogged over. "Everything okay?" He was taken a touch off guard when he found Olivia, Ava, and Yun all at varying degrees of depth inside the woods. Yun was the farthest in, pushing through thick cedar branches; Olivia wasn't far behind her; and Ava, in a pair of heels and dress pants, was hanging back on the edge of the grass.

"Everything's fine," Ava said as the other two headed out. "Just doing a quick round of geocaching."

"Really?"

"No." She gave a soft laugh as she joined him at the curb. With a flip of her hand, she sent her long black hair tumbling over her shoulder. "Fair warning. I tend to lay on the sarcasm as thick as mascara. Olivia says it's a defense mechanism for avoiding the scars of my youth."

When her words left Gabe a touch dumbfounded, she added, "We're just doing some brainstorming."

Although her hair color and skin tone were starkly different from Olivia's, their similarities in face shape were undeniable, which made it tempting to assume he knew her better than he did.

"With the exception of the little gulch, this seems like the best spot for a cut through," Yun said as she and Olivia stepped out from the last of the overgrowth. "But Gabe was an Eagle Scout. He could put up a bridge over that in a weekend."

"I never made it that far in scouting, remember, but thanks for the vote of confidence. A cut through to what?" he asked, giving Olivia a wink in hello.

She smiled, but it didn't seem to reach her eyes and he could swear he detected a hint of tension on her face, making him wonder what might be going through her head. He closed off the distance between them and pulled her in for a one-armed hug and pressed a kiss onto her forehead. "Missed you," he said, dropping his voice.

She leaned into him, releasing a soft sigh. "Missed you too."

Noticing a cobweb she'd picked up, Yun tramped around, waving off the parts clinging to her hair and clothes. "To the property next door."

"To the jewelry store? What would be the point? I heard that guy hates this place."

"I heard that too," Olivia said.

"I hadn't." Ava swatted away an invisible gnat or mosquito flying by her face, making Gabe wonder if she was triggered by Yun's cobweb-removal endeavor. As far as he could tell, the late-afternoon skies were bug-free.

"But after meeting him," she added, "I can't say he came across as the animal-loving type either. Honestly, it'd probably be safe to go with not the loving type in general. But if that's the case, I'll make sure not to draw any undue attention to your connection here."

"Are you saying the jewelry store's for sale?"

"The building's about to go on the market," Ava confirmed for him. "From what I gathered, the merchandise is being returned or liquidated. He's got some nice stuff. If he has a sale, I'm there."

Finished extracting herself from the cobweb, Yun planted herself a couple feet in front of him. "It's perfect, Gabe. Just the square footage we're looking for, and we wouldn't have to do that much remodeling. And you know what they say about location." With a touch of dramatic flair, she waved a hand toward the shelter.

"We?" Gabe gave her his best skeptical look. "I don't remember saying I'm a hundred percent sold on this idea of yours."

Yun shot the look right back. "Not a hundred percent, but you did say you'd broached the concept with Dr. Washington again and thought you'd made some headway. I've known you for nearly five years. That's as close to a yes as you get without a considerable amount of poking and prodding." Yun closed a hand over one side of her mouth and whispered to Olivia. "Just a hint for you, Olivia." Louder, she added, "Besides, once it sinks in what it could mean to open a business together right next door to this incredible place, you're going to be on board. I know it."

"You've seen inside?"

"We came at lunch. And it's the twenty-third property Ava and I've looked at. I've got a good base with which to measure it."

Gabe looked at Olivia. "Did you know this?"

"Not until I pulled up. I think my sister was going for the surprise factor."

Gabe gave a conciliatory shrug. "So are we just scoping out the side yard, or is there any chance you made a second appointment?"

"We've got an appointment," Ava said, "and fair warning, the owner's going to be there because he isn't comfortable not being there to guard his merchandise while potential buyers are in his store. Despite a security system." She cocked her head. "Which gives us a fresh opportunity to show him we can play hardball. So do your best to keep that skeptical look slapped on a little longer."

Yun stepped forward and poked him in the chest good-naturedly. "Ava's not kidding. He may have spotted me dancing in the parking lot after we left earlier. So give us your crankiest, most skeptical, this'll-never-work Gabe vibe. Even when you realize how perfect it is."

Gabe held up his hands in mock surrender and turned to Olivia. "Have I mentioned that Yun has a flair for the dramatic?"

Olivia clasped a hand over her chest, laughing, and this time her laughter reached her eyes, which sent a wave of happiness through him. "I'm not weighing in on this. Besides, she already had me at hello with a location that's next door to the shelter."

As they headed back into the parking lot, they caught the attention of Patrick, who was almost to his truck, keys in hand. Although he said nothing, he gave them a dubious look.

"We're on a mission to check out the jewelry store," Gabe offered.

Patrick looked from Gabe to Olivia and nodded. "The sidewalk would be an easier walking route."

"Yeah, it seems so."

At this point, it seemed premature to say anything more about their purpose for visiting the store, so Gabe let it drop. If Patrick thought he was in the market to buy Olivia some jewelry, it was fine with him—certainly less complicated than starting premature rumors about the possibility of relocating his office next door.

"Patrick, I can't remember if you've met Yun or Ava. Ava is Olivia's sister, and I went to vet school with Yun. I gave her a tour a few months ago."

Patrick glanced from Yun to Ava, then stared at the asphalt as he nodded. "Yes. To both."

"It's nice to see you again, Patrick." Ava spoke first, and Yun chimed in in agreement.

"You as well." After a swift nod, he added, "Good evening," and got in his truck without another word.

"Think it'll be weird if the owner sees us walking over?" Yun asked as they took off across the parking lot.

"A little, but he might assume we street parked," Ava said.

They headed across the parking lot and fell into twos at the sidewalk, Ava and Olivia in front. They were of equal height, except that Ava was in two-inch heels. Olivia was in jeans and a pair of unassuming Top-Sider shoes. Ava's walk was not without a touch of swagger, while Olivia's reminded him of someone who was just stepping into her confidence—tall, straight, and purposeful—which he realized was one more thing about her that moved him.

By the time they were halfway across the jewelry-store parking lot, Gabe spotted an older man staring out a wide bay window. Like the shelter, the jewelry store was a brick, single-story building, but this one had a steeper peak in the roof and more windows along the front.

Yun's right, he realized, a rush of excitement surging through his veins. He'd helped at a few big shelter events this winter that had drawn crowds that spilled off shelter property. And whenever customers had realized he was the shelter's primary vet, they'd asked for his contact information. He could only imagine how much new business he and Yun could get if they were right next door.

They stepped through polished double-glass doors into the main showroom, which was lined with cases of jewelry.

"Olivia and Gabe, this is Mr. Bouchard," Ava said. "Thanks for letting everyone have a second look around today. Lots to think about, as I'm sure you know."

At best guess, Mr. Bouchard was nearing seventy, though there was a cloudiness in his gaze and an ashiness to his skin tone and that didn't do him any favors. He was lean, had once been tall but was now stooped across the upper back and shoulders, and had a thick magnifying headband resting atop his head.

Gabe shook his hand.

Ava clapped her hands against her thighs. "So, if you don't mind, we'll leave you to your work, and we'll have a look around."

"As you wish. I have security cameras in every room."

As if anticipating Gabe was being triggered, Yun shot him a "be nice" look. Not that he needed it. He didn't care what a crotchety, old jeweler thought of him. What he cared about was figuring out if Yun was on to something here. His pulse was racing as he took in the building's features: thick molding, newer windows, hardwood flooring that had just enough dings and stains to add a touch of character and forgiveness to the possibility of countless paws traversing it day in and day out.

Olivia was quiet, taking everything in, as was Yun, though her eyes were big in that way they got when she was plotting out graphs and flow charts in her head. Not that Gabe blamed her. His mind was racing too. He'd never been one to brag about his imagination, but he had easy visuals of customers seated with their pets near the windows up front, fresh, bright coats of paint refreshing the muted burgundy walls, blown-up pictures of clients' pets decorating the place, and a registration counter in place of the main display case. And they could have fun going all out to make it as welcoming as the shelter.

"What's the square footage?" he asked Ava.

"Just over two thousand square feet. Yun said your current place is a little under thirteen hundred?"

"Yeah."

"There are two rooms behind this one that could be used for appointments, and another two in back that could be converted into pre-op and op rooms," Yun said.

About ready to pace the room in excitement, Gabe remembered he'd been tasked with coming across as skeptical, so he folded his arms over his chest instead. "What are your thoughts about all this space up front?"

"It's a lot of space for a waiting room and reception area," Yun agreed, "but we could build out another two appointment rooms along the side here. Three even, if we keep them on the small side."

"Yeah, or we could keep it to two and save room to separate out the dogs and cats as they're waiting."

Noticing Yun was starting to glow with excitement, he shot her a look. Mr. Bouchard wasn't just listening as he hung behind the counters, seemingly doing inventory of his stock. He kept throwing suspicious glances in their direction. "Just keep in mind, all that costs money," Gabe added. "Might not be feasible to do all that work when the place you looked at yesterday wouldn't require half the up-front investment."

As if she couldn't decipher whether or not he was bluffing, Yun frowned, her eyebrows knotting into peaks. "I swear, Gabe, sometimes you forget to see the possibilities."

"I see possibilities; this place is a diamond in the rough. The question is how much are you willing to spend to get it into the shape that would work for us?"

Suddenly Yun seemed to remember the role with which he'd been charged and nodded. "You're right. I'll put some comparison charts together tonight."

Across the way, Mr. Bouchard didn't seem to like his store being called a diamond in the rough. He scoffed loudly, then shuffled his paperwork, mumbling something under his breath. All Gabe caught of it was "You can never count on the boy when you need him."

Since he didn't seem to be directing it their way, Gabe opted to ignore it. He headed over to Olivia, who was looking out one of the big side windows at the line of trees that separated this property from the shelter. He could just make out the building through some of the thinner spots in the cedars, hickories, and overgrown honeysuckle bushes.

He closed a hand over her back. "You okay?" Rather than looking at him, she dropped her gaze toward the floor, clueing him in for the second time tonight that something was wrong.

"Yeah, I'm good. I just have a little headache, that's all." After closing her eyes for the space of a few heartbeats, she opened them, and her shoulders dropped an inch or two. "This place is great," she whispered. "Almost too good to be true."

He cupped one hand over the side of her face. "Whatever it is, we'll talk about it in a little bit. Okay?"

"Yeah, okay." A flood of moisture seemed to wash over her eyes but not enough for tears to well up. "That sounds good."

"You know what else? It's not the only thing that's almost too good to be true."

His words seemed to cut through her. He locked a hand around her elbow, but with her sister approaching, heels clicking on the hardwood, Olivia gave a little shake of her head and pasted on a bigger smile that for the second time in a few minutes didn't reach her eyes.

"You two want to check out the back rooms? Or have you seen enough?" Ava asked in a tone that seemed to say she'd picked up on Gabe's quasi disappointment.

Seeing in his peripheral vision that Mr. Bouchard was craning his head in their direction, Gabe shrugged. "Wouldn't hurt to take a look."

Locking Olivia's hand in his, he fell into step behind Ava to check out the rest of the place, even though he knew he already agreed with Yun. He was just as sold on it as she was. If they could make this place work financially, buying it and going into business with her would be the best business decision he could make.

Chapter 25

BY THE TIME THEY'D MADE IT BACK TO THE SHELTER'S parking lot, it was just after six and the lot was empty aside from their cars. Olivia climbed into the passenger seat of Gabe's truck, buckled her seat belt, and tucked her hands under her thighs.

A thousand thoughts swam in her head, some of them wanting to race out her throat more than others. Knowing most of them would lead to having to tell Gabe she'd lost her best hope of a teaching job for next year, she swallowed all of them back and let him scroll through on his phone as he searched for a nearby place to eat.

"What are you in the mood for?" He rubbed two knuckles along the ridge of his chin as he scanned through his choices.

"Some place outside. It's a perfect night."

He was quiet a minute or two, then said, "Got it! Big Sky Café. Locally sourced. Sustainable. Great patio. And not only is it less than a mile from here, it's dog friendly."

"Sounds perfect. You want to go back to your place and grab Samson?"

"Ah, no. He'll be good till we get back. I was thinking maybe what you need right now more than anything is a breakout." He arched an eyebrow, the playful, boyish look in his eyes immediately melting some of her sorrow away.

Olivia bit her lip to keep from laughing as the arched eyebrow morphed into a waggling one. "You're going to have to explain yourself. Because right now I'm having dine-and-dash visions, only I know that's so not you."

He grinned. "Not us. Your dog."

"Morgan?"

"Is there another?"

Olivia scoped the empty lot. "I hate to break it to you, but it's after hours. I don't think we could bring him even if they allowed that sort of thing, which I'm not entirely sure they do."

"I'll text Megan and let her know."

"Don't you think everything's all locked up?"

He slipped his keys from his jeans pocket. "I don't have eight keys on here for nothing. As their vet, I've been granted twenty-four-hour access to this place."

Olivia stayed quiet a few seconds, processing this. "I *so* want to bring him, but you may have more faith in the training I've put in him than is deserved. He only sits for a couple seconds at a time, and when he's excited, he pulls up a storm even in a no-pull harness. And I'm sure he won't be one of those dogs with table manners."

Gabe shrugged. "Gotta start somewhere. What do you say?"

"You don't think Megan will care?" she asked before realizing he was already typing out a text.

"I doubt it. She knows you're giving serious thought to adopting him."

Olivia unbuckled and hopped out of the truck. "I hope you didn't put it like that to her," she said, shutting the door. "I'd adopt him in a heartbeat if I had a place to keep him." *And a job. Don't forget about that.*

The hopeful mood that had begun to build deflated a touch. Determined not to let it ruin what was turning out to be a special night, she did her best to tamp down her fears.

"That's what I meant. And she's met you. She knows."

"Are you saying my love for him is written all over my face?"

"That's a hard yes," he said, jiggling open the door with his key. He waved her in as he opened the door. "Extraordinary women first."

She laughed and pressed a kiss onto his cheek as she stepped inside. When the short kiss wasn't enough to satisfy her, she planted another on his lips but let it linger a touch longer. "Thank you for this."

"You'd better watch it," he said, pulling her close after he let the door fall shut behind him, "or you'll get an entirely different hard yes."

"Mmm...enticing, and we *are* alone." She gave him another kiss, pressing his mouth open with hers and slipping her hands low around his hips.

He ground against her, his growing bulge pressing into her low belly. After drawing out the kiss enough to superheat her blood, he pulled away, closing both hands over the sides of her head. "And here I thought you were sad about something."

She blinked and stepped back, trying to slip back into armor that had shed itself with that kiss.

"I see I wasn't wrong. Want to tell me about it?"

She shook her head. "Not tonight. It's such a good night for you. I just... I'm not ready to talk about it."

His mouth clamped tight, the muscles along his jaw

growing rigid and defined. "If you don't want to talk about it, I'll honor that. But I'm here for you, Olivia. If there's something I can do, then let me do it."

"There's one thing you can do." Her lips found his again, and she kissed him harder than she'd ever kissed him before, that same need she'd experienced in his truck a few weeks ago waking like a long-slumbering giant when it hadn't even been a full day since their bodies had joined together.

She made quick work of the button of his jeans and was slipping one hand into his pants when Trina hopped up onto the closest counter, meowing to get their attention and reminding Olivia they were in the main room of the very shelter where she volunteered.

She scanned through a list of places in here where they'd have a bit more privacy. She gave a second or two of serious thought to the couch in the break room but changed her mind and pulled him toward the staff bathroom instead. The fact was, she wasn't in the space for quiet and contemplative lovemaking. She wanted him standing, and she wanted it hard enough there'd be hope of washing her thoughts and insecurities away.

He was going into business with his best friend right next to this wonderful place. How very close to perfect. If only she had a job to keep herself up here in this new and exciting city. If only there was a way to remain a part of it.

The bathroom was small but clean and cozy enough to serve her needs. He trailed inside after her, and she did her best to ignore the blend of skepticism and intrigue written on his face. She locked the door, shutting out Trina and Chance, who'd just gotten up from his bed, too, and anyone who might swing back by for some unknown reason.

Olivia didn't check, but she was willing to bet the look of skepticism fell away as soon as she sank onto her heels, making deliberate, exaggerated work of unbuttoning his jeans and then savoring him long enough to bring him to the edge of climax. When she knew he was almost there by the saltiness washing over her tongue, she pulled away and tugged out of one leg of her jeans, leaving the other hooked around her ankle.

He wrapped his hands around the backs of her thighs and lifted her, and she locked her legs around his hips. She was thankful when he was able to ride it out long enough to enable her to find a release that matched his. He pressed her against the door, drawing it out through rhythm as the first unexpected tears slid down her face.

Before she knew it, she'd wrapped her arms tightly around his neck and was sobbing into the crook of it even while he was still inside her.

Freeing one hand, he swept back her hair and brushed his lips over her wet tears. "Whatever it is, we've got this. *Whatever* it is. You'll never be able to convince me otherwise, because I love you, Olivia Graham. More than I ever thought I could love anyone. And I'm damn sure that's all that matters."

She wanted to say it back, wanted to tell him she'd felt the same way for a while now. Almost from the very beginning. But the fears and sorrow swelling inside her locked her throat too tight for words. Instead, her tears colored his shirt like drops of wet paint. So many that she feared the release of them might sweep her away.

The color of the sky in the west had Gabe wishing for a view not blocked by buildings and tall trees. From what he could see of it, the western sky was a wash of brilliant oranges and soft reds. He remembered camping with his family as a kid of about nine or ten in Grand Canyon National Park, watching the sun sink below the horizon from the South Rim. He'd been bored and fidgety and not interested in hanging around for half an hour to see the sunset. But even at that age, his hands sore from spinning in circles around the metal railing as he waited, there was a moment when the sun finally dipped below the horizon and everything got quiet—and he felt a sense of awe wash over him he'd never experienced before.

Wisps of that same feeling had been returning these last few weeks; it had just taken this sunset for him to make the connection. It rushed him when he least expected it—threatening to sweep him away the same way the river had. It was strongest in the quiet moments after making love when the intense rush of an orgasm was fading and what remained was a quiet awareness that he was one piece of something bigger than he could comprehend.

Would she believe him if he told her how certain he was that everything in his life had been leading him to right here, right now—to this career, to that store next to the shelter, to her?

The server approached, carrying their entrees on a tray, and Morgan, who'd been showing the first hint of relaxing, bolted to all fours and let out a single woof.

He wasn't the only dog on the patio that was

crowded with diners, but he was the biggest and clearly the most out of place. Thankfully, they'd been able to snag one of the tables in the corner where it was quieter. Even so, Morgan had drawn his fair share of attention with his powerful build, big ears, striking coloring, and sable eyes.

The two other dogs were a Maltese who never left its owner's lap and a lively Boston terrier named Gus two tables away who had a—thankfully—broken squeaky toy that provided him seemingly endless amusement once he determined that Morgan was not going to come over to play.

The server approached with their food and, seeing that Olivia was attempting to get Morgan's attention and asking him to sit at attention, paused a few feet away. Morgan eventually realized he was being beckoned by the one human he had clear and continuing interest in. He stopped huffing at the server and sank to his haunches, looking between Olivia's closed fist indicating "sit" and the hand at her side that he sensed held a treat.

"Cute dog," the server said as she headed around the table to drop off the entrees on the opposite side where she wouldn't be as big of a distraction. "Hound?"

"German shorthaired pointer." Knowing Olivia was still a bit nasal-sounding from the tears she'd shed in the shelter and wasn't in the mood to bring attention to it, Gabe answered for her.

"What's the difference?"

"Hounds use scent to hunt and typically have even longer ears. Pointers use scent, too, but they're also sight dogs. Once they hone in on something, they're better at posturing, so they make good gun dogs."

"Huh. Who knew?" the server replied, pursing her lips. "Enjoy your dinners, and unless I can get you something now, just, ah, posture if you need me."

Once she headed back inside, Olivia rewarded Morgan with the treat and an affectionate pat on the shoulder. "Good boy!"

Head and back as tall as the table, Morgan finished gobbling up the treat and attempted to shove his head over the side, hoping for a bite of Olivia's locally raised trout.

Whoever had owned him had clearly worked with him enough for the dog to have learned some basic boundaries, or he wouldn't have backed off so easily when Olivia gave him a firm "No."

When he retreated, Olivia stuck out her lower lip. "Why is it that establishing boundaries feels so harsh?"

"If it helps, I don't think they process authority that way. They're pack animals and naturally obey alphas. It's good that he's listening to you as easily as he is."

Olivia slipped a travel-size bottle of hand sanitizer back into her purse after offering Gabe some. "That makes sense, and I get it. I don't want him swiping food off the table when I'm not in the room." As if realizing the permanency of her words, she gave a light shake of her head. "Or anyone's table, I guess."

Her words stirred up Gabe's desire to know what was bothering her tonight. He'd been patient, hoping she'd confide in him when her emotions ebbed along with her tears. Thanks to that wash of tears, she was makeup-free and as enchanting as ever, just in a more vulnerable way.

"How's the trout?"

She nodded, following a bite with a sip of water. "Great. What about the salmon?"

"Perfect. I was tempted to go with that blue cheese burger, but I have no regrets."

"Neither do your arteries," she said, laughing. "You're really doing good getting a handle on that cheeseburger addiction."

"Odds were I had to grow up sometime." After chasing down another bite with a swallow of wine, he took a risk and added, "The truth is, with you in my life, it's much easier to think long-term."

She froze with her fork hovering over a roasted grape tomato. For several seconds she stayed frozen, then she dropped her fork and sat back, refolding the napkin in her lap. "I—I found out today there aren't going to be any open positions I can apply for next year. Not at my school. And so far, I've gotten zero interview requests from the positions I applied for around here." Her voice pitched midway through, but she paused to clear her throat and got control of it again.

Gabe set his fork down and leaned forward. He wanted to tell her it was okay but checked himself. It clearly wasn't okay to her. Olivia lit up when she talked about teaching, about the small but essential breakthrough moments she'd had with her students, the moments that got them better tuned in to her lessons and caring about their performance in her class.

"I'm sorry," he said instead. "That's…tough, I'm sure. Thank you for telling me."

"Gabe, if I don't get a job next year…"

He waited for her to finish, but she didn't. He wanted to tell her it would be okay, but that wasn't his to say.

Clearly fighting back a fresh wave of tears, she shook

it off and picked up her fork again. A foot away, Morgan sat on his haunches, watching her with keen interest.

"Olivia, I believe it when people say things happen exactly the way they're supposed to happen, even if it doesn't always seem like it in the moment."

She stabbed at a half tomato, then wound her fork around a bit of steamed spinach. "I like being a teacher. The only reason I didn't go to school for it originally was because of fear about not making enough money, and that was me being one hundred percent reactive to the environment I grew up in. My parents... That's a story for another day, I guess. Like I told you, thank goodness we had my grandparents to turn to, or I'd have spent half my childhood in a car or on someone else's couch. But when I was a kid in elementary school, I had a friend whose mother was a teacher. Every summer just before school started, I'd get to go in with her while her mom got her classroom prepped. We used to play school in empty classrooms, and I don't know, it was just so clear teaching was what I wanted to do. Then money was so tight just before college that I made a different decision and majored in something that worked with both my dyslexia and the employment market.

"Once I had my degree, nothing felt right. I wanted to do something that would let me make the difference I wanted to make—connecting with kids and getting them passionate about math or science. And now that I've been through the Teach for America program and am certified, it just feels like the right doors open just enough for me to get a good look at what's inside but not enough for me to really step in."

"They'll open all the way; I'm sure of it. From the

stories you've told, you're a great teacher, the kind that gets nominated for teacher of the year and all that other stuff."

Olivia rolled her neck in a slow circle. "Thank you, but what if they don't?"

"They will. Trust me." He leaned forward and cupped his hand over hers. "Better yet, trust yourself. From personal experience, I think that's the biggest step a person can make."

She pulled in a slow breath and turned her hand over to squeeze his. "Trust myself, huh? I haven't exactly mastered that, but I'll give it a whirl."

Morgan instantly picked up on the hand-holding. Whether it was because he wanted in on their moment of connection or because he'd lost patience with waiting at attention in hope of a bite of food, he stood up and shoved his head underneath Olivia's arm, giving her mouth a thorough sniff that made her pull away and brought a delighted smile to her face.

"Gabe's the only one who gets mouth kisses, goober."

"You got that right."

Olivia was patting Morgan on the shoulder when, in the space of a mere second, he yanked the trout fillet off her plate and onto the concrete patio floor. Before she could even begin to reprimand him, he gulped it down in two quick bites.

"Oh my God. What do I do?"

Gabe shook his head, laughing. "I think we're best chalking that one up to experience and ordering you something else."

Olivia curled forward, overtaken by laughter for the first time all night. "To be honest, the way my stomach feels after all these waves of emotion, that blue cheese burger and some fries seem like they'd go down a whole lot easier than that fish was about to…but only if you eat half."

Gabe clasped a hand over his stomach. "I could be talked into that."

Olivia let out a contented nod. "Then we'll start over tomorrow on the healthy eating."

Two tables over, Gus, the Boston terrier, had dropped his squeakless toy and pressed to the edge of his leash as Morgan inhaled the trout. He was continuing to let out a series of sharp barks in clear reprimand.

"Yeah, about that, little dog, I don't think Morgan cares," Gabe said, chuckling.

As if in agreement, Morgan stretched out across the patio in obvious contentment and let out a single woof that sent Gus back to the other side of the table with his toy.

Gabe chuckled. "You know what that is?"

"Disobedience?"

"Yeah, that, but I was going to go with having trust in oneself. He's got zero doubt in the world he could kick that terrier's ass, and no one's going to tell him differently."

Still laughing, Olivia nodded in agreement. "It only makes sense that he's got some things to teach me too."

Chapter 26

OLIVIA SPENT HER FREE TIME OVER THE FOLLOWING week and a half checking the websites of every middle school in drivable range of the shelter—the spot that was turning out to be the perfect location for both her and Gabe. Disheartening as it was, her search confirmed that for whatever reason, there was no shortage of math and science teachers this year. Upon applying to the handful of schools with open positions in the area, she learned each school had received upward of fifty or sixty applications. With numbers like that, it was no wonder she wasn't being called for interviews.

A part of her wanted to give in to panic and shut down, but instead, she threw herself into ending the school year with the best effort she could give it, including organizing what was turning out to be a giant supply drive for the shelter. Her last-hour students were creating a buzz that was expanding through the school. With Principal Garcia's consent, they'd hung posters, passed out flyers, advertised in the school newspaper, and publicized the drive twice over the intercom during morning announcements.

As a result, the back corner of her classroom was overflowing. Olivia was thankful they'd secured a full-size school bus to transport the kids and supplies to the shelter next week. Some of the items—towels, blankets, and dishcloths—required nothing more than a cleaning out of closets or a redirection of recycling—nonglossy newspaper for shredding for the shelter's few rabbit cages—while others had required a financial investment.

Not for the first time, Olivia realized the financial difference of where she taught now, a top-rated magnet school that attracted some of the brightest kids in the city, from the continuously-struggling-for-funding school where she'd done her teacher training and the one where she'd taught near her hometown last semester that had been on the verge of closing its doors.

Perhaps it shouldn't have been as surprising as it was to see how giving the Westbury Middle families were, but expensive bags of dog and cat food, cat litter, nylon bones, cat toys, leashes, and grooming supplies were piling up as well. Olivia was particularly touched by some of the donations being made that weren't on the list, particularly ones meant for the staff and volunteers—prepacked snacks and bottled drinks and even a gift certificate to a Webster Groves takeout pizza joint for a weekend-volunteer pizza party.

When Olivia wasn't at work, she spent her time with Gabe or at the shelter where she always made time for Morgan, who she was bonding with more each visit despite knowing it might only end in a broken heart. After giving it some thought, Aunt Becky had come forward to say she could be talked into allowing him to stay at her house as long as they made an effort to keep Morgan and Coco apart until Coco had adjusted, or indefinitely if she didn't. But without promise of a job, Olivia was having second thoughts about being able to provide the kind of life Morgan needed. As much as she adored the tenderhearted and stubborn dog, maybe it was best to wait and see if an adopter came forward who could give him a better life right now.

Both firm believers that everything was going to work out, Gabe and Ava were encouraging her to adopt Morgan regardless of the uncertainty. But Olivia just wasn't sure.

After the final bell rang for the day, Olivia helped three of her students who were staying after for track and hung around to do a quick sorting and counting of the supplies that had been brought in so far. To keep the supply drive related to math, everything was being counted, and the students would be using algebra to figure out how many animals would benefit from the drive based on their individual needs.

"Should we track the food that's being collected by bags or total weight?" Addison asked. The drive had been her idea, and the kid had more than impressed Olivia with the way she'd continued to be a strong leader in ensuring the drive came together.

After mulling it over, Olivia said, "How about both for now? Since we're getting bags of all sizes, it makes sense to record weight too. Hopefully we get an average weight of food consumed each day at the shelter by both dogs and cats and really provide some good data when you all present your results."

"What about the nylon bones?"

"For everything else, I think we can stick to number only."

It took about fifteen minutes to get everything counted and sorted and marked since the collection was still growing, and Olivia sent them on their way with the last three granola bars from her snack drawer.

She was almost brought to tears when Addison hugged her on the way out. "Ms. Graham, you're the best teacher I've ever had. I wish you were coming back next year."

"That's so nice to hear, Addison. I won't lie. I wish I was too."

"Do you know where you're teaching yet?"

"Not yet." She left it at that. There was no reason to bring some of her favorite students down with her troubles.

After they headed out and she got to her desk, she found she had two new voicemails on her phone. The first was from the shelter, and she listened to it first.

"Olivia, hey, it's Megan. I hope I'm not overstepping here, but I wanted to give you a heads-up. We had some serious interest in Morgan today. It was a family with two young kids. They were close to deciding to adopt him but decided instead to sleep on it tonight. Since they have young kids and no fence, we'd have to do a home visit before adopting him out." There was a pause and then Megan added, "I just wanted you to know. And I know they were unfamiliar to him, but he looked pretty much the same way he did when we were giving him a bath, which I suspect is enough not to have to say any more about his excitement level." After an audible sigh, Megan finished with, "That's it. Sorry, lady. No pressure. Just thought you needed to know."

Olivia's heart pounded in her chest. How young were the kids and what kind of kids were they? Were they gentle and laid-back or the rough-and-tumble sort? Morgan was obedient enough, but he wasn't playful like some dogs. Would he take having his ears or tail tugged or being ridden like a horse? She could never imagine him snarling or snapping, but she also couldn't imagine him finding that fun either.

With shaky hands, she listened to the other voice-mail. It was a 573 area code, which meant the caller was most likely from her hometown.

"Olivia Graham, this is Principal Rutherford. Give me a call when you have a minute, will ya?"

That was it. Nothing else. Her heart raced harder as she remembered him walking into her classroom a little over five months ago and telling her that with their budget crisis, combined with the three students they'd lost to relocations, they'd made a proactive decision to combine classes. She no longer had a job for the spring semester.

That brought you here. To these kids. To Gabe. To Morgan. To Aunt Becky and that little town that was so healing when you most needed it.

She took a long drink of water and dialed back his number. He answered on the second ring.

"Olivia. I was hoping to hear from you yet today."

"Hi. Sorry I missed your call. I was with my students."

"I'll cut to the chase. Rumor has it your contract up there wasn't extended next year. That right?"

"Ahh…yeah. The teacher who took the extended leave of absence is coming back."

"Well, you know what they say. 'One man's tragedy is another man's treasure.' Looks like we get to split the eighth graders into the two classes again next year. You're our first choice at bringing in a teacher. And while I can't guarantee anything beyond next school year, I *can* guarantee you wouldn't be cut midyear again.

We've got the budget to carry us through even if there's a drop in class size after the start of the year again."

Olivia's pulse burst into hyperdrive. "I, uh, don't know what to say."

"We're even giving salary increases next year. First time in a couple years. Three and a quarter percent."

"Um, how many have applied so far?"

"Not a one. Everything was just finalized today. Given that you technically held a contract here this school year, added to the way you handled things and the effort you gave those kids, I won't post it. If you want it, that is."

Even though she'd just had a drink, Olivia's mouth had gone dry and it was hard to swallow. "How soon would you need an answer?"

"Ah, today's Wednesday. Any chance you could run down here this week sometime? I could have the contract drawn up and ready."

It was happening too fast to think. "I, uh, could probably come down Friday after school lets out. It would be close to six before I could get there though."

"Tell you what. Why don't you come on down, and the wife and I will take you out to dinner? Bet you miss the Big E's place."

"Oh. Wow. That would be very nice. Thank you." Her vision had gone blurry, and in her mind's eye she kept seeing Gabe, that remarkable mouth of his twisted in disappointment and a heaviness in his gaze. *No, no, no. Tell him no. You're not leaving Gabe.*

She thanked him again and hung up. She dropped the phone and covered her mouth in shaky hands. First Morgan, now this city. Gabe. The shelter. Everything.

She wanted to teach. More than anything. Hadn't she just said that? But *did* she? Enough to go home again where everyone knew her—or at least thought they did—and made enough judgments to last her a lifetime?

But a teaching position that was guaranteed for an entire year could open doors up here in St. Louis next year. And it wasn't as if she'd be moving to Alaska. She and Gabe could make it through. She'd come up on weekends. She wouldn't even have to stop volunteering at the shelter.

What would Ava think? She shook her head hard, sending her long locks tousling over her shoulders. She knew full well what Ava would think. She'd think she'd lost her mind.

Knowing it would be completely useless to attempt to sit around and plan lessons with all these thoughts roaming through her head, she logged off her computer and headed out for the day. She needed to tell Gabe and Ava, and even owed Aunt Becky a call.

But right now, there was something she wanted—no, *needed*—to do more than anything else.

———

Memories of his home flashed through the dog's mind as he dozed in his kennel in late afternoon. He woke up to the scents of the grasses, birds, and squirrels just beyond reach as his dreams faded.

He'd been here in this new place long enough that he no longer shook with fear at all the strange sounds and smells, and he'd come to trust these unfamiliar people meant him no harm. He was also beginning to trust that the dogs flanking both sides of his kennel weren't a threat either, no matter how much they'd barked and growled when he was first placed between them. They were beginning to tolerate him just as he was them, though he disliked not being able to move away and claim a space of his own far from where they slept.

His life before coming here had been a solitary one, as far back as he could remember. This life was different. The day here was filled with commotion almost as long as the sun was in the sky. People of all shapes and sizes stopped by his kennel to stare at him and to call out the name that he recognized was distinctly meant to call his attention. Morgan.

Some of them sank to his level and flattened their hands against the metal for him to sniff and even lick when they tasted of food. Others opened the door and clipped a leash to his collar, sometimes taking him outside where he could stretch his legs and catch new and unfamiliar scents on the wind. Other times, like today, he was taken into a small, confined room where strangers were waiting to run their hands along his body and give him commands for savory pieces of food that made his mouth water in anticipation.

Some of the people pleased him; others, like the anxious and loud ones who'd been in the room today, he preferred to get away from as fast as he could. But none of them held the same appeal as the woman whose smell and look and sound and touch were distinctly familiar to him now. When he was awake, and people were coming and going, he watched for her to appear.

Whenever she pushed past the doors, locking eyes and calling out that word—*Morgan*—the dog grew so full of happiness that his whole body shook. The sound of her voice made him want to pounce and jump and left him wanting to hear it again and again, the same way he wanted her to take him with her when she went away, wherever she went.

She'd done it once, her and the man who'd pulled him from the water when he could no longer swim. That night the dog had been more content than since before he'd left his home. She was the one who'd brought him to this place. He knew by the scents in the air that it was too far from his home to ever find his way back.

At first, the dog had longed for her to bring him back there, back to the quiet land near the river. As he grew strong here and never felt the great hunger or thirst again, he remembered the long stretch of days before the water rose, and he no longer wanted that.

He thought of the man who'd cared for him most of the dog's life—the one whose voice had been stern but whose touch had been gentle much more than it had been rough—and missed him. But the man had stopped coming, had stopped caring for him, and the dog no longer yearned for him the way he once had during the long, quiet days by the river.

Here, the dog was never hungry or thirsty, and no one's touch was ever rough or painful. Still, the dog wanted something beyond this place even though he couldn't imagine any life other than the one he'd lived before and the one he lived now.

He was dozing again when he caught the woman's scent wafting through the doors. He barked and strained to hear her voice. Finally, he heard it but just barely, muted as it was by the doors and the walls. Hoping she'd come to him, he barked and barked till the dogs flanking his sides joined in, barking wildly enough that he could no longer hear her.

The dog waited, but she didn't come to him the way she always did when he first heard her, bringing him something delicious to chomp up and showing she was as pleased to see him as he was to see her.

He whined and sank to the floor and waited in hope she would come to him. His eyelids had grown heavy again from all the waiting when his kennel door began to rattle. He jumped to his feet, a rush of delight at the realization that she was the one opening it. She sank low so that she was level with him and pressed her face into his neck and wrapped her arms around his body.

The dog didn't mind. Her affection was pleasing, just like the muffled "Morgans" she spoke into his fur.

He whined and wagged his tail and licked her neck, hoping this would be one of the times when she took him outside to stretch his legs. When she pulled her face away, her cheeks were wet and salty, and he licked them dry, remembering the salty fish he'd savored when she'd taken him to that crowded place with so many wonderful smells.

Something was different this time. She clipped a leash to his collar and led him into the part of the building where he'd only been a few times rather than out the door that led outside where she usually took him. People crowded him. Most were ones he was beginning to trust. They patted him and praised him and locked their arms around her just like they did him. Soon after, she knelt on the floor close beside him, a treat hidden in her hand as she asked him to sit while one of the people who brought his food loomed over them with an object in his hands, stirring up worry in the dog over what might happen. When the woman wasn't frightened but smiled up at the man, waiting for something the dog couldn't comprehend, he let go of his fear too.

When it was over, she brought him out the door she'd first brought him in, all those days ago when his muscles had been weak and he'd still been hungrier than he cared to ever be again.

Then she spoke words that conveyed a tone that made his tail wag just to hear even if he didn't understand them.

"Come on, Morgan," she said, patting him again in that special way of hers, "let's go home."

Chapter 27

GABE HEADED ACROSS THE METICULOUSLY MAINTAINED backyard and stepped through the open door of Dr. Washington's detached garage where Carol, his wife, had said her husband was finding new ways to keep himself busy now that he was largely on the mend from his surgery.

Gabe had been here once before, over Christmas, for a staff party. Albert was a model-train hobbyist and had transformed his garage into something worthy of comparison, on a smaller scale, to the display at Chicago's Museum of Science and Industry. Albert's collection of Lionel trains ran on a track at tabletop height that traversed tree-covered mountains with ski runs, elk, and bighorn sheep and passed into a model-scale village of nineteenth-century America at Christmastime replete with carolers and tree trimmers and a house that even could have smoke coming out the chimney. A second track circled from the town's depot to a representation of the Great Plains where Albert had created a display of the Old West with buffalo, horses, grizzlies, and an old mining town.

Today, he was seated on a stool at a tall craft table in the only area of the garage not devoted to his train collection. He was wearing the same thick-rimmed glasses he wore in surgery, reminding Gabe of all the highly skilled things he'd watched Dr. Washington do over the months he'd known him. As it turned out, today Albert was working on something that had nothing to do with his model-train collection.

"I wondered how that was done." Gabe watched as Albert threaded rigging lines through the sails of a still-collapsed miniature model sailing ship that, based on the image on the nearby box, was supposed to be displayed in a narrow-mouthed glass bottle. "I assumed they were assembled inside with long tweezers or something."

"Now that you know the secret, don't spread it around. As it is, this is an art that's nearly been lost to history." Showing off his work, Albert pulled the rigging lines hinged to the mast and running under the hull, cautiously raising the sails into position so that the ship was its full height. "Once it's inside, you tie and cut away the extra rigging lines, and no one is any the wiser as to how it was assembled."

Gabe shook his head. "Impressive."

"I have another one on order that's a good deal more complicated. A Spanish galleon from the sixteenth century."

"Oh yeah? And I wondered how you were spending your days."

"When you've spent forty years honing and challenging your fine motor skills, you've got to find something to occupy your time."

"That makes sense. Don't let this get out, but as a kid, I went through a phase where I loved to paint model soldiers."

"From the Revolutionary War?"

"No, marines from Nam. An uncle of mine gave me a kit for Christmas one year."

As Albert finished hooking in the rigging lines, Gabe headed over to the train's control station. "Mind if I run it?"

"Help yourself."

Gabe started both tracks. A Sante Fe train ran on the line from the village to the Old West, and a Union Pacific one ran along the mountains and surrounding woods and into the village depot. As they circled the separate tracks, Gabe strolled along, appreciating the level of detail he'd not noticed on his first visit here, including an outhouse in the woods behind a cabin that had a roll of toilet paper hung inside its open door and a book on the bench seat titled *The Yellow River* by I. P. Freely. On the outskirts of the village, a fox was hidden in a bush, eyeing chickens who were safe inside the chicken yard behind a farmhouse, and an arrow was subtly placed in a dry creek bed outside the mining town.

"What you did here is amazing. How long did this take you?"

"Can't really say because it's still not finished. I can tell you when I started. It was back when my daughter was three, and I thought it would be fun to get a train for Christmas. She's forty-one now."

Gabe huffed. "The level of detail here—it's impressive. Beyond impressive."

"The most important parts are always in the details. If you don't pay attention, so many moments get lost as they turn into memory."

Gabe glanced his way. "I'll remember that."

After Gabe met with his consultant last week, Olivia had helped him and Yun assemble a spreadsheet that impressed even detail-oriented Yun. At the end of last week, he'd officially presented his proposal to purchase Dr. Washington's clientele list and equipment but not his building, and Albert had been thinking it over.

Since he'd texted Gabe earlier today asking if he could pop over at lunch, Gabe suspected Albert had made his decision, and the minutes had been ticking by slowly ever since.

Considering he'd been managing the practice completely on his own the last couple months, Gabe wasn't sure what would happen if Albert didn't agree to the split sale. But the fact of the matter was, with his student loans added to the business and building loan for Dr. Washington's old place, he'd barely have been able to scrape by. Even before Albert admitted he'd been turning away clients during his busiest months for the last few years, Gabe had known the biggest limitation to growing the business would be the building's small size.

If Albert would agree to sell him the business and equipment only, and he and Yun were to split the costs of it and the new building, they'd be able to create an entirely different financial picture. Especially considering that once the cost was spread over a thirty-year payment plan, the jewelry store wasn't much more expensive than Albert's property.

"This friend of yours you want to go into business with," Albert asked, apparently ready to get to business. "She's the one you've talked about? Who took a position over at Warson Landing?"

"Yeah. That's her."

"I know it's not my place to ask, but your relationship, it's platonic?"

Gabe blinked. Of all the questions he was prepared

to address, that one hadn't made the list. "Uh, yeah. Completely."

Albert nodded and switched off the long-armed lamp before slipping carefully off the stool and walking over to join Gabe in front of the ski lodge. He had been admiring the miniature hot chocolate stand and the small group of people standing huddled around a campfire.

"I take it you think you would work well together?"

"We studied well together, and we're close."

Albert dragged a hand over the thick, gray stubble covering his chin. "I'd just hate to see everything I've built torn apart in a business disagreement one day. I worked with you for eight months, and I wouldn't have offered to sell you what I spent a lifetime building if I didn't think you had a good head on your shoulders. I hope you don't take offense, but work partnerships can be tough. More so if they were ever to evolve into anything more complicated."

Gabe felt a spark of anger igniting in his gut but fought it back. It made sense that Albert would be concerned. A sole proprietorship was one thing. This was a partnership. And while Gabe had worked with him for nearly eight months before Albert's back surgery, Yun was a practical stranger to him. *It's in the details*, he'd just said.

"It won't," Gabe replied. "If that was ever going to happen, it would've by now. Besides, I'm pretty confident that a month ago I met the person I'm supposed to be with. You haven't had the chance to meet her yet, but I'd like you to."

Albert gave him a sharp look. "Did you? How'd the staff take that?"

"What do you mean?"

"Just that it may have killed a few quietly smoldering crushes."

"None that I would've intentionally fostered."

Albert nodded. "I know, or I wouldn't be selling you my business."

Gabe ground his bottom teeth into his top, waiting for more. The Union Pacific was passing by, filling his nostrils with the smell of the smoke fluid.

"Does that mean you're still selling me your business?"

With a touch of dramatic flair that was warranted for someone who was about to embark on one of the most dramatic changes of his life, Albert extended his hand with an uncharacteristic flourish. "The wife says she'll divorce me if I don't, but between me and you, I was going to anyway."

Gabe took his hand but stepped in to give him a careful hug, not sure of the condition of his back. "I can promise you, you won't regret it. It's going to be good. Better than good. It's going to be incredible."

Albert chuckled and adjusted the thick glasses he'd stuck on top of his head. "I have nothing but faith in you, son. Nothing but faith."

~~~

More days had passed than Olivia could remember since she'd headed back to Elsah so early in the evening, and she was half-surprised when doing so put her smack-dab in the middle of rush hour. As much as she disliked driving in traffic, sitting parked on the highway and then riding her brake lights through Alton to get to the Great River Road gave her plenty of time to think.

What had started out as a nondescript Wednesday was turning out to be a momentous day. She'd adopted Morgan, who'd been much more content watching out her back window in traffic than she'd been driving in it, and—even though she was having a hard time believing it—she'd pretty much accepted a job she'd not even known existed a few hours before. A job that would keep her away from all the amazing things—and people—up here that she was starting to love.

Or already did.

Her belly flipped in a wild circle as traffic opened up and she drove along the Great River Road. Flanking her left side, the sprawling Mississippi had finally retreated to a full but nonthreatening level as the spring rains eased up.

"You've been here once. Do you remember?"

In the rearview mirror, she noticed how Morgan turned his head toward her at the sound of her voice.

"You may not realize this yet, but you're my dog now, and—hopefully—I'm your person. I know you had another one before all this, but I'm crossing my fingers you have no regrets. I know I won't."

As he turned his attention back to the window, her thoughts went back to wondering what Gabe would say about all this. And the strain it might cause on their relationship. She'd called on the way to the shelter to get Morgan, but it had still been his workday, and he hadn't picked up. He'd called back a half hour later, but she'd been in the middle of filling out adoption papers.

What kind of girlfriend was she? Gabe had told her he loved her, and her response was going to be taking a job that would keep her away from him for nine full months.

Sure, there were weekends. She'd drive up here most of them, after she traded in the Cruze for a newer car.

It wasn't going to be a picnic, moving back in with her grandparents, especially with her parents still living in the prefab house on the other end of the property. Ava was going to read her the riot act for this. But a three percent raise on the salary she'd gotten for teaching in rural Missouri wasn't enough to pay a car payment, apartment, and her student loans.

You could always call Principal Rutherford back and turn it down. Work as a sub up here to get you through. Maybe pick up a second job too.

Olivia rolled her neck in a slow circle and dropped her hands away from ten and two after realizing she was still in full-traffic driving mode.

The longer she waited, the more telling Gabe all this was going to sound like an afterthought. He didn't even know she'd headed home to Elsah and he wouldn't see her tonight.

With another ten minutes to her aunt's, Olivia picked up her phone to make the much-needed call, only to have her phone ring in her hand.

Gabe.

"Hey there. I was literally picking up the phone to call you."

"Yeah? Guess that means we're connected. Hey, so, I don't know how you're going to like this, but my mom invited us over for dinner."

"Did she? When?"

"Tonight. If you're good with that. She's making spaghetti. I think I told you she's not the best cook, but she makes a killer spaghetti sauce."

"Oh…" *You're going to tell him you'll be leaving him in a few months, and he's inviting you to his parents'.* "I, uh, should've called you earlier. The thing is, I'm headed back to Elsah. I'm almost there."

He was quiet a second. "Everything okay?"

"Yeah, it's just…*so* much, actually. It started with getting a call from Megan. A family came by today who was giving serious thought to adopting Morgan, only Megan didn't seem that excited about the match, and—I don't know—it just made me realize how close I could be to losing him."

"Wait, does this mean—?"

A grin curled her lips. "Yeah, it does. I went right after school."

"That's awesome. I'm proud of you, Olivia."

"Thanks. He's in the back seat and seems pretty chill. Aunt Becky's headed to the store to buy a couple stair gates to close off different parts of the house and to pick up a few supplies for me."

"He'll figure out Coco's a pet, not a potential chew toy, I'm sure. He's got the same temperament as other dogs I've known who've gotten used to things like that. I've got a client whose farm-raised bloodhound's new best friend is a lop-eared bunny."

"Cute. And reassuring. I have to say as reality sinks in, the whole thing is a touch intimidating. I've never actually had a dog of my own. I'm glad to have you to give me pointers. And I can't wait for him and Samson to officially meet."

"Me, neither. I'm surprised you didn't swing by first."

"I should've. I was going to. It's just… Ugh." She let

out a huff that blew the hair on her forehead. "There's something else, something a little more complicated, and I guess I just needed the drive to process it all. I wanted to tell you in person, but waiting doesn't feel right either."

He was quiet, leaving her an opening to continue with no interruption.

"I got a call this afternoon from the principal of the school where I taught last semester. He's offering me a guaranteed position for next year. No chance of it falling through in the middle of the year this time."

"The one in your hometown?"

"Yeah, that one."

A handful of seconds passed. "Did you take it?"

"He's asking me to drive down Friday so we can get everything signed this week. I think that way he won't have to list it. Technically, I guess I'm still on their list of contracted teachers this year."

"Wow. So, it sounds like you're taking it."

She pursed her lips. *Yeah, it does, and it sucks*. "I think I need to," she said aloud. "It's looking less and less likely that I'll get offered anything else this late in the game. But we still have the whole summer ahead of us. And there are always weekends."

"Yeah, there are weekends." He was trying to sound optimistic, but she was still able to pick up on an underlying layer of disappointment.

"Gabe, I—I know this sucks. I know we're just starting out, and I don't want to be away from you five days out of seven. But if I don't find work this year, I can't help but think it's going to be that much harder next year."

He cleared his throat, and Olivia could picture a perfect furrow between his brows. "I can see that being a legitimate worry. Look, I'm not going to lie and tell you I won't miss you. But you're right. You've got to do this." Her ear tingled from the sound of his exhale against the receiver. "We'll make it work."

Tears stung her eyes instantly. "Thank you." *I love you. More than I thought I could love anyone. It means so much that you're taking this so well.* Why couldn't she say it? Why was she so afraid of losing herself? "I'm sorry, really sorry" was all that came out.

"Don't be sorry. We'll figure it out. I mean it. Samson's always up for a drive. We'll alternate weekends so you're not always driving."

"You might not want to do that when you realize I'm most likely going to be staying at my grandparents'. I'm pretty sure if you sleep over, you'll be sequestered to the guest room."

He laughed. "Whatever it takes, Olivia."

She sucked in a shaky breath. "What did I do to deserve you? I thought… I don't know what I thought. I just… Gabe…" *I love you.* Her throat went as dry as cement. What was wrong with her? She cleared it hard as she flipped on her blinker to turn into the little village of Elsah before it came into view. Towering, mature trees blocked the entrance on both sides until she was practically upon it, adding to its hidden-gem allure, but she'd memorized the turn by now and could find it on autopilot. "I don't know why it's so hard to find the words. It's just… It's different with you. It's real."

"I know. And that stuff about deserving; you may be forgetting how extraordinary you are. If anything, it's the other way around. But I'm good going with us being a good match for each other."

She laughed softly. "Me too. Thank you. For everything."

"You're welcome. You know, I had something I wanted to tell you, too, but I'll wait till I see you in person. I'd better hang up and call my mom to let her know she doesn't have to do a rush clean of her house."

"Tell her thanks, please, and I'm excited to meet her. Both of them. This weekend could work. I'll be back Saturday afternoon. And please tell her I'd love to bring something."

"I'll tell her. And hey..."

"Yeah?"

"Enjoy that dog. Just try not to let him pull a Samson and get used to hogging the other side of the bed, because it's not going to stay empty long."

She laughed. "I won't. He's sleeping on the floor. Promise."

"Good, because none of the places your sister has lined up to show me have room for those California kings. And with both of them on the bed, we'd need one."

After a shared laugh, she said goodbye and hung up, regretting she hadn't made the decision to swing by his place before heading home. She should have told him in person. It enamored her to him even more to realize he probably felt the same way but wasn't holding it against her. He seemed to understand her fears even better than she did.

Maintaining the mandated snail's pace of a speed limit, Olivia drove through the picturesque town reminiscent of stepping back in time to the late eighteen hundreds, complete with cobblestone sidewalks, gazebos, and even an old dance hall. As if anticipating that the drop in speed indicated a bigger change, Morgan poked his head between the seats.

"Hey, buddy." She pressed her forehead against his soft jowls. "We're home. For the time being, anyway. But you know what they say. 'Home is where you hang your hat.' What matters is that we're together."

As if agreeing with her, Morgan gave a thorough sniff of her hair that ended in a swipe of his tongue across her temple. As she slipped the car into Park on the narrow strip of driveway her aunt had reserved for her, she swiped her temple dry with the back of her hand.

"I'm going to take that as you being in agreement. So, this is it, Morgs. Welcome to the first day of the rest of your life."

Chapter 28

"ANYTHING BEGINNING TO SMELL FAMILIAR?"

Now that they were less than ten miles from their hometown, it sounded as if Morgan was taking deeper sniffs of the air from his spot in the back seat.

It was still hard for Olivia to believe she was a dog owner. Had been for over forty-eight hours. Coco hadn't exactly had a heart attack, but the vocal bird wasn't happy. So far and for the foreseeable future, only one of them was allowed in Aunt Becky's main living area at a time. When Coco was on her perch between the dining area and couch, Morgan was either in Olivia's loft bedroom or outside in the small, fenced-in yard. Once Coco was taken to Aunt Becky's room for an early evening, Morgan was being given a cautious free rein of the living room and kitchen.

Even though it was unlikely he'd spent much time indoors most of his life, potty training so far had been a breeze. Olivia's fingers were crossed, hoping that as he got more comfortable, he wouldn't regress. For now, he seemed eager to relieve himself on the plants, grasses, and trees as he'd grown up doing. She was committed to giving him plenty of opportunity to do so until she was certain he'd figured it out.

When it came to swiping food off the table, it was another story all together. Even in-peel bananas weren't safe, which came as a bit of a shocker to Olivia. She'd known a few food-snatching dogs but had never met one with a hankering for fruit. Or with his stealth at swiping food off plates.

Knowing he was still adjusting to having an abundance of food again, she was committed to optimism that he'd be trainable in this regard too. And he hadn't even come close to leaving some of his kibble in the bowl at his morning and evening meals. The opposite, actually. He spent a few minutes each time licking his bowl spotless.

"Considering how rough your last few weeks were down here, you may not be psyched about spending nine months in this place. To be completely honest, I'm not either."

Now that they were on the outskirts of their mutual hometown, it was clear Morgan was smelling long-familiar scents. He was practically shoving his nose in the corner of the side window where the trim was loose.

The closer they got, the more real this whole thing became. She was going home. *Again.*

"You want to know something crazy?" When Morgan licked his jowls, she took it as being as close to a yes as she'd get. "I've never lived on my own. Ever. There was dorm life. But I don't think that counts. I've always lived with someone, and mostly it's been with an authority figure. What does that say about me?"

When nothing but silence filled the car, she added, "What if I never live alone?" If things kept progressing with Gabe the way she expected them to, they'd very likely be moving in together when this year was over. And she'd welcome it, but still, would she be losing out on something if she never had this experience?

She was still reeling over this new awareness when she pulled off the highway and stopped at the U Gas to fill her almost-to-fumes tank. While it was filling, she got Morgan out to stretch his legs, remembering how impressed she had been with Gabe that first day she'd met him when he'd done nothing more than point to the grass and trustworthy Samson had trotted over to do his business.

She could hardly fathom being able to do that with Morgan someday. Even if he didn't run off, it seemed like a far stretch to imagine him becoming as calm and easily obedient as Samson.

It didn't matter if Morgan was never obedient like that, she thought, heading back to the car with him. He was charming and affectionate and already loyal in his own way. Even if she did have to guard her plate with the attention of a night watchman.

"Olivia Graham? Well, I'll be! Look at you. All grown up and still a Graham at that. Got a lot of your grandfather in you, don't you?"

Olivia blinked at the woman who'd just gotten out of the truck on the other side of the pump. It took a couple seconds to connect the considerably older but familiar woman with the voice that didn't seem to have changed a bit. "Mrs. Tilby?" She could hear Ava saying it was just the kind of town where your fourth-grade teacher remembered you even when you hadn't seen her for the better part of fifteen years.

"In the flesh."

Morgan let out a loud bark when Mrs. Tilby stepped around the pump, her gait having stiffened considerably since Olivia had last seen her.

"Hush, Morgan. It's okay."

"I heard you've been teaching up in St. Louis this spring. City kids, of all things. Bet that was an adjustment compared to the good stock we get around these parts."

The hair on the back of Olivia's neck prickled. "The new school was a bit of an adjustment. But not because of the kids. They've been great. Better than great. They're motivated and caring and passionate about making a difference. A lot like our kids, only their focus is a bit different."

Mrs. Tilby let out a huff that implied nothing Olivia could say would change her opinion, reminding Olivia of some of the things she'd been one hundred percent fine leaving behind back in January.

"Well, you don't look any worse for the wear. I'll give you that." Mrs. Tilby wasn't at all shy about looking Olivia over from head to toe.

After letting Morgan sniff Mrs. Tilby and tolerate a pat on the head before shying away, Olivia opened the back door of her car, and he hopped in with easy grace. "Thanks. It's actually been an incredible experience, if you want to know."

"As they say, better you than me. I would've guessed that breakup with Trevor might've left its scars, but you look good. Real good."

"Life's been treating me well, thanks." She hung up the nozzle and closed her fuel-tank lid, determined to get out before this turned into a full-scale interrogation.

"I guess you heard he's still living in that pretty little ranch out on the 4 County Road."

"I wouldn't have guessed he'd live anywhere else.

It was willed to him, after all." She threw open her car door, a dozen things she'd not liked about her fourth-grade teacher circulating freshly through her mind. "It was nice running into you, but I'd better go."

"It'll be a lucky girl who catches him, that's for sure."

Olivia had one leg inside but froze. "My hope for Trevor—and whoever he ends up with—is that they're better matched than he and I were. Good afternoon, Mrs. Tilby."

Olivia slipped in and shut the door before anything else was said. Fire was flowing through her veins.

What are you doing coming back here?

"That's the thing about this place, Morgan," she said as she drove off, pulling onto the two-lane highway and hitting the gas pedal a little too hard. "Just about every-one thinks they know your business, when they don't know even the half of it." She gripped the steering wheel like she was about to pull onto a motocross raceway. "And another thing. They're never going to let me live it down. Ever. Trevor is a Jones. And the Joneses are as good as legend." She took a handful of long, deep breaths in hopes of calming down, but it did little to chill the fire in her veins.

Pulling over onto gravel, she scanned through her music for something to help ease the tension coursing through her. Spotting Rachel Platten's "Fight Song," she pressed Play and turned up the volume, singing along in hopes of finding some release. After a few stanzas, Morgan joined in, letting out a series of barks that rolled into a bay, and more than anything, this is what cooled her anger. By the time the song was over, she was laughing at her dog's excitement.

"Is my voice that bad? Wait, don't answer."

Before even contemplating it, she turned down the dirt road where she and Gabe had found Morgan, and her blood began to heat all over again. It felt like much longer than a month ago that she and Gabe had driven down this road together. And it looked it too. Back then, most of the world had still been the dull brown of winter with sporadic hints of yellow-green. Now, the trees and grasses were the bright, healthy green of full spring, the corn, soy, and cotton fields were bustling with new growth, and the river had receded after the deluge of spring rains had ended. The evening sky was a brilliant hue of bright blue, and the heat and humidity that were sure to come were holding off awhile longer.

"You know where we're going, don't you, Morgs?"

He was sniffing the air with such exuberance, she cracked the windows, letting in the wind.

She wasn't sure what was drawing her down this road, or even if it was in his best interest, but she couldn't turn back. She needed to see the house. Morgan's house. And for some reason, she was strangely certain he needed to see it too.

"Do dogs need closure?" Her heart leaped into her throat as she spotted the house ahead and slowed to a snail's pace to finish their approach. She'd forgotten what terrible shape the home had been in. Peeling paint. Broken shutters and a broken window. Seedlings growing out of the gutter. Dark, gritty stains running down the roof. Discarded furniture and trash strewn about the front porch.

She pulled into the empty driveway and shut off the ignition. "We don't have to get out if you don't want to."

Morgan stuck his head out the half-rolled-down window and woofed at the house.

"Is that a yes?"

She got out and opened the back-passenger door. When he hopped out without hesitation, she grabbed his leash and decided to let him lead her wherever he wanted to go.

He beelined for the porch, sniffing everything along the way but turning twice to look back as if to reaffirm she was still with him. He sniffed and paced back and forth the length of the leash, then abruptly pulled toward the far end of the porch. What had earlier felt like a long time ago suddenly seemed right upon her again, as if she could turn around and see Gabe's truck parked in the driveway and, if she listened, hear the rush of the floodwater surging in the backyard.

An image of Gabe that afternoon rose clear and crisp in her mind. He was soaked and exhausted from his struggle in the water. He'd tugged off the life vest and out of his shirt and was drying off with a worn towel he'd had in the back of his truck. In just a glimpse, she'd committed that torso—long and lean and naturally muscled—to memory. Maybe it was spurred by how close he'd come to not getting to the dog in time, or because of the spill he'd taken in the water, but he'd looked as vulnerable as he did strong and capable. She'd wanted to be there for him, just like she'd wanted him to be there for her. And a half hour later, she'd been unable to stop herself from initiating that first kiss in his truck that had been so unlike anything she'd ever done.

How was it that on that stormy afternoon a month ago, she'd taken a leap down the path of becoming wildly in love with both a person and a dog when neither had been in her plans?

She remembered back to being a kid in preschool and playing with the bin full of red cardboard construction bricks. She'd painstakingly assemble an imposing tower, hoping her creation wouldn't fall, and then, when it inevitably tumbled apart, cringed as if the impact of the cardboard bricks would hurt even though they never did. She felt the same way now—as though she was watching something she'd built fall apart; only, in the very same way, the crashing bricks didn't hurt. More surprisingly, as they fell, they were reassembling into something else entirely. Something new and foreign and exciting.

Before she knew it, Morgan had tugged her around to the back of the house, nose to the ground.

Even though she'd witnessed the power of the water firsthand, the flood damage came as a shock. The trees still stood, but branches littered a yard caked with mud and other debris. As she spied the remnants of the shed and pen, her shock was so great, she nearly let go of Morgan's leash. Most of what was left of his old home had been washed more than fifty feet from where it stood when he'd been rescued. Broken sections of fence and strips of wood were wrapped around the bases of the trees they'd been washed into. The rest had been washed away.

With ears pricked forward and nose still to the ground, Morgan tugged her forward. Did he have any idea how close he'd been to dying?

Morgan sniffed and sniffed around the base of what had once been his pen but was now only splintered wood and bent, galvanized metal posts jutting up from concrete mounds. Finally satiated, he stopped sniffing and raised his head, looking at her before turning his attention to the woods.

She waited as still as could be, wondering what he'd do next. His body remained as still as stone for close to a minute, his only movement an occasional sniffing of the air as he took in his surroundings. A steady, gentle breeze blew, carrying the earthy scent of the river mixed with the new growth of spring. Finally, he sank to his haunches, head cocked at attention and big ears dangling, watching her the way he did when she had a treat in her hand and he was waiting for direction.

She sank to his level, resting on the backs of her ankles and draping her arms over his neck. With no hesitation, he melted closer into her, his wet nose burrowing in her hair and along her face and neck.

She closed her eyes and soaked in his warmth. She couldn't say if seconds or minutes passed as a calm swept over her deeper than any she'd experienced in a long time.

"You know what, Morgs," she said when she finally pulled away. "I'm pretty sure you and I have come to the same conclusion. This isn't our home anymore."

As if he was in complete agreement, he stood up and began leading her back through the yard and around the house to the car.

Chapter 29

SAMSON WAS PRESSING AGAINST HIS SIDE, SNORING INTO his ear, when Gabe stirred from a deep sleep. He flipped sides, turning his back to his dog, trying to retreat into sleep again before his mind began to race. He was starting to drift when he was awakened again. This time, he was alert enough to identify the sound.

Someone was knocking on his door.

He sat up, swiping his thumb and forefinger across his lids before opening his eyes. He reached for his cell and lit the screen. 1:17. He didn't need to spy the missed call from Olivia a few minutes ago to know it was her knocking at the door.

He got up and headed across his apartment, clearing his throat and adjusting the only thing he was wearing, a pair of old boxers, so they weren't gaping open as he greeted her.

He was still too sleep-ridden to attempt to guess what had brought her here when she was supposed to be over three hours away, but he was still relieved when he opened the door to find her beautiful face a wash of what could only be happiness.

"I know it's late. I'm not even going to ask if I woke you." She bit her lip, a wide, happy grin spreading across her face. "And I'll apologize later. I just… I didn't want to waste another minute."

He pulled her in for a hug and pressed his lips against

her temple as she stepped inside. "I'm glad you're here. You know, you can always use the code so you're not stuck in the hallway."

"I used the other one to get in downstairs. But when I got up here, knocking felt more right."

It wasn't until he shut the door that he realized how dark it was in the room. He flipped on the overhead light and winced. There was a lamp on the side table next to the couch that hadn't been on in more than year. He headed over and turned the switch. He was half-surprised it wasn't burned out.

Still standing by the door, she read his thoughts and flipped off the glaring overhead light.

"Thanks. You, ah, want something to drink?"

"Sure. A glass of water would be nice."

She followed him in and, as he filled two glasses, stepped behind him and wrapped her arms around his torso, pressing a cheek against his shoulder blade.

"I missed you."

"I missed you too." After setting the glasses on the counter, he turned and locked his arms around her, his body responding in more ways than just the warming in his blood. When she was near, he experienced a sense of being alive more profound than anything he'd felt before. The words *I love you* attempted to push their way out, but he held them back, not wanting them to get in the way of anything she had to say.

The water was still running. She flipped off the faucet and closed her hands over both sides of his face. "Thank you. For letting me go. For letting me do this when everything between us is so new. You have no idea what it means to me for you to just—I don't know—to let me figure this out for myself."

"Figure what out?"

"That I wasn't trusting myself." She slid her hands down his neck and let them settle over his chest. She stepped closer still and pressed a soft kiss against his sternum. "It's crazy, and maybe it's because I was raised on a farm a stone's throw from a river, but all my life, I've been super aware of... Ugh. I don't know how to explain it." She pressed her forehead into his chest for a few seconds before meeting his gaze again. "The ebb and flow of life, I guess. Sometimes there's never enough, and sometimes there's too much, and sometimes it's just right. At times, I catch myself thinking things will never be perfect, but the truth is, I'm starting to think most of what comes our way is exactly what's supposed to."

She pulled in a deep breath, and the same smile returned that had been on her face when he opened the door.

"What I'm trying to say is I realized tonight I'm ready to trust myself. I don't know how I'm going to get there, but I *do* know what I'm supposed to be doing, and I know where I'm supposed to be. And just as importantly, I know who I'm supposed to be with."

He ran a hand down the length of her hair, lightness filling him like a balloon. "I'm hoping I know the answer to that last part. Actually, I'm hoping I *am* the answer."

She rose up and brushed her lips over his. "You're the best answer I could have in that regard. I love you, Gabe. I've known it for a while, maybe even since that first day I met you. And the more I get to know you, the more it grows."

Her lips met his in a kiss that sent a rush of energy over his spine and through his limbs. As it progressed, she slipped her hands into his hair. The need in her fingertips and the gentle pressure of her body against his heated his blood from warm to hot.

"I love you too," he answered when she pulled away to meet his gaze.

"I know you do. And if Morgan wasn't waiting in the car, I'd be very tempted to head into your room to show you all the ways I mean that."

He kissed her again, and his boxers began to gape open for a different reason than the disarray of sleep. "I wondered where he was. We can bring him up, if you want. But full disclosure, Samson's hogging the bed, and he's out like a light. If you're serious, we could always settle for the couch."

Her smile grew wide, her teeth shining in the lamplight. "How's your stock of peanut butter looking?"

He cocked an eyebrow. "Enough to fill the big Kong, at least."

"You know, Morgan's really food-focused. I think that would do the trick." She lifted his hand in hers and pressed his palm against her lips. "Only there's something else I want to tell you first. Two things, actually."

"Yeah. Anything."

"The job back home... I turned it down. I told you that I know I'm meant to be a teacher, and that hasn't changed. But the shelter, you, my sister... I'm meant to be here, Gabe. Now. Not in another year. I'll pick up subbing or maybe even a teaching assistant position if nothing opens. Not getting a position for next year doesn't mean the end of my career."

"I want to ask if you're sure, but you look really clear."

"I *am* clear."

Their lips brushed again, and tears unexpectedly stung his eyes. He cleared his throat and did his best to blink them back. "I can't tell you how happy that makes me."

"You don't have to. I already know."

He laughed, shaking his head. "It opens everything up. *Everything*, Olivia."

"I know. Pretty much everything, I guess. I do have one disclaimer."

"Oh yeah? What's that?"

"It's the other thing I wanted to say. I don't know how I'm going to do it yet, considering I don't have steady employment, but I do have decent savings built up. I realized tonight that I've never lived alone. Ever. It may be a little early to lay out all my cards like this, but I feel I need to say it now because I realized how important this is to me too."

"You want to get a place of your own?"

"A lease on an apartment or something. And that's the awkward part. I won't sign anything too long in the event that…you know, things between us keep progressing like they have been. But this is something I feel called to do."

He shook his head, laughing off what felt like a potentially surreal connection. "I understand that. And I'll honor it. Happily. As far as I'm concerned, what's between us is for the long term, Olivia. And I'm fine with you taking the steps you need to get us there. The funny thing is, when I told my landlord I'm house shopping, he asked if I knew anyone who might be interested in moving in. It's something to think about, but if he doesn't have to advertise or lose out on rent if it goes unoccupied, he said he won't raise it for the next person. I know for a fact my rent is practically unheard of in this market."

Olivia chewed on the inside of her cheek as she looked around. Gabe's place had called to her from the first time she stepped inside. From the tall ceilings to the molding and brick, it had amazing bones. All it needed was bit of a homemaking to really shine.

Finally, she gave a giant shrug. "You moving out for your dog, me moving in here for a bit with another dog—it's a touch nontraditional, but I like it. And so long as we consider still doing that weekend thing we've been talking about, I think it could be just what I need right now."

He wrapped both hands around her hips and pulled her close. "Thank you for telling me. For trusting me." He kissed her, holding nothing back. Just when he was becoming seriously tempted to lift her to his counter, he stopped. After honesty like that, this wasn't something he wanted to rush. "How about you grab that dog and I'll fill the Kong? And I'm pretty sure I have a few candles shoved in a drawer around here somewhere."

Olivia pressed her body even closer just long enough to get his blood boiling. "It sounds like we've got a plan."

Chapter 30

THE SKY WAS PARTIALLY OVERCAST WITH PUFFY, DARK-gray clouds racing across and revealing patches of brilliant blue behind them, making it a bit unclear whether it would rain as forecasted. Knowing all the supplies she and her seventh-hour students needed to haul into the shelter, Olivia was hoping it would hold off for another half hour at least, ideally longer since she'd been told at least one of her students' service-hour activities would be outside.

She'd settled in for the bus ride in the seat behind the driver, an older woman who wasn't very talkative. This gave her time to savor the drive from Westbury Middle to the High Grove Animal Shelter in relative quiet. The fourteen kids who'd been able to attend were scattered around the middle and rear of the bus, and some of their conversation—borderline inappropriate at times as it seemed most middle school conversations tended to be—floated up as far as where she was sitting. Thankfully, the kids were sticking with crude humor and a bit of flirting, but no bullying or anything that she needed to call them on.

Feeling her phone vibrate in her purse beside her, Olivia pulled it out to find new texts from both Ava and Gabe, who were headed to the shelter separately. Ava was on her way with Morgan, and Gabe was ducking out of his office for an hour after getting Yun to cover a few of his appointments.

Olivia sent off a text to her sister first.

Hope my baby boy wasn't much trouble today.

Then one to Gabe.

Can't wait for you to meet some of these kids. Thanks for taking time out to make it happen.

Gabe texted back first.

Wouldn't miss it. See you in a few.

Ava took a full ten minutes to respond.

Here. He did great aside from the items he swiped off the counter.

This text was followed by bread, apple, banana, and hairbrush emojis.

Please tell me he didn't eat the hairbrush.

He didn't, but you owe me a new one.

After half a minute, a new text arrived, this one a photo of a mangled hairbrush.

Laughing, Olivia sent a thumbs-up and a thankful emoji, then returned her phone to her purse. The bus driver exited Interstate 44 and was heading along the ramp toward Webster Groves when Olivia rose to her knees, facing the students, to relay a handful of last-minute instructions.

"Listen up, kids!" She clapped her hands to get their attention and waited till she had it to continue. "We'll be there in just a couple of minutes. Most importantly, remember to keep together until I take another head count after we get off the bus. This is my first real-life field trip with students all on my own. And for those of you who have someone meeting you here, just a reminder that your mom or dad or guardian needs to sign you out tonight before you leave. If not… Let's not even go there. Raise your hands please so I know you understand and are in agreement."

It took a quick repeat of the last part of instructions, but all fourteen kids had arms raised overhead by the time they pulled into the parking lot.

"Great." She clamped a hand over her heart. "I also want to say that you guys are amazing kids. Each and every one of you. Thank you for everything you did to make this happen. More than anything else, the compassion and enthusiasm you've all shown for this makes my year."

From the middle of the bus, one of the girls practically squealed. "That's your dog by that tree, isn't it? I recognize him from your pictures."

Olivia ducked her head to look out the window. She spotted her sister waiting with Morgan off to the side of the parking lot. He had one back leg raised and was doing his business. "Yep! In the flesh. And you guys can thank my sister for turning down a spur-of-the-moment afternoon property showing to get him here."

"Can we get a picture with him for the student paper?" Addison asked.

"Of course. And I'm sure the social media guru here will want to post it as well."

Even though it was hard, Olivia resisted heading around to meet Ava and her dog—who'd already smelled her and was wagging that docked tail a mile a minute—until the kids had filed out and all been counted. "Good boy, Morgs," she called, giving him a few seconds of petting and additional praise.

"Guys, this is my sister, Ava Graham, and as you know, my dog, Morgan." She took the leash as Ava said hi. A new wave of happiness rolled over Olivia when Morgan seemed perfectly relaxed and content to hang by her side. Any worry that he might assume she'd be leaving him behind again washed away.

She was about to give Ava a rundown of the kids' names when Megan, Patrick, and Tess filed out of the building, each with a cart or dolly, and Olivia started fresh with the round of introductions. She listed all the kids by name but suspected she should probably grab a handful of blank name tags before the tour and service projects started.

"So, where would you like everything?" she asked.

"We were just talking about that," Megan said. "I think we'll unload and get it all to the back room. Then organize it from there. The kids can help sort stuff or pick another project."

"Sounds great," Olivia said as she spotted Gabe's truck pulling in out of the corner of her eye. To the kids, she added, "Let's work hard, guys. I may or may not have packed a bag full of snacks for a break later."

The group groaned appreciatively, and a few begged to have them now with pleading looks as sincere as Morgan's could be.

"A half hour won't send you into starvation, will it?"

"It could" came with a few grumbles.

Choosing to ignore the side comment, Olivia waved Gabe over. "Guys, you might recognize Dr. Wentworth from the rescue video of Morgan. I wasn't sure if he'd be able to step out from his office this afternoon, so I didn't tell you he was going to join us."

Gabe nodded at the group of kids as he locked a hand over Olivia's shoulder. "Nice to meet you, guys. Olivia has talked my ear off about you. And just call me Gabe. Honestly, if you forget that, I'm fine with 'Hey, Ms. Graham's boyfriend.'"

Olivia rolled her eyes at the collective snickers, shuffling of feet, and even the few gagging sounds that rolled over her students in a wave.

"Nice, Gabe," she said, giving him a smile.

He winked, then nodded toward the back of the bus. The bus driver was opening the doors at the back so they could begin unloading the supplies that took up both sides of the last two rows. "Want me in there or down here?" he asked her.

"Um, how about you lower them down and we'll load the carts?" She glanced Ava's way. "Since you're in heels, can you do leash duty again for a few minutes?"

"Sure. Just don't ask me to hold that snack bag too. He certainly isn't afraid to test authority." When Morgan gave her a guilty-as-charged look, she added, "And chase perfectly innocent cats."

Olivia clamped her lower lip to hold back her laughter. "They'll get used to each other. Promise." She was willing to bet Ava was as smitten with her newly adopted cat as she was with Morgan.

With the kids pitching in, the supplies were unloaded and stacked in the back room behind the dog kennels in just minutes, and then Megan and Tess herded the middle schoolers back to the front to start the tour.

After taking Morgan off Ava's hands again, Olivia joined Gabe and Patrick, who were off to the side talking about one of the kids' service project options. Samson was sprawled against the back wall, as comfortable as if he owned the place, reminding Olivia that he'd been coming here with Gabe since well before she had started.

"Assuming the rain holds off," Gabe was saying to

Patrick. "And without hand tools, we'll stick with raking and pulling weeds where we're going to carve out the trail."

"Are you talking about *the* trail?" Olivia asked. "You're just going to start and hope for the best?"

For the last week and a half, Gabe and Yun had been in negotiations—first with Dr. Washington, and for nearly a week with the owner of the jewelry store. Since Ava was acting as a dual agent on the sale, Olivia had been worried about the pressure her sister was under to make the sale happen. So far, though, she hadn't been showing signs of any real strain.

"Sort of." Looking a bit like he was holding something back, Gabe gave Patrick a nod and promised to catch up with him later. "Can you take a quick walk while your students get the tour?"

"Sure." Olivia slipped her free hand into Gabe's as they headed out the back door. With a sigh of reluctance, Samson took his time rising to his feet, then trotted happily out after them, at first single file behind Morgan who was confined by the leash.

She leaned in to Gabe as Morgan's attention was caught by a robin hopping about on the ground, and she needed to urge him along. Samson, who remained leashless as always, hung by Gabe's side when something wasn't calling his attention to give it a quick sniff.

He and Morgan had been together several times now, and on walks and outings, years seemed to shed off Samson in Morgan's presence. It was only when they were hanging out together in Gabe's apartment or Aunt Becky's that they retreated to separate spaces and largely ignored each other, acting a bit like stepchildren who were still more focused on carving out their own space than sharing with their new companion.

"Did I tell you yet how happy I am that you were able to come?" Olivia gave Gabe's hand a squeeze.

He grinned. "Once. Maybe twice." He draped his arm over her shoulder as they headed around the building to the strip of woods separating the shelter from the jewelry store. "Did I tell you how much it means to me to be here for you? And to get to meet your students?"

She laughed and pressed a kiss against his cheek. "You may have."

He stopped about halfway around the side of the building and guided their small group toward the short dog-walking trail that circled through the deepest section of the woods. Olivia had walked Morgan through here several times before he'd become hers. He'd loved the scent stations, especially the boxes with the squirrel and groundhog scents. He could've stood around sniffing those boxes for hours.

Proving his memory was as good as hers, Morgan beelined straight toward the first box as they started down the path.

"Fair warning, once he comes in here, it's hard to get him out."

"You know, now that he and Samson are hanging out as much as they are, Samson may help instill some manners in him. Morgan's a sharp enough dog to figure it out, that's for sure. It just takes awhile to come back from neglect like he's had."

"I bet Samson does teach him a few things. Especially once they get over that cool, indifferent phase they're in with each other."

Gabe chuckled. "We're already seeing some signs of that, don't you think?"

They'd reached the first scent box, the trail's newest addition, that contained an abandoned beehive. Morgan went to town sniffing and sniffing, the sound reverberating through the air holes in the box.

As if proving their growing camaraderie, Samson noticed that something interesting held Morgan's attention and trotted over to sniff the box as well. Their noses touched as they sniffed, and Samson's long, bushy tail kept almost identical time with Morgan's short, stiff one.

"It would certainly seem so." Olivia glanced down the trail as far as she could see. "So, what are we doing out here anyway?"

"Patrick pointed something out to me earlier. It's a bit windier this way, and the ravine's steeper, but the bridge would be no wider, and the trail's mostly already here. We could start on the bridge this weekend and have most of it done by Sunday."

"Don't you think we should wait? Till it's official?"

Gabe had pulled out his phone. Olivia assumed he was checking a text before he passed it her way, but she realized that he had an e-doc pulled up—one that looked very official and had a series of signatures, including his and Yun's.

She gasped. "It's final? Oh my gosh, when did it happen?"

"Around eleven o'clock this morning." He grinned, happiness radiating off him. "I'd have called, but I wanted to tell you in person."

Olivia threw her arms around him. "Gabe, I'm so happy for you!"

"Thanks. I'm happy for *us*. Good things are coming for you too. Trust me. I can feel it."

"You know what? I believe you. I feel it too." She pressed her lips against his for a congratulatory kiss. "How's Yun? Ecstatic?"

"You could say that. She spent her lunch break drawing up plans. I think I told you, the jewelry store owner's son just moved back home. We agreed that he could be the general contractor on the remodeling. It was the one thing that finally tipped that cranky old man's scale."

"The one who was away at the Peace Corps?"

"Yeah, him."

"Do you think that could be weird, having the previous owner's son doing the remodeling?"

"Maybe, but he's a legit contractor and from the pictures we saw, a talented one at that. Besides, with the money we've saved on the contract, it's a win-win. I'm guessing there's more to the whole thing than I know, but the old man really wanted his son to stay in St. Louis for a while. And honestly, I'm not going to have to manage much on the construction end of things. Yun lives for project management. As you may have guessed."

Olivia laughed and hugged him again. "In a few months, you're going to be working right next door to this place. It's practically too good to be true."

"I hear you." He pulled her in for a hug, one hand closing over her back pocket. "Hey, I think you're getting a call."

"I thought I felt something. But I also thought maybe I was just happy to see you," she said, grinning. She pulled out her phone to glance at the number. It was a local one, but not a number she knew. Just as she started to answer, it was lost to voicemail. "I'll check it later," she said when her phone vibrated to indicate a new message. "I see a pair of lips I'd like to spend a couple minutes kissing before I have to head back inside to those kids."

Gabe kissed her just long enough to warm her blood before slipping Samson's leash from her hand. "You know, all those résumés you've been sending out... Why not take a few seconds to see who it was?"

Olivia shrugged. "You're right. As always."

Maybe it was because the afternoon had already been so perfect, but after pressing her phone to her ear and listening to the voicemail, she needed to play the short message a second time for it to sink in.

When it finished the second time, she had to steady herself by locking a hand over Gabe's arm. He'd been watching Morgan and Samson take turns sniffing around the base of a crooked sapling. He looked her way at the touch and cocked an eyebrow. "Judging by the look on your face, I'm guessing you don't regret that lost minute or two of kissing. I hope you're about to tell me you're getting called in for an interview."

She shook her head, keeping her hand on his arm. "Uh, not exactly. Maybe, I guess."

"It's got to be something good, because you look like Christmas just came about eight months early."

"It was Principal Garcia. That must have been her cell phone. She said they've had a string of new-student applications. Enough to be over limit by one."

"Over limit by one? That's enough, isn't it?"

Olivia bit her lip, but the smile still spread across her

face. "It would seem so. I can hardly believe it. Gabe, it's the one job I wanted all along."

Gabe enveloped her in a tight hug. "I'm sorry you had to go through this, but no one deserves a position there more than you. Not after all you've done with those kids."

"She didn't exactly say the position was mine, but she asked me to come to her office first thing Monday morning. Here, listen, because I can hardly believe it."

Olivia pulled up the voicemail again and played it over the speaker for Gabe to hear. Sure enough, it ended with the words she'd thought Principal Garcia had said: "There are the formalities, of course. We can never skip those. But I know who I want back here next year. And after this field trip of yours, there's a motivated group of incoming eighth graders who are hoping for the same thing."

"Listen to that," Gabe said as Olivia hung up. He brushed the tip of one finger across the ridge of her brow. "Olivia Graham, not even finished with a full semester there and already making waves."

"Oh, Gabe, I can't tell you how many ideas I've been storing away in hopes of having my own students next year."

Gabe locked her hand in his and pulled it to his chest. Morgan had finished scoping out the area and was ready to move on and made it known by tugging the leash in his other hand. Samson had wandered a few feet ahead and was busy sniffing out the next scent station, making Morgan whine with envy.

Gabe looked from the dogs to the jewelry store just visible beyond the trees and then back at her. "You know, all my bets are on next year being a really good year."

As their lips met somewhere in the middle, Olivia couldn't think of a single reason to disagree.

Acknowledgments

One of my favorite coffee mugs reads "Please don't confuse your Google search with my medical degree." As a fiction writer, I often find it necessary to dive headfirst into a subject I know little about, soak in what I can, and hope to do the subject justice in the manuscript. Understandably, one of the questions I get asked most about my writing of this series is, "How am I so versed in animal rescue work and dog training?"

While Google searches are helpful, they can't compare to life experience or in-person interviews. Fortunately, the animal shelter world is one in which I'm fairly well versed. I've had considerable experience working for nonprofit conservation organizations and volunteering with animal shelters. When it comes to dog training, I know the basics and have taken my own dogs through obedience training courses, but I'm not a professional trainer. Fortunately, my two adequately trained shelter dogs fit right into my at-times chaotic house with teens!

There are many other aspects of the canine world that I've written about in this series in which I'm not as well versed. For help in portraying Gabe and Samson's search-and-rescue (SAR) work, I'd like to thank Brenda Cone for sharing her expertise as a SAR worker with her beloved dog, Max. I'd also like to thank Linda Swoboda for sharing her behind-the-scenes expertise as a volunteer rescue transporter. In regard to portraying Gabe's EMT-firefighting work, I'd like to thank Battalion Chief Eric Heimos and his crew for sharing their knowledge and expertise on firefighting and emergency rescue services with the Missouri Romance Writers of America. In regard to Gabe's veterinary work, a special thanks to Dr. Rebecca Hodges for looking over the manuscript with her keen veterinary eye. Thanks also to Patsy Donaldson and her knowledge of all things Missouri Bootheel.

For helping shape *Head Over Paws* from story development to cover design and more, I'd like to thank the wonderful team at Sourcebooks and Sourcebooks Casablanca, most especially my editor, Deb Werksman. I'd be remiss not to also mention Susie Benton, Stefani Sloma, and Diane Dannenfeldt by name. Thanks to my beta readers of this book, Sandy Thal and Theresa Schmidt. And of course, there's my agent, Jess Watterson, at Sandra Dijkstra Literary Agency, who's always there when I need her and who brightens my days with pictures of her shelter dogs whenever I'm surfing through Instagram due to a bout of writer's block.

Last but never least are my family and friends whose support means so much. Amanda Heger and Angela Evans, thanks for helping me stay grounded through the at-times chaotic life of being a published writer. Ciara Brewer and Bree Liddell, without our consistent goal setting in our mastermind meetings, I doubt I'd ever make these deadlines. And finally, there's my family, who even with book number five, are still just as excited for release day as they were for my debut. Thanks for your support, love, and inspiration.

About the Author

Debbie Burns lives in St. Louis with her teens, two phenomenal rescue dogs, and a somewhat tetchy Maine coon cat who everyone loves anyway. Her hobbies include hiking, gardening, and daydreaming, which, of course, always leads to new story ideas.

Debbie is an award-winning author and 2019 HOLT Medallion Award of Merit recipient. Commendations for her Rescue Me series include a Starred Review from *Publishers Weekly* and a Top Pick from RT Book Reviews for *A New Leash on Love*, and an Amazon Best Book of the Month for *My Forever Home*.

You can find her on Instagram and Twitter (@_debbieburns), on Facebook (facebook.com/author debbieburns), on BookBub (@AuthorDebbieBurns), and at authordebbieburns.com.

Also by Debbie Burns